I0733534

The View from Gleninagh North

By K.D. Norris

Chapbook Press

Schuler Books
2660 28th Street SE
Grand Rapids, MI 49512
(616) 942-7330
www.schulerbooks.com

The View from Gleninagh North

ISBN 13: 9781957169422

eBook ISBN: 9781957169866

Library of Congress Control Number: 2023906323

Cover Design by Vintonmedia

Printed in the United States by Chapbook Press.

Dedicated to:

Else Steiner, who introduced me to Ireland

Kelly Roach, in whose coffee shop I wrote a first draft

And, of course, my beautiful wife, TJ,
the model for every strong, confident, loving
female character I will ever create

I believe in the sun when it's not shining,
I believe in love even when I feel it not,
I believe in God even when he is silent.

–Irish saying

"One small statement (marriage) and it holds the risk of tragedy,
the chance of happiness,
the probability of mere endurance—choices wide as the world."

–From "The Quiet Man" by Maurice Walsh
Originally published in the Saturday Evening Post
Feb. 11, 1933.

An tús

(The beginning)

First let me say this is not the book I wanted to write. It is not the book I was paid to write: a sequel to *The Quiet Man*—an attempt to imitate and yet not—a sweet, simple story glorified and gorged for Hollywood, which is what Maurice Walsh's original short story eventually became.

Had this been that book, I would probably have come up with a better book title than simply what I saw out my front window and better chapter titles than Chapter 1, and on, made however fashionable by using Walsh's Gaelic, *Caibidil a haon*.

But I did not.

This is not that story, that book, that sequel to *The Quiet Man*. This is another story about Ireland, about Irish people and the Irish landscape, a moment captured in time that is neither today, yesterday or tomorrow.

And it is certainly not a story written by someone who really *knows* Ireland. But it is a story of the Ireland that I know, that I learned, and learned to love, and let love me.

I knew I had to write this story, this book, when I accepted that love.

* * *

Walking up behind the house, on the edge of The Burren, on a circular path where I often find myself these days, I reached the top of Gleninagh North and stopped to take it all in. There is a bird in the air, a hawk. Not sure what kind of hawk, but from somewhere I remember a poem. Yeats, I think. Something about a yellow-eyed hawk.

"Call down the hawk from the air," it starts. "Let him be hooded or caged. Till the yellow eye has grown mild …"

I forget the rest, too much archaic language, probably. But I remember an essay, some dissection of the poem I must have studied in college, something about the hawk being the poet's symbol of the soul. The hawk glides freely through the sky, touching the heavens, yet still risks all by returning to earth, to the ties that bind it, and us all, to the ground.

The bird slowly circled out over the rock landscape, again and again, letting the wind carry it, its wings spread wide but barely working. As it circles, it flys over my head. I stop my walk and stand and watch. And then I circle with it, a clumsy pirouette to keep it in view. The sun, high in the sky, blinds me, sporadically, as the hawk circles and is lost in the glare. The landscape flashes like a kaleidoscope, first an expanse of rocky landscape, then the usually quiet village of Rathmorgan and the always uneasy waters of Galway Bay.

I followed the bird, maybe half a dozen times.

Is it watching me as I watch it? Am I an intruder in its world? What is it focused on? Prey? A mouse maybe? Another bird? What does a yellow-eyed hawk eat? Hell, maybe it is actually a falcon. There are peregrines in Ireland, lots of them. Maybe that's what it is.

It stopped circling, worked its wings quickly with purpose as it made headway against the wind, flying a little to the north, then to the east, then circling again.

More distant from the high point where I stand, I see the road, the only road in and out of Rathmorgan, and then the castle and the pub and the bay beyond. From my vantage point on the backside of the crest, my house and Cathleen's house are hidden below the rocky crest. But I know they are there, her home of beautifully sad memories and exquisitely fashioned hope, and my home of indecision.

I stand a moment longer, watch the hawk—or the falcon, whatever—circle once more, and admire for the hundredth time the lovely view from Gleninagh North.

But then the bird folds in its wings, becomes little more than a spot in the infinite blue sky, and dives to the ground, disappearing from my sight, somewhere down the slope from the rocky crest.

Will I find evidence of its presence as I walk home? The remains of its prey, of its successful hunt, or even the remains of its ultimate failure?

On one of my walks with Cathleen, we found a bird dead on a rocky point. A yellow-eyed hawk, she said. One of its wings was clearly broken. I wondered if it had been mortally wounded in a fight with another bird or from its impact with the ground, a fatal mistake as it sought prey. Or, if the bird had an old soul, and on on that day, that special day, its brittle wings failed and it fell to Earth one last time.

Had fate played, as it has always played, its unfathomable hand?

* * *

If you visit Ireland, especially County Clare, the tourist books tell you, you have to see The Cliffs of Moher. True enough. But the locals, should you be lucky enough to have one show you around, will invariably make a stop on the *boireann*, The Burren, a great karst-rock landscape that is about as tourist friendly as the dark side of the moon.

Moher and The Burren, when you listen close, each whisper stories of Ireland. The cliffs tell of fate risked, of adventure and hope to the west, of a sojourn across the Atlantic in hopes of a better life. The barren landscape tells of fate accepted, if not hope lost, of living out one's life amidst the hard stone of the west Irish highlands.

I visited Moher once, many years ago, as a tourist. Crawled out to the edge, just like all the tourists, and peered down to the rhythmically crashing waves from 700 feet above. Maggie refused to join me; she stayed well back with our Irish host, and I teased her repeatedly for her timidity. As awesome as it was, I had no desire to go back, no desire to alter that memory when I returned these many years later.

The Burren, Ireland's great rock garden, stunned me from the moment I saw its stark lushness, on that first day, just after noon, as I stood and looked south, away from Galway Bay, standing on the top of a stone wall surrounding the house on the hillside of Gleninagh North, my new home away from home.

The short, steep-sloping hill rose up from the shoreline to an undulating ridge alternately covered by lush green and exposed, grayish stone. It stands watch over the tiny village of Rathmorgan, on the south shore of Galway Bay.

While Rathmorgan lies in County Clare, to the locals who later schooled me on the subject, all the land that touches Galway Bay is undoubtedly Galway even if it is not County Galway.

Rathmorgan is a hamlet most notable for its easy access to the bay. The town has docking for more than a dozen boats but only half a dozen houses, one petrol station and, of course, the mandatory public house pub, all of which I could see from my hillside perch. Its appearance is not unlike a picture-perfect postcard.

Not surprisingly, the pub drew my attention. "Cassidy's" it proudly announced in large green letters on one of its white-washed brick walls It has a more modern looking brick two-story addition on the seaward side, a nondescript inn with a smaller sign advertising "Pub and Bed Inn".

I'd never heard of Rathmorgan, let alone Gleninagh North, before I'd agreed to live there. Never laid eyes on it until the day I moved in. I drove down from Galway city after spending the previous day in a blur of jet lagged activity and then stupor.

Arriving at Shannon on the red eye from New York City, during which I slept little, I packed into a few hours the renting of a small SUV, a crash course on navigating Irish freeways leading to Galway, a late lunch and a couple Smithwick's beers at an Indian restaurant just off Eyre Square, and finally an early turn-in for what I hoped would be a sound night's sleep in a modern hotel on the waterfront.

My sleep, though, was fitful, at best, and in the morning, with my internal clock struggling for a reset, I stocked up on the bare essentials of housewares, toiletries and bachelor-chow groceries, and then again risked my life on the freeway.

I arrived at Rathmorgan, just before noontime, followed the emailed instructions from Else's housekeeper to drive .3 kilometers further on the main road and then to turn off to the south on a rough, unnamed dirt road that turned out to be little more than a driveway to the two houses located up the hill, both on the left. A single power line ribbon loped along the side of the road up the hill, first to the lower house and then on to the upper house.

The scene had likely not changed in decades. Subtract the power poles and it might have looked the same for a century.

As happens often to me, a writer's imaginations ran aground in worldly reality.

Turning off the main road with only a moment's preparation I was forced to downshift the car quickly, the engine dragged, and my rental car crawled up into the highlands, to the edge of The Burren. Passing the first house about midway up a half-kilometer hill in slow motion, I took a brief exam of its many details before picking up a little speed as the road neared its end. At the second house, where I braked and came to rest in a parking area to the side of the house where I was to stay for the next few months.

Else Hensch, Maggie's old boss and good friend to both of us, offered the house when I told her I intended to live in Ireland for a time to write a book.

"Vhatever you vrite, it vill help," she said, never able to pronounce her English "W" words properly even after 40 years of living first in Ireland and then America. "It is Ireland."

I offered to pay rent, but Else would have none of it.

"Please, no," she said, gently, as we talked on the phone a couple of weeks before I left Philadelphia. "Friends, Matthew, you and I. Maggie vas more than a friend. It is a lovely house, with a lovely view of the bay. Oskar loved the view. But I do not, not anymore."

Her voice trailed off from her usual Germanic volume and vigor, remembering her deceased husband and happy days in the house, days now past.

I knew what she felt, just as she knew my feelings.

After parking the car, I walked around the house.

Else's house is all gray stone and white-painted doors and windows, two stories in height with a chimney on one side. It looks like a good, secure place that had weathered many an Atlantic storm. Else was correct in her assessment of the view from Gleninagh North, too, from the front of the house.

This is Ireland.

The instant I climbed the stone wall at the back of the house and looked at "The Burren", I knew this was a good place for me to retreat, to rest, to write.

I also knew Jasper had been right. That coming here, writing his book, was what I needed to do.

This was a place I might even forget the pain, for a few minutes, for a few days.

Maybe.

Caibidil a haon
(Chapter 1)

It was just after 4 p.m. when my initial inspection of
Gleninagh North was complete; the day was growing old but the
evening was young. I was going to open the bottle of Absolute I
had brought with me, but decided drinking vodka on the rocks
alone in the my new home, before dinner on my first day, would
set a bad precedent.

That sort of thing should wait for the second day, at least.

And, after all, there was that pub down the hill …

I thought about walking. But didn't.

Thought about parking in the front parking lot, entering at
the inn like a tourist trying not to seem so desperate for a drink.
But didn't.

I nearly changed my mind, thinking it was too early to drink,
standing outside the pub's backdoor, on a well-worn circle of dirt
littered with the ghostly remnants of dead cigarettes despite a
butt can filled with sand. But didn't.

Was thinking I think too damn much as I opened the door
and heard a low rumble of a few conversations almost drowned
out by the voices of sport announcers on a television: "Tommaso
number 7 shirt beats Mateo. He charging through the midfield ...
it's up for grabs now!"

The conversations paused, until the announcer's "Shot 's
high o' the cross!" echoed as if the announcer was in the room
before being met with a collective groan of the patrons and the
television audience. The quiet remained, however, as a few faces

turned momentarily to me. The singular, heavy "clunk" of the door closing behind me only amplified the lull. Most of the faces quickly turned away and low rumble of conversations mercifully returned as I slid into the mix, such as it was.

I glanced at the bar—a massive, elbow-height, wooden beauty clearly more than long enough for a dozen or more solitary men standing shoulder to shoulder, but still ample room for 20 or so sets of leaning elbows and associated beers on a really busy night, which this evening was not. There were only three men at the bar, leaning back into their drinks. I glanced around the room. Elsewhere there was a group of four, sitting at a single table, now back to jabbering away and seemingly oblivious to all but themselves. One of the men wore a Seattle Mariners baseball cap. Tourists. The only other person, a lone man sitting in a booth about as far from the bar as possible, was oddly hunched over his table.

I turned back to the bar and approached.

"Mr. Maybourn, I'm guessin', down from the shoulder of Gleninagh," the bartender called out, as he sprang from his bartender's roosting spot, leaning casually against a liquor shelf, an old fashioned cash till off one shoulder and a row of half a dozen beer taps off the other.

"They call me Cassidy," he continued as he neared the open area of the bar I had chosen, halfway between two old men and one young one. "And what ya drinkin' sir?"

"Smithwick's," I announced, having fully prepared for just such a question.

"You got it," Cassidy said, stepping smoothly toward his taps, grabbing a pint glass from a neat row of the same, waiting patiently, and taking the proper time to make a proper pour.

"And how did you know my name, Mr. Cassidy?" I asked as he returned, snatched up a Guinness paper coaster, tossed it casually onto the bar near enough to my vicinity, and set the pint in front of me. All with the skill of a task done a thousand times.

"Cassidy, if you will," he said. "And how do I know your name? Well, that's a story."

"I got time," I said as I tipped my glass to him.

"*Sláinte!*" pronouncing the traditional Irish toast—"to your health"—as Else had taught me. I wondered if her words would make me sound like I, too, were an old German lady. "That about right?"

"Near 'nough for a Paddy."

There was a murmur from the spectators on both sides of the bar, especially from two older men nearest to me, to my left, who groaned as if they wanted to laugh but were trying to hold it in.

I glanced at the two. One had the look of old Hemingway, but on a diet: gray crewcut and beard contrasting a decades-old sunburned face. The other had a little Popeye thing going on: big nose, cheeks and chin devoid of even the hint of hair, same sunburned face.

Cassidy briefly glared their way.

"No offense," he said, turning back to me.

"None taken," I said before taking a good quaff of beer.

Cassidy leaned in as I drank.

"Know some American is set to stay in the high house, up the old road to Gleninagh North, up beyond widow O'Brian's," he said. "Been all the talk for two weeks, since Kenny's father learned of your impending habitation from a realtor down in Ballyvaughan who keeps care o' the place. Kenny's only good gossip in weeks."

"Meet Kenny," he said, waving off to my right, toward the solitary young man standing by himself at the far end of the bar, enamored with the soccer game as if the television was his only friend, sipping a bottled Stella Artois as gently as if it were the last bottle on Earth. "Lay-about son of Sargent Jones, at the *Garda* Station o'er at Ballyvaughn. But a true football fan."

I quickly and silently tipped my beer in the general direction of the seemingly oblivious young man.

"Feckin lives for the sport," one of the old men said. I could not tell which.

"And not much else," the other said, after which they both laughed.

"Feck off," Kenny said, glancing our way but looking past me to the old men, then back to me as he raised his beer, returned my toast with a slight bob of his bottle.

I wondered if I was wrong in the meaning of feckin?

Two Irish slang words I had to learn, according to Google anyway: "craic" for fun or enjoyment of just about any kind, and "feckin'" for, well, just about anything one wants to bring attention to. But "feck off" sure sounded like a curse.

I was sure, however, that the *Garda* Kenny's father was a member of was the national police force, and that *football*, on this side of the Atlantic, meant soccer.

Kenny was quiet. Seemed as though he could barely muster the energy to raise his beer. He looked a little ragged for a young man, especially a "lay-about." His shoulder-length dark hair hung lifeless around a gaunt face, his jeans and light sweater hung equally lifeless from an equally gaunt frame.

I glanced up to the television game. He noticed my glance.

"Feckin Italian league," Kenny said. "But it's football."

I nodded.

Cassidy interrupted our bonding moment and went on with his story.

"House up Gleninagh North. Everybody knows the owners, the Hensches. Good people. Have a small factory in Ballyvaughn and a larger one, newer one over the bay in the suburbs of Galway city. Used to visit the house regularly, a getaway for themselves or guests, even flew their little airplane in and landed it on an open field beside the coast road. Mr. Hensch died a dozen or so years back. House sits mostly empty these days. Occasionally rented out, maybe given out, by Mrs. Hensch, to friends and family. Local realtor handles the business side of such things. Local woman hired to keep the place clean, shine it up when someone visiting. Local pub gossip always a brewing 'bout new residents, even if just that someone was arriving on this day and leaving on that.

"So, Mr. Maybourn," Cassidy concluded. "You a friend of the good Mrs. Hensch or you a renter?"

"Little bit of both, I guess. And my name is Matt," I said as I tipped my glass and took a long drink. "But how did you know I wasn't just another tourist," nodding my head toward the tables of obvious tourists, "just stop by on my way to the cliffs?"

"Sure of it, Matty. Saw your car pull up and park this side of the building," he said, nodding his head to the windows that faced the dirt parking lot. "Tourists drive around the building, enter through the main doors. Want to see the view of the ocean, or don't want to appear too bent on finding a drink."

"I was bent, I guess," I said, after nearly finishing my beer with another big swallow. Cassidy took note and took the glass, filled it again, and returned. While he worked, I walked over to one of the windows, looked at my car and the road and my house in the distance. Then I walked back to my spot at the bar. "How far is it up the hill?" I said as I sidled back up to the bar.

"You drivin' or walkin'?" Kenny asked.

"Driving," I said. "Car had it at two Kilometers, but seemed more than that."

"Miles," one of the two old men said; Popeye, I thought. "Still can't get used to the change."

"When was that?" the other chirped in. " '04?"

"No. '05 ya ol' man," Kenny said, as the chorus of my three bar mates began in earnest, sometimes so fast I could not tell who was saying what.

"Ya. '05. A bunch of euro fools. Changin' what didn't need changin'. Just to be different from the Brits."

"All started in '04. Remember those stickers an' all."

"What a feckin waste of me taxes."

"Feckin waste of paper."

I listened as the discussion bounced from one side to the other of the bar, until Cassidy jumped in. "You goin' let Matty get a word in?"

He then turned to me: "Two miles driven'. Little less. Mile as the hawk flies."

"Good," I said. "Two beers is my max to drive, but that's close enough to stumble home."

I then lifted my freshly poured glass, and took that perfect first swallow. "*Sláinte!*"

Cassidy laughed. So did my bar mates on either side. The barkeep then leaned into the bar again, settling in for real conversation.

In preparation for his asking me a few more questions but trying to not seem too nosey I assumed, he first told me his story.

His name was not really Cassidy, he confided. Even though he owned the establishment for nigh on seven years, almost everybody who stopped by, both the long-time locals and the wayfaring tourists, refused to call him anything else, especially after they had a couple of drinks.

"So, Jimmy Harrington answers to Cassidy these days," he said, touching his forehead as if he were tipping a hat.

"Hey Cassidy," one of two old men standing at the bar—
Hemingway, I think—called out as if on cue. "Two more or'
here."

"Ian and ol' man Mulligan," Cassidy said, nodding their way
as he stepped away from me and as the two men slid their empty
glasses a couple feet down the bar toward me and nearer to
Cassidy.

I noticed they did not have coasters. No reason to waste
them on regulars when a bar towel will do.

Proper introductions ensued as the barkeep swooped in to
get the glasses.

I found out Popeye—the thirstier, more talkative one—was
Ian. Mulligan remained mostly silent. As Cassidy referred to the
quiet one as "ol' man Mulligan," the man's response was
appropriately and simply a scowl toward the barkeep, followed by
knowing smiles between the two. I assumed it was a private joke.
Barkeeps and regulars do such things.

"You're drinkin' 'em like water today, boys," Cassidy said as
he carried the two glasses to the tap. "No charter today, I'm
guessin'."

"Still early for tourist fishin'," Old Mulligan said, finally,
looking around a bar with only the few other souls in sight. "But
you talking as if you're not needin' our business. Don't look all
that busy yourself."

"True enough," Cassidy said aloud as he poured the two
another round of Guinness.

"True enough," he repeated, muttering, as he walked the
beers back, and then returned his focus to me to finish his
Readers Digest version of the story of Cassidy and his pub.

After working 25 years at a truck and rail shipping company
outside Galway city, his story went, Cassidy and his wife of 30
years retired and bought the establishment "to stay busy and wait

our government pension." They lived and worked the inn, but really didn't need to make a lot of money from the place. "Kind of like a hobby," he said. "Barely pays the bills, but can't complain 'bout the view."

It certainly did appear that Cassidy's Pub and Bed Inn could use all the business it could get. I wondered if Tuesday might well be a slow day, especially in the late afternoon, before the working folk got off and wanted to wash away their workday, and other locals stopped off to start their evening. Even though it was spring, I expected to see more tourists stopping by to drink up a little local color.

The inn part of the business, connected to the pub by large, ornate wood and stained-glass double doors, did good business in the tourist high season of summer, June to August. "Not great business," Cassidy insisted. But the regular business was mostly as a drinking establishment. Cassidy's wife, Eileen, provided a limited menu of food in a small dining room for house guests, not for the pub crowd, he pointed out.

"She don't fancy servin' the ungrateful," he said. Although, he added with a wink, "She does offer up the occasional meal to a bar patron she's takes a fancy to."

Sounded like a bit of advice to me. I decided then and there that I would look to get on the woman's good side. I am a decent cook when cooking for others, but when feeding only myself the menu was usually various versions of pasta or rice. "Purina bachelor chow," Maggie had called it.

As the afternoon flowed, and a third beer came my way while a few more locals came in to increase the noise level, I sporadically learned more than a little about the regulars in the pub, some from the good barkeep and some from just listening to the banter along the bar.

Old Mulligan and Ian were retired commercial sailors, now deep-sea fisherman with a boat docked out of Gleninagh Quay, up the coast. "Now two ol' salts with nothing better to do with their day," Cassidy said loud enough for everyone to hear. Neither man argued the barkeep's description.

In the back of the pub, almost hidden from view, was Séamus, whom Cassidy described in a mumble that passed for a bartender's whisper: "Defense Forces, army. Put to pasture too young. Sips his Irish whiskey, smokes his American cigarettes inside the pub."

He then shrugged his shoulders in silent commentary.

"Pretend not to see him breaking the rules if only locals are in. Served his country and all."

He also introduced two other men who had recently occupied leaning spots at the bar between Kenny and me. Public servants, maybe road workers, I assumed by their youth, their worn uniforms and their even more worn hands offered and shaken. But I can only handle so many new faces and names in one day, especially with me working on my third beer, so their names escaped me.

"So," Cassidy said, finally, after he made a round of the three regulars, the new customers at the bar and refreshed Séamus' drink, and then settled back in, leaning at the bar across from me.

"So, what's your story, Matty?"

"I'm a writer," I said. "Least that is what I get paid to do."

As I began my story, Old Mulligan and Ian moved a little closer on one side, and Kenny picked up his Stella, broke away from his football game and stepped around the expanding herd of unnamed workmen.

"You write anything I might have read?" Cassidy asked.

"Kiss of Treachery?"

"Tha's what your Eileen said," Ian nodded to Cassidy before returning to me. "Wife and I saw the movie, few years ago. Don't like those American cop movies all that much, but it was all the rage that year."

"The book's better," I said.

"Course it is," Old Mulligan said, more to Ian than to me. "Now let the man tell his story."

"Well, I'm here to write about Ireland, I guess. For a few months, the summer anyway. Thought I'd just hang around. Talk, listen, travel. See what comes."

When I stopped talking, a silence descended around my section of the bar, and most of the pack of working men up the bar glanced over, abandoning even trying to pretend they weren't eavesdropping.

They, too, must have seen the movie.

"Feckin all," someone from the pack said.

"Staying up on Gleninagh …" another someone said, as the conversation bounced around again, of even more confusing origins than before.

"Got to tell the wife, she readin' all the time."

"Wife will say I'm tellin' lies."

"You always tellin' lies."

"Might have his book. Maybe get it signed."

"Bet he charges."

I couldn't tell who had the wife who might have my book, but had to jump in.

"Sign it anytime, just buy me a beer."

There was laughter and unintelligible murmur from the pack, but before the conversation could continue Cassidy sent a glare their way. The pack returned to small talk among themselves and pretending not to hear my conversation.

"What's your story goin' to be about?" Cassidy asked, turning his attention back to me.

"Don't know yet."

"And you gettin' paid to come here to write a story what nobody knows about?" Cassidy said.

I nodded.

Kenny jumped in. "Sounds like a job I should look into."

"You wishin' you had such a job," Ian said.

"Not puttin' him down. Just wondering, old man."

"Old man? I knocked your papa on his ass once or twice. Can still do the same to you."

I took the opportunity to sip my beer.

"Drink up and shut up," Cassidy said to all but me, then he looked back my way. "Do continue Matty."

Damn, now everybody will be calling me Matty …

It seemed everybody moved a little closer, and I continued.

"Plan to make Galway home but travel around. Got to be some stories waiting to be told here. Maybe something about Gleninagh Castle. Read it has an interesting history. Poke around Galway, maybe up in Connemara, out to the Aran Islands. Burren seems like quite a place, strange landscape and all. Maybe I'll write a story about fishing in the area. Don't really know just yet."

The conversational jig started up again, and again I lost track of who was speaking.

"Fishing? You talkin' about business or pleasure? Business all but gone away from Galway Bay."

"He's not talkin' business of fishing. He's talking about the fly rod. That what you talking about, right Matty?"

"Aran's all tourist these days. Like the cliffs, all tourists."

"Connemara's nice. I'm from up that way."

"How you know what he talking about? Just met the man."

"Well, I'm listening to him. More than you're doing."

"Drink up and shut up," Cassidy said, finally.

I took another sip.

"Grew up a John Wayne fan," I said. "Thinking about taking a visit up to the Quiet Man cottage. Up in County Mayo. On the Galway border, I understand."

"Up in Cong. Not far really."

"Big tourist crowd in the summer, I guess. Ain't been in years."

"Now it's a good drive, that's sure."

"Hated it when I toured a cousin, Boston Irish, he was. Drank like a fish. Took him and his brats up there a few years ago. Hated every minute of it."

"It's a drive, ya, but he got the time."

"And someone's paying him. That's a job I want."

"Bet that's the way in Hollywood. Bet ya."

"That's a right feckin movie," a growling voice announced from beyond the bar crowd. "A right feckin story."

The jig stopped abruptly. Everybody turned to look at Séamus, sitting alone across the pub.

"Quiet Man," he continued. "That's an Irish fairy tale dreamed up by feckin Americans with the right soundin' names. Nothing more."

"Hold on there, ya pecker," Cassidy said, the firm voice of a man used to dealing with drunks in general if not this man in particular. "Man's a guest here."

"No offense meant."

Séamus awkwardly twisted to look at me and held up his whiskey glass in toast.

"No offense taken."

I toasted him back.

My writer's radar told me this man was a story just waiting to be told.

"He's right, you know. Most think the Quiet Man's a bunch of *shite*, nothin' more," Kenny said.

"Just an idea," I said, turning back to the bar.

"Matty's beer gettin' stale," Old Mulligan said. "Get him a fresh one on Mully, and fill this one and my deckhand's while you're at it."

Ian, quietly standing beside Old Mulligan, seemed ready to argue his need of another, if not his job title. I guessed both men could handle a boat in a gale, need be. But he simply surveyed his empty glass, smiled and nodded.

I gave up on the idea of driving home, gulped down the dregs of the beer in front of me so the glass could be taken and refilled. For the next hour I listened as the clatter around me swirled and swirled, with sometimes informative talk of The Burren and Gleninagh Castle, Galway city and bay, Connemara and the Aran Islands.

At some point, one of the workmen got the idea that only a photo would prove his Hollywood story to his wife. A quick round of selfies ensued before Cassidy put a stop to it.

There was more talk about fishing Galway Bay, for business and for pleasure, as that is what the two old men talked about most. I liked them both, and Mully—at some point, he asked me to call him "Mully", which I considered a compliment—was also someone I knew had stories to tell.

But there was no more talk about *The Quiet Man*, and not another word from Séamus, the lonely whiskey drinker.

I lost track of how many beers I had, but at some point in the early evening, four tourists staying at the inn but enjoying an early beer were notified dinner was ready and escorted to the dining room by the lady of the house. Eileen, too, was fifth-ish, with shoulder-length hair colored too dark a jet-black and pulled back in the tightest ponytail I'd ever seen. She was short in stature but big in personality.

A few minutes later, she came strolling back into the bar area to get a small glass of some sort of liqueur. She wanted to talk, being the good gossip I understood her to be. But the pub was filling and the noise was growing and without even my asking, she offered a meal of sliced beef steak in gravy and chips.

"She's butterin' you up with no delay," Cassidy quietly warned me as I paid my bar bill and accepted the meal offered in the inn's dining room. "And know this as God's truth, that woman can't keep a secret."

I washed down the good dinner, and Eileen's gentle inquisition, with strong black coffee as dusk settled in over the bay beyond two large windows at the front of the inn. I felt sober enough to drive back up the hill, but didn't; rules are rules.

The path across the field was darkening, and new, so I took the long way home. Wasn't that long. I swore to myself, as I trudged the road on foot in a darkening twilight, that I'd never drive down again. Cassidy's was, indeed, close enough to stumble home if need be, as every neighborhood pub should be.

There were no lights on yet in the house halfway up the hill, but I thought I heard a dog barking from inside. What did Cassidy say? The widow O'Brian?

Someone else to introduce myself to. Should know the woman to be neighborly, and know the dog because this would not be the last time I'd stumble by at night.

After playing with the house's lights to see what illuminated what in my new world, I sought out and downed two aspirins with half a can of 7-Up, both of which would be appreciated as I slept off my unplanned beer binge.

I read a few emails. One from the man paying for my new adventure, the friend who convinced me to write a book I had no idea how to write. When it was finally dark, I introduced myself to a strange bed.

* * *

"That idea I told you about, that Irish story," Jasper Kelly had said months before my arrival on Gleninagh North, as we sat in his Santa Monica film studio office. The curtains covering two large windows behind him slowly raised, flooding the room with smog-defused California late afternoon sunlight. "I really want you to write that for me."

"I don't want to write anything right now."

"I know, Matty. That's why you have to do it, my friend."

The logic of his argument was as simple as simple human nature. But I still hated hearing it, especially from a friend I valued as much as I did this friend.

Simple human nature. The moment you realize you have been avoiding a difficult task is the moment to start it. The day your body, battered by fate or misfortune, hurts the most is precisely the day you have to get on with your life, however altered. The morning you wake up, look in the mirror and think that you have become invisible, that is clearly the morning when you must go out into the world and make your presence known again.

In those days, I did not like what I saw in the morning mirror. Some days I almost didn't recognize myself.

A week earlier Jasper had called, asked me to come out to L.A. for some "creative consultation" as he was in the final editing of his new movie, "Breakfast with Mossad", a short story

I wrote that he and his screenwriters had turned into a movie script.

Now, Jasper, of all people, was using the logic of human nature against me.

A one-time star football player, current Hollywood golden boy actor and producer, and occasionally the most naive multi-millionaire I'd ever known, Jasper sometimes struggled when it came to grasping human nature. But this time I knew he was probably the wiser man.

Jasper always had the ability to get noticed, to make himself famous, to make money, first by his knowing when something was right and then from seizing upon it, learning from it, and exploiting it.

Being a fine high school student-athlete allowed him to get a scholarship to the University of Wisconsin. Being a smart, coachable and often effective college quarterback allowed him to take his Badger teams to a couple of bowl games, sign a professional football contract when he graduated, and then spend three years as an over-paid, little-used back-up with the Seattle Seahawks.

The semi-fame of his being an NFL quarterback allowed him to gain *entrée* into Hollywood entertainment circles and to get some bit parts in television and movies. His paychecks from playing pro football, two off-seasons spent taking acting lessons from the best acting coach in Tinseltown, and the connections made from several "ruggedly handsome white guy" character-actor roles, allowed him to partially produce and co-star in a mildly profitable action movie with a decent plot and featuring several experienced character-acting professionals he had met and made friends of along the way. He learned about the business of moviemaking from those experiences. He learned to be a decent actor but an even better producer.

It was his next film, though, that made Jasper an international star, and made him very nearly rich. He bought the rights to my first moderately successful novel, *Kiss of Treachery*, hired me, as well as a truly experienced screenwriter to adapt it into a screenplay, and then made a blockbuster film which he produced and took the lead role in. The movie briefly pushed my novel onto a New York Times bestseller list.

The success of *Kiss of Treachery*, the novel and the film, made both of our careers. But Jasper's dearth of skill in human nature, in mature relationships, and his inflated opinion of my skill in that same social realm, cemented our friendship.

Jasper's biggest Hollywood-career mistake was marrying the most beautiful actress he could find, which led to a beautiful daughter but a fatally flawed marriage that ended in less than two years. During the filming of his follow-up to *Kiss*, based on another of my novels but more critically using a lesser screenwriting partner, his star powered marriage imploded, partially because of his not having anybody within his entourage who would tell him he was being a piss-poor husband if not a classic Hollywood jerk.

He was running the wrong plays, making stupid decisions, for maybe the first time in his life, and he knew enough to know it when somebody pointed it out to him. In this case, me.

During a conversation at an outrageously priced dinner at a really swank Malibu Beach bistro where we were supposed to be talking about his having bought the rights to another of my books, he, instead, started bitching about the cruel current state of his pampered life: how delays in the building of his new Santa Barbara home were costing him money, how rare Southern California rains were delaying his current film shoot and costing him money, how his soon-to-be ex-wife was playing hardball and costing him money.

"Jackie's divorce lawyer is really being a dick," he said, a moment after he finished his second scotch before our main courses arrived, angrily returning the empty tumbler to the table with a little too much emphasis.

Not without my own sins, I was working on my second martini and, my inhibitions diluted, not buying into his pity party.

"You know you're being a jerk, right? You know you paid more attention to our damn movie than you did your wife, right?"

Maybe it was that second martini. Maybe I just really liked Jasper. Maybe I just didn't give a shit if he bought the rights to any more of my books. But I bluntly offered, and more importantly he quietly accepted, relationship advice from a man 20 years his senior, but one he knew was being brutally honest.

"You left her alone when she was carrying your child. You left her alone, your baby alone, to go off and make movies. That's not what a husband does. What a father does."

I think he took that wise counsel ass-whipping because, ultimately, he had probably noticed and admired how Maggie and I handled life's successes and failures because he, quietly, witnessed the forever love she and I shared, the good kids we raised. I think he admired that, wanted that. He wanted to know how to do that.

He was always the coachable kind, and that night in Malibu, I was simply pointing out flaws in his game.

Now, sitting in his office on a sunny California day, it is his turn to be honest with me.

"You're over thinking this, Matty."

He often called me "Matty" with an ever-so-slight Irish accent, which I thought humorous as, despite his last name, any linguist evidence of his Irish ancestry had long ago been lost in America.

While I went by Matthew Maybourn on my book covers and in general public, I am simply "Matt" to my family, friends and business associates, including Jasper, who is both friend and associate.

Jasper only called me Matty when he has been drinking or was getting a little emotional.

"Need a job done, Matty, and you're the man I want to do it."

I thought he sounded a little like an Irish mobster in a bad 1950s B movie. I fought back a laugh, and tried to fight logic with logic.

"First, I am not a screenwriter and you want an original screenplay written. And, second, what the hell makes you think I can write a sequel to *The Quiet Man?*"

"I'm not hiring you because you're Irish or because you're a screenwriter or because I think you fuckin' need a job. If that is what you're thinking. I'm hiring you because I own the rights to a sequel to *The Quiet Man* and the screenwriters I want to work with need a good story to give me a great screenplay. And I want this to be a great screenplay. Need it. I want to do this in the next few years, and the first step is a story and when your head is in the right place you write great stories."

"I don't know, maybe later."

"I need the job done now, soon at the latest," he said, talking right over my meek rebuttal. "I have maybe 10 more years of doing these Action Jackson things before I look stupid doing the stunts. I have to grow up, get some big-boy roles under my belt. I have an Irish sounding name and I think this is something that will be good for me as I get gray and fat."

There was a moment of silence as we both recognize our separate, now exposed, truths be told. He was using that logic thing again. I hated when he did that.

I had misunderstood him when he first brought up the idea, in a FaceTime call a couple of weeks earlier. I thought Jasper *was* simply trying to be a good friend. He wanted to be supportive in what was a difficult time in my life. He had offered kind words, and more, routinely during Maggie's illness and immediately after she died. "Whatever you need."

I accepted his kind words but needed nothing from him.

With this Quiet Man thing, I again assumed he was offering to help, financially, if needed. He probably felt he needed to reach out to me, as I had reached out to him during his days of reflection and uncertainty. That's what people in big-boy relationships do.

In his time of need, at that Malibu dinner, after I pointed out that he was really screwing things up and needed to stop doing so, I also offered him what I thought was practically throwaway personal advice on how to handle his pending divorce, advice he apparently mistakenly took for true wisdom.

I have had a little experience in moving on from marital mistakes, from a first marriage which came and went in my 20s, when I, too, was still learning about human nature. Most of my advice to him that night was actually passed on directly from a very good marriage counselor, who, during two short, to-the-point sessions, helped me understand that, above all, I would never completely understand why people fall out of love any more than why they fall into love.

The crippling mistake, she counseled me, was looking for fault only in others. The healthy path was forgiving, yourself and others, and then accepting your own mistakes and trying not to make them again. After that she helped me see some of my mistakes, to accept them and more importantly to understand why I made those mistakes. She then counseled me that I didn't need her counsel anymore unless I had some other, more challenging personal problems we had not yet discussed.

I admired her directness, her honesty. I later made her a character in one of my books.

I had repeated most of her advice to Jasper as we lingered over post-dinner coffee that night at Malibu, an evening punctuated by honesty, accountability and the echoing heartbeat of waves pounding the shoreline in aftermath of a Pacific storm.

Seeking fault in others usually leads nowhere, I told him. He had to look, first and only, in the proverbial mirror. Look for what he could have done better and what he might be able to do better the next time. Then move on as best as he could and try to be a better man.

As he tells it, I guess I also told him that he came off as a fucking jerk when he tried to lay all the blame on his ex-wife, in public or private. I had polished off that second martini by then so I have only vague memories of the latter parts of that evening and my diatribe. My advice, he pointed out, was precisely what his media people had advised him to say when the divorce was announced, when the TMZ-and-company media circus pitched their blood-red camera tents.

"You hire professionals, listen to them," I told him. "But I'm worried more about you and your daughter."

"I'll get visitation, my lawyers will make sure of that. Jackie will use that against me, but I'll get visitation."

"That's not the question. The question is do you want to be a father?"

"Of course."

"Then be her father," I think I said, "not her mother's ex-husband."

As I said, the conversation was a little fuzzy in the rearview mirror, but I remember how he looked at me: like I was a coach who had just called a play from the sidelines that he had no clue how to run. I guess my rambling became a little more specific. Apparently told him that he could be, should be, an occasionally absent but still loving life-long father, a caring and involved father, no matter how difficult his soon-to-be ex-wife might make it in the short run.

Essential to having a good relationship with his daughter, I think I said, was never saying bad things about her mother to his daughter, or to anyone else where it might get back to his daughter. Never throw blame. Never. No matter how much crap was thrown your way.

The same rule applies to ex-lovers, I learned long ago, for much the same reasons; such actions throw more doubt on your character than they do onto the other's.

"Take the high road," I told him, or some similar version of the simplistic *cliché*, words of wisdom induced by honesty and, undoubtedly, too much vodka. That bumpy road might cost him money, but would allow him to forever look at his daughter, and his ex-wife, and all their friends, and never glance away in regret.

Jasper might have had trouble with human nature, but he knew in his gut what was right, what was true, when he heard it or saw it.

After that "man-to-man" conversation, and for the last half a dozen years, he and I had maintained a surprising friendship, usually all business and somewhat distant, but occasionally exciting and in-person. Our friendship, our history, was not one of walking the red carpets and such flamboyant things, but small dinners at my place or at his, private talks over drinks, sometimes more discussion of the roadmaps required to stay on life's high road.

That history is why, on that sunny day in Jasper's Hollywood office, I assume my friend's job offer was just his way of being a friend, of his seeking to continue to walk his high road.

Not for the first time in my life, I was wrong.

"What did you once say to me, Matty? That I was being a jerk to Jackie? That if I wanted to be a father I needed to act like one? Maybe now you need to look in that mirror, you know? You grieve the way you want to grieve. That's your business. But you are worrying your daughter, your friends. You're worrying me."

His next words come at me like a boxers' jabs, one after another after another, each hitting the same weak spot.

"You're not dead yet. You have to quit acting like it. You need to get back to living your life."

Not for the first time, I knew I was defenseless.

"You need to get out of that house, for a while, maybe forever," he says. "You need to get out of Philly. Get the hell out of Dodge, you know. You need to see something new, to find something new. It's been, what? More than a year? And from what your daughter and your agent say, you haven't done shit but sit around and drink and be sad. You got to go out and find some happy, Matty. You fucking need to get back to work."

He paused again, letting the words sink in. He was acting a little, but the script was from the heart.

"Take this job. Go to Ireland. See the sights, drink a little less, write me my story. It will be good for you. It will be good for me."

Leaning back into his chair, he said nothing; I said nothing. The whole lot of nothing mercifully ended as his secretary slid into the room like a stealth cat, placed a cup of coffee on the desk, leaned in and whispered something I could not understand.

Jasper looked away for a moment.

"Thanks Carrie," he said. "Ya. Push that off for a while. I'm talking to a friend."

She exited as stealthily as she entered.

He looked back at me and took a sip from a sissy-looking coffee mug adorned with the word "Dad" in big red letters, surrounded by little red hearts, on it. He now had a lovely 3-year-old daughter, Lexi, from his second marriage and is just as attentive, as loving with his just-as-lovely 6-year-old daughter from his first, Bre. Both adored their father.

"I know you think I'm just doing this because you're my friend, because I want to help. Ya. I am. But I need this story written too. Take my money. Go somewhere and write me a story. We'll get it published. I'll make my movie. Do this for me, will ya Matty?"

Again, I detected a little of an Irish gangster character at work. That's Jasper; that's Mr. Hollywood.

I nodded. He was right. I needed to get out of the damned bed and walk off the pain. I needed to get away for a while.

As I sat there, pondering my future, I became conscious that I was unconsciously twisting my wedding band on its new home, the ring finger of my right hand. It still felt very strange, my wearing it there. But I was doing so for some reason I could not really explain.

I also thought about what I was getting into …

I had no idea, back then, about where my decision would lead me, to this first day on Galway Bay.

I had no idea of what a continuation of *The Quiet Man* story would be, what a sequel to the famous John Ford film could look like. I'd never even read the story the film is based on. But I know I can do the job. Knowing nothing of what I am writing about until I start researching it, having no idea of plot or characters until they came to life in my mind and on my pages. That's the way I write.

He was right that my taking some time in Ireland, getting out of Philly, might be good for me.

"Okay. I'll write you a book," I told him.

"Good. I'll have my people talk to your agent to work out the details. Tell me when you plan to head off for Europe and I'll fly out to New York and we'll have dinner. Maybe we'll sample some Irish whiskeys, so you know what you like when you get there."

"Don't they have any good vodka in Ireland, Mister O'Kelly?"

He laughed a little. "When it Rome, Matty. When in Rome."

He smiled. I smiled back.

"Can you stay around through tomorrow. Having a little birthday party for Lexi. Bre will be there. They love your bad jokes."

"Wouldn't miss it for the world Hollywood."

"Good. Good. And your script consulting services will not be needed tomorrow."

* * *

Admittedly, I did not get started until late in the morning that second day on Gleninagh North, thanks too few days on Irish time and my too many hours at Cassidy's Pub. It took a good part of the afternoon to fully unpack and, with a cup of strong Italian roast coffee in hand, explore the house in more depth.

I had expected the house would need a good cleaning, at least dusting and exorcism of spider webs, their creators, and other creepy things, but, as Cassidy had promised, someone had very throughly cleaned.

The house was small, comfy for two and more than big enough for one.

Upstairs, a tiny shower room was accessed through the single cramped bedroom with the double bed I'd crashed into the night before.

Downstairs, a large front room served as both a seating area and dining area, including a round wooden table I knew would be my work area the moment I saw it. A separate room, a fair-sized kitchen, included a two-person breakfast table and one of those old school, oversized split back doors that could be opened fully or just the top window.

From the back of the house, standing at the rear door, I looked out to a small back yard ending at the low wall of piled stones that surrounded the house. Beyond the wall, after a slight rise of scrub grass, there appeared not a single manmade obstruction to the view of the stone highlands. The crest of the view behind the house, appeared as a breaking grey wave at the edge of an ocean of Burren stone.

From the front door, and either of two front windows, you look toward the sea. With my SUV parked to the side of the house, out of view, I saw the dirt road as it fell away down the hill, past the first house — larger, painted in a dull red that still made it stand out starkly against the green fields. A cute little car, a Mini, also red, was parked on a small dirt parking area between the road and the house.

My new neighbor apparently liked red; she likely also liked order.

The rear of her house was one of a manicured landscape: a back yard maybe twice the size of mine but defined by a stone wall similar to mine but even higher and much sturdier in appearance, with an immaculate garden area within its confines.

There were already plants growing in the garden; spring greens possibly.

To the side of the house opposite of the road, was a single gnarly tree, bent low to the ground and sloped down the hill by what I soon discovered were nearly unrelenting prevailing winds, usually blowing to the west.

Further down the dirt road, there was a low hedge row, maybe five feet high and stretching a hundred feet or so to either side of the paved coast road which appeared to be wearing a neckless of modern power poles and lines. Beyond, the landscape was a pattern of squared off stone fences surrounding bright green cattle pastures dotted with more houses and their own neatly fenced yards, and then the buildings which made up Rathmorgan.

For the first time, I noticed the tall square landmark tower of the ruins of Gleninagh Castle, its base rising out of a field of green and its top appearing to touch the blue-grey water of Galway Bay.

Beyond that, across the water, a ribbon of land that was the bay's north shore.

This would, indeed, be a good place to write.

As I began setting up my work area, I noticed there was even a little stereo on a bookshelf in the great room which to my delight my iPhone would mate successfully with. There was no television, which was just fine with me. My computer, where I did my business, would not operate properly in the same room with a television. At least that is what I told people, only half jokingly.

I had brought my own liquor supply unnecessarily as it turned out. A closer inspection of the cabinet reviewed Else's little bar area, which had clearly just been restocked. Else knew I was a martini-on-the-rocks guy, so there were new bottles of French vodka and Italian vermouth, the names of which I could not pronounce. I figured they were both top shelf. Else knew her liquors, and she knew me. There were also two bottles of wine in a rack, vintage French reds I assumed, knowing Else. The bottle of Absolute vodka I bought in Galway took its rightful place, but out of deference, slightly behind its Euro brethren.

I plugged my phone into the stereo, found a U2 recording and started blasting *Beautiful Day*.

My phone was loaded with all the Irish and pseudo-Irish music in my CD collection, from James Galway to Van Morrison, The Cranberries to Dropkick Murphys. But I had nearly everything U2 and Sinéad O'Connor had ever recorded, so their sounds would dominate any random play.

I drank my coffee and ate a light meal as I finished set-up of my writing area, figured out the wireless internet router with a little help from a note left by someone, likely the housekeeper, and answered a few emails.

I spent a couple hours writing stunted, directionless notes about my day's drive from Galway and my evening's adventures at the pub. Sentences and paragraphs that kept my lazy fingers and my fuzzy brain busy but did not overtax my imagination. Before I realized it, it was mid-afternoon, and I felt like a nap was in order. I guess I was still fighting off the jet lag.

Or maybe the hangover.

* * *

I woke early the next morning. So much for the afternoon nap. A hint of dawn danced on the bay as I looked out one of the bedroom windows. Or maybe it was a dream; I often dream vividly.

Or maybe I was sleeping. Doesn't really matter.

I stood and looked out the window. Either the outside world, or my mind's eye, was a little foggy. Gray masses of nothing moved across the landscape, from the base of Gleninagh North to the water. Galway Bay appeared as flawed glass from this distance and height, smooth but with faint rippling lines that give it movement. More nothingness encroached from the far side of the bay; maybe a mile was visible, maybe twenty.

On my side of the bay, the nebula of fog undulated, sporadically ripping open here and there, to reveal secrets. My neighbor's not-so-distant house, lit with morning lights, stood out for a moment. The roadway at the base of the hill moved like a black snake, rippling from side to side, as the fog moved past in broken waves. A row of distant trees look like a line of human figures bowed in prayer. And the castle, a recognizable bit of reality, appears in the middle distance, at first the top and then more and more until, for a moment, it stands clear and bright in the soft light of the setting gibbous moon. Then it is gone.

Twin, parallel lights cut through the night's nothingness, a worker on his morning drive to someplace bigger and more populated with people and jobs and noise and other early morning lights. Another brief flash of light cuts the darkness in the distance: a ship on the bay maybe, or a plane, or the momentary clearing of the far shore. Then the lights are gone.

Unexpectedly, the house lower down the hill again fully emerges. The bent tree at first, then the top of the house. Briefly there is more, including the back yard. I see someone, a lone woman, standing straight and tall and appearing to my eyes or maybe only in my imagination, to look up the hill, to this window, to me.

I rub my eyes and the woman and the house are gone, obscured again in fog and nothingness.

The dawn was advancing on the world now; the fog receding in deliberate, orderly fashion.

Ah, Ireland.

Caibidil a dó
(Chapter 2)

My friends know me too well, and I like it that way. I am indulgent in that way.

Thanks to my friends, my little Irish cottage was well stocked in liquor; some might say too well stocked, for a wandering writer in search of a story. But then again, my friends know the river from which my best words ofttimes flowed.

Jasper's contribution to my supply arrived by a parcel delivery company I had never heard of and could not pronounce if my life depended on it: two bottles of Connemara whiskey. One of the sturdy Irish lads immediately took its rightful place, beside Else's bottle of French vodka, a slim Parisian beauty with her face turned away. They were not unlike an awkward couple waiting for a good song to dance to. In front of the pair were a glass fit for either and the smaller bottle of vermouth. Behind the pair stood Connemara's brother and his more commoner cousin, a bottle of Jameson, both earnestly awaiting their hoped-for turn on the dance card.

The Jameson, a gift from my literary agency, awaited me at my hotel in Galway city the day I flew in, part of a care package for the carefree in the form of a huge gift basket filled with an impressive spectrum of decadence including, I immediately noticed, Belgian dark chocolates. From the shotgun approach to its contents, I guessed it had been a task assigned to an agency intern. The gift basket had remained unopened until this morning.

The intern knew I was visiting Ireland; Jasper knew I was *living* Ireland.

Jasper knew my writing habits and drinking habits, knew that strong coffee got my writing juices flowing in the morning while hard liquor did the trick at night. The difference was that when I was caffeinated I wrote clear, nearly perfect, often boring words and sentences and paragraphs. Under the influence of alcohol I came up with great ideas, great dialogue, poor grammar and syntax, and often some of the best pages I would ever write.

Both writer's excuses, I know. Both crutches. For me, the trick was to know when to use which crutch.

I also used alcohol as reward for good grunt work done or an easy means to break through any writer's block, which for me was a nearly non-existent condition. I often could not write on the subject I wanted to write about, but I could always write about something.

So, I placed my entourage of Irish, French and Swedes out to see, hoping to set the mood as I pondered the task of writing the sequel to a story that really required no sequel.

Then again, I was writing for Hollywood, and these days Hollywood was all about the sequel.

After sleeping in late, my internal clock finally reset on the morning of the third day at Gleninagh North I made strong coffee, had some toast and jam, and sat at the computer with *The Quiet Man* on my mind.

I knew the film, of course, in a general, film-buff, kind of way. But I needed to dig a little deeper. But not too deep. Writing fiction, I long ago decided, required enough facts to get the place and time right but not enough to where you actually thought you knew how something happened, or why it happened, or what people were thinking when they made it happen. That was history, a branch of fiction all by itself; this was popular, commercial fiction. Two very different beasts.

As usual, my starting place was the internet, a place where a few basic facts, often mostly true stories, echoed again and again, like the image of oneself reflected deeper and deeper into the hall of mirrors, slightly more distorted with each echo.

* * *

The Quiet Man is a 1952 Hollywood paean to Ireland, created and directed by Irish-American filmmaker John Ford, and once described as a "love letter" to his parents' homeland. It is an utterly romantic and completely unrealistic image of the country in the early 20th Century. It may well be the most watched, best loved, B Movie ever made.

Seventy years after it debuted at the *Festival de Cannes*, where the scars of World War II were still fresh on the southern French countryside and everybody in the Western world wanted a little romantic escape, it is still one of the best Valentine's Day flicks available.

Despite all its faults and fallacies, it was one of my favorites growing up and, despite my best efforts, continued to be as I grew older.

I was raised a John Wayne fan, in an age before the internet brought every person's personal flaws into the public realm. It was one of the few things my dad and I would watch together on television. In the 1960s there was a weekly series of old movies on television on Saturday mornings. John Wayne Theater, or something like that. Dad would watch with me sometimes. We sat in the living room together, in the late morning, after the cartoons were done for the day and he finally woke up from a deep sleep following a week of brutal labor as an asphalt paver

and a long night of drinking at his current tavern of choice—
sometimes with and sometimes without my mom. Dad liked his
leisurely wake-ups after five days of being up at 5 a.m. or so.

John Wayne Theater consisted of "old" films, ones that were
old in the mid-1960s anyway. I watched them, again and again. I
remember, almost by heart, many of the plots, starting with his
star maker, 1939's *Stagecoach*. But my fascination focused on his
wartime films. The most notable of the lot was 1949's *The Sands
of Iwo Jima*, the film that gave Wayne his first Academy Award
acting nomination. My favorite Wayne film as a kid, however,
was the *The Fighting Kentuckian*, also released in '49. It is easily
forgotten in Wayne's filmography but was unique in that its plot
focused on a bit of little known French-America history and
because it also had Oliver Hardy, of Laurel and Hardy fame, in a
supporting role. There were good films and bad films in the
series, and one really bad film: 1956's *The Conqueror*, wherein The
Duke played Genghis Khan. And, of course, there was all his
1950s westerns, starting with 1950's *Rio Grande*, one of his most
critically acclaimed films, and his first of five films with Quiet
Man female lead Maureen O'Hara.

The westerns, which were my dad's favorites, included the
likes of *Hondo* and *The Searchers*, which critics sometimes list as his
best film. The film rerun series seemed to end with a pair of
westerns from 1959: *Rio Bravo*, the basic storyline of which he
repeated several more times in the 1960s, and *The Horse Soldiers*.

Smack in the middle of the John Wayne Theater rotation
was *The Quiet Man*.

Actually, my dad would not watch Quiet Man, which he
called "a damn woman's movie." And he really did not like
Wayne's war films. He fought in World War II and not enough
years and beers had come and gone for him to easily revisit that
time. But the westerns, those he and I sat and watched, he in his

recliner, sipping a can of beer, Schlitz or Rainier, a bit of the hair of the dog that bit him the night before, and me on the floor usually lying with my head on a pillow about two foot away from the television, an empty bowl of some super-sweet cereal beside me.

Those Saturday mornings were among the few times he and I were together, alone.

While *The Quiet Man* was a part of the Saturday morning John Wayne film ritual, I really did not get into it all that much until I was an adult. It was my "chick flick" of choice when I had a woman over at my apartment. First when I was just out of high school and in the military, or later in college, and then finally out on my own and dating with a purpose — to fall in love, whatever that was, and to get married.

Maggie and I watched it together. Not every year, but every two or three, usually on a rainy fall day.

The Quiet Man is billed as a romantic comedy and it is, technically. There are sparks and fire galore between Wayne's character, Sean Thornton, a handsome and decent man, and O'Hara's Mary Kate Danagher, a fiery, red-headed spinster who is too much a woman for any of the locals. But the film's central relationship, really, is between Thornton, a physically and emotionally-scarred American of Irish descent with a Hollywood-scripted past, and Victor McLaglen's "Red" Will Danagher, a bigger-than-life caricature of the hard-working, hard-drinking, hard-fighting, semi-literate Irish ruffian. To marry Mary Kate, Thornton must prove to be the equal if not the better man than her brother, Red. And that, of course, involves drinking, and horseback riding, and drinking, and brawling, and some more drinking.

The most memorable scene in the film, in my strange way of looking at such things, is a long, comic, brawling and drinking scene focused on Thornton and Red.

The film's cast, in addition to Wayne, O'Hara and McLaglen, included what seemed like every Irish actor (or actor who could act Irish) available in Hollywood, right down to having someone named Paddy O'Donnell billed as the train platform conductor.

The Quiet Man story is, to be kind, an Irish fairy tale.

It is based on a short story by Irish writer Maurice Walsh, originally published in the Saturday Evening Post in 1933. The story is set in the 1920s. Thornton, a child of the Irish Diaspora, comes "home" to his abandoned family farm in Innisfree seeking privacy after a public tragedy, wherein he killed a man in the boxing ring.

But *The Quiet Man* movie was a very different story. It is all old-school courting and love, including escorted dates, torrid romance in an abandoned castle during a lightning storm, a contested dowry, a meddling community including the kindly priest who knows but keeps secret Thornton's boxing past, and, of course, the focal point of all good Irish stories, the local pub.

In the end, the Quiet Man story and movie are clearly dated but romantically transcendent fiction created by the fertile minds of a fine Irish writer seeking to expand his audience to the shores of America and a great American film director seeking a lost heritage with a return to the shores of Ireland.

I understood both quests. But I also understood their Ireland was their individually framed portraits of the past, and I somehow had to find my own way into that past and carry a modern audience, if not a modern Ireland, with me.

* * *

I gained a glimpse into the window of modern Ireland a little later that first week, in the form a young Irish woman.

It started with a call from my agency in New York, from "Young Saul" Meyers. Technically Saul's father, Saul Meyers Sr., was my agent. But the senior, as he eased into retirement and eased his only son into the top management position, did not like dealing with Hollywood anymore and the junior loved the bullshit games. I mostly dealt with the son these days. Saul Meyers Jr. hated being called "Junior," though. So, when he started in the business right after barely graduating from Williams College and his father deciding any further higher education for his son would be a waste of hard-earned money, somebody in his father's office called him "Young Saul" and it stuck whether he liked it or not.

"Matthew," he boomed out when I answered the phone. "All tucked in and at home on the Emerald Isle, I trust."

"I'm in, Saul. Found a local pub, got lost on the roads. Life is good."

"You got the gift basket, right?"

"I did. Thank you."

"Excellent. Excellent," he said, pausing about a nanosecond before getting to business. "Down to business. I've asked one of our Euro people to contact you, woman out of Dublin. You'll love her. She's a hoot. I've asked her to set up a series of bookstore talk-talks, you know, plugging your latest, maybe what's next. You can talk about the Quiet Man thing, or not. Whatever. She should get to you later today. It's what, like early afternoon there? Right? It's like 10 a.m. here, so it's like 2 p.m. Right? Whatever. She'll call and you two just do what you want to do. OK? How's it going? The writing, anyway?"

I waited until Saul took a breath. He was naturally a little high strung but, if it was still morning in New York and he was working, he would be additionally pumped with one or more of his Starbucks espresso macchiatos.

"I've been here a week, Saul."

"I know, I know. Just checking. Small talk. Anyway, her name is Jennifer, the woman who will be contacting you. Last name is O'Reardon, like the singer. Cranberries. I know, I know. About as Irish as it gets. She's good though. She's out of Dublin, I said that, didn't I? She'll set up some trips for you. Flights, trains, hotels. Whatever you want. She'll set it all up. You just need to OK some dates and she will do the rest."

He took another breath.

"I'm working for Jasper these days, right? That's what the deal is, he's actually paying me to be here and write his story."

"I know, I know. His people understand that you will be doing other things, though. We talked it out. It's all business, all part of the deal. Good for everybody. You get to travel around, talk a little. Get your name out there, pump your books. You could use more sales in Euro. Maybe you come up with an idea for a Euro crime novel. For later. You could use a little international stuff. People love that stuff. Hollywood loves that stuff. And Mr. Kelly's people? I told them they get to start a little accidental buzz on the film before it is even scripted. Good for everybody."

He was slowing down. Fewer words between breaths.

"I get to accept and reject dates?"

"Sure. Sure. Your call. Just take a few, OK? Good for everybody."

"OK Saul. OK."

"Good. Good. Next time you're in the big city. Let's talk. Love to talk to you. You know how to listen. Do business. Love it. We'll talk."

"OK Saul. Best to your father."

I am not sure he heard my last words before he clicked off the phone and moved on to the next task on his list.

I assumed, however, that what was next on his list was calling Jennifer because it was mere minutes before I got another call.

She too was all business, at least initially.

"Mister Maybourn?" she said. Before I could even respond, she rolled on. "Good day sir. Jennifer O'Reardon."

Young people and their caffeine; same on either side of the pond.

She pronounced her first name as I expected, but the last was almost unpronounceable: it was sort of "Ah-rear-nun."

"Yes. Please call me Matthew. May I call you Jennifer?"

"Thank you. Yes, of course, but then please call me Jenn, everybody does," she said. "Mr. Meyers has explained what his plans are, I assume. So we just need to get together to discuss your schedule and see what I can set up for you. I'm in Galway for a few days next week, big literary conference, Cúirt Festival, writers and those that want to be. Editors and publishers from all over. So I can come over and meet. Anytime you want. Shouldn't take much. Couple hours at the most. I understand you're writing a book about Ireland. Wonderful. When might you like me to come over mister, ah … Matthew?"

She had an accent, but it didn't sound very Irish, I thought. Vaguely English; maybe what is now called Euro. But she did pronounce my name as "Matt-you," like she was sneezing, which somehow sounded Irish.

"What about I come up to you. I'll need another shopping day in the city. Restock the kitchen. Get a few things I missed the first time."

"Sure. I'll be in Wednesday to Friday, and what day would you be thinkin'?"

"Thursday. Morning. Maybe about 9?"

"Sure. But maybe we make it 11. You'll be havin' the hell fighin' traffic until after 10."

Now she sounded Irish. She must have the ability to drown her accent when business called for it to be drowned.

"Good. Where?" I asked.

"You know the Eyre Square, Kennedy Park?

"Yes."

"Café Euro, up Shop Street a little. There's tables outside to smoke. You smoke, right? Americans smoke. Do you?"

"I'll find it," I said, thinking it must be crazy when she and Young Saul got together. "I don't smoke, but I don't mind it."

"Good. Lookin' to meet you, ah … Matthew."

"Me too, Jenn."

"You have my cell?"

"Do now. Right here on mine," I said, glancing down at the new Euro iPhone I'd bought for the trip.

"Good. I'm looking forward to our meeting," she said, talking a little slower, slipping back into her business voice.

When she hung up I took my phone over to the music box, plugged it in, and started to play some music. Cranberries, of course. Dolores O'Riordan singing. Maggie loved the Cranberries. I liked them. Young Saul snagged me a couple tickets last minute, to a sold-out show a few years back. He has a good memory when it came to his clients.

The music put me in the mood to write; or maybe it was talking to Jenn. Maybe it was an Irish thing; maybe an O'Riordan thing.

There was something about Jenn's voice, when she slipped into her true Irish, something about the way she talked, the sound of her words. There was the same something about Delores' vocals. There was a sing-song lilt to their voices. A dance from high to low in the same sentence, sometimes in the same word. The slightly hypnotic music of the English language flavored with Gaelic.

For the first time I could hear the faint whispers of an Irish woman's voice, saying things I wanted her to say. I wanted to get that voice into print while I could.

* * *

A few days after setting up housekeeping, and still wrestling with original source material, I decided to visit the Quiet Man Cottage and its accompanying but dubious "museum" despite the dire warnings from the drinkers at the pub. So set off to find the town of Cong, in County Mayo, which I was assured was just 30 minutes north of Galway city, less than 30 miles.

Sometimes you have to listen to the doubters; sometimes you have to learn from them.

Seemed simple enough to get the cottage, according to app, N84 north to Route 334 to R346 to R345 and on to Circular Road, on which the cottage was located. There were even advertisement signs all along the route. But driving unfamiliar roads, in a new country, with a foreigner's driving mentality, proved frustrating as I missed turns and circled and missed turns again. It took me almost two hours to find it, and then took me all of 10 minutes to decide I should have paid heed to the warnings to avoid the place.

The Quiet Man Cottage Museum *is what it is*. There are some interesting displays devoted to the making of the film, proudly displayed photos of John Wayne's family, but not the Duke himself, visiting the museum, and a portion of the building included a replica of the 1920's era "White-o-Mornin' Cottage" where Mary Kate "made her married home" with her American husband. But there was also a politically incorrect and actually rather scary statue of Thornton carrying a seemingly angry Mary Kate into her wedding night or away from the train or some other scene from the film. And, of course, there is a gift shop with all the trinkets an American tourist would ever possibly desire.

It was a place of noise and crowds and a distorted if earnest view of Irish history.

I was on the road back toward Galway city before the engine of my rental car cooled.

Luckily, accidental adventure has always been more to my liking, and my drive home proved the point.

On my way out of Cong, I ran across something truly worth a stop. I initially passed the Ballymagibbon Cairn on the way north, at least I saw a sign for it. But heading south I decided to stop. Hell, I had fuel to burn and interesting roads to drive, as a Neil Young song sort of says.

From the road, the cairn is just a circle of trees with a stone structure atop a hill in the middle of the trees. As you walk up near it, however, the structure if not the purpose reveals itself to you: a nearly perfect mound of stones and grasses. Too perfect to not have been manmade. Atop it, a circular pile of stones that was clearly manmade. A sign, discovered as I circled the mound, described it as an unopened passage mound, with a limestone cairn atop it.

These circle mounds abound in Ireland, I came to learn, each unique in modern remnant but common in ancient purpose.

I lingered at the burial place that was Ballymagibbon Cairn for much longer than I did at the Quiet Man cottage.

It was a place of peace and quiet and contemplation. It was ancient Éire, a glimpse into its early inhabitants. As I departed, I picked up a rock from the trail, a small flat one the size of a silver dollar.

It was my only souvenir of the day.

* * *

Sometimes my computer screen, its Microsoft Word cursor blinking at me like a puppy eager to play, is a willing co-conspirator in my writing. Sometimes it just mocks me.

This morning, it was mocking me.

I sat, sipped coffee, and lost a staring contest with the computer.

Maybe it would be better for me to get some exercise, to get out and blow America out of my lungs and my head, to fill it with Irish air and Irish dreams. It couldn't hurt. I sure as hell had no idea of what I should do to even start wrestling with my story.

I did occasionally jog so changed into old jogging pants, an even older t-shirt and sweatshirt, and brand new Saucony running shoes.

And about the only thing that got my creative juices flowing better than good alcohol was a good heart attack.

I run in much the fashion which I write: plodding at best, ungraceful but efficient, workmanlike in duration I like to think. And I concentrate more on the journey than the finish line, which will always make itself known in its own good time. At 55, and fighting to keep my waistline and my cholesterol within acceptable boundaries, workouts are a necessary evil.

Spinning bike classes were once my favorite, but not since I lost my riding partner. So I mostly jog.

As I completed a mostly for-show perfunctory stretch in front of my new house, I couldn't help but think of Philadelphia, of Maggie. But as I started my jog, with gravity giving me unexpected initial momentum coming down the hill, I inspected the mysterious red house with more than a passing interest. The car was absent and there was neither movement nor sound, human or canine. Then the unexpectedly stunning landscape demanded my full attention. The view ahead, as I neared the bottom of the dirt road, appeared strangely new when not viewed from a car; more beautiful, maybe more timeless.

It was, I poetically conjectured, a postcard come to life.

Pausing at the intersection, jogging in place, I glanced to the left, and then to the right, looking for careening cars more than a directional decision. There were no cars, just a little white house with a bright blue door across the street and to the right, a house which I came to use as a marker for the break in the roadside hedge row and the road to my house. For the first time, I noticed the haphazardly situated trees and sporadic overgrown natural hedges which dotted the fields on the far side of the house, both to the left and right. Through the vegetative breaks I could see a stone wall, two foot high or so, covered with undefined greenery.

From there, the land fell away, out of sight from ground level, and the bay provided the backdrop.

Both directions of the road looked worthy of exploration, but nearly straight ahead I could see the top portion of the square tower of the castle, in the distance, maybe a mile or so away. As good a destination as any. I knew approximately how to get there. To the right on the road. Back toward Rathmorgan, and the bay. I'd find my way from there.

Today, this was the Irish road that would rise to meet me.

As I sprinted up to my slow jogging pace, I felt strangely energized. It had been a while.

Jogging is good for the brain; any exercise really. Dopamine, or endorphins, or some other big word like that. For me, the mind wonders easily. This morning, it wondered mostly over my borrowed homeland.

In Ireland, like America, like anywhere in the world, there is both natural beauty and urban decay; there is profound and irreplaceable history, and the fleeting fad of the latest cell phone; there are lovely, friendly people and there are desperate, violent people. I read a saying once—or did I make it up one night at the keyboard? Maybe: "No man is as evil as his enemies would say, nor as pure as his mother would pray."

No matter how perfect the landscape from a distance, there is often dirt in the details; the world, and Ireland, is that way. As I jogged, this land appeared, to paraphrase an Irish saying, "a bit of heaven on earth." But I understood it is also a land washed by centuries of tears.

I had to keep that in mind as I started to write about this country. I wanted to remember that the makers of *The Quiet Man* film consciously created an imaginary world of splendor, if not perfection, in a land enduring a bloody civil and religious war. Ireland, at least this rural countryside south of Galway Bay, is beautiful but not all the country is such. Rural Galway would be a great setting for a *Gaelic færie* tale but maybe not the story I intended to write. I appreciated the view from Gleninagh North, its landscape and my new place in it, but also understood its isolation.

Love that endorphin high.

This is why I jog: my body gets focused by work and my mind gets lost in inane, sometimes brilliant thoughts. As I plodded through the Gleninagh countryside, I tried to decide if this morning's musings were inane or brilliant.

I traversed the coast road, toward Cregg, before almost doubling back on the narrower paved road that headed back to Rathmorgan, keeping the landmark of the castle in sight in the distance. I knew the castle was by the sea, if not on the beach itself, and my Google Earth program later placed it about a mile, as the crow flies, from my house. There and back, on my serpentine route, somewhere between two and three miles. Maybe a perfect distance for me—and it passed the pub, just in case.

As I neared Cassidy's, I noticed several rental cars in the front parking lot. Good, maybe there were some tourists visiting. It was too early for the pub, so they must have stayed the night. If there were lodgers at the guest house, Eileen had told me, it would usually be a good day to come down and purchase a morning or mid-day meal. She would be cooking up something more than the simple evening pub fare and she habitually prepared more than she needed for the number of guests. She had refused payment for dinner the first night, but then the meal was at her purposeful invite; if I were to invite myself, I came to understand, payment would be expected. Seemed like a fair deal to me.

Passing the petrol station, and the small group of half a dozen houses, I was pretty much alone in the world. But not completely. From one house an old lady's face peered out at an unfamiliar figure plodding from the inn to the beach. In this case, a pudgy, middle age American, wearing a Philadelphia Phillies sweatshirt and jogging pants.

I looked back, waved, and she shrunk away from sight.

The paved road ended past the pub, and shortly after the final pair of the handful of buildings making up beautiful downtown Rathmorgan, at a dirt parking lot providing access to several footpaths. One led directly off to the beach, another toward the castle, and another back toward the coast road — maybe a direct foot path to the main road which I had missed and would need to check out later.

I maintained my focus on the castle ruins.

O'Lochlainn castle, research reveals, dates from the 1500s, when the family *O'Lochlainn* built it. According to the web, what was visible was really just the single remaining tower of what was likely a larger "L" shaped structure in days of yore. At one time it included a basement also likely used as a prison if not dungeon. It was, apparently, occupied by the O'Loughlin family well into the 1800s.

It would make a great setting for a little horror story, or maybe a quirky love story. Hadn't the most romantic scene in *The Quiet Man* been in an abandoned castle?
Definitely inane thoughts.

I approached and slowed from a slow jog to a fast walk. Checked my little Japanese jogging watch: heartbeat of 165, about my max but the thumping felt good; 1.8 miles, perfect; 20 minutes, slow as shit, as usual. I looked away before the watch communicated my always-disappointing calories burned.

I walked around the castle once, getting my breath back, then stood on its sea side, scanning the shoreline. Someone sat alone on a large, rocky protrusion bordering a small beach. At first glance, maybe with the endorphins still running rampant, I saw Spencer Tracy, from film version of *The Old Man and the Sea*. The closer I walked, the more reality came into detail. The old man was Ian. I made my way across the rocky beach recalling what I knew, and didn't know, about the man.

Ian had the rough, but always ready, look of a working man. A weathered face; not unlike my dad in some ways. It was a fairly nice spring day yet still he wore a black high-neck sweater, maybe it was all those years fishing the North Atlantic, where the cold winds sink into your bones and never leave. He had a funny corduroy hat with a little bill, cocked a little to the left on his head. He always touched the right side of the hat when he said

"Hi" to friends and strangers, so the hat tended to lean in the opposite direction.

Always clean shaven, I considered the possibility that hair would never even grow on that dark, weathered face. But grey hair peeking out the sides of the hat, and especially his bushy eyebrows, proved that facial hair was possible, just not allowed. His right hand habitually hovered near his face as he talked in the bar, and now, with a cigarette held loosely between his index and middle fingers, only a second away from his addictively impatient mouth, I understood why.

His eyes were bright. Not unlike an old dog noticing everything but only reacting to something promising adventure or something hinting danger. His eyes were the facial feature I remember most from the shadowy-lit pub. I pictured them as steel-grey, but in the daylight they were the light blue of a cloudless day.

The light of day often changes one's perception of others.

"Good morning," I said as I neared.

"Tha' t'is," he said, glancing from the bay toward me before looking back to the sea.

I came to a stop beside what I assumed was his ritual resting place.

"The bay is beautiful this morning," I said, following his gaze to the sea.

"Lovely as a woman waking in your unkempt bed," he said.

We glanced at each other, smiled the smile of knowing men.

"You fished the North Atlantic, think I heard," I said as we looked back to the bay.

"Any work done on the ocean, I done in my time," he said. "You been on d' water?"

"Navy. Four years. Like to say the first two were some of the best of the life and the last two were the worst. West Pac sailor, middle and south Pacific."

"Spent a little time in warm waters, off Spain and Portugal, off the Azores and the Canaries. North Atlantic mostly. Feckin froze my ass off."

"British Navy?" I asked, thinking I heard a little of a blended accent in his banter. Ireland was neutral in World War II, but some Irish joined one enemy to fight a greater one, I read somewhere.

"Few years, ya," he said, turning back to the ocean. "Too late for the war. Just a wee boy hiding out in the country them years. Spent my time in uniform in the '50s. Grew up on a farm, over Limerick way. But after seeing the sea, farming held no love for me. Never wanted to leave the water."

"You're retired now though?"

"Mostly so. Me and ol' Mully do a little work. Fishin' charters mostly. He knows the sea better than any man I ever been on the water with, but I know the fish. Mostly we are two salts, run aground and rusting."

I studied his face, the morning light and our discussion illuminating its details.

"Why do you call him old? You two must be near the same age."

"He's got almost 10 years on me. But I've married. Guess that what makes me old. Work for him sometimes, on his fishing boat."

"What kind of fishing?"

Ian took a long drag on his cigarette, blew smoke out that the breeze off the water just blew back into his face.

"You *inner*-viewing for your story?" he said.

"Always a possibility."

"You go talk to Mully then. He's the interesting one. He got more stories to tell than I could ever dream up for ya. He's lived a life, ya know? Me? Just a family man made his living on the sea. Nothing more."

I nodded.

"Mully traveled the world. I stayed close to home. Spent most of my life working those waters." He waved the back of hand out toward the bay as he talked. "Galway Bay my home. Used to be lot o' good fish out there. Off the North Sound, down the Slate. Really good off the back of the islands, west of the Arans. Out on Porcupine Bank 'bout as far as I worked it."

He took another drag, then let out a big sigh with the smoke.

"Had wife and kids to be around. Wanted to be home when I could."

"Wife and kids?"

"Two great girls. Both of 'em smart enough to get an education and leave home. One in Galway city. An accountant. One immigrated to America, living in Boston. She a nurse."

"And the wife?"

"Nelly," he said, a smile coming across his face as he said her name. "At home. She's grown used to me being gone all day, so I get out the house when I can. Give her time. Nearly 40 years been married. Count the bad days on one hand."

"You?" he added, after a pause. Maybe a prayer of thanks.

"Widowed," I said.

He looked at me with shining but slightly sad eyes. Again I thought of that old dog who had lived a good life. I glancing out to the sea and just letting our words fall away into silence. I did not want him to see the secrets my eyes held.

"Hope you had good years," he said, gracefully breaking the silence.

"We did."

"And now you running around Ireland, smelling the world a'fresh," he said, as he gave a once over to my jogging attire, shrugged his shoulders in acceptance of another man's faults, and then took another drag off his cigarette as he turned back to the water. "That's good."

"It is good."

The silence of secluded memory, from both of us, followed.

The sound of the gentle tidal waves dancing around the rocks soon overwhelmed our silence.

Seemed to me as he was talked out for now. Interview over. Needed a beer in his hands to really get an Irishman talking, I guess.

"I'll start making my way back up the hill," I said.

"Yes sir,' he said. "Met widow O'Brian's dog yet? Hound don't much like visitors. Always barking and growling, least when I see him, when I take Nelly up to clean the house where you're staying. Good dog for the widow, though. Just got to show it due respect."

"Heard him once," glancing back up the hill. "We'll probably get to know each other better."

Ian took another hit off his cigarette, made another futile attempt to blow smoke against the wind. I liked the image and imagery.

"See you at the pub," I said as I turned to leave him, the old man and the sea, alone on the beach.

"Yes sir. Do occasionally stop by for a pint."

Quickly off the rocky beach, back on the dirt path, I started to run at an unsustainable pace. Guess I wanted to make an impression, in case Ian watched me.

Out of sight, I quickly reverted to my slow jog and maintained that all the way back to the base of my hill. I turned up the road, saw how steep the hill was, and decided enough was enough when it came to jogging.

But then I noticed the widow O'Brian, outside her house, and shifted into a quickstep run.

An occasional running buddy back in Philly advised early in my training to always attack hills. Good hill running technique, however, was not the reason for my decision.

* * *

Nearing Cathleen's house, I saw her in the front yard, crouched, working in a flower bed within a stoned-fenced area.

She is oblivious to me, it seems. I cannot look away.

Jet black hair juts out wildly from under corners of a bright red bandana. Her off-white dress is spotted with dirt and sweat. Knee-high yellow muck boots.

Finally, she notices my passing, stands up, and looks my way. My legs are protesting the sprint uphill, but I put down the revolt. Be strong; look strong.

I cannot look away. It is her eyes. Not really the color, but thick black eyebrows crowning a pale, seemingly colorless face despite a weathered look of someone accustomed to the sun. Only her sharply-molded lips offer a hint of red hue. The dress is baggy, but a belt tied just under her bust defines her figure. I cannot help but admire what I see. Feminine, yes, but not the corseted, red-haired Irish beauties of Hollywood. She could be my age, or 20 years younger.

Despite my lungs now joining my legs in protest I fake an easy breath and am about to say something when my distraction, my shuffling stride and the rough dirt road conspire against me. I catch the toe of a Saucony in the dirt and nearly fall. A quick bit of dancing the funky chicken allows me to catch myself, but by the time I am righted, my eyes are on the ground in front of me.

It is better to just jog on by and save introductions for a less clumsy moment.

But there is another distraction to deal with: the dog. He, too, is taking note of the stranger's passing.

At first, all I see is a mass of dark kinky hair. On closer inspection eyes peek out from under tufts of hair, as does a muzzle, fronted with rather large teeth, part of a silent growl. He stands off to the side of the house, between his home and the road, between his mistress and the stranger. He is not big, but has that coiled-energy of a hound poised to jump into action without warning.

We watch each other, warily, as I pass on up the hill.

Half a dozen strides farther up the hill, after I have broken eye contact with the widow O'Brian's guardian, I heard a clear, firm woman's voice.

"Michaeleen," she calls out, with the "eeeeen" seeming to last for several seconds. "You come now!"

I glanced over my shoulder, quickly, as not to have a repeat of my stumble. The dog is following me. I stop, turn, and look him eye-to-eye—a mistake realized the moment it is made.

Michaeleen stops, locks his eyes on mine, bares his teeth just a little. It's that Alpha thing.

"Michaeleen!" she calls again.

I will come to know my neighbor is an Irish Blue Terrier, or at least mostly descended from such a breed. Also known as the Kerry Blue Terrier, but often considered to be the dog of Ireland not just County Kerry. Medium in size, maybe two-foot-tall at the shoulders and 40 pounds.

He looks larger at that moment we are eye-to-eye.

To understand the breed's temperament, one must understand that its primary historic job was vermin control, which included not only rats but the occasional badger. It is said to be a loyal family dog, gentle with its housemates, but known to often have real attitude issues with other dogs and strangers. It is known to be playful if not downright mischievous when bored.

Also, using the athletic idiom, its motor is always running.

It is loved in rural Ireland due to its farmhand work ethic, and loved in urban Ireland due to its historic link to the country's nationalism. Michael Collins supposedly named his terrier "Convict 224".

Having learned all this only *after* my face-to-face with Michaeleen that day, when I Googled Irish dog photos until I found a mug shot of my neighbor, at that eye-to-eye moment I rely heavily on Ian's opinion of the dog's attitude issues as I realize my mistake in stopping to face him.

The widow O'Brian's "Michaeleen!" fades into the quiet.

I drop my gaze, but stay aware of his location. He stands firm, squares himself up, not unlike a boxer in the ring. He shakes his head once, to clear his head and maybe the hair from his eyes, and then steps half a stride forward and emits a low growl.

If I were into anthropomorphism, which as a writer I am often wont to do, I would say he is laying down a challenge.

"I am Michalleen O'Brian, of Gleninagh hill," he says. "You think yourself my better? Come then and prove it!"

He stands as solid as the stone that defines his landscape, air whistles through his nostrils; his dark eyes and steady glare dares me to take his challenge. In that moment, I am not even sure I could prove as tough as an Irish rat, let alone a badger.

Again, I hear a voice, an actual human voice.

"Michaeleen," she calls out, this time with more emphasis. "You come here!"

Both Michaeleen and I look to the source of the command.

I back up slowly, a couple steps. The growling ceases; he takes a couple quick steps back toward his house, then glances back at me. I turn my back to him and walk toward my front door, keeping watch out of the corner of my eye at the movement of the reigning king of this hill.

Michaeleen, a true Irish gentleman at heart, I would also come to learn, continues back down the hill. He glances back at me as he prances away, barks once: a soft bark, as if to say "see you later" if not "welcome to the neighborhood."

Caibidil a trí
(Chapter 3)

It was a weekday evening and after a good day of work accompanied by a lack of planning for a suddenly desired evening meal, I set off down the hill in hungry hopes of a seat at Eileen's evening table.

The pub side was crowded with mostly strange faces watching Ireland play a "friendly" soccer game that meant little more than national pride and serious practice for the next year's World Cup qualifying. Portugal was the opponent and, as I had no reason to root for "The Machine", as I once heard the Porto squad's nickname translated. A dozen or so hard-drinking Irishman also provided ample reason for me to root for The Boys in Green.

Kenny was the only recognized regular at the bar, other than the good barkeep, busy at the taps as usual. Even Séamus was absent, which was rare in my limited census opportunities. While the bar was nearly shoulder-to-shoulder with young men, there was an open spot at the bar beside Kenny and I took it. It seemed to me he was usually avoided by the other local young men who patronized the pub; maybe it was his father being one of the *Gardaí*, maybe it was another story I had yet to hear.

Kenny and I exchanged perfunctory greetings and he returned his attention to the game. It seemed he knew every player, on both sides. I was never much of a soccer fan, but I came to enjoy his "football" while standing beside him, sipping a beer, and listening to him give an almost play-by-play account of the match. This evening, he sported a deep-green, retro Irish national football jersey, with "eirecom" emblazoned on the front. I assumed the Irish communications company either is or was a national team sponsor.

Like just about everything he wore, the jersey hung loosely on his gaunt frame. He also had athletic wrist bands which he seem to always have on for some unexplained reason. He had a habit of scratching at the bands, I had observed before and noticed again that night.

Within a half hour of my arrival, the game came to a dull, merciful end after a couple minutes of anticlimactic extra time and my first beer not yet off to meet its maker. The local boys lost 2-nill to a better team and Kenny knew it. Apparently, the Irish side has been doing a lot of losing the last few years.

"And we have to face the Germans in World Cup qualifying this year," he said. "Worse match ever saw in m' life was them runnin' us off the pitch in 2014. Feckin worst ever."

I had made a short list of people I wanted to interview within the first few days of residence on Gleninagh North, and I added to it all the time. I had a good mental picture of the Harringtons in place and in printed note form, and a pretty good grasp of a character in my yet to be written that looked and sounded a lot like Ian. Old Mulligan just had to have a good story to tell. I knew as much even before Ian advised me so, but his personality was as elusive as his story. Jenn, and maybe the Widow O'Brian, would probably have their own unique stories.

Séamus, too. But that would be a very, very difficult interview.

Kenny fascinated me because he seemed such a simple young man, but clearly wasn't.

That night, I really wanted to ask him why he kept scratching at his wrists, but didn't. Maybe I would have, eventually, if Eileen hadn't made an appearance in the pub, saw me, and quickly, quietly invited me to a meal in the inn's dining room. I accepted before she could mention the menu.

Kenny was not invited, the reason for which I added to my mental list of unanswered questions about the young man. I paid my bar tab, including Kenny's next Stella, and thanked the barkeep.

"Thanks for the play-by-play," I said to Kenny as I excused myself.

"Thanks for listening."

His thanks was more meaningful than mine.

The meal was nothing fancy: shepherd's pie topped with champ, a mix of mashed potatoes with peas. But it was fresh and filling, and beggars cannot be choosers.

The only payment Eileen required was a little discussion about my book in progress, Hollywood in general and Jasper specifically, with an audience of two quartets of tourist couples more than able to eavesdrop and quietly speculate on my personal celebrity.

A smart business woman, that Eileen.

She must have been pleased with my playing along with her not-so-subtle advertising as she offered to refill my beer in addition to my meal, twice, but I nursed my second and final beer throughout dinner and had coffee before desert.

The walk back up the hill was becoming as routine as it was pleasant.

* * *

Walking around Galway city's Eyre Square, on the agreed morning of my meeting with Jenn, I had a strange *déjà vu*. Not so much that I have been here before, which I had, but almost that I was seeing it afresh, through someone else's eyes.

Since my last visit, my research found a YouTube video of President John F. Kennedy speaking in Galway, from June of 1963, just a few months before his assassination. It is an old black and white television video of a short speech he gave in a crowded square on one of the last stops he made during a visit to his family's native country.

"If the day was clear enough, and if you went down to the bay and you looked west, and your sight was good enough, you would see Boston," the beloved president of Irish Catholic heritage told the crowd. "And if you did, you would see down working on the docks there some Doughertys and Flahertys and Ryans and cousins of yours who have gone to Boston and made good."

He then asks the crowd for a show of hands as to how many people have family in America, drawing a response from nearly every person in the crowd.

A speaker known for his humor, his funniest line is about inviting the crowd to visit him sometime, in Washington, D.C., and advising them to simply tell the guards that they are from Galway and that "they are friends of the President."

He thanks the audience for their gifts and warm wishes, and in a slightly macabre touch, given his impending assassination, he bids farewell with the line: "I must say that though other days may not be so bright, as we look toward the future, that the brightest days will continue to be those we spent with you here in Ireland."

For some reason I pictured myself present that day, in 1963, in Eyre Square, which would be renamed President John F. Kennedy Memorial Park in 1965, after the pain of the city's

revered Irish descendent's death became the dull memory of a
serious wound healed as best as it would ever heal.

I saw myself as one of the people in the video, hanging
precariously from the side of a building, as some in the crowd
were, or as a man shimmied up a sign post, a few feet in the air,
seeking a different view of a memorable sight. "There he is, it's
Mr. Kennedy," I would shout, as he approached, a line of
motorcycle *Gardaí* on either side of his car, the crowd surging to
get a glimpse.

I wondered if the crowd, seeing Kennedy riding open-air in
a convertible on that day, later had a *déjà vu* of their own when
seeing the film of that November day in Dallas, when another
open-air ride in a convertible would be the last moment of the
President's life.

Wandering feet and a wandering mind. I returned to the
present.

The view from the square could serve as a good microcosm
of all of Ireland: a blend of the old world and the new, living in
often uneasy coexistence. There is a bank building that dates
from the first half of the 1800s, and there is the glass enclosed
entrance to a shopping mall complete with a Gap and an Apple
store. There is a fountain that commemorates the city's birth
more than 500 years ago, and there is a street musician playing
bastardized modern versions of ancient Gaelic ballads using a
crude electric guitar and vocal amplifier, collecting coins from
unknowing, uncaring tourists.

As happened the first time I walked the square, maybe 15
years before with Maggie, I became disoriented. Enveloped by
the chaos of the city, I lost track of north, and which way to the
water; really all orientation points. I searched and found the big
hotel where we stayed. *Has it really been that long ago?* How could it
be 15 years since our first romantic vacation after starting our

family, when the kids were old enough to be left with their grandparents while we adventured?

The hotel changed names but not its landmark status, nor its value as an orientation point, over the years of my absence. I stood with my back to the hotel's doors and look out to where the main route through town, R863, bends and heads north. The appropriately named Shop Street is off to the left from where I stand.

There is my destination. I think.

I walked through the park, this time with a clear direction in mind, now with gentle memories of Maggie walking beside me. For a moment, I let the memories carry me, but they quickly flow on to places I do not want to go. Longing for my partner in adventure, I stopped and the crowd moved around me as if I am just another bird-stained statue of which few remember its significance.

I forced myself to notice details of the square, of the people, of the way they are dressed, the way they talk. I give them imaginary motivations for their being here, at this place and this time. I pick one or two and give them fictional storylines.

Memories, good and bad, mercifully, fade.

I think instead of my coming task, my Irish book, still very much hiding in the shadows of idea and yet to even begin to come into the light of my imagination and my computer screen. How might it fit into this changed yet familiar landscape? I know, at some point, I will need an Irish editor. Someone whose advice I could listen to, heed, or ignore, as necessary. But my first decision, my pivotal decision, was whether this book would be simply a cinematic echo of *The Quiet Man*, another travelogue to an idyllic Ireland, or something more?

Could it be something more?

My wonderings, and my inherent my writer's ego, are brought back to earth, and my attention back to current place and time, as, taking another step, I stepped onto direct evidence of an unidentified Irish dog recently walked and rudely left unattended.

Scraping the sole of my left foot with each step, first on the grass and then on the cement walk and the asphalt streets, I put aside thoughts of my future works and focused instead on the past work I would be promoting on the planned book reading tour.

Crap such as this is, alas, the business of novelists.

After walking purposefully down Shop Street, approaching the Café Euro, through a fenced-in outdoor seating area that had a few customers braving a cool spring day for the sake of much-needed sunshine, I scanned the faces of a dozen or so female customers, looking for a reciprocating face in response. My attention rushed past a few modish teenagers, lingered on a couple of 40-ish feminine faces, burnished with proper business makeup, topping prim and proper business-hours outfits.

My mistake.

After gaining hardly a glance from one of my suspected Jenns, and nothing from the other, I was about to enter the café's glass double doors when a voice from behind called out.

"Matt-ew?"

I turned to look into a face that could easily had been one of my daughter's girlfriends: a 20-ish *colleen*—a rather too familiar Irish term, I think, for unknown young women—styling red-tinted black hair cut short, just above the shoulders and swept back, and a kind of Goth-lite makeup style that includes slightly over-applied dark eye shadow and slightly too-dark lipstick. For all the immaturity conveyed initially, there were also large, square, black-rimmed glasses that did a good job of convincing one of the innate intelligence of the wearer despite other fashion statements.

"Ms. O'Reardon?"

"That's me, sir. And how you be enjoyin' Ireland?" she said, holding out a hand for me to shake.

A good handshake. No limp wrist for this one.

"The view from Gleninagh North is great," I said as I finish the handshake and forced my awkward stare away from her hair and makeup, glanced down, and instantly notice her tight sweater and the attractive view it offered. I shot my eyes back to her face as quickly as they had left. The lessor of two revealed evils.

"Glad to hear it. No trouble finding the place?"

"No trouble. I've explored the square and the downtown before, with my wife many years ago. And briefly a few days ago, when I flew in."

"Hasn't changed much in recent years. Maybe a few less tourists as the dollar has fallen against the Euro. Sitting outside good with you?" She pointed over to a nearby table with a jacket hanging on one of two chairs, as well as a small note book, an even smaller cell phone, a large paper coffee cup, and what looked like the crumbled remains of a pastry on a plate. The essential accoutrements of business all spread out on a café table, as young professionals often do.

"Had a bit of a hunger on me," she said. "Can I get you something?"

"I'll get something to drink and come back," I said, deciding to take advantage of the opportunity to break from the initial and uncomfortable first eye-contact moment.

I returned with a paper cup of coffee of my own, a smaller one. I had them brew up an Americano to make sure it was fresh and strong, which the brewed coffee rarely was in Ireland.

This time, I had my business face on.

"So, you and Saul have a little book tour planned for me?"

"We do. Starting here, in Galway. Then a sort of dance around the island. Cork and Dublin and Belfast." She had pulled a pen out of her notebook as she talked. She, too, was ready for business.

"Sorry I'll be pushing it a bit," she continued, "but there is a literary fest next week in town. Be a perfect time to get you into a bookstore here. Not far away, on Foster Street on the other side of Eyre Square. Could you start as early as next weekend?"

"I don't see why not. I can make it there by myself but I assume you will be taking care of the rest of the travel. I just need to show up. Do my song and dance."

"Taking care of you I'll certainly be doing. At each bookstore, I'll make sure all is well, books are available, signing table — you do sign books?"

"If they're going to pay hard cash for a book these days I'm sure as hell going to sign them."

"*Foirfe*," she said, nodding.

I guess I looked at her with a confused expression, because I was confused.

"For-fay," she repeated, slower. "Perfect."

I nodded.

"Do you prefer flying or Irish Rail?"

"I have the time."

"So rail? You'll need plenty of time with the rail."

"I have the time, and I need to see more of the country."

"Modern hotels or small inns?"

"If all I am doing is sleeping the night, hotels. But they don't need to be modern."

"You're a U2 fan, I hear? Mr. Meyers said he had the hell to get ya some tickets for a New York show some time back?"

"Both true," I said. "Isn't all Ireland a fan?"

"Well you'd be surprised by that, but yes. Mostly. So, be putting you up in the Clarence in Dublin. They're part owners of it, ya know. Tourist place, little expensive, but nice and in good area too, near Trinity, the college, you know it?"

"Never been to Dublin, or Cork or Belfast."

"And you be writing a book on Ireland?"

For just the briefest of moments, she had a sour look on her face, a disapproving look. The Irish were usually poor poker players, I knew from personal experience long before seeing this youthfully beautiful new bit of empirical evidence. The Irish, I think, all too often wear their emotions on the outside, clear for people to see.

She recovered, quickly. Maybe she thought I didn't notice.

"Good for you to get around, then. Mr. Meyers said you would have need of a little touring. I can plan to be spending a day with you at each stop, if you like. Show you around a little."

"That will be fine. But I'm a good traveler. Don't want to be a pain."

"No problem at all. Sorry if it came across that way. Happy to be of any assistance, really."

"Actually,' she continued, choosing her words a little more carefully. "I wanted to spend a little time with you. Hoping you would be gracious enough to give me a little tour 'round of the writing business. Do a little writing myself. Hope we could talk a little 'bout the business. Maybe you might even take a little look … sometime, if you have the time."

"I would be happy to," I said, then taking a sip from my still too-hot coffee. "But I am not much of an editor."

"*Foirfe*," she said. "Editors. Bane of creative writers. Necessary, but not 'til all the bleedin' be done and the readin' to start. Know what I mean?"

I did know what she meant.

There is the writing, and then there is the business of writing. Two almost totally exclusive things.

* * *

I am slow to judge people, usually, but seldom misjudge. I usually think the best until proven otherwise. There are exceptions.

I hadn't shared a dozen words with Séamus O'Dennehy before I decided I did not like him. He was a man clearly filled with anger, justified and unjustified, and, more dangerous, a man who could not tell the difference.

Séamus oozed inherent risk. I sensed it.

He was the dark alley in a strange city, the car drifting in and out of its lane as it sped past you, the stranger watching people come and go from the bank cash machine you had intended to visit.

Séamus' dislike of all things American was clear the first day in the pub. His disappointment with life in general, and his seemingly tragic fate in specific, came to me as I learned about him, bit by bit, often from off-hand remarks by the rest of the pub clan, selectively from secretive observation. His mean streak was hinted at, but it was, evidently, something you had to witness to fully respect. I witnessed it one night, still early on in my stay on Gleninagh North, sometime after my first Smithwick's of the night was finished and before the bitter end of my second ended up spilled on the floor and over a perfect stranger.

I had a ringside reporter's seat, in fact.

I was a wrestler in high school; may have already said that. I repeat my stories; may have said that as well.

75

Thought I was a pretty good wrestler, actually, but really wasn't. Wrestled a little in college too, as a club sport, after I realized I wasn't really all that good. Finally got tired of the abuse, and found other ways to stay in shape. I was also a sports writer in college and for a couple years just after, as my first journalism gig, before I started my decade-long stint as a hard news reporter. Those two facts, I guess, are why I can follow athletic action as it unfolds in front of me; I can understand what is happening and, usually, why it is happening. I can anticipate who will win and who will lose and why; and I am only rarely completely fooled.

That's why I remember so clearly exactly how Séamus came to put the young Burke boy, my beer, and a perfect stranger all on the floor.

I had been talking with Eileen, leisurely fishing for what she planned to cook up for her lodgers that night. But our talk was interrupted by about half a dozen related, cascading events occurring within seconds.

Séamus, who was sitting and talking with an unknown young local leaning over his table, uttered a half-understood growl of "feck off ya' mog." As both the lady of the house and I turned our attention, I wondered who he was calling an idiot.

There followed quickly a brief, overlapping and indiscernible conversation between Séamus and the unknown mog that ended with the mog's clear declarative of "Goin' to kick your crippled ars", leaving no doubt who was talking to whom at that point.

A split second later an unknown male American tourist in a day-glow-green tourist sweatshirt let out a high-pitched feminine squeal of "Eeeeee". In roughly the same instant, the unknown mog stumbled back away from Séamus's table and every face at the bar that hadn't already noticed the impending fight turned sharply to see the burgeoning entertainment.

At first, I was stunned by the speed of movement of the usually slothful Séamus. Before the unknown mog could regain his balance, Séamus was up, out of his booth and moving purposefully, if awkwardly, toward his opponent.

Then there was more yelling.

"O'Dennehy!" someone called out authoritatively. Sounded like the barkeep.

"Fast ol' arse, for a feckin cripple," the mog said as he regained his footing.

Overlapping everything was the resumption of the "Eeeeee" squeal, from the same tourist, or another. I cared not to discern.

A few people moved forward, as if to intervene; for some unknown reason me included. I stepped in front of Eileen and the squealing tourist, took a step toward the action.

"Leave 'em," Mully said as he stepped in front of a man he had been talking with. Eileen pulled me back as well. "No," she said.

I glanced back at her. Despite my growing dislike of Séamus, I felt the urge, the need to protect him. It wasn't a fair fight, I thought, his injury and all. He'd get hurt, maybe badly. I had to help. That Captain America Syndrome kicking in. Protect the weak, challenge the bully, and all that other world-leader pretend shit the good old U.S. of A. was known for.

"Worry about the Burke boy," she added, knowingly.

I turned, again, to the looming fight, noticed again how quickly Séamus moved. Then I understood. I took back my step forward and continued to mentally record the sequence of action. Good fight scenes, ones that looked and felt real, were the bread and butter of my novels.

Cassidy quickly moved from around the bar and toward the combatants, but then he stopped after he placed himself between the combatants and the rest of the customers. It seemed that most of the locals had seen this little dance of destruction before, maybe repeatedly, and those that hadn't were being held back by those who had.

The dance didn't take long.

The two men, fists at the ready, circled. There was a lot of boastful cursing from the Burke boy, most of which I did not really understand. It was clear he had a few beers in him, both from his slurred speech and from his slightly sluggish movement.

There was now nothing but silence from Séamus, who despite his everyday awkwardness, moved with a deceptive smoothness, clearly purposeful.

At first I thought Séamus entered the fight as a wounded animal might fight, favoring his bad left side, turning it away, shrinking away from a war he was ill-prepared to wage. The Burke boy sensed his apparent weakness, and circled, moving to attack the man's bad side. Séamus' ploy, and what I soon witnessed was a wounded soldier's skill in such dances, became clear.

I decided it was, in fact, a fight between a boy and a man.

Without warning, at his chosen moment, Séamus ceased his movement, squared up and stood face to face with his opponent. His right fist was poised at chin level, to protect his face but also ready to strike; his left hand, barely made into a fist, was held chest high, inviting attack to his weak side. The Burke boy blindly obliged. With his first approach the boy launched and easily landed a right over the man's bad arm. It seemed to do little damage, though, as the man simply laid his head over forward and onto his hunched shoulder, and the incoming blow mostly. glanced off his arm and slipped off the back of his head. Again both squared up. Again the boy attacked the obvious weakness; again he landed but did little damage.

Having sized up his opponent's power punch, the man then seemed to retreat back into his wounded animal mode, and the boy, either hubris or beers blinding him, sensed retreat and maybe advantage, recklessly pressed the attack, almost sprinting as he circled around to continue his attack to the man's bad side.

As it turned out, a very bad decision.

The man, pivoting slowly on his good leg, stepping back on his bad leg and turning his bad shoulder away as the boy attacked, drew his opponent close, especially close to his good right hand. But the man held his good right at bay, for the moment.

The boy threw a series of awkward-looking punches, first jabs with his left, finding only air or the man's parrying right knocking it away, then with his seemingly advantageous right again, and again, sometimes landing glancing blows but still doing little damage. Frustrated, the boy tried another desperate, heavy right with his full weight behind it, clearly seeking a fatal blow but now also opening his chin to attack from the man's right which I now knew was clearly held in reserve for just such an opportunity.

The man, after easily slipping another awkward punch to his bad side, waited until the boy dropped his defending left again, and then he unleashed a flashing, punishing right of his own.

There was dull thud as fist met jaw; it sounded like pain.

The boy moaned. The audience groaned.

The sequence repeated itself, more or less in the same sequence, only twice more, each time the action more deliberate by Séamus, the result more painful for the Burke boy. Each time, when the wild right came and went, Séamus purposefully, punishingly, struck back. Each time connecting, and snapping the Burke boy's head back with same dull thud, the same moan, the same audience groan.

After the third hit, I knew the argument was settled. The boy was defenseless, his left held low, inviting continued destruction. Cassidy's opinion on the eventual outcome was one punch behind mine. Once more, Séamus drew near to the Burke boy and delivered a lunging roundhouse right, his full body weight backing the punch that I watched as if it were delivered in slow motion. It rocked the kid, buckled his youthfully foolish knees, and sent him reeling back toward the bar.

He stumbled, lost his footing and fell into me before Cassidy could move to intercede. I fell, as stacked dominos fall, back into an American tourist.

That was when the Burke boy, and my beer, unconsciously still held in my hand, and the perfect stranger all hit the floor, roughly at the same moment.

Eileen moved from protecting me to aiding the American tourist, who seemed to be enjoying the show right up to the point that he became part of the show.

Cassidy stopped the fight as his wife minimized the customer damage.

"Enough O'Dennehy!" he yelled. "Enough."

"He started it," Séamus said. "Feckin *buachaill dúr*."

"Ya, he's a stupid boy, drunk to boot, and you finished it. You're done for the night."

Séamus stepped back, nodded, smiled a smile you see only in the movies, the kind of smile a guy acting crazy smiles, or an insane villain smiles. Menacing, yes, but mostly for show, I thought. He turned and slowly walked back to his booth, grabbed a jacket and pulled some wadded up Euro notes out of his pocket, counted some out, and tossed them onto the table.

"Buy the boy a beer," he said to Cassidy as the barkeep knelt down to check on the young Burke boy. "One for the feckin writer, too. Seemed to have spilled his drink."

Séamus looked my way, nodded again, as he finished his instructions. It was a look not unlike Michaeleen's. A challenge to a stranger sniffing around his turf?

"Say one more word, Mr. O'Dennehy, and you'll not be welcome here again," Eileen said from behind me.

The woman of the house had spoken and nothing more need be said.

Séamus nodded her way, glanced again at me but paid not another moment of attention to the Burke boy. There was almost a bounce in his clumsy step as he departed the pub. A couple of the boy's running dogs helped the young Mr. Burke out shortly thereafter, without collecting on the beer, but only after hearing Séamus' car tear out of the parking lot.

I declined the beer as well. I had some manly thoughts to get down in print when I got home, before I slept and forgot them.

* * *

I have played the ego game of writers' publicly tours for coming on 20 years now, so like any repeated task, it gets monotonous unless you do it with some degree of spontaneity. It is similar to sex after marriage in that way.

The basic sequence of book readings and signings are pretty much the same everywhere, every time, for every writer. I show up an hour or so before the reading is to start, as I hate to be late and rarely have been. I take a quick look at the room and the place I will sit or stand to read. I like a podium, but have performed fine with nothing but air and a little distance between me and the audience. I don't like using a microphone, as my voice can boom when necessary, but some large rooms or elderly crowds necessitate it, so I can deal.

I brought notes to my first couple of readings, before I realized they ended up of little or no value, as I go off script easily and often. I find most audiences are more appreciative of casual conversation than the conveyance of a multitude of facts. I always mark two or three spots in the book I am currently hawking for reading, usually one long passage of description of scene or character. Reading dialogue is harder to convey properly, but I am at my best in writing dialogue so I usually include a section with a long soliloquy. I am careful, though, to be ready and able to talk in detail about the character I am speaking for because, when the reading is done and the questions begin, someone will inevitably ask about the *motivation* of the character.

Motivation is the most used and least useful word in any description of character development. I understand this and usually I am honest about it—my motivation for having the character say something lengthy and profound is simply the writer advancing the plot through slow moments of description, explaining that some ideas are too complicated or too simple for description or action to explain. Occasionally, I joke that I am simply taking up space on the page and increasing the word count. The crowd usually laughs but other writers know I am not really joking.

After the reading, and the questions, comes the most difficult part of the ritual: the signing of the books.

The experience always seems to be a little like those pitiful one-time celebrities selling something of little or no usefulness on those cable television stations that specialize in selling things nobody really needs to bored people who already have more useless things than they will ever use. At a signing, there is usually an assembly line consisting of someone standing and lining up the customers, one or two people usually sitting at a table selling the books and passing them on to me, also sitting at the table signing the books and making quick, sequential small talk, and someone usually standing at the end of the line and making sure the customer does not dawdle and slow the assembly line too much.

My part in the assembly line is multifold and sometimes mysterious: I look up and smile, as casually as possible, to the standing buyer. I find out the customer's name or take a special request to address it to someone else. I usually sign books something like: "Marion, Thanks for being a reader. M.Maybourn", with the two Ms written large and with flourish. If I know the person, I usually make it a little more personal, but I rarely know the people. My family and close friends all get my newest book as Christmas or birthday gifts, and usually get a little handwritten story imbedded inside the cover extolling the last time we were together, or the planned next time.

It is funny, though, that several of them, including Jasper, send me checks for the cost of the books.

"It's business," Jasper once told me about his checks. "It's how you feed your kids."

And then, as part of almost every book signing process, sometime during the assembly line, there is always the answering of an innocuous question or the reacting to an awkward compliment. There are stock answers to stock questions:

"What made you start writing?" …

… "I had things I wanted to say and nobody was listening."

"How do you get over writer's block?" …

… "I don't accept writer's block. I only accept any words on the page, any words on any page."

"What was it like meeting Jasper Kelly?" …

… "He's a nice guy, just a little into himself."

Jasper once poked me about that response, after someone more loyal to him than me ratted me out after a reading in Los Angeles. I said it made him sound human, he said he did not want to be human, he wanted to be a movie star. We both laughed and agreed that he was, truth be known, a little too into himself.

So, for me, such was pretty much the normal book signing event; but every signing is also unique, and the one in Galway city that weekend was a little more unique than most. Maybe it was the fact that there were a lot of great writers in town for the literary conference; maybe it was the fact that American crime novels just are not the Irish cup of tea; maybe it was because, as I scanned the audience of 30 or so, seeking an attentive, friendly face to escape to if the talk went really bad, I noticed Eileen and the widow O'Brian were in attendance. It took me a moment to deduce the identity of the woman with Eileen, though. She was dressed in a colorful sweater and had some color to, if not make-up on, her face.

Had they been standing off to the side, I would have walked up and made small talk, but they were seated already and I learned early on in my public reading experiences that is was not a good idea to mix with the audience before the event, before I was officially introduced.

Had they been looking at me, which they were not, I would have waved.

So I simply wrote a note to myself: "widow O."

Then, as usual, the reading took on its own life and carried me along.

Jenn and the bookstore owner, a man roughly my age introduced as simply Albert, set up things well. They sat together off to one side near the front. I publicly thanked the owner at the beginning and again the end of the talk; always thank the bookstore owner. For the most part the listeners were attentive. There was a couple of old people in the front row who fell asleep; there always seems to be a couple of old people who fall asleep. I do not take it personally.

Most of the questions were softball, lobbed up softly for me to hit easily. The only curve was thrown by an intense, glassy-eyed young man who probably wanted to be a great writer and had correctly decided that I had little to teach him about attaining such a lofty goal.

"I understand that popular pulp fiction is not great literature, but your books seem to have a consistent theme of violence, even from the protagonists. Do you think that violence in entertainment is degrading the American society?" he asked, after being picked at random by the owner.

I was thoughtful for a moment, first impressed with the young man's sentence structure and then taking a moment to study his face. I noticed Albert also took a good look at the young man. The experienced bookstore owner probably wanted to make sure the intense young man was not unobserved later, while strolling through the philosophy section of the bookshelves. Jenn also took a good look. I almost laughed musing that the punkish PR assistant probably wanted to make sure she was kicking the right ass if the two met up later at a pub.

"I am a writer of popular crime fiction, and writers of such usually have a fairly simple vision of the world," I said. "My characters usually have a tendency to violence, it is in their DNA, both the, quote, good guys and the bad guys. That is nothing new to popular crime fiction or to classic literature. In the *Iliad*, in *Moby Dick*, in *Dune*, all great literature in my opinion, almost everybody had a tendency to inner anger if not outright violence."

I paused, impressed with my self. *That* was sentence structure for you, young man.

"As far as the degradation of American society is concerned, I am no social anthropologist so I will leave such questions to others. But the American crime drama, in print and on the small and big screens, continue to find an audience, on both sides of the ocean."

The owner made sure the young man was not allowed a follow-up, and we moved on to another questioner. Softball.

As is common, after the questions came the few minutes of less formal meet and greet and small talk before I was ushered away to where the book signing would be, in this case, at a table set up near the front doors of the bookstore. I guess they figured they could put on a little show for passersby at the same time they sold some books. Fine with me. Business is business.

I signed a couple dozen books, including one for the glassy-eyed young man, who declined his chance for the follow-up question. Maybe Jenn had already gotten to him. But he did say he enjoyed a particular character in *Kiss of Treachery*, an avenging angel in the form of an old biker bent on righteous self-destruction.

I was surprised he had actually read it. Impressed but surprised.

All and all, a good book signing. The only problem with the evening was that when Jenn and Albert came by to say good night, after the book sales and signing had ended, I realized that neither Eileen nor the widow O'Brian had come to talk to me.

The bookstore owner thanked me for my time, then asked me to do a signature-only signing on half a dozen books — in Ireland as in America, I assumed, that meant he could sell them for above cover price. Business is business.

As I bent over the table, creating my own little assembly line of taking the first book from the stack, opening and simply signing my name on the books' title page, and then stacking the books back up again, my little PR punker girl slid up beside me.

"Good night, I'd say," she said. "You?"

After finishing the last of the owner's books, I sipped the last of the now-tepid tea someone had given me at the beginning of the book signing assembly line. And, for the first time that evening, I took notice of how the young woman was dressed: a modish black leather skirt and a white long-sleeve blouse buttoned to the top with a mannish red tie loosely knotted around the neck.

"Nice," I agreed. "Everything went really well from my view."

"*Foirfe,*" she said, as she started to slip the tie loose. "We do this again in Cork in three weeks, then Dublin after that."

In short order, as I continued to take note, the tie was off and the top two buttons of her shirt were opened. She then shook her head, her hair flying around her face, and let out a big sigh as if she had just finished a boring task.

"Yes we will," I said.

She nodded. Smiled.

I made sure I was looking at her eyes.

"Don't get out much here in Galway, but have few pals here. Going out for a little *craic.* Care to join?"

I could use a drink, or two. But I wanted to get back to Gleninagh before I started doing so. I also wanted to check up on my two local groupies who hadn't even stuck around for the signing.

"Thanks," I said. "Not tonight."

"No worries. I know lots of great places in Dublin too, all walking distance home. Know what I mean?"

"I do indeed."

"By the way," I continued. "Can I get a couple copies of the book?"

"Sure," she said. She then stepped away for a moment, as I grabbed my jacket, and when she returned she had two books, which she sat on the table. "I'll email you the details of the Cork trip in a few days."

"For-fe," I said, over enunciating before smiling.

"Not bad,' she said. "Not *Foirfe*, but not bad."

She then smiled back and, probably without even knowing she was doing so, unbuttoned another button of her blouse, exposing the hint of a bra.

I took my books and started the walk back to the car. The streets and the park were buzzing with life. There were couples enjoying the early spring evening, groups of youth, overly loud boys and giggling girls and mixed group mash-ups in aimless motion; and there were several young, yet fully mature women mostly in pairs and trios, joyfully unveiling new summer dresses despite an obvious need for a light sweater, joyfully flaunting their femininity if not their actual beauty.

I felt every bit the middle-aged man.

* * *

As I drove home, I thought mostly of Maggie despite trying to think of something else. But thoughts of Jenn snuck their way in. Both led to dark, empty rooms, neither of which I really wanted to enter.

To escape, I first blasted the stereo, but neither Bob Dylan nor Miles Davis succeeded in untangling me from my blue notes. As I pulled off the N18 south and onto N67, heading west to Ballyvaughan, I then tried silence and the briskness of open windows on a cool night. But my heightened awareness only focused my senses when, what I really wanted, was to feel nothing at all. When I pulled off N67 and onto R477 for the last few miles, I was already thinking about the bottles of forgetfulness awaiting me at Gleninagh North.

I knew I was probably going to drink a little too much that night. But when I reached my decision point, I turned toward Cassidy's.

From the number of cars parked in the front of the pub, I knew there were plenty of locals tonight. From the two travel company mini-vans parked on the other side of the building, in front of the inn, I knew there would also be several tourists.

Good. The more witnesses to my melancholy the better.

I learned my new normal for drinking too much quickly after I lost Maggie. Actually as I was losing her, when she was under hospice care, during those last days when her pain meds allowed both of us to sleep, her more at peace than I.

If I wanted to drown my sorrows in alcohol I needed to do so in public, not in private. I drink alone at home to relax, or sometimes to free up my mental inhibitions and allow me to write more freely. But, maybe counterintuitively, for me there is a certain dampening of dark moods by my being around strangers. I drink less, seeking to avoid regrettable behavior in front of witnesses. And in crowds of strangers my mind drifts away easier from my private pity party and toward the people around me, in no small part because none of them are saying how much they feel sorry for me.

In a bar of strangers, even in a rural Irish pub scene straight out of a Hollywood movie, or a travel industry advertisement, I thought that I could drink alone in a crowd.

But this was Cassidy's, and I should have known better.

Mully, always the watchful sailor, was the first to recognize me as I entered and made my way toward the standing bar.

"An' here be our own *scríbhneoir*, in the flesh," he said. Just loud enough for those around him to hear. There was an audible, "ah" as several in the crowd turned to look. The knowledge of my presence in town had grown a bit, obviously. It had a vaguely staged feel, like the trademark scene from the bar in the television series *Cheers*.

"One Smithwick's comin'," Jimmy shouted as he moved to get the beer.

"So Matty be gracing us tonight," Ian said, holding up his half empty beer in toast.

As Ian and Mully parted at the bar to give me a place to belly-up, a quick glance around the bar showed me who I knew and who I didn't.

Kenny was absent from his usual spot at the bar; replaced by a couple who were obvious American tourists, she in an expensive but still gaudy-green pullover sweater with the Irish flag, something only tourists would buy and wear, and he in a Williams College sweatshirt only a proud American father or an alum would wear.

I continued to scan, but had about given up finding another familiar face when I spotted Eileen sitting at a booth. She had a short glass in her hand, drinking what I assumed was her usual Porto wine. I notice what people drink, one of those odd people-watching habits which I have. Across the table from her was a man with his back to me. Séamus, I assumed. The widow O'Brian was nowhere in sight.

I finished my scan. The rest were strangers, local or tourist. There were an unusual number of locals, in fact, mostly working-class men with females of their social strata: a few wives, a few lovers or hoped for lovers. There were also a couple tables occupied by more tourists, mostly keeping to themselves, talking in soft voices and people-watching themselves. I glanced at the tourist couple at the bar and decided I needed to reward their bravery by talking to them at some point in the evening.

But first I would pay some respect to my new Irish groupie, and find out from Eileen what happened to her and the widow after the reading. My wandering eyes returned to the bar just as my Smithwick's arrived. I stepped back and raised my glass to the boys.

"*Sláinte*," I said, "A night of telling lies about yourself makes one thirsty."

"That be God's truth," Mully said, as he and Ian raised their glasses before all three of us drank. Cassidy just smiled and glanced to the ceiling, started my bar tab in his head.

After my newness in the bar settled in, which included having my story of the reading in Galway city promptly given short-shrift by the boys. When Mully's attention was diverted to another new arrival in the pub, I asked Ian quietly what Mully had called me when I came in.

"*Scríbhneoir?*" he said. "Writer. A compliment, really. All knew you had a readin' in Galway. Mully and I just not ones for bookstores."

I nodded. "No offense taken," I said.

Ian smiled. I felt a little like a true Irish drinking buddy.

As I finished my first beer, which happened way too quickly, I bought myself a second, and Ian and Mully a round. Got to keep my fans happy.

Awaiting my turn with Eileen, I bided my time, nursed my second beer, and made small talk with the boys, the bellied-up tourists, and a few others who drifted in and out of our section of the bar while always keeping an eye on the inn keeper.

When Eileen finally parted ways with Séamus' booth, she
first came around behind the bar, a situation which Jimmy took
quick advantage of, rushing to relieve himself with a quick
exclamation "Off to the jacks. You be the boss."

As I found out my first night at the pub, "the jacks" meant
the pub toilet in this neck of the Irish woods, if not the whole
country, a helpful language oddity I discovered in no small part
due to one door in Cassidy's being labeled *Fir Jacks* and other *Ban
Jacks*. Those unfamiliar usually waited to see who entered or
emerged from which to find the distinction, or just asked to the
great amusement of the locals. Jimmy entered and exited the one
marked *Fir Jacks*.

When he returned, Eileen escaped from the working side of
the bar, but not before a close encounter with her husband.

"Always the boss," she said as she brushed intimately past
him, face to face, pausing for a brief kiss.

"And don't I know it," Jimmy said as he returned to an
adjacent leaning area while his boss settled into her usual leaning
area at the end of the bar after pouring herself another Porto.

I took that moment to excuse myself and spend some time
with the woman of the house. I was hungry, but not for food.

"Pardon me my good men," I said. "I'm off to be with a true
fan."

"And good riddance to ya," Ian responded. Mully merely
tipped his beer to me in appreciation of the round. No wasted
words from that one, that's for sure. He'd be a fun interview
when that time came.

"You're quite the talker with an audience listening," Eileen
said as I neared.

"I'd have thought you were bored. You two left quickly."

"Not bored at all. But Cathleen said we should not bother
you if we weren't buyin'. I disagreed but she'd have none of it.

Myself don't mind a good American shoot 'em up. But Cathleen, she's a little more of a Hibernophile, if you know what I mean."

I was good with words; I did know what she meant.

"Well then," I said. "She is going to have a very good paperweight. I have a couple books in the car, one for each. I'll deliver yours when I'm not drinking. When I come up with something pithy to write in it."

"Look forward to it. I'll read it before it gets lost in my bookshelves."

About that time, Cassidy sauntered down to our end of the bar, either out of professional interest or marital curiosity. I assumed the first as my second beer was getting a little low, and, as with any good marriage, he probably rarely butted into his wife's *tête-à-tête* without invite.

"You walking or driving home tonight?" he said, having picked up on my habit of a two-beer limit if getting behind the wheel as opposed to my having walked down or my leaving my car in the parking lot overnight.

"Driving."

"Can we brew up a tea for you?" he asked, talking to me but touching his wife's hand gently. She would be the one brewing up some tea if needed.

I shook my head. "Thank you though."

He nodded, then headed off to check other glasses.

"You were talking about Cathleen," Eileen said to me as the barkeep went back to work.

"Was I?"

She gave me that look that women give men when they are tired of playing whatever game a man has been playing.

"You and Cathleen both be dancing a *seachain* dance. She asking of you. You asking of her."

I shrugged my shoulders. "We are neighbors."

"Truth be. And both ya know I'm a gossip at heart. What d' you want to know?"

"They call her widow O'Brien around here. When did her husband die?"

"Not dead. Left her alone coming on three years, for work in America. Stupid bastard. He worked for a company that rode the Celtic Tiger for a while but the work went back to Boston when hard times returned."

"And she didn't go?"

"He wanted her with him, but Cathleen's Irish born. Anyway, stupid bastard was half a Hun. You know? English. Not a bad bloke, really. Loved her, I guess. But he had to follow the money. Cathleen follows the heart."

"She married kind of late in life?"

She nodded, but paused, thinking, choosing her words carefully now. "Follows the heart."

"Ahh …" I either said aloud or thought quietly; sometimes it is hard to know which after-the-fact.

"You said we were both dancing," I said, clearly aloud. "That word, the dance?"

"*Seachain?* Not really a dance. Avoiding something, really."

I paused, choosing my words carefully: "So, what did you tell her about me?"

"You? I told her that you were a nice guy, a little into himself, but a nice bloke. Told her the whole writer's sojourn story, 'bout you being here to write the Quiet Man book and all. She thought that was a joke. Laughed. Stopped laughing when I told her it was God's truth. She must of Googled you after. When we went out to dinner before your talk tonight, she knew all about you and your work. Widow, children, the movies and all. Knew more 'bout you than I did."

There was another pause in her ramble.

"Cancer, uh? Tragic that."

"We had many good years. Great kids," I said. "Sean and Alice—Ally. Both on their own. Both look like her."

Eileen raised her Porto in toast. "*Go maire na mná go deo*," she said. "May women live forever," she echoed.

I toasted Maggie myself, finished my beer. Decided I should not appear too interested in Cathleen. Decided it was time to call it a night.

I said my goodbyes to Eileen, and then the boys, leaving enough Euro on the bar between them to pay my tab, and headed off.

The night was void of moon and full of stars, and after driving back I stood outside my house on Gleninagh North and let it all soak in. I recognized the stars and constellations, mostly. But things looked different too. My thoughts were mostly of Maggie, a little of Jenn and a little of Cathleen, but mostly of Maggie.

I miss her most in quiet moments. She would have enjoyed a night like this, standing here, talking to the stars, listening as, for the hundredth time, I found and pointed out the Belt of Orion, blue Rigel to one side and red Betelgeuse to the other.

We did have good years, she and I. Always said I would take every day the man upstairs would give us and thank him for it.

I paused, looked up into the starlight, and said a quick prayer of thanks.

Maybe it was simply the beers. I thought not. But as I entered the house it felt a little more like a home.

* * *

The next day actually dawned with rain, first a hard rain that woke me and then a soft, steady drizzle that drowned out the sound of the occasional truck rumbling along the coast road and invited me to spend more time in bed. But with the rain, and no excuse for procrastination, like book signings, I decided to spend the day turning some of my research into written ideas if not actual scenes for possible use in the book.

Strong black coffee helped fuel the writing, as it often does in the morning. Toast and jam helped balance out the caffeine. It was a good hour or so before I heard a car start and then rumble down the hill. I rose and arrived at the front window just in time to see Cathleen's car turn onto the coast road and disappear into the hedgerow. Before I could return to the table and the computer and the blank pages awaiting words, there was a scratching sound at the door.

I listened to it without reacting, at first, thinking it was a blown branch that would pass with the next gust. But it did not pass and I returned to the door, opened it and saw Michaeleen, his nose quickly poking into the doorway, making clear his desire. He was wet, and strangely timid in his stance, his ears unsteady and his tail tucked behind. His eyes were bright but not threatening. We stood facing each other for a moment. Then, for some reason, maybe it was his eyes, I stepped aside. The dog entered, cleared the door and circled a couple times, off to one side, and curled up while laying down on the floor.

"Well, yes, you can come in."

I have always loved dogs, but not really liked dogs. It is complicated.

I get along great with friends' dogs, when they are well mannered, don't jump on me, like to get scratched and are polite when offered doggie treats, taking the morsel gently from your hand instead of snapping at it.

When Maggie and I were first married, we had a dog, Winnie. Winston Churchill, an English bulldog, who was a perfect companion for an urban couple living in a Rittenhouse row house. Winnie liked her walks short with plenty of stops to read the pee mail. She slept, or at least lazed around, for half the day and most of the night. She couldn't jump on you if her life depended on it. But when the kids were born, and she a few years old, Winnie took to them like an old Tennessee nanny, watched them constantly when they were infants, allowed them to crawl all over her when they were toddlers. She never raised her growl to them that I saw, although she would occasionally offer deep and an amazingly loud bark when the kids and she were confronted by a stranger on the street or at the door.

She died in her 13th year, old for the breed, and still had all her teeth and still loved her belly-love. Hind-quarter arthritis caught up with her and we were not one for personality-dulling drugs. Winnie was laconic enough as it was. So when she had trouble sleeping and squatting to do her business, we had her put down by a very respectful vet, who commented, rather strangely, that Ms. Churchill "did good work" as he administered the fatal drugs.

Maggie and I had decided she would stay outside during these final moments, with the kids, the oldest not yet 10 years old, and I would be with the vet to give Winnie some goodbye love and scratches. But at the last minute, Sean, then age nine, asked if he could be with me. He was strong-willed even then. He accepted childhood's hard lesson of death with impressive grace. Ally not so much.

I left it to Maggie to decide on getting another dog and, while we talked about it, she never pulled the trigger and I told people I didn't care one way or the other. Maybe the truth.

There is something I really do like about dogs, however. Looking into their eyes you can read them like a book. Winnie was always a happy dog, from a puppy when we first got her and gave her a warm place to sleep, occasionally our bed instead of her bed, and a life almost without want. Her eyes were always bright and smiling, even at the end. But I have seen shelter dogs, with the dull, sad eyes of a neglected if not abused animal. I have seen mean dogs, with their dark, focused eyes, made that way either by cruel fate or cruel training.

Michaeleen's eyes, that morning, where different than I had ever seen. He was fearless, but not aggressive. He was, shall we say, polite. He was the one asking for shelter from the storm.

"Just make yourself at home," I told him.

I returned to the table and my writing, for much of the morning. The dog hardly stirred. He never really slept, but watched me intently, particularly when I got up for coffee in and coffee out. I am not sure if he got up when the rain stopped, or when Cathleen came back; I did not hear the car come. But at one point he rose to his feet, went to the door, looked back at me and uttered the softest, shortest bark I had yet heard out of him. I let him out, his tail wagging and his butt jaunting away was the only goodbye he gave me.

But as he walked home, I stood at the front window and watched, and saw that Cathleen noticed the direction from which her dog came.

She saw me, waved a kind-of forced, beauty-queen kind of wave. I waved back.

When the dog came face-to-face with the mistress of his house, she bent down and talked to him, then she turned to look, again, back up the hill.

I was still in the window, but she did not acknowledge. Neither did I.

My presence on Gleninagh North is no longer new. Just neighbors.

Caibidil a ceathair
(Chapter 4)

The real pleasure of my occasional meals at Eileen's "invitation only" dining table is not the food. Not that the food isn't worth the price, in Euro or Hollywood stories, depending on her mood. She even cooks up a more than acceptable version of corned beef and an "Irish" breakfast — the tourists, apparently, demand such tourist accoutrements.

I particularly enjoyed her Sunday breakfast, falling in the habit of noticing if there were tourists in the inn on Saturday nights and, as a result, knowing there would be a Sunday morning menu. I would stop off without invite after a walk along the beach and gladly pay for it. Like the classic Irish breakfast, she served both sausage and bacon, with eggs, and traditional brown soda bread. But she served it without either white or black pudding — the stereotypical blood sausage made with all sorts of pork and beef byproducts mercifully diluted by traditional oatmeal.

"Even when properly prepared, it is *shite*," Eileen informed me one morning, after that day's tourists were gone and I asked about it. "I have my limits."

As I became an occasional regular at Eileen's table, however, what I really came to appreciate, more than the menu, was the interaction with other dinners, local and tourist.

Food for nourishment; food for thought.

It was at one of her tables that Cathleen and I were formally introduced and, I guess Eileen would say, we continued our dance. However, our initial interaction was brief, inconclusive and mostly unsatisfying.

Cathleen also had a chaperon at the time: The Reverend Thomas Ronan.

Actually, at first, I felt quite the ugly American when Eileen unexpectedly directed me to sit with them. I carried a nearly full beer to the dinner table before I knew who I would be dining with. They were both drinking tea.

The good innkeeper glanced at the good Reverend first.

"To your liking?" she said.

She might have been asking about his mostly devoured meal, or she might have been asking about her placement of dinner guests. Didn't matter. If he, too, were a routine guest at Eileen's table, she was probably reminding him of her largess as well as her prerogative to sit who she wanted with whomever she wanted.

"Of course," he said. "The colcannon was delicious tonight."

The tone in his voice was one of honest humbleness, maybe more related to a desire to stay in Eileen's good graces than any priestly habit.

"Good," she said, waving her hand toward me. "I introduce Matthew Maybourn of America. Make a new friend."

Eileen then glanced at Cathleen. Her returned stare to the hostess was not nearly so passive.

"We have met, but not introduced," Cathleen said.

"Well then, Cathleen O'Brien of Gleninagh," Eileen said, first looking to me and then to her. "You two get to know each other. I'm done with it."

The two women share smiles of secret sarcasm offered and understood.

Cathleen turned her gaze my way; we share smiles.

"Please call me Cathleen," she said, standing but not offering a hand for shaking despite my shifting my beer from my right hand to my left in expectation of the handshake that never comes.

"Matty, please," I announced, instantly aghast as I tip my beer her way before I realize how uncivilized it probably appeared.

Eileen giggled. Cathleen smirked as one would to a rude child. The Reverend merely stood and offered his hand.

I held the beer down, almost behind me and out of sight.

"Thomas Ronan," he said, as we shake. "Of Carnserfin, just up to road. But of Vatican City, truth be told. My parishioners often call me Reverend Tom as I don't object to informality."

"Smithwick's?" he added, his eyes darting toward my beer hand.

I nod. Cathleen joined Eileen in finding humor in my uncomfortable situation.

Feeling that I could do no more social damage with honesty, I sat my beer proudly on an unoccupied place setting at the four-person table, and purposefully sit my butt in a chair opposite Cathleen and to the Reverend's right as they return to their seats.

I searched for something pithy to say. Nothing came to mind.

"Boiled ham and colcannon tonight, if that is to your likin'," Eileen said.

"Yes please," I answer quickly but having only a vague idea of what would be served with my ham.

As the good innkeeper turned away, I glanced at the recently emptied plate in front of the Reverend.

Only a half-full cup of tea occupied Cathleen's dining space. I smile, wait for the good innkeeper to be out of earshot.

"Colcannon?" I asked, probably butchering the pronunciation as I looked her way. "Potatoes and cabbage?"

"Creamed mashed potatoes, and kale, in this case," Cathleen answers. "Much better than cabbage."

I nod. "You get potatoes with every meal here, don't you?"

I was talking about Eileen's table, but I could as well have been talking about the country as a whole I guess.

"Tourists kind of expect it, she says," Cathleen added. "But she does a good *cál ceannann*."

I look to the Reverend.

"Wouldn't argue with that review," he said, taking a finger, swiping it dramatically across his plate, and then licking it off.

"Beggars can't be choosers," he added. "And she's promised some apple cake."

He and I share beggars' knowing winks.

Cathleen shook her head, took a sip of her tea, but reacted to the drink with a frown I could only assume was a result of its tepid condition.

Another ensuing awkward moment mercifully ends as she pushed her tea cup toward the center of the table and started to slide her chair back.

"Think I'll be leavin' you men to your dinner."

The Reverend and I raced to stand. I win the race but gain no reward for my over-eagerness. She's up and standing before I could even think of being chivalrous.

"I do appreciate your work," she said, as she first glances to the Reverend and then lowers her eyes and offers a slight bow of her head. "I don't mean to be impatient."

"Not at all," he replied, reaching to touch her gently on her shoulder. "Patience is a virtue we must share at this time."

She nodded her head, then turns to me.

"We must have tea sometime soon," she says, reaching out and touching me with her bright smile, her even brighter eyes, but still offering no hand to shake.

This woman is old school proper, if not old-country Catholic.

"Love to."

She nods again, walks away.

I turned back to the Reverend.

His head cocked to one side, he studied me with serious diligence, his priestly duty of tending the flock hinted at.

"So Mr. Maybourn," he said as we return to our seats, my now playing musical chairs to sit opposite of him. "Eileen's relayed a little of your story. Fascinated, must admit. But it all sounds a bit too fictional, a writer's sabbatical in our lovely bit of God's green acre. So, may I ask a bit of your plans?"

I paused, gave him a questioning look, unsure of the source of his interest—personal or professional—and the corresponding goal of his inquiry.

"You're writing a book about our lovely country, I hear," he continued, leaving the direction of his inquiry still unanswered but a path forward for our conversation revealed.

"I am," I said, and proceeded to give him my now automatic, for the people, abridged version of the story I had now told a dozen times and pretty much had down pat: *The Quiet Man* and Jasper and Mrs. Hench and the house on Gleninagh North.

He listened, made a few comments of little consequence, and never mentioned Cathleen once. But, were I a conspiracy theorist, I might say his priestly duty revealed itself a little when he asked about Maggie.

"Pardon my blunt question," he said. "You are a widower, I understand?"

"I am. Coming on to two years."

He nodded. "May God hold her in the palm of his gentle hand. And two grown children?"

"Eileen's got it all correct."

He smiled, shrugged his shoulders.

"It is a small world, here about," he said.

"I am finding that out. And, in case you are interested in such things, I am a fallen again Baptist."

When the Reverend stopped laughing, he tipped his nearly empty tea cup to me and I toasted my half-full beer to him.

"Excellent," he said. "I now know something the lady of the house doesn't."

Our conversation went quiet as Eileen approached, a plate in one hand and a tea pot in the other.

"I'll get you silver and a napkin," she said as she placed the plate of ham and colcannon, with a hunk of brown bread on top, in front of me.

"Ready for apple cake Reverend?" she said, as she sat the pot in the center of the table.

My "Thank you" and his "That'll be splendid" came as if in chorus.

A moment later, she was back with a delivery for each of us.

I liked the look of my meal, and the Reverend's apple cake. He probably noticed my lustful eyes. With a great flourish, he tucked his napkin into the white-collared neck of his short-sleeved, black clergy shirt. He had just finished a meal and there was not blemish on his crisp attire, so I assumed his protective nature was not all for show.

"Gentlemen," she said, softly, so as the nameless occupants at two other tables probably could not hear. "I'd appreciate a little gratuity tonight from ya both."

Both of us nodded, smiled pleasantly. I glanced over to the Reverend's plate; she noticed.

"And there be plenty of the cake remaining."

My smile expanded exponentially.

Eileen asked but I declined another beer. We agreed upon tea with my dessert, however, before she moved to tend to her tourists and left us to resume our conversation.

As two polite strangers often do at the dinner table, we took turns talking and allowing the other to eat. I had more to eat then the Reverend, so he did most of the talking.

His parish was in Ballyvaughan but he also conducted services in Fanore, another small village further west, and actually had a residence in Carnserfin, just north of the inn.

"Half an hour behind the wheel 'tween the two," he said.

"Why live here?" I asked, taking a break from my meal and allowing him a polite moment to finish his cake. "You've a place in Ballyvaughan? Priests do still live on the grounds of their church, don't they? Think they do in America, anyway."

"They often do in Ireland as well," he said, as he poured his tea anew, spooned in some honey, and then stirred with great intent. "There is a place for me. Just as there's place for me in Fanore. Both have fine quarters, private quarters and soft beds that are remade once a week despite my rarely sleeping in 'em."

I figured there was more to the story to come, so I just nodded my head in between bites as I returned to my plate.

"Part of it be lack of priests, part of it be lack of parishioners," he said, pausing to take a sip from his cup and test his precision in tea preparation. "Old priests get older. They die, or retire due to health before they die. They just leave the life sometimes. And young priests are a rare breed these days. Much the same in America too, I read. Way of the world. Certainly is here in Ireland."

He took a moment to stir in just a bit more honey, with slightly less intent, then sipped it again, nodded before following up with a good gulp.

Looking at the Reverend, I guessed he was neither old nor young; maybe 30 years old, maybe 40. His close-cropped hair obscured but could not hide the early evidence of grey. But significant lines around his tightly-held mouth and his soft eyes made him look older than he might actually be.

"Can't expect my parishioners, especially older ones, to drive all that much a distance. In the cities, you can just close a church or two to be more efficient. Out here, in the countryside, the distance between the church and the flock can't be made any shorter.

"So I go to the flock," he added, before taking another gulp of his tea, then reaching for the tea pot before pausing and apparently deciding he'd had enough of a good thing for one night. "You should stop off sometime in Ballyvaughan. Good bit of history. I'd be happy to show you around."

Sounded like a good idea to me.

I made a point later of driving by the Reverend's home-away-from-home on a drive back from a Galway day trip for supplies. I discovered that I routinely miss St. John the Baptist Catholic Church each time I come through town. When I did see its consecrated setting, I was impressed with its postcard-perfect appearance. I knew immediately that the building had been there a while; the gnarled, mature trees surrounding it gave ample evidence. I found out later, from Google of course, that St. John's foundation was laid in 1858.

The Reverend's assessment was correct: it held a good bit of history.

The Reverend, I also learned, as he allowed his meal to settle and I awaited my Irish cake, had been moved from another rural parish, someplace in the south, in County Cork, two years before.

"There was quite a bit of movement that year," he explained. "Some for good reasons and some for bad."

I was going to press him on the reasons for the "movement",
but I didn't. I hoped we would share another meal together and
be able to dig a little deeper into such things.

I was going to throw up some softball questions, about his
family, but he excused himself as Eileen returned to collect
plates.

"Delicious," he said as he neatly removed and folded his
napkin onto his near spotless plate.

"Good to meet you Mr. Maybourn," he said, rising, turning
to me.

I, too, stood. "Matty, please."

"And I am Reverend Tom, then. Can Baptists say such
things?"

I shrugged. His big, playful smile showed me he was
probably nearer 30 years old than 40.

His leaving some euro notes on the table, in full presence of
the good innkeeper, give me a lead to follow after my cake was
devoured in solitude.

* * *

I got a call from Ally one day; I forget which day. My days,
now weeks, on Gleninagh North were starting to blur.

"What time am I catching you, daddy?" my daughter said
without introduction, when I answered my iPhone's FaceTime
call, a call announced by the chorus of Emerson, Lake and
Palmer's song "Oh, what a lucky man, he was." It was an inside
joke between us.

"Middle of the afternoon, young lady. No early classes
today? It's, what, eight your time?"

"Nine, daddy. And, yes, I am skipping a class. Nothing big.
Islamic lit. I'm up on the reading and ready for a mid-term this

week. The professor is doing a prep for a few basketball and football players.”

Ally was in her third year at Temple. Great school, mostly good students; but they did kind of coddle the jocks.

“How do you always know that I am skipping class?”

“I skipped too.”

She giggled. It was good to hear her laugh, to see her seemingly happy. I needed her to be happy these days.

The call was a little of a surprise. We rarely talk these days, since Maggie died. A distance had grown between us that was mostly my fault. I see a lot of her mother in my daughter, which I once thought was a Godsend but now feel is a little divine cruelty.

Not my daughter’s fault, I know. But the truth. And, following the advice of the grief counselor I had a few sessions with, my life was all about trying to accept the truth of the moment these days.

Another reason for our distance was that, like me but unlike her mother, Ally could find dark places in the mind.

Maggie handled the rare real disasters and occasional near disasters of our life together with great calm and a seemingly un-orchestrated thoughtfulness. I often went practically sleepless for days at a time, lying in bed beside her for long hours each night, listening to a soft nasal snore that usually, eventually put me into blissful sleep.

While I frittered through the endless permutations of life’s decisions, she seemed to make a decision and never look back with uncertainty.

Whether it was her father’s accidental death, our son’s diagnosis of mild Attention Deficit Disorder or, near the end, the realization of her own mortality, Maggie remained optimistic. I, in truth, had a depressive bent that bordered on a personal darkness.

So, despite inheriting her mother's facial features, Ally often took after me in dark times.

But, I suspected the moment her face appeared on my phone, such was not the case on this day.

"How you doin', daddy? Getting lots of good writing done?"

"Mostly research now. Haven't quite got a handle on the storyline yet, just getting the setting, the characters, you know. I have to build the world, and populate it, before I make things happen."

"Sounds kind of God-like, to me."

"What are you saying? And you better not be calling for money, my child."

She giggled again.

"Well, as long as you're bringing it up," she said, stretching out her words like a comedian setting up a punch line. "Just kidding. I'm fine."

I smiled, hearing echoes of Maggie's voice.

Ally was fine, financially. I paid for her college costs, as Maggie and I had done for Sean before her. And her college experience was much more frugal than her brother's, as he was hell-bent on attending the "Little Ivy" Middlebury College after a high school skiing trip to Vermont.

Ally also worked for her college fun money, as Sean had, as Maggie had. The G.I. bill and my bartending skills paid for both my college tuition and my fun money.

Ally did not need to work, however. She had more than $50,000 in the bank, in long-term investments, actually, as a result of Maggie's will. She wanted the kids to have a "pillow," she called it, since she wouldn't be around to pick them up from their inevitable financial falls. She knew I would take care of their needs, if not their wants, but she was always more of a soft touch than I.

Ally never touched her pillow, I knew. Falling into inheritance money at too young an age, I set up the kids with the same financial advisor I have had for 25 years, partially because I knew Anthony would have told me, in an off-hand way of course, if anything was happening to Ally's portfolio. Anthony, in his subtly professional way, had given me the head's up when Sean took $10,000 of his money a few months back: "Sean is becoming quite the young entrepreneur, buying into a ski shop," the advisor told me the last time we talked, without going into any detail that would obviously betray confidentially. A little fatherly prying made Sean come clean about the need to keep alive his youthful dream of owing a Vermont outdoor sports store.

Maggie would have approved, I decided. So I had no opposition to his plan.

Just as I would probably have no opposition to whatever plans Ally had in mind that she now thought she needed parental approval for.

And there had to be a reason for the FaceTime. Ally was big into texting, which is how she usually checked in with me — a form of communication I really hated responding to, so there had to be a reason for this modern version of a face-to-face.

"So, young lady, what's new in your world?"

"I think I have a boyfriend, daddy."

"You think?"

"OK. I have a friend and he is a boy and we have been spending time together."

"And my part in this is?"

"Well, he's a basketball player."

I thought for a moment, running through the scenarios of what such an admission might mean, then deciding my opinion really didn't matter all that much in this matter.

"Does he treat you well? Does he respect you?"

"I think he loves me, daddy."

I could see her face, small but clear, could see her struggle to choose her next words.

"But, ah, I'm not sure I am there with him."

My turn to struggle.

"Young men fall in love easily, especially with pretty young blond girls."

"Kind of where I'm going. Not sure what love means, to him or me. You know?"

"Not really. But, once again. Does he treat you well? Does he respect you?"

"He treats me well. The respect thing is a little harder to figure out. You know?"

There was a joint pause. We just looked at each other. It was kind of strange to do that on FaceTime; it was a little hard to read emotions when you are looking up someone's nose. But such is modern times.

I thought of Maggie. Knew this would be a question Ally would have brought to her mother instead of me. But now there was just me.

"Everyone deserves to be happy, Ally," I said, finally. "Sometimes to be happy you have to take chances in life, take chances in love. That's the way it is. Sometimes you get hurt."

I thought of what I had just said without really thinking much about why I said it, how shallow it probably sounded. Then that truth-of-the-moment thing appeared.

"I hurt your mother, when we first were together. Didn't mean to. Hated myself when I did. She never really talked about it, but I could see it. I learned, I guess. But it took time. To understand her. Myself, you know. Us. To understand us."

I did not know if I answered her question. Not even sure I understood her question or my answer.

"That's the best I got," I said when another, longer, pause turned awkward. "You sure you don't need a little money?"

She shook her head.

"I'm good, daddy. Just wanted to talk."

"OK then. Go take a walk. I miss springtime in Philly. Loved to jog in the springtime. It cleared the head, you know."

"Love you daddy."

"Love you too, young lady."

She smiled at me, then clicked off, leaving me with the remembered image of a happy child that looked a lot like a happy Maggie.

I felt good about the image, the memory.

A moment later a text came through, it was a little tiny photo of Ally with a young man, one of those big-faced selfies. I clicked on the tiny photo and it became merely a small photo. They both had big toothy grins, lots of white teeth. The young man's smile stood out in sharp contrast to his very dark skin; her short blonde hair in sharp contrast to his shoulder-length jet-black dreadlocks. He wore an Owls basketball team sweatshirt.

I did not recognize him, but then I did not follow Temple basketball much, not until March Madness time, anyway.

As I looked at the photo, I found myself absentmindedly twisting my wedding ring on its new finger. Maggie would have liked what I just saw.

I decided it was time to take a walk myself.

Caibidil a coign
(Chapter 5)

Trains play a center-stage role in *The Quiet Man,* and in the history of rural Ireland. But there is a certain melancholy, a certain sadness, associated with the comings and goings of trains for small Irish towns and their residents. While the railroad occasionally brings people home, it is often a home they wished they'd never left, a place now offering an uncertain homecoming. And more often the trains take people away from their homes, their land, their heritage, on the first step to a ship outbound to some far distance land of dreams that rarely came true.

It is the returning home that is the opening scene of the film. John Wayne's character Sean arrives at a fictional rural station titled Castletown, near his destination in the aforementioned equally fictional village of Inisfree. He is instantly immersed in the local Cinemascope color: solid, if artificial, deep Irish green.

One of the film's pivotal late scenes is also at the train station, when Maureen O'Hara's Mary Kate has threatened to leave Inisfree, and Sean, for faraway Dublin. It is not that she does not love him, or he, her; but Sean has refused to stand up for Mary Kate in her dowry battle with her brother. The resulting romantic resolution in the scene would not pass politically correct muster these days, him dragging her away. But it is, ultimately, enduring and weirdly funny.

The modern Irish Rail system does not have the same train-travel allure as the scenes in the film, although the train station used in the film, the real town of Ballyglunin, has been refurbished as a tourist attraction.

But I wander; as you know I am wont to do in my writing before an editor gets hold of my pages.

My trip from Galway to Cork was enjoyable but also a little lonely. Jenn was not all that hot on taking a train, while I wanted to see more of the country than airports and Google Earth views. But she wanted to please Saul, if not me, telling me she wouldn't send me off into strange lands by myself. I assured her that I was fine traveling alone.

Before she acquiesced, she tried to change my mind.

"Hate the train," she argued, as we talked travel details on the phone. "It'll be four, maybe five hours each way. More if there's rain and they'll be running late. Rains a lot. They're late a lot."

I couldn't help but remember the train scene in the movie as she talked. The quaint train into and out of Inisfree was habitually late and nobody really cared then. I didn't care now.

"I don't care," I replied.

"The plane takes about the same and you have to go through Dublin," she continued. "But at least you spend most of your time in the airport between two short flights, not bouncing along the rail. There is a great noodle bar at the airport. Thai food. Love Thai food. Good burger place as well. You like burgers better than noodles?"

"Not really. But no flying, please."

"We could drive in two or three," she added, finally, reluctantly. "But I don't drive all that much and you don't want to drive by yourself, I'm guessin'."

"I'll be fine on the train," I reiterated. "You ever been on the New York subway system?"

"London. Paris. But not New York."

"Wear boots and always stand."

Nothing from Jenn. She either did not understand the joke or find it funny.

"Believe me," I said. "I can handle the trains."

"Very good."

She seemed to be relieved that she was off the hook; it wouldn't be her fault if I got lost on a rail trip that had only one transfer.

It was a week after the Galway reading that we talked; two weeks after that was the Cork reading. It was a good three weeks of good writing; not that the story was falling into place quite yet. But scenes were becoming clearer: places and people, probable histories and possible futures.

I was walking around the countryside a lot, running every other day, almost, and rewarding myself with drinks at the pub only when I ran, or wrote a lot. So, with my conscience as my guide, I was at the pub a fair amount. Mostly just sipping my beer and drinking in the small talk watching soccer—excuse me, *football*—and listening to Irish life flow past me, sometimes lazily, sometimes torrentially, like the River Corrib as it flows about four miles from Lough Corrib through Galway city to Galway Bay.

The train trip to Cork was also a good day to listen, to hear and see Ireland and the Irish, to watch everything flow, both the hodgepodge of passengers on the trains with me and the kaleidoscopic scenery flashing by outside the windows. I took it all in, and it tasted as good as the Smithwick's.

My train left from a station outside of Galway, Athenry. I could have taken it from Downtown but I would have changed in Athenry anyway and it was on the road north around the bay and had good parking. The names of the towns, the stops, along the way south often sounded as fictitious as Inisfree: Craughwell, Ardrahan, Gort, Ennis, Charleville and Mallow.

My favorite names were Sixmilebridge, even though it did not sound Irish in origin and undoubtedly wasn't, and Limerick, a city of mostly functional modern buildings and a smattering of beautiful old edifices, including several castles, but with a name that was, in America, an Irish pun. I changed trains at Limerick Junction, which, I noted, is not in County Limerick but Tipperary. Just another reason to love Ireland.

My favorite place we did not stop was just south of Crusheen, just north of Ennis. There is big lake, Inchicronin Lough, and a small town on what looked like an island in the lake, Inchicronin. It seemed like one those places that you would never want to leave. Seemed like a good location for a story, or a scene in a story, and I made note of it as such.

When I stepped off the train in Cork, at Kent Station, it was nothing like Sean Thornton's jumping off adventure at Castletown. But the station looked like a set from a movie all the same; it is a great curving building of glass and metal that looks not all that different from the same building more than 100 years ago, as shown in a photo of the station.

It had that funny feeling of Old World charm washed in modern technology that Maggie and I often found so beautiful on our various travels. She would have gasped at the view as we stepped off the train and took it in. She would have kissed me, as we were starting another adventure and she loved adventuring.

After admiring the building a little, and reminiscing a little, I found a cab waiting outside, its trunk open for luggage and its driver eager to open and close a back passenger door.

"Baily's Hotel Cork," I said as the driver slipped into his seat. "Near Merchant's Quay."

The driver gave me a glance in his rear mirror, a glance that I instantly interpreted as a *This is my town, sir. And I know very well where the hotel is!* look. But his politeness to paying fares, if not tourists, forced him to simply say: "Only one Baily's in town, sir. Welcome to Cork."

Jenn said she picked the hotel because it was only a short walk from the bookstore where the reading would be, the exquisitely named The Three Scribes, which was located near the Cork Opera House on the River Lee and just off Merchant's Quay.

"If you were just another tourist I'd have put up in the Hayfield Manor, but it is a little off the river," she explained. "Taxi to Baily's should cost you less than 10 Euro. Keep your tip small, you Americans spoil the taxi drivers. Waiters and bartenders too."

The fare was 8 Euro 50 and I gave the driver a 10 Euro note; we ugly-tipper Americans have to keep up our reputation.

The hotel was an old but well maintained building, with a modern, modish lobby, and an intimate room off the lobby that doubled as a breakfast area in the morning and a casual bar in the evening.

Just the way I like my hotels.

There was a note awaiting me at the front desk as I checked in; the clerk passed it to me with the introduction: "Pádraig left this for you."

I must have look confused.

"Proprietor of Three Scribes," he continued. "I assumed you knew him."

"I do now. Say his name again."

"Paad-rig," he enunciated. "Patrick in the English."

As the clerk ran my credit card, I read the note.

Mr. Maybourn,
Sinead has been delayed in Dublin. She will arrive tomorrow morning.
Please join me for dinner tonight. Farmgate Café. Short taxi fare or good

"How far is the Farmgate Café?" I asked when the clerk returned my credit card and gave me a key card.

"A mile, give or take. Nice place. Bit of a tourist romp, but nice, not too expensive. Pádraig likes it. He's a bud of mine. We agreed it was a proper place to meet tonight."

I checked my watch: 4:30 p.m. Perfect. A quick shower, freshen up my traveling clothes, then a walk to find the book store and then the café.

"Perfect," I said.

"7 p.m.? May I call him for you? Asked me to describe you to him."

"7 is good. Thank you," I said as I pulled a couple euro coins out of my pocket and slid them across the desk to him. "I'll be wearing the same jacket."

"My pleasure," he said as he slid the coins back. "A bud, he is."

Jenn's advice on tipping came back to me.

The room was nice but not as nicely refurbished as the lobby.

The evening walk was pleasant. The ocean air smelled different than back in Galway. Maybe more industry, maybe different ocean currents, maybe all in my mind. The bookstore took only a little searching to find. The restaurant was a little farther and a little more difficult, but I found it well before the appointed time. It was probably two miles of walking, with all the adventuring, and I liked the walk.

* * *

The café's façade had a modern look: all glass and metal and brightly lit. Only a single wooden sign of general Irish design broke the modern feel. A pair of smiling, happy people were exiting as I approached and we brushed past each other, had a moment of shared holding of the open door and fleeting but sincere smiles. The inside smelled of food and sounded of camaraderie.

As I entered the café I scanned the crowd and found one man sitting alone, with a book in his face. Seemed like a good bet. Upon closer inspection the first detail I noticed was a schlock of dark but greying curly hair topping a somewhat receding hairline with the rest of his face hidden by the book held high in one hand. He was hunched over the table, a half full glass of beer in his other hand, still resting on the table but at the ready for an appropriate break in his reading.

I stood for a moment to allow somebody from the business to approach me or give my suspected dinner date a chance to take notice of me. He acted first. As I watched him, he moved his beer closer, ready for action, and dropped the book slightly. His eyes were dark and colorless in the low mood lighting, but I could see them glance at me, then to the beer, then quickly back to me.

In one smooth motion, he slid his chair back, stood up, closed his book with a finger marking his page, and slid the beer to a more secure, central location on the table.

A huge smile, made distinctive by a couple of crooked front teeth and surrounded by a clean-shaved and tanned face with a ruddy complexion, told me I had the right man.

"Ah … Mr. Maybourn," he said.

It wasn't until the blur of introductions—"Please call me Matt" … "Please call me Pádraig"; a hand shake, and my taking a seat opposite him at the table—that I noticed he was reading a paperback copy of *Kiss of Treachery*, which he more permanently place-marked with the folded ear of a page and then set aside.

Small talk followed: the train trip, the walk, the weather and such.

I had a Smithwick's in hand before I had a chance to follow up on the book.

"You're reading Kiss."

"Indeed. Like to know what my authors are about. Not much for American crime stories, really. An easy read though. A strong style, for the genre, I would say."

"I think that's a compliment."

"Indeed," he said, after which we shared smiles, shared a "Sláinte" toast, and took a good drink of our separate beers.

"Sinéad tells me you are writing a little something different while you are visiting," he continued. "Not that 'tis any of my business. Though 'tis a little of my business if you'll be planning to read a little of it in my store."

"I am working on a novel of Ireland, but I will be reading from my latest and talking only about my published books. I assume that's what you expected."

"Sure, sure," he said. "Personally, though, I am more interested in the new work. Something along the line of Quiet Man? That true?"

"Not really. But Hollywood may think so."

"Ah, Hollywood. Mind of its own I expect."

"It pays the bills."

"Indeed. We all have to pay the bills."

More smiles and another toast.

"I am curious about Jenn … should I say Sinéad?" I said.

"Sinéad is Jennifer in Gaelic. Pádraig, Peter. Just harder to pronounce. You do a good effort with Sinéad, though."

"I had a thing for the singer, O'Conner, in the day."

"As did we all," he said.

We shared smiles of knowing.

Always had a thing for Sinéad O'Conner, back in the day, which in my case was the late 1980s and early '90s, just before I married. Had a thing about Euro-trash girls. Just thinking about her, I can hear "Just Like U Said It Would B" in my mind's ear.

Our talk, Pádraig and mine, and my background playback of O'Conner's song, was interrupted by a waiter coming to take our order. I had barely glanced at the menu. But Pádraig ordered "chippers" without hesitation.

"Fish and chips?" I asked; he nodded.

I did the same, adding a Caesar salad to start.

"To our young Sinéad," he said. "She's quite, ah, a different kind of lass."

I said nothing, just took another drink of my beer; he took that as an invitation.

"Came out of a tough neighborhood in Dublin, she did. Even has the tattoos to prove it. In a good postal code now. Worked her way out. Worked at my book store when she was at UCC, University College, here. Kind of private about her past. Never talks about her father. Never ask. Mum died when she was a teen. Think that's when she got her life on the straight. Don't think it was a nice end for the mum. Anyway, she wants better for her story."

I took another drink. Said nothing.

"She wants to be a writer too. Don't we all? She tell you that?"

I nodded. Still said nothing.

"She's got the right idea. A good education, journalism and marketing, I think. Always hanging around writers wherever she goes. Working her way up in the publishing world. Pleasure to work with her, really. Very organized. She's working on the next great Irish novel. She talk to you about that yet? She wants to. She will. Says you're famous, because your books go Hollywood. I tell her great novels do not make good movies. You agree?"

He paused, possibly wondering if he had offended me again but probably desiring a long drink of his beer after talking too much. I obliged.

"I might argue the point. Some great books do make great movies. *Doctor Zhivago* comes to mind. Maybe *Godfather*. At least one British version of *Pride and Prejudice*. But in general I agree great novels do not make good films, at least that has been the case for my books."

I smiled. He smiled, then, eventually, a polite, petite laugh.

"Your book is good, but I like you better than your book," he said.

We both laughed genuinely, he a nanosecond after me.

The kitchen and the waiter had good timing. My salad and a basket of soda bread came, followed shortly by our chippers and more beer. It all allowed us to take turns talking and listening while eating. There was more small talk, mostly general family stuff, our educations and careers, and sometimes interesting life stories. Told him mine. He told me his.

Pádraig was single, always been single. "Always have my face in a book or a beer," he said. Raised in Dubin but moved to Cork 20-odd years ago. "Fled the big city madness." Bought a book store because he loved books. Said he had to get into board gaming to help make a go of the bookstore, but didn't seem to mind. "Most of 'em just a modern way of telling epic stories."

Then he gave me the lowdown on Cork; later, I remembered most of it.

"The City of the Marshes, they call it," he said, "City's name, *corcaigh*, means marshy place, or somethin' similar."

But a better nickname might be "Rebel Country", I concluded, as he went on, and for more than one reason. First, due to its great harbor's attractiveness to conquering forces throughout history, from the Norse to the English. Also, as the third largest city in the Ireland, and home of many an independent sea-faring Irish cuss, it was also the scene of a fair amount of fighting in the Irish War of Independence.

Cork's history, apparently, dates back to about 900 AD, or CE, depending on how you were taught such things, as it served as a Scandinavian trade stop. There was probably a monastery dating from the 6th century already there, however; just no proof of it. It became a city in the 1100s: a walled, fortified English city on the edge of an often hostile Gaelic countryside. As with most locations where seafaring merchants traveled, it lost about half its population in the mid-1300s when the Black Death paid a tourist visit. As with much of urban Ireland, it became more and more a surrogate English city where cheap labor mixed with a vibrant maritime community, making the locale's locals ripe for revolution.

In addition to the history lesson, Pádraig also advised me on some of the tourist highlights of Cork, such as the Red Abbey, which was a Medieval red sandstone building of which only the bell tower remains.

"Quite a history, the Abby," he said. "Dates from 13th Century, Augustinian friars. Focal point of more than one battle in the city. Much of it was destroyed by a fire in 1799, not in battle, though. It was part of a commercial building then."

"Most tourists like the Shandon tower, all white limestone, with the clock telling you the time, and the big fish telling you which way the wind blows. I like the Red Abbey. That's Ireland."

Pádraig was an easy talker, a knowledgeable talker. He seemed to be self-effacing about the good and bad of his life, his city, his Ireland. I took advantage of the opportunity.

"Would it be rude to ask you about the revolution?" I asked.

"Yours or ours?"

"Yours."

"Be rude to not ask, you writing a book on Ireland and all."

He paused for a moment, thinking about how he wanted to approach such a serious subject, or, maybe, approach such a naïve questioner.

"Been several revolutions, really. You could date it back a thousand years to good ol' Henry II of England and his taking Éire for himself. Then the Pope got involved in the 1500s, tried to get the good Catholics to turn against Elizabeth I. Nine Years' War they called it. Start of troubles up north. Not *The Troubles*, mind you. Troubles none the less. Problems between Catholics and Protestants. First real independence revolution came about the same time as your American one. Just not as successful. 1800s was all big famines and little rebellions. You know about the potato famine I assume?"

He paused. Took a long drink of his beer; history is a thirsty business.

I nodded.

"My family dates from the mid-1800s in New York," I said. "Probably immigrated due to the famine, the story goes."

"Was a million of them," he said. "With a million sad stories, I say."

"Then there was the Easter Rising …," he continued. "1919. The War for Irish Independence. Free State. The division up north. A lot of Cork was burned in 1920 by the Black and Tans. As retaliation for a rebel attack. Town center was fought over for during the Civil War."

He took another pause.

"Then there was the late '60s, the real troubles …" he said, his voice fading to quiet.

My eyes must have been glazed, because he stopped. Not his problem. I asked a bookworm about a history subject. You get what you deserve when you do that.

"If you really want to dig deep," he said after another swallow of our drinks allowed both of us to take a breath. "Mary Collins has a huge work on Ireland before and after 1919. M.E. Collins. She's American, so you'd expect a tome and you'll get one. Peter Cottrell has a good revisionist book on the subject. But he's Brit, so you expect as much. Still he argues well. Two sides, as they say. There's a good book, *Making Sense of the Troubles*, worth a read."

"Thing is," he said after a pause, "everybody has a story to tell. Everybody saw something, or knew someone, or did something they don't really like to talk about. Those are the people you need to talk to."

"Do you have as story to tell?" I asked.

"Me?" he said, shaking his head. "Not me. Just a reader of books who looks away when somethin' bothers him. Different up north. They lived it for generations. Walls are still separating Catholic and Protestant neighborhoods in Belfast. Better up there now, but bloody grudges die hard."

"Me," he reiterated. "Just looked the other way. Kept my face in the books."

There was a tone of regret in his voice, a tone of a man who maybe wished he were brave but was merely pragmatic. Maybe it was just too much beer. We all have places we care not to revisit.

"Thank you. Sorry," I said, not knowing what else to say.

"No, No. Good question," he said. "Got to be asked. But other people have better stories. Tha's mine."

Pádraig had slipped into a slightly different voice, not as precise English, as un-Irish, as before. Maybe it was just too much beer. Maybe it was his Dublin past coming back to haunt him.

The waiter came with our bill, again interrupting us at an appropriate time. He grabbed it. I protested; he declined. "I'll ask you to sign some books for me. Should sell a bit better at the store."

I nodded and finished my beer.

"I understand one of your stops will be in Belfast?" he said, after he pulled out some Euro notes and dropped them on the table.

I nodded.

"It is much better," he said. "There are a lot of people working hard to put it all behind them, especially the youth. When the Millennials grow old, it will be something mostly for the history books. But not yet for their parents. Find a good guide when you're there. Someone to show you around, the good and bad. Sinéad should know people. She knows a lot of people in a lot of places."

"Now I know someone in Cork," I said.

"And I know an American writer who might be more interesting than his books."

We laughed as we got up and headed outside as two drinking buddies might do so, almost shoulder to shoulder as we dodged tables while making small talk on the quality of the meal.

I was going to walk back, but he insisted on hailing a cab, then handed the driver some notes. "Take 'em to Baily's. Drive him by the Red Abbey on the ride, if ya please. Enough for the fare?"

It apparently was; though I later tipped the driver anyway, just a couple of Euro. He seemed pleased.

The abbey was beautiful at night. The drive was pleasant. The driver and I made small talk; tourist stuff. There was a message for me at the hotel from Jenn. *Sinéad*. I'd have to get used to that. She would arrive in town late tomorrow morning, and asked forgiveness for not being there for breakfast.

I slept well and left a phone message for her the next morning that all was well and I would see her at the bookstore that night, which I did, after doing a little window shopping.

The reading went well: no pain-in-the-butt questions. I already drank enough beer in Cork, so I again declined an invitation from Jenn, this time for dinner. She offered to get me back to the train station the next day, but I declined that as well. She hinted that she wanted to take an early morning flight back to Dublin and told her I was fine with that. Business is business.

The best part of the reading night, though, was Pádraig giving me a gift before I left and after I signed half a dozen books. *Fidchell*, I read on the box. His pronunciation was unintelligible to non-Irish ears. It was an ancient Celtic board game: a round wooden board with simple wooden blocks and kind of rustic. Looked a little like Checkers.

"Same name in old Irish and Welsh," he said. "Shows you how old it is. Basis of chess, we like to say. But there is some argument 'bout that. You move your men around the board and battle other men. Fighting has always been a sport in Ireland."

* * *

The train trip back to Galway was an adventure of a lesser kind.

True to Jenn's word, there was a delay in the train moving out of Limerick Junction. It was raining, but not storming, so it couldn't have been that. Or maybe it could have.

Once I started the trip north, toward Galway, I could see little out the windows and what I did see did not reveal as much as what I saw on the trip south. I spent much of my time with my notebook out, writing. Yes, I have an old pen and paper journal, not some flat-screen, book-sized computer to take my notes. I did have my iPhone in use, however: my earbuds plugged in and playing some of my Sinéad O'Conner collection. Her early stuff, when she was having babies and railing at the big cruel world, not lost in her own small cruel world.

As Ireland rushed by my windows, I was thinking about Irish women, about the two Sinéads, about Maureen O'Hara, both her character in "The Quiet Man" and the real woman. And then there was Cathleen.

I made notes, gave impressions, of Irish women I didn't really know but whose personalities were forming the identity of a character or two in my head and in my story.

They were an odd set of personalities:

A Dublin singer who used to be bad-ass enough to tear up a picture of The Pope on live television, but then grew up and slowed down; a lot like me.

A young would-be writer, also Dublin born and bred, playing a key role in my introduction to Ireland, but a feminine personality that would probably make Maurice Walsh roll over in his grave.

There was that actress, also born in Dublin. Sad to say, but I knew her better than I knew the others. At least I knew all of her story that was plastered over the internet by writers of varying levels of veracity. On second thought, maybe I did not really know Ms. O'Hara at all.

And then there was Cathleen, a middle aged woman who, I guessed, carried burdens of the past and uncertainty about the future; also a lot like me.

Giving life to the female characters in my books was always difficult for me; I knew so little about the species. Men … men I knew. I knew their motivation for actions; their past, present and future. American, Irish, Martian; it didn't matter. Giving life, giving history, to my Irish men was an ongoing effort but on sure footing, on a clear path. Giving life to my Irish women was proving to be an uneven, winding road. It was difficult to think about them in the past tense, and give them history; only in the present tense was I beginning to understand them.

* * *

I continued to rely on Eileen for two things: a good meal and at least the dime-store version of any gossip, past or present, on any subject I cared to bring up. But you had to catch her at the right time, and that time was usually when the pub was quiet, late in the evening, or when the tourists were off touristing in the early afternoon.

This time it was late in the evening and it was as quiet as calm waters on the bay. I decided to stop for a nightcap after the drive home from the train station, after the long day returning from Cork.

Jimmy's timing was perfect, as bartenders' timing often is. As I entered, and looked around, I caught his eye. He gave me his "Smithwick's?" look, not needing to even ask aloud anymore. I simply shook my head in the negative. He stopped in his tracks and awaited my approach and my pleasure.

"Jameson, please," I said.

He nodded, frowned, and moved away, knowing to serve my Irish whiskey with a few junks of ice, his subtle displeasure with my watering down my whiskey evident but held in check as always.

A quick glance showed a very slow night at the pub: none of the regulars were present, except Eileen, who was standing at the end of the bar, sipping her Porto. There was only one other party in the place, a group of four young men, none of whom I recognized, sitting at a table and making a little too much noise.

As Eileen seemed focused on some paperwork, I found place at the middle of the bar. Drinking alone, I toasted my father — glancing up to the heavens as I raised my presented tumbler — a toast I almost always did so as to not be drinking alone. I savored that first, perfect, sip.

Eileen and her glass of Porto joined me before my glass returned to the bar.

"My I join ya, sir?" she said.

"Please."

"So how was Cork?"

"Nice," I said. "The train ride. City. Reading. Learned a little too. You want the long version?"

"Not really," she said.

"Good," I said. "More in the mood to hear about that little dance, Séamus and the boy, the other day."

She looked at me, her head cocked to one side. Deciding whether I deserved the story.

A good gossip choses carefully what she shares with whom, and Eileen was a good gossip.

"*Sláinte*," she said, before she started her story.

A good gossip always cuts to the chase.

"Séamus was in a particularly bad mood that night, he was. Usually he's a regular *Saint Brónach*, saint of sadness." She paused, took another sip of her Porto. "That was a bad mood, even for him."

"So what's Séamus' story?"

"Well. Modern tragedy, I would say."

She finished her Porto, slowly. Pondering her empty drink and her next words.

"Pardon," she said, stepping away with her glass and grabbing my half-full tumbler on the way up the back of the bar. I noticed her glance around the pub as she poured the drinks and say something to Jimmy, who shook his head in the negative. When she returned, both our glasses were refreshed, and she settled in beside me at the bar.

"Séamus was in the army. Military police. Spent time in Afghanistan, what a troubled place, but poor man found his own troubles. You know?"

"He was wounded there?"

She nodded.

"Bad time for all, really. But he was particularly unlucky. Or very lucky, depending on how you look at it. Only a few Irish soldiers injured in the whole bloody mess. But he was unlucky enough to be one of them. Lucky, though, not to have been the only one to die. Bomb or something, he says. Messed up his whole left side. Not lame, really, but just not right anymore."

She then cast another glance to the booth where Séamus usually sat. She then looked around to see if anybody else was noticing; apparently nobody was.

"Left him less than a man, you know?" she said. "An' left him angry at the world about it. Can't get past it. Too bad. Not a bad bloke. Deserves better."

"You see the good in everybody," I said, knowing she was probably telling me more than she really wanted to, more than I deserved.

"Man's faults are clear. Have to search for a man's virtues."

"Irish saying?"

"Female saying," she said.

"So you know," she continued. "Gave our Saint a bit 'bout you."

My look must have explained that I was confused.

"Asked me after you came in that first day, when he found out you be staying up on Gleninagh North. Told him you were a writer hanging around, getting a little local color."

"True enough," I said.

"One other thing you should know 'bout. He and Cathleen, 'fore he went away, 'fore she married. They were close. Different now, for a lot of reasons. But you might say he will always have eyes for her. One of the reasons she doesn't come to the pub much. He's usually here. Truth is, one of the reasons she's alone too. Séamus never really took to her husband. There was a *comhrac*, a fight, you know?"

Eileen paused again, sipped her drink again, searched for the right words again.

"You've seen our Mr. O'Dennehy can be a mean man."

"Fair warning?" I said.

"Bit of advice," she said.

And we changed the subject, I forget to what, and finished our drinks.

Cathleen's history was a little more in focus as I carefully drove home, up past her house.

* * *

The more I learn, the more I understand that Cathleen O'Brian is a dark woman, in aura as well as appearance.

She is what is still somewhat confusingly called Black Irish. In her younger days she probably had jet black hair contrasting a too pale complexion and eyes of an unnatural green even more sharply contrasted by eyelashes of that same jet black. Almost a

Goth look, but naturally that way. She is now in her late-40s I would guess. Maybe early 40s, but having lived a few hard years that added silver to the color of her hair and shadowy creases around her eyes that lessened the contrast and slightly diminished the vibrancy of her eyes.

I read somewhere on the web that the origin of Black Irish, as a Gaelic tribal subset, might have been from prehistoric immigrants from the Iberian Peninsula, modern Spain and Portugal, or maybe they were descended from seafaring Scythians, from the area of present-day Iran. Both sound exotic, but the second a little too far-fetched. Yet, who's to know?

Bottom line is that the Black Irish, while not uncommon, is still distinctive in rural Ireland; just as Cathleen is distinctive.

One beautiful day, she invited me to share a "cuppa tae" outside her house as I returned from a late morning run and, after begging for a few minutes, changed into a clean t-shirt and not so sweaty sweatshirt before walking back down. Michaeleen, who barely gives me notice on my jogs anymore, left her side to come out to the road to greet me as I neared.

Her dark aura, like the until-then blurred features of her face, begins to come into focus from the moment we are close.

"Morning to ya, Mister Maybourn."

"Good morning, ah, Missus O'Brian."

She giggled on our formality.

"All too much English decorum for us being Irish neighbors," she says. "Cathleen and Matty, I say. Or pardon me, do you prefer Matthew? Good Catholic name that."

"Matty is fine," I say, bending down, scratching the waiting Michaeleen on his neck.

"Well then, Matty, thanks for visitin'," she says as she walks across from her back garden area toward the stone wall that separates her yard from the road.

"What is it about you, Matty? He's not the friendliness of hounds, not since his master left. But he likes you."

"I let him be alpha, and I gave him shelter from a storm."

She nodded, maybe remembering the day, the moment she hadn't until then really understood. Maybe confused but polite.

"Good judge of people, that dog. Should pay heed to 'em more."

I look up from the dog, and my distant image of her fell into perfect focus: her Black Irish-ness, those eyes, her once-youthful beauty flawed, only a bit, by life.

"*Tae*?" she says, then adds. "Coffee?"

"Tea is good."

"Make yourself comfortable," she says, waving her hand toward an area in her back yard with a slightly rusted metal table and three equally weathered metal chairs made inviting by colorful seat cushions.

Michaeleen, seeming to understand the conversation, takes a couple quick steps and leaps over the stone wall with a gracefulness of an act done successfully a hundred times. I take more time and care stepping over the wall, finding I need to sit at the top and swing my legs over one at a time.

"Thank you," I say, once the obstacle was cleared.

As she turns toward her back door, I noticed her confident stride, her well-worn, washed-out blouse and mid-calf kaki skirt meant more for yard work than making a good impression, and her dirty yellow boots, which she deftly slips out of after opening the lower half door at the back of her house and entering in stocking feet. I find a seat where the mid-morning sun is in my face to allow her to sit with the sun behind her.

Michaeleen is torn between a visitor to his yard and actual access to his house, wherein, I assumed, is his bed and food dish. He pauses by the door Cathleen entered, looks out at me, looks in at her, and then prances back to my side for a little more scratching.

"What is it about you and that dog?" she says from somewhere in the kitchen. The question seems like it requires no answer, so I don't.

When she returns, she has a tray with a pot and two cups, none of which match, with a small plate of an unknown bread product and a short bottle of known Irish whiskey, Jameson.

The bottle is half empty. She notices that I notice.

"Know it's a bit early," she says as she puts the tray down. "Like my tea alright, but not the way the English drink it, milk and sugar.

"Dislike most things English," she says, her voice tailing off as her gaze glances off to a distance. I wonder if it is a sadness I see her her face, a sadness as bad memories overcome current events.

My thought, and her mood, lasts only a moment.

"My grandfather always had his morning tea this way. He said soda bread and tea prepared him for his day's labor," pouring the steaming liquid into the two cups, then grabbing the bottle and looking at me.

"Sounds right proper to me," I say, attempting a bad English accent.

She smiles at the attempt, splashes a short shot into the cups: maybe an ounce. *Maybe* just a touch more.

"Soda cookies. Nothing special," she says as she deftly sets a cup in front of me, waves at the tray, and sits down with her cup in hand, all in one fluid, graceful series of motion.

"So, was it rude of Eile and myself, not buying books at that book reading of yours?"

"Not at all. Appreciated the audience. I have read at places where even the management didn't listen."

"Truth is, I'm not much for American crime dramas. Nothing personal, but I prefer Irish writers. The classics. Try to read all the Nobel winners. They often lose something in translation, I imagine. But still great writing."

I cannot, would not, argue. So I nod my head.

"Garcia Marquez. All very lush, like his Aracataca. Hot and humid and full of life. Tranströmer's poetry. Pleasingly sterile, like his Scandinavia. Cold and barren, but only on the surface."

She pauses, awaiting my reaction, a mischievous smile on her lips, a bit of a one eyebrow raised, asking me "What you think of that?"

I know Marquez well and have passing knowledge of Tranströmer's work; but I am momentarily speechless at her impressive literary knowledge.

"Impressed?" she says, impatient for a reply.

"Yes."

"Good. Eile said I should try to impress you. Bit of a matchmaker you know."

"Are you?"

"Trying to impress you?" she said with a bit of a smirk on her face. "Not really. Mostly just don't want to sound simple when I say I haven't read any of your works. Eile will read anything. She read a couple of your things. Kiss o' Treachery, something like that? Said they were good reads. She's a good liar, though. I love literature too much to lie about a book …"

She stops abruptly, a serious look now on her face.

"… that sounds rude. Is that rude?"

The question seems like it requires no answer, so I don't. I smile; she smiles.

"I read an essay you wrote for that Philadelphia paper. After the Trade Center attack in America. A good read, that. We can't condemn all of Islam for the acts of fanatics, then or now, but it was brave of you to speak truth so soon after. You're brave. You get much hate for that?"

"A little."

"Good writing always draws out the hate. Walsh got some hate for some of his works, the rebellion and all. You read anything other than Quiet Man? Of course you did. You research well, I can see that. Assume you're researching the Irish all the time. The pub's a good place to meet people, talk to people. Lot of local stories to be heard. Mully, Ian, Séamus, even sad Kenny. You met them, got their stories to tell."

I sip the tea, which is still very hot, even with the whiskey, and listen. When she takes a break to take a sip of her tea, I break in.

"I am. Talking to people. Listening. Doing a little traveling."

"Good. You being an American and all, writing about Ireland. Finding a voice going to be hard. Not sounding clumsy, you know?"

"You sound like an editor?"

"I am. Thought you knew. Thought Elie would have told you. Medical writer and editor. Nurse by trade. I worked in the field many years. Went to London for work. Good work there but not my best years. Did meet my husband, though. Was some good days."

I think I see the sadness return to her face, for just a moment.

"Now I just edit and ghost write for doctors who want to be published. Kind of a part-time job, really. But don't need much, really. Have all I need right here."

She stops abruptly. Takes a sip, then a long drink; her's must have cooled to a proper temperature. I sip mine, it is cooler, and then take a long drink too. The Jameson is a good addition.

"I'm being rude," she says. "You get in a word. Guess I just know a lot about you. Your Wiki page and all. Most of that true?"

"Most of it. My son posted it. Publisher tweaked it. I avoid it."

"Sorry about your wife."

"Thanks. We had good years. Great kids. You have any?"

She shakes her head. I, again, read her face. This time it is more than simple sadness. It is some other emotion. Or maybe it is just me being me.

"Just a dog," she says.

I take another drink of tea, try to decide how to get out of the line of conversation, and try to decide if I really want to.

"Michaeleen?"

"Husband's dog, really. Ex-husband. I have to start saying it that way. Make that clear. He wanted the hound, then left both of us behind to go to the states. You know the story? Elie told you a bit?"

"Cassidy too. Just a little. Explaining why they call you a widow."

"Good. Saves me from explaining. It must seem rude, you being a widower and all."

I shrug.

"We had a few good years back in London. Then his work went away and we moved back here, to my family's house. Cheaper to live and all. He was never happy here. Worked in Galway but was never happy there. He always thought the states was the better place, for him, and that's all that mattered to him, really. He wanted more than Gleninagh. Can't really blame him, really, a Londoner and all. But this is enough for me."

I shrug.

"Sounds selfish? On me, I mean?"

I, again, shrug. I am shrugging too much. She says nothing
This is an answer she wants, and opinion she demands.

"Sounds like you two just grew apart. It happens. Sometimes.
You just take the high road and move on."

"Sounds Irish."

"Good," I say, then I finish my tea in final gulp.

She offers more but I have had enough, both of the Irish
morning tea, the whisky before noon, and the discussion. For
now.

"No thanks."

She nods. We stand up almost in unison. Michaeleen
demands a goodbye scratch. I give it. Cathleen shakes her head
at her dog, or at me.

"I enjoyed the tea, and the talk," I say as I give a little bow, a
strange habit I have when ill-at-ease.

"Did too," she says, flashing a smile that lights up her face
and ignites her beautiful green eyes. I am sure, at that moment,
that she was stunningly beautiful in her youth.

I turn and walk toward my house. The dog jumps the stone
fence as I approach it. I try to go over it too quickly and catch my
trailing leg and nearly fall on my face on the other side.

"I'm good," I say as I regain my balance if not my honor,
glance back at her.

She laughs, then quickly stops herself, covering her mouth
with a hand. When she removes her hand, she has a tight look to
her face, still trying to suppress another laugh.

I shrug my shoulders, repeat: "I'm good." Turn away.

I hear a soft, gentle giggle behind me.

Michaeleen walked with me for a short period and then
barked once and turned around.

I turn around. Cathleen was already in her house.

Caibidil sé
(Chapter 6)

There is a scene in *The Quiet Man,* the movie but not the
story, where Sean and Mary Kate take shelter from a storm and
share a passionate kiss in the ruins of a castle. In the broad
cinemascope of things, it is little more than an on-screen
opportunity to show off John Wayne's seemingly hairless chest
under a wet shirt while Maureen O'Hara, unfortunately, looks a
little like a half-drowned cat in heat. The scene is probably meant
more for film's female fans, but it did offer a little something-
something for the men, both straight and closeted.

My encounter at Gleninagh Castle with the opposite sex had
no such purposeful scripting.

The ruins of the castle provide a beautiful foreground to my
view of the bay from the house on the hill. It was, originally, a
double-tower citadel but these days it looks like the taller of the
two is a lighthouse without the glass-enclosed light at the top. You
can see the original outside wall, the walk and battlement of the
castle from my hilltop, but until you know the structure's historic
grandeur, the ruins look like just another of the ragged field-
stone walls which surround just about every other structure in
rural Ireland.

Once up close, the castle looks less impressive, less imposing,
than one assumes. And its cold, emotionless walls and secretive
dark recesses reminds one of its authoritarian past purpose.

The castle ruins, as a scene of secrets and revelations, were on my mind as I sat on one of the surrounding stone walls with my notebook and pen taking notes.

"A fine thing it is, viewed from Gleninagh North," Cathleen says, as she announces her until-then unnoticed presence. "Little less impressive this close."

I turn and see her and Michaeleen. She, 10 or so yards down the path leading from the road to the castle; he, half that distance but gaining ground away from her and toward me.

"Post cards of it. Lots of 'em," she continues as she draws near. Michaeleen is already beside me, offering up his neck for a little scratching.

I acquiesce.

"Dog must hunger for scent of a man," she mumbles as she comes to halt a few feet away.

I ignore that particular line of discussion and focus on the scenery.

"It is pretty special," I say, turning my gaze toward the bay and beyond. "What's the far shore?"

"Connemara. West of Galway."

This morning, there are low clouds on the other side, almost hiding what is usually clear evidence of modern industry and multiple industrial buildings.

"With the fog, view must be the same as it has for hundreds of years," I say.

She looks at me, a strange look, as if I am saying something either profound or stupid.

"Poetic," she says, sitting on the stone wall beside me; near but not uncomfortably near.

She looks at the ruins, and I do as well.

"You know the history?" she continues.

"16th Century, build for the O'Loughlin clan."

I turn the pages of my notebook and continue to confidently read from my notes. "Tower is four stories as it stands now. Once a much larger structure. A residence after it was a fortified castle, I read somewhere. People lived there up to the mid-1800s. National Monument now. About right?"

" 'Bout. Still has chambers below the ground. Probably a dungeon, too. Ghosts and all. Was a prison for a while. That fact out there on that wonderful web?"

"Read that somewhere. Not very romantic, though. Travel websites don't mention it. Looks like it could be a romantic place for a wedding, or tourists looking for a photo."

"What's above ground is the tourist part. Government keeps it cleaned up for 'em. Underground is dark, dangerous place. History is like that, you know?"

"You've explored it?"

"When I was a child. My brother thought it an entrance to the underworld, with a door to hell. Tried to scare me by saying demons were down there. Went in with him once, just to prove him wrong. Scared me, but didn't tell him. May be a *cailleach* now, an old woman, but still scares me like the devil."

She pauses. Looks at me like she had just told me a secret. I wonder what the secret was.

"You're not old," I say.

"Going to turn 50 this fall."

"That's not old."

"Not for a man," she says, looking off to the bay, to the foggy far shore.

The mood was turning too dark for a sunny day. I decided it was time to change the line of discussion to something of a little lighter vein. Probably picked the wrong vein to bleed.

"There is a castle scene in the Quiet Man, the film, the lovers take shelter from the storm. Find a little romance."

She looks at me, shakes her head.

I shrug my shoulders as if to say "Ya, I realize, that was not a great change of subject matter."

She laughs, softly.

"Old castles make pretty poor locations for romantic encounters," she says. "Especially 100 years ago, when that feckin story was new. Dirty, dangerous places with fallen stones and bad floors and roofs. More rats than romance, I'd say."

I nod. Make another note in my book.

"Thought St. Patrick drove the rats out of Ireland … no, snakes, wasn't it?"

She laughs out loud.

"You read the Internet too much," she said. "Ain't a seafarin' country don't have rodents."

"Now The Burren, that's a romantic place," she continued.

It is my turn to shake my head. To me, the vast stone landscape to the south of Gleninagh doesn't seem very romantic on its rocky surface.

"You walk back, up past the houses, off the road?"

"A little. Not far," I said.

"Do so, mister writer. Do so."

She smiles at me. A nice smile, a sweet smile.

"I'll give you a tour, if you like."

"That would be good," I say. "I would like that."

I match her smile. The moment lasts all of a nanosecond, but I notice and I think she notices. Michaeleen seems to have noticed I am not so intent on scratching anymore and he steps away. We both turn to watch as he wanders off down the trail toward the bay.

She stands. I stand.

"Enjoy your note taking Matty," she says, glancing off toward Michaeleen's path, then back to me.

"Enjoy your walk Cathleen."

* * *

With my trip to Dublin coming, I asked around the bar for stories.

I wasn't really interested in travelogues, which are usually boring, and often biased, with the bias often based on completely isolated, often dated, experiences that may or may not have any connection to up-to-date realities.

Mully and Ian had little or nothing to say on the subject of being a tourist in Dublin. Neither really liked the city all that much, which was clear without much interrogation, and their experiences in the city, they eventually explained, were mostly confined to the port area.

"Smells of stale sea and garbage," Ian succinctly put it, adding: "Rough pubs and rough women."

I trusted his judgment, however dated. But any international port area, in any big city, is not reflective of the actual city in any meaningful way. I think my Navy days and a few explorations since prove my theory.

Jimmy and Eileen's advice was only a little more useful. They had a short list of famous places to visit and decent places to eat, drink and sleep: tourist small talk researched, rehearsed and repeated.

The rest of the room had slim pickings for stories. But I eventually settled on Kenny, who was watching some talking heads dressed in soccer attire, with the television's volume all but absent. He was clearly bored beyond description due apparently to there not being a televised football game available anywhere in the world.

The boy did, indeed, live football. There were nights when I would catch him watching a Central American Cup game from distance pitches in Mexico City or Rio de Janeiro. Maybe the only person in the place who could tell you the score.

I rarely talked to the solitary young man, but from gossip and overhearing, I knew he had a story or two to tell about Dublin. Maybe not the prettiest story, but maybe one of some truthfulness. I sidled up beside him.

After some meaningless small talk about the weather, and the last football game of semi-importance to him, I directed us to the subject of Dublin by way of telling him I was getting ready to cross the country for another book reading. He seemed to already know. He, too, had access to the Eileen rumor mill.

We danced around the subject, and the city, for a while. Talked a little about the area surrounding his brief collegiate home. I learned little or nothing I did not already know except that we had a little punk rock in common, but for different reasons.

And that is when our dance became interesting.

"Not really up on the tourist attractions of Dub," he said. "Now ask me about the punk scene off Lamb Alley … that I know somethin' about."

"Punk still around? I thought that came and went with the millennium."

"They call it something different now. Alt this or that, pop punk, whatever. Bad music played loud to drunk kids still brings 'em in."

"I had a punk phase," I said.

He looked at me, a questioning slant to the head.

"Loved The Clash, back in the day," I continued. "Have *London Calling* on my iPhone. U2 early stuff is kind of punk — *Boy*."

He looked me up and down. "Just don't seem 'da type, button down shirt an' all."

"In the day."

He nodded, accepting if not believing.

"I'm not a fan of the music, really," he said. "Just the place to go to … ah … find people, find what I needed."

I was trying to figure out how to broach the subject of *what he needed* when he opened the door to his past all by himself.

"Truth be told, I don't like Dub much. Almost died in that feckin town, more than once."

I just shut up and listened. I offered to buy him a Stella but he declined.

"Dub is pretty and all. Tourists runnin' all over. But it has a drug problem too, big problem," he said. "Poor people. Young people. Not enough decent jobs. Lot a ways to find trouble, or trouble to find you."

He looked at me after he spoke; looked and, I thought, wondered how much I knew and how much I really wanted to know.

"Been told my story?"

"I know you went to college in Dublin. Heard it hanging around here, people talk," I said. "I heard you found trouble. Also heard your father maybe pulled some strings to get you out of trouble. That's about it."

"You know more, I'd wager, but too much of a gentleman."

"Maybe."

I did know more, from Jimmy and Ian mostly. Neither seemed to have all that much regard for Kenny. A little pity, maybe, but not much respect. Jimmy put up with him because his money was good, and maybe Eileen had a soft spot in her heart for the kid, but thought the young man was little more than a spoiled brat riding through life on his father's position, other people's money, and his mother's blind eye. Ian seemed to take a little less of a hard line, the reasons for which I guessed from some of his off-hand remarks.

"Young man grown up under hard hand of a hard father," Ian told me once.

Of course, Kenny was about the same age as his daughters, one of whom was educated in Dublin. There but for the grace of God, he might have decided.

Kenny had been a pretty good student, at least at one time, his pieced-together story goes. Also a good but not great football player which helped him get into a good college in Dublin. But, his was also the oldest of stories: youth gone astray. He fell in with the wrong crowd: ruffians and druggies and just stupid young people. He just could not, did not want, to climb out.

Someone, Ian I think, told me he became addicted to an undefined but "nasty somethin' or 'nother" and stumbled down on his distractive downward spiral.

I assumed that was why he looked like death warmed over, on a good day. I had always noticed his being gaunt, too thin for the athlete I understood him to once be. Anyway, he dropped out of college a few months before his father learned the news and stopped sending him college money. Kenny then found his trouble with the law: maybe a drug bust, maybe a drunken night gone wrong; maybe worse. That is when his father, the *Garda* sergeant, called in every favor he could and got his son home. Now, the young man didn't work as far as anybody could tell, sipped his *aqua vitae* in the form of his Stella Artois beer and mostly kept to himself.

"I guess I know a little more," I told him, after finding some diplomatic words. "People talk."

"Good," he said. "So Dub. You ever been?"

"Not really, stopped at the airport once."

"Beautiful city really. Big an' alive. Got bollocks — balls, you know?" Kenny said. "But all that temptation, you know? Pubs and parties and too feckin' many chancers. Bad guys, you know? Lots of homeless, too. Don't really deal with the problem. Some are just mental, some are drugged up. They can't figure which to fix first. Garda just pushes them out of the tourist areas. Most come back. Tha's where the fun is. Where the good drugs are."

"Every big city has its problems, Ireland and America are not that different," I said. "Philadelphia has its mean streets, always has."

"Boston too," he said. "I went to Boston, more than once. I was in America for a year when I was done with my junior courses, ready to take my tests. Ready to graduate on to college. Exchange student. Stayed with a nice family. Not sure who they exchanged for me. But didn't really fit in well at my school. Too much a loner, I guess. Feckin star of the football team, though— er, soccer, you call it. That year made me feel like a feckin Premier League player."

"Wouldn't know to look at me," he added, stepping back and spreading his arms, inspecting himself, his jersey noticeably hanging loose.

"When were you there? Dublin, I mean."

"Came back less than a year ago. Dropped out right after coming home for Christmas. Still had money comin' for a while, but that stopped and I hit the streets. Always drinkin' too much, but then got into the bam, uppers and downers. Lived on those for weeks. Months. Forget. Stayed wasted for months. Summer is an easy time to be on the streets. Corner boys, they call street people sometimes. All fell apart last summer.

"I think my dad would have left me there if my mum hadn't spoken up. But he's trying, I guess. Soon as I get better, says he'll set me up with a little business. Got to stay around Galway,

though, stay the hell out of Dub. I'm thinkin' about a football
gear place. Somethin' I know, my mum says.

"Dad's a good man, really. Deserves better than my being his
only kid. He's a good *Garda*. Not all of them are. *An Garda
Síochána*, guardian of the peace, more like guardian of the posh
and the tourists, especially in Dub. That's for sure. But I was in
the wrong, true enough. I was high, and in the wrong, and I'll
pay for that the rest of my life. Already paid too high a price, just
look at me."

That was twice in five minutes he mentioned being sick. It
begged a question.

"AIDS?" I asked.

"Good guess, but no. Hepatitis B. Needle, they think. Feckin
needle. Only did heroin a few times. Liked the bam more. But it's
not even the feckin drugs goin' to kill me. Feckin needle put
poison in and doctors say my body is slowly shutin' down.
Happened fast, doctor said. Too fast. Fightin' some sort of slow
cancer, they say. Shit luck, I figure."

He took a moment, looked around to make sure nobody else
was noticing, and rolled up his left shirt sleeve over his athletic
wristband and past his elbow. On the inside of his elbow there
was the scarred evidence of wasted nights and days and maybe
ultimately a wasted life.

It looked to me like more than "a few" times, but I didn't say
so.

He then rolled his sleeve back down.

I nodded, not knowing what else to do. What can you do
when a person shows you their secret scars but accept the terrible
gift and try to understand the reason it was given.

"Ireland is more than your Quiet Man, Mr. Maybourn.
There are beautiful places in this country, but there's shit wells
too."

"What do you consider a beautiful place," I asked, thinking we were getting a little too close to the young man's truth. A little too close, a little too quickly.

He thought for a moment, then a smile came across his face. I couldn't remember ever seeing Kenny smile like that.

"The Arans, you been to the islands?"

"Not yet. I want to go."

"I love the islands," he said, his smile decaying into the tight mouth of a wistful memory. "Was the last place my dad and I were happy together. He was stationed out there for a few years, visited often. Spent summer days out there with my mum as he worked. Ever heard of *Dún Aonghasa*? Old fort on Inishmore. Cliffs and old fortress walls. Much more of a view than Moher, you know? Popular with tourists, not so many as Moher though, in the spring anyway. Rain keeps them away. You should see it sometime."

His voice was fading away as he spoke. He was almost whispering when he said: "Love the Arans ..."

I knew the fade to his voice was the fade to his story. I had heard it often, in my years of interviewing people for stories and talking to people for no purpose. It was a fade of good memories decaying into bad.

I knew that fade too well.

I decided, at that moment, that I needed to see The Arans, especially Inishmore, maybe *Dún Aonghasa*, for many reasons but mostly because this was not the first time I had heard it was a place I had to see. One of the most beautiful places in Ireland. They say.

I also decided I had to take a tour of Lamb Alley when I went to Dubin. I always thought you had to see the ugly to appreciate the beautiful, in people, places—in just about all things.

* * *

The River Shannon is the longest river in Ireland. While its 350-or-so-mile length is modest by world river standards, its watershed drains nearly half of the country, some 18,000 square kilometers. It unifies the country in that way, from the County Fermanagh in the north, one of the counties of Northern Ireland, all the way down to County Cork, the country's southernmost county.

But it does not come near Dubin and, the saying goes, the life of Ireland flows to Dublin.

The Liffey, the "river of life" in rough translation, flows down to Dublin from the Liffey Head Bog in the Wicklow Mountains but its entire length is just 125 kilometers to the point it empties into the Irish Sea at Dublin Bay, between the Baily Lighthouse and the Muglin Rocks. And while it provides a beautiful if sometimes polluted scenic backdrop to many a tourist photo of downtown Dublin, it is no longer the waterway that brings the masses from the country to the city.

The heavily travelled M6 motorway, *mótarbhealach* in the Irish, runs from the outskirts of Galway to the outskirts of Dublin, where it connects to the equally heavily travelled M4 to complete the trip into Dublin. It takes about two hours to drive between the two, at the official top speed of 120 kilometers per hour, but like any major motorway in the world it almost always takes longer.

So when Jenn was planning my talk in Dublin, she asked the now cursory question of whether I wanted to fly and received the now expected response: "Nope". She then asked if I wanted to drive or be driven, and I could almost hear the dread in her voice as she readied herself for my wanting to do so, especially if it meant her driving over and back in one day to be my chauffeur. I could hear the relief in her voice when she received the desired response: "Nope".

"Train then," she said. "Catch it at Atherny again? Or you want downtown Galway, at Ceannt?"

"Atherny is good," I said, having grown fond of the functional station, an updated structure but still all old stone and memories.

"You'll be comin' in to Heuston, take you about two hours, station to station. About two miles from the hotel. Still want The Clarence?"

"Yes please."

"You want me to meet you?"

"Taxi 's fine," I said. "How about a noon-ish time out of Atherny. I'll do a little touristing on my own that afternoon, then we meet up for dinner and discuss the plans for the next day. OK? You pick the place to eat. It's your city."

"*Foirfe*," she said. "The area around the hotel is worth some time, river walk and all. Trinity is a grand place to stroll. I know a famous pub and restaurant nearby, O'Riley's. Good local color. Can I throw the net larger the next night, after the reading? There are a lot of great restaurants in Dublin. A little Indian café near the bookstore has great curry. Lots of choices. You have anything in mind?"

I paused. I still hadn't decided if I really wanted to go exploring Kenny's Dublin, and if I did, should it be alone, or with an escort? I decided.

"There is one place I have an interest in. Some music club off Lamb Alley."

"Lamb Alley?" she said, after her own pause.

"You know it?"

"Not so much anymore. Once."

"I can go alone. I understand it is a nightlife kind of …"

"You will not go there alone," she said, emphatically, a certain sound of "no feckin way" in her voice. "We'll talk that out at dinner, the night you arrive. I assume there's a story …"

"Sounds good. Look forward to it."

She again paused for a moment, checking her list of discussion topics, I guessed.

"And that phoner with the writer from the Villager?"

I remembered the email she had sent discussing an interview a Dublin paper wanted to do on the reading.

"Sure, sure," I said. "Nothing planned but writing for a couple of days. You set the time and tell me. Have him call my cell. It's cool."

"Very good. Reading. Train. Hotel. Press. All on my list." Another pause. "And a visit to Lamb Alley."

This time she emphasized the word "lamb", stretching it out, like "laaamb alley", as if she were struggling to grasp her reality of the place and unreality of my request to visit it.

"Anything else you need?" she said.

"Nope."

"Good. I'll email the interview details when I set them up. Have a good week of writing, a safe trip and I'll see you Friday next."

And I did have a good week of writing before the trip to Dub, as my river of research and mountain of scattered notes and bits of storyline were beginning to congeal into a vague form of characters and a skeletal plot of a novel.

So far, though, the skeleton was simply hanging around like those old-school models in an old-school doctor's office: no real life yet, but no danger of some Frankenstein monster emerging either. They say that creative writing takes on a life of its own, sometimes in an unanticipated form, in a form that often needs to be terminated with prejudice and buried in a deep grave. My writing is occasionally like that, when I am in a dark mood or of angry persuasion.

My Irish novel, however, was so far safe but of little interest.

The trip, too, was safe but not of much interest.

When the day came I made sure I had some U2 on my iPhone and a little map of the route as I boarded the train and headed east. It was due in at about 3 p.m. and I had more than two hours to kill.

The train would make stops at Ballinasloe and Tullamore and Monasterevin, as well as half a dozen places between, before Heuston. There is an Irish whiskey named Tullamore Dew, so that was easy for me to pronounce: *tull-A-more*. Ballinasloe was a little harder. *Baal-in-A-slow*. But I was getting used to the sounds of Ireland and the Irish. Monasterevin looked like one of the many words unpronounceable to all but native speakers. Another fact I was getting used to.

As the countryside passed, I listened to something old, something classic, and something fairly new from U2, starting with 1980's *Boy* to *The Joshua Tree and* ending with 2014's *Songs Of Innocence*, a recording that proved even 50-ish artists could still be innovative and interesting, if not at the height of their artistic talent.

I 2 took comfort in that fact.

The scenery along the rail route was pretty much nondescript on the outside: green fields, some pastured and some with unidentified early crops, small towns that flashed by and a few large towns that you pretty much wished would flash by. No really ugly rail corridors, though, as you would see in route almost anywhere on America's East Coast Amtrak lines through cities and suburbs of cities such as Boston, New York and Philadelphia. But, seeing as how you were traveling first through the rural belly and then through the urbanized heart of Ireland, not great photo ops either.

Notes made, and a few quick photos taken.

The Heuston train station also appeared to be of little historical or storyline interest, but only from the inside, as an initial impression. As you pull in there is a maze of rail tracks and transparent roof panels, with people waiting with European patience or scurrying politely but purposefully after too long a wait. But when you leave the building, and see the outside, you see a beautiful structure that gives ample evidence of another time in Irish life. Originally called Kingsbridge Station, after a nearby bridge over the Liffey, Heuston dates from the 1950s when it was built by the Great Southern & Western Railway. Its façade includes the crests of the coat of arms of Cork, Dublin and Limerick cities.

After a moment spent in a slow sidewalk pirouette to fully take in the street scene, the taxi drive to the Clarence Hotel was short and sweet.

The four-story Clarence was both a letdown and a grand sight at the same time, with its back to the Liffey and its front on a street picturesquely named Wood Quay. Its entrance looks more like a bank, red brick and white stone, but a good bank, a strong bank where good, strong bankers do their business. Even the lobby has a little of the feel of a bank, with a big wooden check-in area and, at least when I arrived, a rather husky doorman who could easily have been a guard. I wondered if at night the doorman occasionally guarded the door as much as welcomed guests.

The building dates originally from the 1850s, but its current street side dates from the 1930s. The front is pretty much a façade, however, as the hotel's backside where my room was located, is very modern with shiny metal and big windows and expensive views of the river and city.

I checked in and had time to wander before meeting Jenn for dinner. I decided I would find O'Riley's, find Trinity, find the bookstore … what was it again? Books on Molesworth, on Molesworth Street, of course. I love the simple descriptiveness of Irish places. Pubs named after people and businesses named after their streets.

I unpacked, got into some "dress" athletic clothes: athletic pants, a t-shirt and a sweatshirt glorifying the U.S. soccer World Cup team. The sweatshirt made me look like a tourist but a very Euro-friendly tourist. Now that the weather was nicer, I liked to street hike in athletic attire. Not that I ran, but putting the miles on the tennis shoes was almost as good as a jog sometimes. At least that was a lie some exercise magazine easily convinced me of at some point in the past.

Anyway, on the walk, I just wandered with a purpose and found the restaurant, found the bookstore, then stumbled into the famous Temple Bar tourist area. The crowds and tourist signs just carried me this way and that, including sending me on a mission to find the James Joyce statue affectionally known locally as "the Prick and the Stick", a hipster tourist magazine at the hotel informed me. The statue was a little bit of a walk north of the river, but I was in the mood. The artwork does make the man look like he could be a prick when he wanted to be, with his hat all cockeyed and his gaze somewhere nobody else could see. I wondered if those were his walking clothes when he walked the streets of Dublin. After the statue, I went back on mission and finally found Trinity.

I was feeling a bit thin after the train trip and the walk, so I had a coffee and a bagel at a Starbucks. Don't know why, maybe just to see if it was different. It wasn't. Along the way, I walked along something called "Bachelors Walk". Got to be a story there, I noted. And then crossed the Ha'penny Bridge to the south side of the river. Other than that, the walk was not unlike a walk through Galway or Cork, only bigger and more bustling.

Trinity College, however, was everything I had expected and more: Parliament Square, College Park, the Old Library where the Book of Kells is kept. I passed by and through but did not stop. I have learned to take in one thing fully when you are visiting for a day, and I wanted to fully take in the art at the Hyde Gallery and, of course, find Ireland's version of Arnaldo Pomodoro's *Sphere Within Sphere* outside the Berkeley Library.

Maggie would have loved the Pomodoro. We would have seen totally different things in the piece, however. We always did see art differently. The work, not unlike the artist's *Disk in the Form of a Desert Rose*, a work she and I saw during a visit to Western Michigan, allows different worlds of interpretation.

She and I, as we often did, saw completely different things in Desert Rose, and agreed to disagree.

In the Trinity work, I saw a world within a world, not unlike Ireland itself, both beautifully reflective on the outside and yet somehow dark and secretive, with the secrets held tightly somewhere inside, somewhere deep. I wondered what Maggie would have seen.

I found out with a quick Google search that the Trinity work is nicknamed "The half-eaten Malteser" due to its resemblance to a candy with a bite out of it. I did not see its resemblance, but then I had never heard of that particular version of a malt ball.

I found a bag of the candy and ate one on my way back to the Clarence to rest up before dinner. Still did not get it and tossed the rest.

I was getting hungry, however, and was dressed for the evening in dark blue Dockers and a bright, button-down Oxford bright red in color. I had the strange hankering for some fried chicken, American style, crispy with no adornments but black pepper, something I had not yet found on an Irish menu. I guess I was feeling a little homesick for America. When I looked in the mirror as I headed out, and noticed I was dressed a little like Old Glory, was wondered if it were coincidence or subconscious.

I arrived at the appointed place and time to find Jenn, in what looked like full business attire of dark knee-length skirt, sky blue business shirt and very mannish paisley bow tie. She was standing a little like a posing model for a New Yorker magazine fashion advertisement, soaking up the fading spring sunset.

"Found your way, I see," she said as I emerged from the moving crowd by stopping while they moved on.

"O'Riley's," I said, glancing up at the small sign hanging from the front of the establishment. "Is every pub in this country named after someone?"

"Treat 'em as a friend, call 'em as a friend," she said. "Owner's name, least at one time, usually. Some are street and neighborhood names. I saw a lot like that in America. Did you run across Sober Lane in your adventures in Cork? I love that name. Some connection to an abstinence movement, I think. Some are named just so the tourists think they are spending their money in an Irish pub."

"This one?"

"O'Riley's been here since Joyce was writing."

I nodded, and then ushered her toward the front door with an exaggerated underhand wave of a hand.

As we entered, I noted that O'Riley's Bar and Restaurant looked small from the front only. It was almost a maze inside, starting with a softy lit, dark-wood entryway with hooks for coats that appeared to be rarely used, leading to a fork in the restaurant road, where you could go unescorted to the left into what I assumed was the pub area due to the joyous noise emanating from it, or to the right, where a rather stylish young black woman attentively stood at a short lectern awaiting diners. There was a third path at the fork, a large, unmarked door in the middle that could either have led up to the second floor of the building or down to a basement. I love to imagine what might be behind such mysterious locked doors. A small sign on the door only enhanced the mystery: "None of your Feckin Business." Clearly a solution to a problem of drunk people trying to find a place to piss.

Jenn had made reservations, of course, and we were soon escorted to a fine booth that could have held four comfortably, six if you were really friendly with each other. I sat at one end, she slid in the other but continued to slide around until she was in the middle and within easy talking distance.

When the waitress came, she ordered a martini with a vodka I had never heard of before, something from Brazil, she said. Made with acai, she explained: "a little fruity, I think." I matched her yuppie vodka choice with my own.

"Ciroc, on the rocks, please," I said. "Twist of lime."

The waitress nodded and departed.

"French vodka?" she said. "I thought you were a whiskey and beer man."

"Maybe I want to be a cool kid too," I said.

"I don't think you care all that much what other people think."

"Maybe I just want to keep people guessing,"

"Ah, Matt Maybourn, man of mystery," she said, almost giggling as she faked a serious tone. "Oh, and how did the interview go?"

"Good. Softball questions, you know? Pried a little about the new novel. He thinks it's a crime story set in Ireland. I figured we'd just let him think that. We never touched on Jasper or the Quiet Man angle."

She nodded.

"Story reads that way. it was in the Wednesday print edition and up online. You want to read it?"

I shook my head. I had long since given up caring about what entertainment reporters wrote about me or my books. OK, maybe The New Yorker article, from almost four years ago, mattered to me. But the magazine didn't really like my first new novel after Kiss hit it big on the screen. I hadn't written anything worth publishing since then, since Maggie was diagnosed,

Had it really been four years since I put out a book?

"Well, it got read in London," she said.

I was thinking about Maggie, and not writing seriously for some time, and did not really understand what she meant. I was not really trying to understand what she meant.

"Sorry," I said, returning to the here and now, and Jenn, when the drinks arrived.

I waited for the waitress to set them down and give us menus before departing.

I could tell Jenn was just dying to tell me the rest of her story, but wanted my undivided attention, so I simply said "And?" and then leaned back in the booth with the vodka in my hand.

"The BBC wants an interview," she blurted out. "Maybe they read the local piece and are interested. Maybe someone in Hollywood is talking. They know you are working on some sort of sequel to Quiet Man. If you talk about that, it will make the international wire. Big splash, I think."

There was something about the way she talked, like it was scripted. Like she was telling me a well-rehearsed story.

"The BBC, uh? They want me to come to London?"

"No. No. They want to meet you here, in Galway. See how you are immersing yourself in the Irish life, I guess. They want to send a photog to Belfast, for your reading there next month. I think they will probably be at the reading. Maybe some posed shots. It will all be great press …"

She then paused. "… If you accept." Her voice trailed off.

There was an uncertain look in her face, in her eyes: the tell-tale tight lips, the darting but averting eyes.

"You planted the seed, didn't you, young lady?"

She might have blushed, I couldn't really tell in the low light. But she stuttered for the first time since I met her and I knew the answer to my question before she spoke.

"Well, ahhhh," she said, looking at me, trying to read my face. Was I angry?

"No worries," I said. "Sure, I'll do it. I've been waiting for the cat to be out of the bag, to have that discussion with someone."

"But I need to know," I continued. "Was it Jasper or you? His people or my people?"

"I made contact with a college bud of mine, working as an intern there. I thought it would be a good thing for both of us, for all of us. You think Mr. Kelly's people will be pissed? I don't want to step out bad with them, you know."

"I'll tell him. He and his people will handle it as they want to handle it."

"Good," she said, after taking a long drink from her martini. Her blush had turned into a flush of excitement. You could see it in her eyes, hear it in her short, quick breaths.

"It'll go international. I just know it."

"I'm sure it will,' I said. "Feckin ugly American writing some lousy book about Ireland that'll be turned into another crappy Hollywood blockbuster."

"No. No," she said. "It'll not be that way."

I looked at her. Took sip of my drink, continued to look at her.

"You think?" she said.

"Could be. One always needs to be prepared for the worst in newspapermen. It's fine, though. It's true and I have to talk about it sooner or later. May as well be while I am still deciding what the lousy book will be about."

She took another dive into her martini, maybe getting up a little more nerve.

"I'm guessin' it'll not be a lousy book, Mr. Maybourn."

I nodded. Maybe it would not be after all. Maybe it would be a good book, one that deserved a good movie to be made from it.

"Let's order some food," I said. "I'm running out of steam today."

We both opened the menus, and as soon as Jenn closed hers the waitress was on the spot.

Dinner was good. We both had second drinks, she only after I ordered mine. The details of the reading were just details. I agreed to get a driving tour of her city in the morning; she almost insisted, and I was interested in seeing the city she knew as well, so it was easy to say yes. She didn't ask about Lamb Alley, as I expected, so I did not bring it up. We split up right outside the front door of O'Rileys, after I surreptitiously checked the third door at the entrance fork. It was locked.

"Sleep well Matty," she said as we parted, she slurred her words just a little. I turned, started to walk away, then turned and watched her walk away. She looked good walking away. The two stiff martinis were hitting me as well.

I slept late the next morning. We had agreed to meet at 10 a.m., which we did. While I waited in the breakfast area at the hotel, I had a croissant with jam and an Americano with steamed milk, what they called *café con leche* in Portugal. Jenn then picked me up and gave me a nice driving tour of the city outside of the Trinity College area. She had obviously had her caffeine too and was buzzing as we went exploring.

She was the perfect guide in many ways: she pointed things out, said a little factoid about each point of interest, stopped and found parking a couple times when I wanted to check something out in a little more detail. It was not her first tour.

She knew I had seen Trinity the day before, but she scolded me for not spending time with the Book of Kells. "Nothin' more Irish than the Book of Kells," she argued. We drove past the Guinness storehouse. "There is a great view of the city from the bar at the top," she pointed out.

I declined a stop for a pint and the view. We did stop at St. Patrick's Cathedral, a beautiful building dating from the 1200s which needed no explanation and none was provided by my guide. We drove by Kilmainham Gaol, a former prison and a strikingly attractive, yet stunningly sad, place where a long line of Irish revolutionaries, especially those of the 1916 Easter Rising, were executed by the British, but also a place of almost equal political bloodshed carried out by leaders of the Irish Free State against the anti-treaty Republicans after 1923.

When I declined a stop at at the castle, she admonished me: "You have to know what happened here, Matty. You have to see the scars, you know."

I thought of Kenny when she mentioned scars.

There were a dozen other places we drove by, most of which I lost track of their names and their reasons to be a point of interest, but we did have a nice walk through the National Botanical Gardens. It was during that walk that Jenn broached the subject of Lamb Alley.

"May I ask why you desire to see Lamb Alley," she said. "It's not exactly on the usual list of tourist attractions."

"Somebody I know, back in Gleninagh, told me a story about the place, some punk music club and the alley, what goes on there," I said.

"Not a nice place, really," she said. "Oh, the club has its attraction, I guess, if you like that kind of thing. But it is not a nice place. Feckin rough boys. Working girls. Fights and drugs and other bad things in the alley. You know that, right?"

"I know. Kenny's story is not a nice story."

"OK, then. We're going. Tonight, after the reading? Headline band gets going around 10 or so, but we will want to in by 9 and be out before it gets feckin crazy at midnight. OK with you?"

I stopped and she stopped and I looked at her. "I know it is above and beyond. I can go by myself. I am a big boy."

"No feckin way are you going by yourself. No feckin' way. I've been there, many times. Not so much anymore, but I know the place."

"Good," I said.

We started walking again. The gardens were beautiful, but I could not stop thinking about Kenny and Jenn, and their connection to the alley. I wondered what Jenn's Lamb Alley story was.

The tour of Dublin ended with a late lunch at a curry joint Jenn liked, near The Clarence. The reading went as planned, as they usually do. This one was early, 4 p.m. Good crowd. The local story must have done its job in more ways than one. I was back in The Clarence by 6-ish.

Jenn and I had agreed to meet at 8-ish for my escorted trip to the dark side. I would have been downstairs at 8 p.m., exactly, but I couldn't decide what an old dude, trying not to look terribly out of place in a Dublin punk bar, should wear. A fool's errand. My faded blue jeans were right from the beginning, but a black tee-shirt with the classic smashing-guitar emblem of The Clash, which I had bought in Galway specifically for this night, seemed like I was futilely trying to be a bad boy. A white tee and a "vintage" grey business suit vest, which I also purchased in Galway, seemed liked I was trying too hard to be hip.

I decided on a bright, almost emerald green, button-down Oxford with the sleeves rolled up a little. It made me look like a businessman, maybe American but maybe Euro, out for the night slumming it. Good enough.

When I met Jenn at the Octagon Bar inside the hotel, one of those intimate drinking rooms where deals are done and liaisons planned, I did not recognize her at first. Her hair was more unkempt, her makeup a little darker both in mood and in shade. Her eyes were almost blackened with mascara that faded off into horizontal teardrops that stretched nearly to her ears. The first striking thing was her nose ring. I had never noticed the hole in her septum necessary for such an ornament, but then I had never really looked up her nose and she had worn no such ornament in the now half dozen times I had been with her. The ring was not one of those gaudy bull-ring things, hanging down with balls on the ends. But a thin, closed string of gold that only gave hint of wildness without giving proof of unnecessary pain accepted.

But it was not her hair, or her makeup, or even the ring that caused me to hesitate and stare.

Exposed by the nearly bare shoulders revealed by her silky black tank-top, a flowing series of thorny rose vine tattoos cascaded from the base of her hair on the back of her neck, spread out over her pale-skinned but muscular right shoulder, descended the right side of her chest and dove under the curves of her blouse.

I imagined the continued flow of the tattoo, wrapping around the outside of her breast, continuing a longer journey with a final destination only hinted at by a glimpse of color below one side of her blouse, a glimpse that disappeared behind her waist.

She saw me stare and stood, following my eyes as I took in her full outfit of silky black blouse above a rough-textured brown leather skirt that ended somewhere mid-thigh with her short, but also muscular and strangely-pale legs, ending with above-the-ankle black military boots.

She looked like a different woman, more Sinéad than Jennifer.

"Whoa," I said.

"The skin or the tats?"

"The tattoos," I answered, thinking both but admitting only the undeniable.

"I keep them covered for business," she said as she waved me toward the seat beside her at the high boy table meant for four. "A girl have to have her secrets."

"And anyway," she continued. "Got to dress for the part if we're headin' to Lamb Alley."

She then looked me up and down, a slightly disapproving crimp to her mouth, with its blood-red lipstick nearly in hiding for a moment. As I moved near and slid up into the barstool, I questioned my choice of costume for the urban safari I had requested.

I looked at her as I sat, looked at my shirt, then back to her.

"I look like a rich old man in this, don't I."

"You are going to look out of place no matter what you wear. But at least you are not tryin' too hard to look young or like some punk wannabe. That would look feckin pitiful. You know?"

"I have a leather jacket in my room."

"Only make it worse, being a wannabe and all, and you'd die of the heat."

She looked at the shirt again, then back to me face.

"You look like who you are."

I was wondering if that was a compliment or a putdown, but the temptation to dig further into that question was put to rest by the approach of a waitress.

"You planning on having a drink or two tonight?" Sinéad asked as the waitress neared.

"One," I said. "At least to get the evening started."

She nodded.

"You into good tequila? The drinks will be feckin expensive anywhere we go down there, probably watered as well. Plus, the memory of a shot will cover up the initial smell of the place."

"You make it sound so nice."

"It's lowlife. I assume you know that."

I nodded. "Kenny said he'd go there to buy his drugs."

That disapproving crimp to her mouth returned. But she said nothing.

"Not for me," I assured her. "Few minutes of research into the dark side of Dub."

"That will do it for ya," she concluded.

The waitress stopped and stood by. Sinéad gave me a look like "you in or out?"

I nodded.

"Chinaco Anejo," she said. "Two shots."

The waitress nodded and went away.

"Never heard of it," I said.

"Only when it's on expense," she said, a big, sheepish, seductive smile now blooming over her red lips. "A bit o' market research, you know? What the cool kids drinkin'."

I nodded, smirked, but my mind was not on the subtle humor. It was on the uneasy feelings stirring by being near her, sharing her breathe, smelling her mix of subtle perfume and even more subtle musk. I wondered just what the hell I was doing, with this woman, in this dark Irish bar, making plans to venture into an even darker place. There was a dangerous desire brewing somewhere down deep, a desire that had laid dormant, for quite a while, one I could feel if not actually acknowledge, but one I thought I could simply lie away.

"Just research," I said, drawing a giggle from her, which I took as maybe an understanding that she knew I was lying to myself.

My decent into an unwelcome reality was rescued by the shots, which were placed in front of us without the accouterments of limes or salt, as I expected.

I looked at Sinéad, and she at me.

"No fanfare?" I said.

"Limes? Not with the cost of this," she said. "Trust me, it will go down smooth and kick in a few minutes later."

I grabbed my shot, and she her's.

"*Croi follain agus gob fliuch!*" she said as it neared her lips.

We drank together, then I held my empty up, shooting a questioning look to her.

"Healthy heart and wet lips," she said, before the tip of her tongue darted around her lips.

I shook my head as the tequila gave up its initial hit, sucked air, and fought off a twitch. It had been a long time.

"You ready?"

I looked at her. Nodded.

"An adventure. We go adventuring."

I nodded again as we both slid off our stools.

It had been a long time.

I moved for my wallet, but she waved it off, opened a small black purse only a little bigger than a wallet, and threw a couple Euro bills on the table.

"I'll handle the bills tonight," she said. "Keep your wallet close."

I nodded, then moved my wallet from its usual right back pocket to right front.

There was a line of taxis waiting outside the hotel, some cramped, new-school Toyota coupes with an occasional old-school, boxy model of unknown make mixed in. She bypassed a pair of eager young new-school drivers and settled on an old-school driver leaning lazily on the hood of his vehicle, smoking a cigarette.

Some words were exchanged which I did not understand; either they were speaking Gaelic or speaking very fast or I was reeling from the tequila.

Negotiations completed, the driver tossed his cigarette into the street and deftly opened a back door to his cab. She slipped into the backseat first. I followed through the same door. As she slid across the seat, she turned her back to me, revealing that her rose vine tattoo exited her blouse on her right side, flowed down to the middle of her lower back, and ended at the top of what I assumed was a St. Patrick's Celtic cross, the size of which was only hinted as it disappeared underneath her leather skirt.

As I slid into the back seat with her, two things were clear: Sinéad was all Irish lass and Irish sass, no doubt. And I, possibly, was diving into the river of life in a stretch of dark water well over my middle-aged head.

I breathed it in.

It was a short drive through mostly heavy traffic. The smooth whine of the taxi's engine accelerating and decelerating, the sounds of other cars bouncing around us, made our back-seat quiet even more pronounced.

I thought about the moment before an amusement park thrill ride kicks off, the anticipation of what is to come, the silence awaiting the realization of reaching the point of no retreat.

"There are a couple clubs to chose from," Sinéad said, bringing me to the moment. "Kind of old school punk or EDM."

She paused, started to explain: "Electronic …"

"… dance music," I interrupted. "Got it."

I smiled at her with a smile of smugness. She smiled at me with, I guessed, a smile of amusement.

"Ladies' choice," I said.

"Always ladies' choice," the taxi driver said just barely loud enough for us to hear but enough to know he had been listening.

"True that," I said, looking into a big driver's mirror, seeing a nod of the head from him and a chuckle from the lady making the choice.

Not sure if I had actually enunciated it to Sinéad, but it was the whole experience I wanted from Lamb Alley. The music at some club was just the background noise to the people watching.

And, oh, what an experience it turned out to be.

Lamb Alley may have been the general location, and maybe the state of mind and music, but it wasn't the street address of any establishment in the nearby nightlife area.

The alley was, well, an alley. On one side, the back entrances of a row of warehouses, large doors for trucks to load and unload, and regular doors, each locked and chained and fortified against those seeking hidden places and those with even lower purpose. Nothing could protect the doors and surrounding walls from graffiti interlopers.

To the alley's other side, a battered but unbroken cement
wall, too tall to look over for all and too tall to scale for all but
those being chased by threatening persons or the Garda. I
assumed there were other businesses, or maybe residences, on the
wall's far side, neither of which really wanted to have anything to
do with the alley.

As Sinéad and I stood at the corner where the taxi had
dropped us, I looked down the alley's long block, lit futilely with
three evenly spaced street lamps that created sporadic islands of
glaring clarity but also defined blurry, shallow shadows. There
may well be ample spaces for drug deals, midnight trysts and
drunken brawls, but there was no real hiding place in Lamb
Alley.

As I got my fill of the image, I heard Sinéad doing business
with the taxi driver.

"I doubt we'll be long," she said. "An hour. Maybe two. I
doubt it. We don't want to wait around on the street, ya know?
I'll text ya and there will be extra for you if ya' scoot over and
wait for us right here."

"Nothin' illegal, this, young lady?"

"Quick tour. Strange business but nothin' illegal."

I turned as there was a slight laugh out of the driver.

"Ten minutes 'n' I'll be here. Or one of my buds who knows
the plan."

"*Foirfe.*"

She then turned to look at me as the taxi pulled away.

"Not much to look at after dark," she said. "In the day, the
graffiti is worth a view. Some just no talent, but some fierce. If
you're into such art."

As she talked, I looked past her to the first corner and nearest
business from the entrance to the alley. There was a crowd of
young people, mostly roguish young men, idling to each side of a

three-story blue building serving as an urban canvas with "fierce" graffiti on the top two floors and "no talent" at street level.

"Like that?" I nodded toward the corner.

She turned as I stepped up beside her. "Exactly."

For a moment we just took in the scene.

The blue building was clearly a music club, not only because of the thumping base oozing from its every orifice but because of the crowd outside, all smoking and laughing and cursing, as young people everywhere are wont to do. The corner had a huge, glaringly bright street lamp, with what looked like one of the urban surveillance cameras, a fortified opaque glass tit protruding from a metal sphere. With the lamp, and two other third-story lamps, nearly as bright, and attached to the club, you could see the top two floors were covered with an almost-beautiful mural of an old, angry god of the ocean: Neptune or Poseidon? I always forget which is the old one. He moved in from the left toward the corner, while moving in from the right side was a sea nymph of some sort. He was reaching out, like God on the Sistine Chapel heavens but if you followed his reach it was toward the nymph's more than ample breasts. She, in fact, seemed to be looking down, maybe even falling to the ground, her hair and clothing streaming upward.

Written above the floating pair were the words "Music for Few" on one side and "Drink for All" on the other. Below the English version was what I assumed was the Gaelic version: *Ceol le haghaidh cúpla* and *Deoch do gach*. Right at the corner, attached to the second floor, was a more traditional pub sign that simply read "Rice House".

The artwork on the bottom floor, a mix of crude caricatures and vulgar script, much of it overlapping and indecipherable, offered less to admire.

"This be the place," she said.

We crossed the street, moving from the entrance to the alley through an intersection where the few passing cars crawled to either for an extended view of the freak show or to avoid the crowd spilling into the street from the club.

Just before we entered the crowd, I noticed the buildings to each side of the club. To the left, a row of shops starting with a shuttered tourist store, I think, with several international flags flying from the second story. Then, nearer, a small restaurant or maybe a big coffee shop, open but with only a single couple sitting on rugged metal café furniture out front. Finally, nearest to the pub, a tattoo shop open for business and pain. Farther down the block, past the tourist shop, there were other shuttered businesses of unknown purpose, some with metal curtains drawn across their windows and door.

At the next intersection, there was another pub, with the same thumping base resounding and another herd of young people standing out front. I thought I heard the swaying beat of electronic dance music, but the punishing punk from the nearest club made exact sonic identification impossible.

The block to the right of the Rice House, though, was clearly a residential block. On both sides of the street there were two- and three-story row houses, some appearing to be nicely refurbished and others in partial state of repair or obvious need of repair. It was probably a great little neighborhood from about 1 a.m.—most pubs close between 1 and 2 p.m., even though they have no real "closing time"—to about 8 p.m. when the club opens.

The first half dozen of the row houses, I noticed, had bars on the windows and heavy, fortified doors. It reminded me a little of Rittenhouse neighborhood where I lived with Maggie. Where I still lived, I corrected myself. It was strange that home seemed like a distant place.

The crowd just outside the front door, which I could now see included a few hard looking females as well as the toughs, did little to part as Sinéad slipped her way through, with me in tow, toward a front door guarded by a short, burley man who noticed our approach with as little cultural amusement as he gave to the the rest of the crowd. When they did notice, the crowd, especially the men, bounced their attention from Sinéad to me and back to her, multiple times in quick turn. She, they could understand: a fine-looking local out for a little fun, they might suppose. Me? Maybe a brave tourist from somewhere not named Ireland walking on the wild side. But the two of us? Together? That was a little hard to wrap their heads around.

A couple of the men in the crowd gave me a nod as I slipped by them, appreciating my evening travel guide if not my overly-Irish shirt. I breathed in a strange mix of smoke from cigarettes of tobacco as well as other legal and illegal mixtures of smokable substances. A couple of the women in the crowd also gave me a good long look, wondering just what my bent was.

The attention, following in the wake of Sinéad's stunning confidence, was pleasurable all unto itself.

At the door, there was a brief conversation between Sinéad and the doorman. She leaned into him, almost touching his barrel chest with hers. There was a shared laugh, like a bawdy joke shared, then something passed from hand to hand. She then reached back her hand, which I instinctively took hold of, childlike, and she slid past him, pulling me a step behind. The doorman, all sweat and muscles and flaming tattoos bulging from the seams of a tee-shirt decorated with a faded picture of the Ramones, gave me a glance as I passed.

He wanted to say something; I wanted to hear what he had to say. I held up for a moment. He thought over his words quickly but carefully.

"Enjoy the evening, sir," he said. "Anybody a bother, ya tell me straight away."

His voice rose in volume as he spoke, either because the opening door allowed the throbbing music to pour out in almost physically abusive levels or because he wanted to send a message to the young men within earshot.

We entered, but stood just inside for a moment, allowing our eyes to adjust to the low light and our ears to adjust to the pounding sound of an electric base being abused. It took me a moment to realize Sinéad was facing me.

She leaned forward, put her lips near my right ear, where she only had to talk loud but not yell.

"Told him you were an American writer, doing a story on the Dublin youth music scene," she said. "He was pleased."

When she pulled her face back, I nodded. Mostly true story. She then turned and led the way deeper into the human zoo, her hand still latched onto mine.

There was a long bar to the left side, with a long line of drinkers, most talking in small groups. I glanced around to the crowd, to the back, where the room opened up into a partially visible open area filled with a wall-to-wall crowd convulsing to the music of a band on a slightly raised stage against the far wall.

Behind the bar were two rather hard-looking women, like the bouncer, all black tees and tattoos, and a tall, older man who seemed to be standing back, aloof, maybe the owner—maybe the gofer for the barmaids, maybe the muscle in case the customers got a little too "over the bar" obnoxious. Probably all three. it seemed like a "lean-management" kind of place.

Sinéad hesitated, looked around the club, so I did as well. As she scanned, I noticed that behind the bar, in both prominence and a protected location, there were eight-by-ten photos of bands, signed, by the look of the scribbles on them. There were maybe twenty or so, a few of which I instantly recognized: The Clash, U2; some of which I had a vague recollection of: Black 47, Dropkick Murphys; and some that I had no idea of but were in newer frames indicating a more recent mounting. I felt a little pride that I knew some of them.

I could just imagine U2, in, say 1979 or '80, playing the Dublin club scene, getting high and playing loud. I could almost hear *I Will Follow*, the oldest U2 song I could remember, weaving its way through the throbbing base of whatever song was being played by that night's band. Ah, what dreams a writer will dream?

"U2 played here?" I said.

She did not hear as the band drowned out all but yells. I reached out and touched her bare shoulder; she looked back.

"U2 played here?" I yelled.

She leaned in, close to my face, again loud but not yelling, but it seemed like she was whispering in my ear. "Several times. Last time early '90s, I think. After *Zooropa*. I liked that one, and before that, Achtung something."

I remembered my collection.

"*Achtung Baby*," I said. "I liked that one too. That song, *End of the World*, from the movie."

"Movie?"

I was going to try to explain the Wim Wenders film, from the 1990s. The one that was like an acid trip come to life: mind and machine melded, China in ascendance, and a lot of other crap. It was too much for yelling.

"Good film. Great song," I said.

"Ya. Me mum liked 'em."

She shrugged as she spoke, and pulled back, smiling.

She was poking me. Feeling brave, either due to the tequila or the club or something. I liked her feeling brave.

She then returned to her scan of the club, as did I.

To the right, opposite the bar, was a row of Spartan wooden booths, large enough for half a dozen people but mostly filled with three or four men demanding more space due to their physical size if not their intimidating auras.

I stared a little too long at one booth, at its backdrop—a rough, artist rendering of musical instruments on a cracked stucco—but also the booth's its occupants: four men, not as old as I but not as young as the majority of the crowd. They wore varying forms of urban camouflage: plaid shirts with sleeves rolled up above the elbow, those Irish tweed caps of various colors and state of existence, and sturdy beer glasses in states of partial consumption on a wooden table top in need of refinishing. One of the gentlemen noticed my voyeurism, caught my eye as he tilted his head back and gave me a stare that could as easily have been an invitation to come play or an ultimatum to come fight.

I nodded, recognizing his presence as one would a ragged old dog worthy of being weary of, and then dropped my gaze to avoid any hint of challenge.

Sinéad rescued me from my imagination if not my actual predicament with a tug on my shirt sleeve. I had not realized we were no longer hand-in-hand. I looked her way.

"I see some mates," she said, looking to a booth farther into the club, near the short passage that led to the dance floor area and maybe a half dozen booths distance from the den of my four tattooed reservoir dogs.

"Oh, this is going to be fun," I either thought to myself, or said in a voice drowned out by the thumping base. I'm not sure what I enjoyed more, watching or being watched. I think a writer, at least of writer of real people in real life, is a voyeur at heart—a *voyeur* in the original French definition of the word, as in "one who watches", and not in the pseudo-medical definition of the word, with all its secretive sexual gratification connotations. But a writer also likes to be noticed, even if not appreciated. There is a certain thrill to being read, or heard, or seen; even if for the wrong reasons.

Writers and punkers are similar in that way.

In the Rice House, in that crowd, I was the object of notice as much as I was the *voyeur*. People's heads turned, and paused for a moment, as I passed: the reservoir dogs and their like kind, a couple of uneasy young men in jackets of new leather and silver studs, a tightly packed pack of young women in various levels of punkish persona.

What did they see? Was I the slightly bent tourist? The rich, middle-aged lecher? The music critic, looking for the next U2, as Sinéad's story had proffered?

Hell, maybe it wasn't even me that they noticed. As I followed Sinéad, in our dance and dodge through the crowd, I could see the speculative looks, the assumptions of the possible relationships between us. I was an out-of-place middle-aged man in the rapidly deteriorating pressed dress shirt being led around by a thoroughly modern young women armored for the night in leather and satin and thorns of Irish roses. My imagination was sufficient for only the most rudimentary of possible relationships, and I appreciated that fact.

When we arrived at the destination booth, there were three young men and one equally young woman, maybe all in their early 20s. They, too, were in versions of the uniform of the day, but all appeared to be more comfortable in their skins, like this was not an unusual destination and amusement.

Sinéad leaned in, caught their attention and ignited the woman's joyous recognition. The woman and one of the young men, especially, seemed to be Sinéad's friends, as they both slid from the booth and hugged and shared brief secret stories whispered close. The other two men, evenly spaced in the booth with one sitting on the outside, watched as I watched; wondered as to the occurrence as I wondered. Sinéad then looked my way and waved me forward.

"Matty," she said, nearly yelling so we both could hear. "Writer friend of mine."

"Abby," she continued. "School mate. And Braden."

I offered my hand to shake, which Braden did. But Abby was more the hugging kind, and she moved close and for a moment held her chest loosely against mine. I could smell a sweet alcohol on her breath and my pressed shirt continued its natural deterioration.

There was then a cyclone of other introductions, none of which I really understood, and movement. First Abby spoke to the two young men still in the booth, in a loud but unintelligible volume, then Sinéad acknowledged the two from her standing position before waving her hand my way while speaking to the two in the same loud but unintelligible volume. They looked my way. I waved. Felt stupid for doing so. There was a little more discussion between Abby and the two young men, then they slid a little closer and to the back of the booth, making room for Sinéad and me. I waved her to sit first, as Abby and Braden slid back into the other side of the booth, but she stepped back and waved me in.

"Right back," she said, yelled, and after I slid into the space vacated by one of the two unnamed young men, she stepped away toward the bar.

Left alone, to fend for myself, I offered my hand to the nearest of the two.

"Matty," I said, at a volume that seemed too loud.

First one, and then the other leaned over the table, took my hand in a slightly uncomfortable shake, and said their names, at least what I assumed was their names. One may have been "Colin" or "Coin" or something like that; the other I understood to be "Obama". Maybe a joke; maybe a compliment to an American; maybe just another Gaelic name I could not get my head around.

We all just sat back into a slightly uncomfortable silence. Me, the two young men, Abby and Braden. Sinéad arrived back with six shots of something, all expertly balanced, three in each hand. In quick, experienced fashion, the shots were distributed to be within reach of all, dodging three beer glasses in state of partial use and one tall, iced glass of something located in front of Abby. The two young men seemed to perk up a little.

Sinéad waved me to stand up, which I did, and she slid in to get close to the two young men, the nearest of which perked up even more with her approach.

"Tequila," she said as I slid back into the now intimate booth. "Decent. Not great. I watched her pour."

She then produced a paper napkin from somewhere, and unfolded it to reveal a pile of lime slices.

I nodded, smiled. The rest of the group nodded acknowledgement of the lime's fate.

She then grabbed her shot. "*Slainte*," she said.

In varying degrees of haste, we all grabbed our shots, repeated the toast, and followed her in laying the bitter liquid to waste before retrieving and sucking, sometimes awkwardly, on the lime.

Sinéad then turned to the nearest of the two young men, who was very perked up at this point, followed closely in attentiveness to her by his partner, and slid a little closer to start a conversation I could not follow. Suddenly we were all not only friends, but drinking buddies.

Abby kind of stood up, leaned across the table a little, and just about yelling, said: "So you some big Hollywood writer?"

I shrugged my shoulders, grinned as the Cheshire cat might grin, and, truth be told, felt a little woozy as the second shot kicked in with significantly less subtleness than the first.

As is usual in such situations, with the foreign ambiance and strong alcohol, time and space seemed to move at an unnatural pace. Some things happened in a blur, so quickly that I could not fully understand what was going on; some things happened in a nearly equal blur but I, somehow, either understood what was occurring or thought I understood enough to give validity to false memories later.

As I remember it now, I learned that Abby was a schoolmate of Sinéad, but they rarely saw each other lately. Braden and Abby were married, or at least lived together, and had a daughter. Both of them lived the young Irish working class life now, she a nurse's assistant and he a factory, or maybe a warehouse, worker bee. The child was with her "Mum", Abby said at one point.

"Let's us 'ave a bit a *craic*," she said. "Mum's good 'bout that. We buy her some curry noodles and a little chardonnay, she loves my little *mavourneen*, my little darling."

Abby was in her late 20s, like Sinéad. Braden a little younger. She had the look of a woman making her way in the world, one who would always make her way in the world, no matter what hardships the world brought her. Brown hair, with subtle blonde stripes, cut high in the back and longer in the front. Very modish with her heavy makeup that night, but able to be totally clean-cut and professional the next time she was at work. He was taller, thin actually, with close-cropped red hair and beard. He didn't talk about his work much: it was a job and he had to have a job to have a woman like Abby and their little girl. He was taking some classes, in electronics repair, I think he said.

"People always be breaking their phones, their toys," he explained. "Not as hard on the back. Ya know?"

They looked like young parents anywhere, getting by as best they can in an ever-changing world, working to better themselves and their kids' future. I remembered the early days with Maggie. Those were hard years, sometimes, but ultimately good years.

Abby was especially talkative, mostly just the two women catching up on their lives. Braden talked when talked to. I listened mostly, but interjected when it seemed I had something to add.

Colin and Obama were the quiet ones, the outsiders at their own party. Friends of Braden's, from his work, I think. The three boys decided to go have some beers, listen to some loud music and, maybe, in Obama's words "pick up a bird." It seemed that Abby was in the habit of not letting her man go alone into the land of temptation. Both of the boys wore fairly new t-shirts, Colin's advertising a band I had never heard of and Obama's advocating anarchy and sex. And they both all but drooled over Sinéad whenever the opportunity arose, but did not seem brave enough to get out on the floor and meet the other dancing birds wrestling with the real punks.

After the latest round of shooters, I was about as punked out as I could handle and turned to a can of Coke to keep me refreshed and caffeinated. Sinéad drank nothing of her own, but shared sips with whatever Abby was drinking a couple times over the span of the hour or so that we were in the Rice House.

The most interesting dynamic of the night, however, was the lead-up and aftermath of my one venture onto the dance floor.

Abby and Braden ventured into the area—not sure if they still called it a mosh pit?—a couple times, more at her urging than his initiative. Whenever they did, Sinéad picked one and then the other of the boys to accompany her on a similar adventure. They each bounced up like playful puppies when she motioned, all smiles and eager eyes, more than happy to be crushing with a beautiful woman they probably knew was out of their league. When the four were out, I shared a few half-understood words with the one remaining but mostly just watched the crowd.

From my edge of the table seat, I had a view of the moshing and the band obstructed only by young people moving into the fray eager to engage or moving back more sweaty then when they entered, often looking exhausted and probably focused on a cool drink inside if not fresh, cool air outside.

The band was a trio consisting of a tall, gangly drummer who pounded more than played his kit, a mostly skinhead base player with a thin, short Mohawk running fore and aft, and lead guitarist and singer, a little older than his mates and dressed in a sweat-soaked white shirt and black vest while sporting big Elvis Costello glasses. He screamed his lines to be heard over the loud music mix but actually seemed to have some vaguely poetic lyrics. They blasted their tunes, jumped around, sweated as much as those in the mosh pit, but kept the crowd moving almost non-stop. All you could ask, I decided.

I asked Obama at one point what the name of the band was, but he either did not hear or did not know as he just shrugged his shoulders. There was some Gaelic writing on a poster behind the band, but it seemed too many words to be a name, and I assumed it imparted some deep Irish message like "Live fast and die young." I was going to ask Sinéad on one of her stops back at

the table, but the thought came and went as new distractions
came and went.

After the two women had apparently satisfied their need to
crush, we were sitting around, mostly quiet, and I was about
ready to call it a night and ask my tourist guide to call up our
pumpkin and take Cinderfella home.

Instead, the Lamb Alley lesson of my night was really just
about to start.

A group of three, maybe four, overtly rowdy young men,
pushing their way forward past people and toward the band with
a bit of pomp and too-noticeable gusto, paused in front of our
table as the platoon's point man glanced at the table, noticed us,
and abruptly stopped. The point man was a rather overly pretty
punker with the barest of a 5 o'clock shadow, a fairly normal
haircut, and what looked like a brand new jean vest covering
bare but recently and sparsely tattooed upper arms and chest.
Compared to much of the usual clientele of the place, he looked
like the poser I assumed him to be.

He drilled in on Sinéad.

"Feckin all," she said, almost growled, as she noticed.

The overly pretty punker stepped to the edge of the table,
almost touching my shoulder.

"Sinéad," he said, then shouting to his pack as much as
talking to us: "Look at this boys. Sinéad be slumming it tonight."

"Evening to ya Niall," she said, pronouncing it as one would
the river Nile.

"Been quite a spell, uh?" she continued. I could detect a bit
of a sarcastic tone in her voice, like she wished it had been a
longer spell. "How are you?"

"Feckin great," he said, squaring himself up to the table,
leaning in a little to get his face closer to her. "How long has it
been, since you moved t' a better post code? Two years now?"

He glanced over to me, then back to her.

"And what's with the daddy," he said. "You a brasser, now?"

I didn't really understand what the hell he was talking about, but I assumed Sinéad did not appreciate it.

"Don't be a feckin *eegit*, Niall," she said. "Tryin' to be nice."

"Oh, I know you can be nice," he said, nearly spitting out the words like someone who had already drank too much or had some other recreational chemical imbalance. "Real nice, as I remember."

About this moment, Braden turned and started to slide out of the booth, and both Colin and Obama leaned forward onto the table as they made motions of figuring out how they, too, could get up and get out. One of Niall's sidekicks stepped up to his side, near Braden.

I was about a half a moment slow. But it dawned on me that there just might be a row coming on.

"Boys!" Sinéad said, talking to Braden, and maybe Niall, but loud enough that everybody heard. "Boys!"

Niall looked around the table, maybe counting the number of boys on his side and comparing them to the number of boys on her side, judging the probability of his getting his pretty punker persona trashed. I looked to Braden: his jaw was set and his intention to protect his wife clear. There was even a little bit of a grin on him. Colin and Obama had now positioned themselves to spring out from the back of the table, intending to back up their bud. I hoped I had the same determined aura.

"Not lookin' for trouble," Niall said, as he finished his assessment of the friend-or-foe masculine firepower around the table and settled his gaze on Sinéad.

"Then don't be callin' me *shite*," she said, a little attitude in her voice. Maybe she had done a little counting herself.

He leaned back, away from the table, looked at her and the back to me.

"Just noticin' your company," he said, still a bit of smart-assed tone to him, but one with a little less aggression. "Goin' to introduce me to your daddy?"

She was already right on my shoulder, but she slid a little closer to me.

"What's it matter to you who my fella is?"

Did I detect a little more attitude?

"Just wonderin' who you be doing a line with these days."

Once again, I did not quite understand what was being said, but did get the general message. I didn't like the message or the messenger.

Before I thought it all out, I stood up, coming nearly face to face with Niall. I noticed Braden stand up as well, coming face to face with Niall's bud, backing up my play, whatever the hell that play was going to be.

Such moments are not moments of thought, they are moments of decision and consequences. It may have been a bit of delusion, but this overly pretty punker was not a fighter I was sure, and even if he was, I just knew Braden was a better fighter. If Niall could take me he could not take Braden, and he would have to take Braden too.

I felt my heart beating, felt blood rushing to my face, anger rushing to my fists. It felt strange. I had not felt like this, acted like this, for more years than I could remember. It felt good. Scary but good.

"Matthew Maybourn," I said, reaching out my right hand to shake while fisting up my left, just in case. "Sinéad and I work together."

He declined the hand, so I pulled it back.

"Plastic paddy, huh?"

I was picking up Irish slang as I was picking up Gaelic: slowly but with some proficiency.

"Ya, I'm American," I said. "So *Niiile…*"

"So what?"

"So I don't know what the fuck you said, but I think you owe an apology to Ms. O'Reardon here."

Niall looked at me, looked at Sinéad, glanced over his shoulder to see his bud slowly moving away from Braden, whose grin had become even more pronounced. Both Colin and Obama were now crouched up on the booth seat, one leap away from being right in the middle of the scrum.

Niall looked back to me. He looked a little pale.

"Not lookin' for trouble," he said, trying his best to smile the smile of a man who had just lost a bluff.

"We're not either," I said, smiling the smile of a poker player raking in his winnings.

We stood for a moment, then he took half a step back.

"*Tá brón orm,*" he said, looking to Sinéad.

I glanced over to her. She responded with: "*Sláinte chugat,* Niall."

I somehow knew she was wishing him good health rather than bad health.

I also knew it was time to take my winnings and walk away from the table.

"Excuse me but we were about to dance," I said, not really knowing why. I really did not want to dance. Did they even call it "dancing"?

Niall looked to Sinéad, then back to me, then back to her.

"Sinéad," he said, nodding his head to her, after which he turned and began pushing his way through the crowd, followed by two of his buds. One must have faded into the crowd when it looked like there might be a little row.

I took a big sigh and looked at Braden.

There was a huge smile on his face, a sparkle in his eyes.

"That was feckin fun," he said, almost yelling.

"Ya think?" I said. We smiled at each other. Colin and Obama gave what I thought was a little cheer.

Sinéad stood up beside me. Close.

"So," she said. "You up for a little moshin' 'fore we call this done?"

She laughed. I laughed.

What the hell.

I grabbed her hand and we moved toward the band. Braden and Abby were close behind, maybe because they wanted to mosh a little, maybe because he wanted to make sure there was no trouble lurking. As we moved out of sight from the table, I saw Colin and Obama standing at the edge of the now-empty booth, maybe also just to make sure there was no trouble lurking.

There was no trouble. There were only a few minutes of jostling with the crowd.

The band was screaming out lyrics of a song I somehow knew. I had heard it before, not sung all that much differently.

"Those are people who died, died … Those are people who died, died … They were all my friends, and they died."

The name Jim Carrol came to mind, either correct or close. The song always creeped me out, in a pleasing kind of way. I sang along, in my head or out loud, not sure which.

"Those are the people who died, died …"

There were flashing colored lights, with the occasional white flash illuminating faces. Was someone photographing us? Did I look as stupid as I felt, the old man trying to be young again?

I glanced at Sinéad; she was looking at me. I stopped bouncing; she stopped bouncing. She brought her face close to mine, almost yelled into my ear: "Enough for ya?"

I nodded.

The band, still on the same song, was singing something about someone dying in upper Manhattan. I had enough.

She looked around, spotted Braden and Abby, grabbed my hand and led us toward them. She and Abby yelled at each other for a moment, then they led both of us guys back toward the table, where Colin and Obama were guzzling down fresh beers. I noticed there was fresh can of Coke, along with fresh drinks for Braden and Abby, on the table.

I took a hard hit from my soft drink. Seemed fitting.

Goodbyes were said. As the ladies hugged and talked and laughed to an unknown joke that I could only assumed I had some part in, I toasted the boys. Braden offered me his hand and, as we shook, he leaned in: "Feckin fun," he said. I then shook the hands of the other two, but we just nodded to each other, said nothing. All manly men, you know.

It was then that Abby came close. We hugged; she was a hugger, and maybe a little drunk. I am not sure who was sweatier. My nice shirt was a mess, but neither of us seemed to care.

"Pleasure to meet you, Matthew," she said. "Goin' to read some of your stuff."

I figured that was the best compliment I could ask for.

"*Sláinte tú féin agus do theaghlach*," I said, wishing her and her family health, I think, and probably with terrible pronunciation.

She looked at me, giggled a little. "Not bad," she said. "Not great."

I shrugged to Abby; we smiled as we parted. Nodded to Braden, then again to Colin and Obama; they, again, nodded back.

Sinéad was already on her cell, to the taxi as it turned out. She put away her phone and led the way to the door.

The air outside hit me almost as hard as the second tequila shot, not quite as hard as almost getting into a fight, though.

I felt a little woozy, a little excited. I felt old and young, at the same time.

I felt alive.

I wondered how long it had been since I felt alive.

We stood outside in the crowd, inhaling the cool air mixed with various smokes for just a few minutes before an old school taxi pulled up in front of Lamb Alley. Sinéad started to cross the street but I stopped her.

"A moment," I said.

She stood and watched as I turned and made my way back through the crowd to the doorman, who had noticed our exit but said nothing as we had slipped by. He noticed my return.

"Gonna write something good about the club?" he asked.

"I will. Thanks, One thing …"

He focused a little closer.

"Some chancer. No shirt, just a vest. A clean-cut poser."

He nodded, like he either knew Niall or knew the kind.

"Tried to pick a fight with me. My friends would have none of it so he backed off."

He nodded again, smiled the smile of a guy who had a job to do and liked his job.

I turned and walked back, pleased in knowing that young Niall was probably going to get his ass kicked out of the club and not understand why. We walked across the street to the waiting taxi. She got in first, but before I climbed in I took a long look up the dark alley, thinking of Kenny. Trouble finds you in places like this, at times like this. But sometimes you just have to venture into the dark.

I slid into the back seat of the taxi, came close to Sinéad. There was some light in the back seat for a moment, but as the door shut, the only light was illuminating the driver. Same guy who dropped us off.

"Good adventure, sir?" he said.

I wondered if they had shared a story while I was outside.

I tried to respond with *"mór eachtraíochta"*. Great adventure. My pronunciation came out badly; maybe really badly. Both of them laughed.

"One Gaelic phase a day?" I said, glancing her way.

"If that."

I liked her honesty. I laughed. She laughed some more. The driver turned his light off and drove off, under instructions, I assumed.

As we drove, we were silent. I alternated my eyes from outside to the inside of the taxi. The traffic and street scenes came and went like a kaleidoscope, light exposing places and people and things, then darkness hiding them. She never moved.

She looked outside the other window. I looked at her. She looked like lust.

I looked away, back outside. We never spoke, until the driver let us off in the neighborhood of the hotel, maybe three blocks away. I never told the driver where to let us off, I assume she had.

"Little walk along the Liffey?" she said as she handed the driver his fare, and an American tip, and then looked at me. "Little fresh air?"

"Sure," I said as I slid outside and offered my hand to help her out.

I had lost track of time, but there was a pretty good crowd along the river walk as we headed in the direction of The Clarence.

"It's strange you wanted to go there, to the alley," she said after a few moments of walking. "Mostly bad memories for me there. I left those memories behind. But it was big part of my life, at one time."

"I hope my friend can leave those memories behind," I said.

"Dublin can be a hard road," she said. "They have a word: riverdance. Heard it?"

"No."

"Suicide, in the river. Drowning. It's what they call it on the streets."

The cool air from the Liffey flowed over me, as well as a slightly stale, disagreeable smell. I was smelling myself.

"Rather dark turn of phrase," I said.

"Rather dark, unforgiving river, our river of life."

We neared an area on the river walk where you could either enter The Clarence or walk on by. We stopped. She turned and we stood close. Very close. I could almost feel her breasts rise and fall as she breathed. I was a good foot or more away, but such is imagination at such times.

"So," she said. "You plannin' to invite me to your room."

I felt my breath slip out of my lungs, logic fade out of my brain, blood rush where it had not rushed for a long while.

I wished I was 30 years younger. I was glad I wasn't 30 years younger. I wished I had drank more. I was glad I had not drank more.

I looked into her eyes; she did not look away, she did not blink.

I glanced away, then looked back.

"I think that would not end well for either of us," I said.

She moved forward, just a little bit more. Now there was no space between us and no imagination required. "I'm bettin' tonight would end well for you."

All I could do was smile, and, in the same instant, think about Maggie and think about Cathleen and think about the fucking train wreck I was stepping into.

"You have no idea how much …"

"Just a fuck," she interrupted. "I'm in the mood and I'm going to fuck someone tonight."

"That's just it," I said. "If I'm going to do something, move on, you know, it has to mean something. More …"

Her fingers were at my lips, stopping my awkward words.

"I'm sorry," she said, stepping back until there was a gulf between us as wide as the river. "I thought, you know, the night. The alley. Thought you were lookin' for somethin'."

"I'm sorry too. I shouldn't have crossed the line. Not your job."

She shrugged. Then she reached out a hand again. It shook ever-so-slightly as she touched my face.

"I think you're a good man, Matthew," she said as she withdrew her hand.

"Have a good trip back," she said, after a moment of silence.

"Thanks for the experience," I said, not really sure what it meant.

As I turned and headed for the hotel entrance, she turned and started to walk away. Then I heard her footsteps stop. I stopped, and glanced over my shoulder to see her locking back.

"Can I still read your book?" I said.

"Please," she said. "Good. Good night Mr. Maybourn.

"Good night, Sinéad."

* * *

I woke up a stranger in my own world. It was a strange bed. Not uncomfortable, really, the king-sized hotel bed covered with

the cool, black coverlet but strange. It was certainly a strange
room, a dark world, my head made thick by fitful sleep and a
tequila stupor. I strained to remember if I had been dreaming
but I could not remember a dream.

With my mind a void, I thought of Maggie, and twisted the
ring on my finger.

I don't dream about Maggie much anymore and, truth is, it
really doesn't bother me.

She consumed my dreams the last few weeks before she died
and the first few weeks after. Not in a bad way, or a creepy
cinematic way, like her falling and my not being able to reach
her, or other manifestations of my impotence in matters of
mortality. They were mostly dreams of her being in the
periphery of the story line, an extra in the movie. She was
working in the kitchen while I was hunting for something I could
not find. She was driving me around as I was writing on some
sort of invisible computer.

My dreams rarely make sense. And they are mostly pleasant,
if sometimes confusing or frustrating. I never have nightmares,
not for long anyway. I simply wake myself up when I am
frightened by a monster or a menacing figure. I see something
that disturbs me, I say to myself that this is not real. I wake up. It
saves me from ever remembering much of my nighttime fears
and anxieties.

I wished that I had possessed the ability to wake myself up,
those last days, when Maggie was dying. I wished I could have
said the breast cancer was not real, that the aggressive chemo
was not real, and that the inevitable end was not real. But I
couldn't simply wake up and have it gone.

I remembered when the doctor and nurses brought her out
of the drug sleep for a while and she said her goodbyes to the
kids. Now it seems more like a dream than almost any dream I

have ever had. It just doesn't seem like it was real. There is distance there, for me.

Ally told me later that Maggie and I didn't even talk to each other, those last few minutes, when I just sat there beside her bed and held her hand and looked into her eyes, even when she took a pause from looking toward the kids and looked over to me, for just a moment, before returning to the beauty she had brought into the world.

I don't remember much what they said, the kids and her; there were words of love between mother and child, and words of pride between mother and child. But there were no words between us. We had said all we needed to say well before those last few minutes, in the hours we talked in bed together during the months she fought the good fight, in the hours we talked over coffee at our dining table or at her favorite coffee shop. There was no need for last words between us.

But I now wished I had said something, something really special, something a great writer would say, as she went back under the drugs and slipped away quietly. I was ashamed of my quietness when the doctor checked her heart and checked her eyes and simply said "She is gone."

I remember the kids crying, and crowding around me and hugging me, and my looking at Maggie seemingly asleep. I cried too, more because I wanted to cry with the kids than because I had to cry myself. I had cried many times before and, had I been alone, I don't think I would have shed a tear.

I said nothing, not even to the kids when they left, nor when the doctor and the nurses left, and then I was alone with the body Maggie had left behind, for a moment. Or maybe it was an hour; there is a distance there for me as well. I stood there and looked at her, and strained to see if she was still breathing. She wasn't. She wasn't there anymore. She was off on an adventure that I knew someday she'd tell me about. An adventure, God willing, we'd share.

And in that moment I was selfish. I have always been a selfish man, but at that moment there was no moral shadows to hide selfishness in.

My overwhelming feeling was emptiness, an empty feeling of being alone. And that feeling of loneliness made me angry, at myself, at God, and worst of all at Maggie. I quickly buried that feeling, that day. But it is a shallow grave that sometimes beckons me but I try hard not to visit.

I felt very much alone when I woke, as I sat there, in my big empty hotel bed, with nothing but darkness surrounding me, I wished I had dreamed about Maggie.

But I hadn't. And I felt guilty.

You see the Poulnabrone Portal Tomb from the roadside where Cathleen parked, where we stood outside her car. On my map it was just north of Corrofin, on R480, a rural, two-lane road through the heart of The Burren.

"I know it's a place associated with an ancient religion," I say, trying to impress her, I guess. "But it strikes me as being a piece of modern art."

She nods, in agreement I think, and smiles as she looks my way.

But then I betray my impressive attempt.

"I feel like Floyd when he first glimpsed the monolith."

Her smile fades to puzzlement.

Clearly she's never been with Kubrick on the dark side of the moon.

"Arthur C. Clarke? 2001? Space Odyssey?"

"Not much into science fiction," she says, nodding, but with little enthusiasm.

I shut up and we move on, walking closer.

The tomb stands solitary, vaguely reminiscent of Stonehenge for those unaware of its history, in a garden of grey stone sewn together with ribbons of hardy scrub grass. A flat horizontal stone perched at an angle on several vertical stones, its closer inspection brings to mind an ultra-modern home constructed of ancient materials, as if designed by prehistoric Frank Lloyd Wright.

For many tourists the well-known portal tomb, surrounded by the great Irish sea of stark stone that is The Burren, would have been the climax of a tour, as evidenced by a small tourist bus parked in front of us and the pack of people surrounding the tomb at the proscribed distance.

For Cathleen, it was the first stop on my promised tour.

"Get this done," she says as we first turned off N67 and she announced our first stop. "Then we'll wander thart."

As with many aspects of my growing understanding of Cathleen, our adventure started at the conclusion.

I have come to notice that discussions with her, the mundane or the serious, often start at what eventually would be the end point. They then progress from there, with only reluctant regression to fill in the blanks as necessary to whomever she is talking.

She'd ask "Your list of groceries?" when she planned to go into Galway and was willing to shop for me. The first time she did so I did not understand and she needed to follow up with "Do you need anything from the market?"

Or she'd simply say "On the stove" as she headed out somewhere, when she'd made something impossible to make for only one, such as this stale bread and milk desert she knew I liked, inviting me to enter her house at my leisure and grab some should I choose.

In political or social intercourse, she had the same habit, only more subtle. If the news of the day was the government falling in Italy, she'd say "Greece 'ill be next" and a couple days later there would be rumblings of Greek government in turmoil.

I was coming to understand she treated encounters, and adventures, with much the same "cut to the end" attitude.

I have lately been thinking more about the woman who shared my view from Gleninagh North. I thought about her that night in Dublin, and in the morning, in the aftermath of my dreamless night. I was glad when, the day after my return from the Dublin reading, she asked if it was a good time to take the tour of The Burren she'd promised. It was a good time. I needed to change the storyline of what had become an increasingly confused Irish immersion. Road trips always cleared my head, or allowed me to focus on certain elements of my always racing mind.

To say that day's guided tour of The Burren started at Poulnabrone was a slight exaggeration, it actually started standing in her yard, before we got into her car, when she pointed to a high point on the horizon, just west of where we stood.

"You know?" she inquires.

To me, it is only another very slight high point along the Gleninagh ridge, the rocky highlands that quickly slopes down to the bay. I shake my head.

"Gleninagh Mountain. Not much of a mountain, 300 meters or so, but often considered the northern end of The Burren. 'Course the highest point on the island, *Carrauntoohil*, is just over 1,000. Down in Kerry. Mere hill by American standards."

I nod weakly, able to think of nothing to add to the conversation, just before 8 a.m., and still struggling to come fully awake.

My agreed-upon 7:30 a.m. arrival from down the hill had been greeted with soda bread, jam and coffee at her house — "an experiment in alternative caffeinating," she told me, as she proudly showed off the completed action of a new stovetop percolator I assumed was purchased specifically with me in mind. It was coffee, but in name only, especially when compared to the dark, strong brew I make and drink each morning to get the body and brain working. It was the thought, though, and I appreciated the thoughtfulness.

As we moved to enter her car, Michaeleen attempted to climb into the passenger seat where I was planning to sit. His usual spot.

"No Michaeleen," she states in no uncertain terms. "Not today."

He looks at her with a bit of disappointment in his eyes, then at me with a bit of a more aggressive emotion, then back to her with what I decide is a look of resignation. He stood at the roadside as we started to drive down Gleninagh North, then jumped the back fence and disappeared into the landscape.

Every man likes a day of freedom every now and then.

We drive straight to Poulnabrone, with some brief discussion on the weather and a short conversation on the status of my writing. Once at the tomb, we stand outside her car, in silence, just taking in the warm summer day, as the tourist herd finished their grazing and their photos and retreated to the van for their next stop, probably the Cliffs of Moher.

When they are gone, and we were alone, I break our silence.

"It is beautiful."

"True enough. Though some say it was most likely a place where people were brutally sacrificed to some unknown god or gods. Not that I believe it."

I look at her, she looks around, first over one shoulder and then over the other, looking into the distance, or maybe the past.

She then walks, at a slow, reverential pace, toward the tomb. I follow.

"Seems hard to imagine," she says as she nears. "There are some small farming areas nearby, lowlands where soil and water collect, so this was probably a burial place for a Stone Age farming community. It is called a portal tomb, the two side and one back stones support the roof stone."

"Looks like a portal to somewhere I don't want to go," I say, trying to peer into the shadowed room the stones created.

" 'Tis actually a small one," she continues. "One in Carlow has a roof stone of 100 tons, I understand. I've never seen it. They had a professional dig here, some time ago, and found human bones laid out in a ritual fashion. Men and women and children. Maybe buried here long after their death. Just the bones, maybe burned for some reason. Purification ritual, maybe. Some say it was a place of sacrifice, I say it was a holy place. A peaceful place, where the leaders of the community were buried with honor and ceremony."

"Kind of the way the Catholics do such things," I say.

She glances at me, nods her head once, in the way a teacher would acknowledge a student who got the right answer to a math problem.

"An' like a good Catholic, often buried with a treasure or two. In their case the treasure was stone beads or a crystal."

She breathes in, deeply, taking in the fresh air if not the mysterious, ancient aura.

"You want a photo?" she says, still looking out at Poulnabrone.

"No. Don't feel much like a tourist anymore."

She nods again. And we turn and walk back to the road.

From Poulnabrone we go west, not really sure exactly where, I must have missed a road sign, but west. Much of the roadways crisscrossing the The Burren look the same unless you know them: winding, two-lanes wide, with slight rises and falls as the landscape rises and falls. Some of the scenery is more grass than rock; some more rock than grass. A few hardy, solitary trees make a stand against the wind. There are areas where the rocks seem to have been cut into sharp faces that rise up three or four feet, like a wall or a fence. There are areas where the rocks seem to have flowed out like the flows from a Hawaiian volcano, but they are grey and not black, mostly limestone sanded down by wind and rain. There are areas where the stone has been broken down into stones and the stones piled up into walls, walls that could have been around for 500 years or built last year.

As we drive. I tell her what I know about The Burren; she amplifies or corrects my knowledge as necessary. We pass through Lidsoonvarna, heading north. And, again, we are mostly silent. At Lisdoonvarna crossroads, though, I point out a sign for Spanish Point and express my intrigue.

"One of the graveyards for the ships and crews of Philip's shattered Armada," she says, glancing my way quickly, I assume to confirm I knew the basic history.

"After Gravelines?" I ask, knowing that the Armada had tried to escape south, along the west coast of Ireland, after repeated, crushing naval losses at English hands, the last being off the now Belgian port city of Gravelines.

She nods, assured that I do, in fact, know my basic history.

"Storms along the Irish coast were as destructive as English cannon," she says. "They say two dozen ships were wrecked and 5,000 men were killed at sea or put to death when they washed ashore."

"Civilized people, those Brits," I add.

"Very. Always the civil conquerors."

We stop not far outside of Lidsoonvarna. After climbing up a little to a plateau, at a wide spot off the side of the road.

She exits the car and I follow. We hike up a little rise, to what may be a high point. She stands and looks into the distance.

On first glance I see nothing; just more of the grey rock and green grass fading to brown. Then I notice some splashes of yellow and pure white, blurs on the grey and green scene. I am seeing color when there is none?

"250 square kilometers of rock," she said, as she kicks at a crack in the rock and a hardy little patch of what looks like thyme growing in the crack.

"Nobody lives here?"

"Not really. You can put a house here, but you can't grow a garden. Every Irish home needs a garden."

"Looks like nothing grows here."

"Don't always believe your eyes, Matty. They say this is the land of the fertile rock."

I laugh a loud laugh that echos off the hardscape, thinking about all the rows of field rocks pulled from farmland and used as walls and building material.

"You could say that about the entire island," I say when my solitary laugh finally fades into the quiet.

"You could. *Eire* has always been a hard place to live off the land."

"Is that why it is so beautiful?"

"Beauty grows in rocky soil."

"Can I steal that line?"

It is her turn to laugh, a soft laugh that is lost quickly in the wind.

"Orchids grow here," she says. "Maybe not the most beautiful orchids in the world, Maybe just the hardiest."

"Orchids?"

"You have to look hard to find beauty on The Burren."

She walks a little ways away and stands over a short white flower. As I near, she turns away from the plant.

"I thought it might be a young spotted orchid, an O'Kelly," she says. "Wasn't."

"Google it," she adds. "It is quite beautiful, and rare. Big and showy white flower. Named after an O'Kelly of Ballyvaughan. Blooms in July or August, depending on the season. Little early yet."

In the silence of the moment I think, maybe for the first time in weeks, of the time of year, of my time spent in Ireland. It is late June, and I have been in Ireland for three short months. It is easy to lose track of time sometimes, in some places.

"Maybe we'll come out again, later this year," I say, not really understanding why I do so.

She kneels, touches a plant, its thin rugged leaves, not its flower. "Another month for an O'Kelly."

She then touches the crack in the rock where the plant is growing. "Grikes, these cervices, provide almost a micro climate, they say. Arctic plants are found here. Orchids and Arctic plants."

She stands up and looks around again. "Plants grow here that shouldn't grow here. The Burren is warmer in the winter than the lowlands, the grasslands. It absorbs the sun's heat and holds it. Lot of light too. No trees, just the rocks, I think. Not much pollution, either. I think."

She notices something else and heads off. I follow.

She talks about this plant and that, this flower and that. I listen. Her voice is soft, her descriptions almost lyrical. I listen to her but remember little of the detail.

As we walk, a car passes by on the road, its engine noise growing and then fading, like all things, into the insistent quiet of the sea of rocks and the waves of wind.

She kneels again, touches a line of green overflowing from a grike.

"In the early spring, this would have been a vibrant blue. Spring Gentian. One of the first flowers to bloom when the rocks warm. Too bad you missed it."

"Maybe next year."

She looked away from the plants, glances to me, then back to the plants.

"Spring is a gift *Eire* gives to the Irish," her voice soft. I almost do not hear her. Maybe she wants it that way. "A gift for enduring the winter."

I say nothing. She says nothing.

"Off we go," she continues, turning and heading back to the car.

I follow, saying nothing. She, too, is quiet.

Strangely, or maybe not, the silence seems right.

Cathleen gets me lost on the way home. There appears to be a road back to Ballyvaghan, but she veers left and follows the Caher River to the sea. She gives me a little history of the river. I see a big creek that occasionally becomes a small river, mostly rippling clear water in a stone-strewed riverbed. I see a castle for a fleeting moment. I see fishermen, waist-deep in fast moving water, for several fleeting moments. I see horses, grey horses, in a field near the river; they are beautiful.

These places, these things, are not our objective.

Cathleen stops, finally, after reaching the Atlantic and turning north for a few minutes, and after passing a road that leads to the village of Murroughkelly. I think that's what was written on the road sign, and I wonder if it has a pub like Gleninagh. She finally stops on the roadside, at a lonely dirt road that turns east.

"Care for a view?" she says. But she exits the car without waiting for an answer.

I follow her lead.

Standing outside the car, there was a single view of note, other than the expanse of Galway Bay getting lost in the Atlantic. I see a solitary lighthouse that looks like it could barely provide enough guidance to the entry of a small port let alone to a bay that was, once, maybe, the first safe haven for eastbound mariners escaping the brutal whims of the northern Atlantic Ocean in a bad mood.

"Black Head point," she says, as she looks out, to the west, into the distance. "To me, this is where Ireland ends and the future begins."

I wonder if she is always in the present tense.

We both look at the lighthouse. It is a small white box with a light on the top. Nothing else. It is the last line of defense from the fates. Somehow, it is simple but deeply meaningful.

We stand and look at the lighthouse, at the ocean, at the past and the future.

"Thank you for showing me The Burren," I say.

"Thank you for allowing me,' she says.

She turns to me. We are close. Maybe closer than we have ever been, physically and otherwise.

I see her beauty. I see the grey in her dark hair. I see the depth of her indescribable eyes.

I see, I think, a slight look of frustration in the tilt of her head.

"I hope you're plannin' to kiss me," she says.

"I was thinking."

She leans forward, puts her hands on my cheeks, gently. I barely feel them. She brings her lips to mine. I meet her halfway, I think.

When she leans back, she smiles.

"You Americans think too much."

I smile back.

She turns and heads to the car, leaving me to my thoughts.

I think about John Wayne and Maureen O'Hara, and I laugh.

Cathleen glances over her shoulder. Shakes her head.

"You think too feckin much, Matty."

I barely hear her.

"I know," I say, wondering if she can hear me.

* * *

Dún Aonghasa is only one of several pre-historic fortifications in the Aran Islands; some date from maybe a century before Christ, this one from maybe 500 BCE. Sources vary due to an almost complete lack of historical evidence on an island swept clean by time, harsh inhabitants and invaders, and even harsher weather.

It is clear, however, that the islands and their fortress were strategically important from the time Galway Bay and its villages became worth raiding and in need of protecting. Like many island fortresses, an invader could bypass the obstacle, but it would always be a source of a constant threat of attack from its defenders. Any long-term invasion plans would require their capture or at least their total isolation and military neutering.

Dún Aonghasa, on Inishmore, currently stands as only a small part of what it once was. Maybe as much as half of the original walls have fallen into the Atlantic Ocean, along a rough-edged 100-meter high cliff.

The land's ragged cliffs, and the ocean's ferocious attitude, could not be more different on the western side of Inishmore than on its eastern side, at Kilronan, the small-town dock area where Mully put Kenny and me ashore after a leisurely hour voyage from Gleninagh Quay. We were lucky because Mully timed our arrival in the port so as to avoid the regular ferry service coming from either Doolin or Rossaveal, avoiding any crowd of tourists disembarking.

When I decided to take the adventure to the Arans, I asked Mully if I could hire him and his boat to take me out there. What ensued was maybe my longest discussion with the usually low-keyed mariner who rarely said anything about himself.

"You lookin' for a tourist sail, or a day on my workin' ferry, out and back," he asked.

"You have two boats?"

He shrugged his shoulders and smiled a kind of sheepish smile.

"I worked for others more than 40 years, last 20 as a captain, and never married. Bought some toys when I retired. I have a beautiful sail, a Laurent Giles. You familiar?"

I shook my head. He looked disappointed.

"I also have my Tyrell 38-footer, great for fishing. She'll work all day long."

"I want to spend a day hiking the Arans, at Inishmore, really," I said. "Me and Kenny."

"The Tyrell it is," he answered the question for me. "Best for getting somewhere on time against the wind."

The Tyrell, I later learned from Ian, was was a 40-year-old wooden powerboat of an unattractive but tough and efficient design.

After a short, very business-like negotiation, in which we agreed I would pay for his fuel and a small fee he'd use to pay Ian as deckhand, we set the date. I think he was just happy to have a reason to take his boat out. He was a little surprised that I wanted Kenny to come along, but this would not have been the first time he had ferried cargo or passengers he did not particularly care for.

Putting in at Kilronan left us about 5 miles from *Dún Aonghasa*. Mully called ahead and had a friend waiting with his car. "Give him 10 Euro and he'll take you there and bring you back. Give him 20 and he'll take you all around the island," he said.

Mully's friend was a fairly scraggly guy, not unlike Mully: well worn, also probably by the sea. His name came and went in a blur of Gaelic words between him and Kenny. His Japanese SUV was not as old as he, but just as well worn. Kenny and I and he agreed he'd drop us off and then wait a couple hours for us.

Once we got to the road's end, it still took us about half an hour to get to the ruins, due in equal parts to the need to climb a rocky hill, my young companion's very labored gait, and because I was in no rush to get through my first visit to the island.

"I love the Arans," Kenny said, as we stood on a promontory to the west of the old fortress and I looked, for the first time, at the ruins. "I love this place."

I could not have agreed more.

We stood outside a low stone wall that arched from cliff's edge to cliff's edge, from our left to our right and then back to our left again. Inside, another low stone wall made the same arch, only tighter. Inside of that was a third, taller, stone wall that would have been the line of last defense. Some of the walls seemed to have been rebuilt, for the tourist trade no doubt; some seemed to lie in ruin but in place. The whole walled area was an acre or two in size, maybe more. I was never very good at guessing such things.

"See the stones around the inner walls?" Kenny said, pointing out things like a tourist guide. "*Cheval de fries*, it's French for some kind of barrier. Must have been a bitch to cross with things being thrown at you."

The barriers, something about a horse if my limited French served me right, reminded me of the photos of the obstacles in the ocean at Omaha Beach on D-Day.

Inside of the final wall, which was maybe 15 or 20 feet high, was the citadel. The inside was hidden by the heights of the hill and the height of the wall.

"They call it *Aonghus mac Úmhór* in the Irish," Kenny said. "Named after some god of old, or a king. I forget. Cliff is about 100 meters on the other side. Good place for a king or a god. They say it was as much a religious place as a place for warriors to make a stand. Druids maybe."

We climbed over the outer wall and Kenny sat down on it as I started to move forward.

"You take a look at the inside. Seen it … I'm tired," he said as I looked back.

So I went in alone, except for the 20 or so other tourists wondering around the grounds. It was easy for my writer's imagination to visualize the defenders and the attackers, the battles. It would have been a terrible place to attack but an even more terrible place to defend. You either defeated the attackers or you faced the choice of undoubtedly vengeful death at their hands or hopefully merciful death at the hands of the gods of the cliffs and the ocean below.

The strangest thing, though, was inside the citadel, which was cut off by a sheer cliff to one side. There was a round raised platform. I wondered what it could have been used for. It could have been where the king, or the gods, watching the battle, gaining the best view of the surroundings. It could have been a place where bad things happened to captured soldiers or other unfortunate sacrifices.

The place kind of creeped me out, so I did not stay long.

I stayed a few yards away from the cliff's edge, too. I was not as brave as I had been at Moher, those years before. I had no need to look over the edge.

When I returned to Kenny, he was still sitting alone. I sat beside him.

"My dad and I used to come here, when he worked out here as the *Gardaí*. I told you that didn't I?"

I nodded.

"This was the last place we played. My father used to play with me, when I was small. Hide and seek. Seems like a million years ago."

I nodded, remembering weekend mornings with my father.

I noticed, as he talked, he was again fidgeting with his FIFA wristbands. This time, if not before, he noticed me notice. He looked at me, then looked at his wrists, then back to me. He pushed one up on his forearm, then the other, slowly, methodically. Turned his arms over to show me his wrists. There were more scars, still raised welts of red from not too-distant wounds, on each wrist. A crude X-shaped scar on one and just a short slash on the other. I guessed he passed out before his chosen blade could complete the second X.

"Dublin?" I said.

He nodded.

"I told you. Almost died there, more than once. This was the last time," he said, raising his hands to look at his wrists as one might inspect a piece of fresh fruit in the market, emotionless but judgmental. "Feckin sloppy at that too."

I didn't know what to say about his skill at suicide, so I tried to change the subject, to give him a way out if he wanted.

"We've all made mistakes Kenny," I said. "I have. If you're lucky you live through them."

He nodded, but probably not in agreement.

"I lived, but just about killed my mum. That's what dad really went all crazy about. She's a real *Bean Phádraig*, a St. Patrick's wife, a very devout Catholic. She just couldn't understand the drugs, this. My running away the only way I knew how. I just about killed my mum, and I was a holy show to my dad, disgraced him to all his guys. She's forgiven me, I think. He never will."

"Was it only the drugs?"

As soon as I said it, I wondered where the question came from. Wondered if I had asked the too blunt a question that often stops interviews in a heartbeat.

He rubbed his X with his other hand. It must have still itched like a bitch.

"Drugs gave me the courage, I guess. Failure really. Failure at everything. Not the footballer I thought. Not the student my mum wanted. Not the son my dad wanted. Not many friends, and the ones I had were damaged like me. Drinkin' and drugs. Laughin' faces with empty futures mostly. My prospects in Dublin were slim to nothin' but there was less than nothin' for me back home."

He paused for a moment, brought his X up to his lips, kissed it gently.

"One night I just ran out of bam, ran out of friends, ran out of money. Seemed like the only thing left. Funny, some nurse told me the downers might have helped me live. Slowed everything, including dying. Girl I was sharing needle with fund me in her tub. I almost remember her screaming. Almost remember the medics. Not really. Remember my dad, though. That look on his face when he came to the hospital. Not the son he wanted. Don't matter much now. Just fading away now. My liver is rot. My guts is rot. Feckin' needle."

He stopped talking. I stopped talking.

We just sat on that stone wall and let the wind and the sun wash over us. It was clean, there and then. Fresh and clean and I felt like Kenny actually was happy. He had spoken his truth, given his confession to someone who would go away in a few months and he'd never see again, someone who might understand him, might write a story with a character that looked a lot like him.

I think that is what he wanted.

He stood up, pulled his wrist bands back down over his wrists, and walked a few steps away before he turned back to me, as if he forgot to tell me something.

"Thank you for bringing me here Matty. Love this place."

I nodded.

He then turned and walked, with his slow, labored stride, toward the nearest cliff. I watched him pass some other tourists, they hardly noticed him. Everybody was in their own world. I watched him as he neared the edge, for a moment he was silhouetted by the empty blue sky beyond. I watched him as, without a pause in his labored stride, he stepped up to and then off the cliff's edge.

I shook my head, not really understanding. It seemed like a scene in a movie, but a subtle scene, a surreal scene, not one scripted for shock effect. I didn't understand until a woman screamed, a man yelled and then, like the sound of the waves repeatedly crashing against the land at the bottom of the cliff, a wave of gasps and screams and yells bounced around the ghostly expanse of *Dún Aonghasa*.

I was as quiet as the stones.

There are moments in one's life, moments of moral if not religious clarity, when one decides upon a good lie which you know must be told, retold, carried to the grave. Gratefully, I carry very few of those. As I stood up and moved slowly to a few yards from the cliff's edge — where I had witnessed Kenny stop, look to the sea, lose his balance, and then fall — I knew this would be one of those moments.

I never looked over the cliff. Others did.

I did not listen when they described what they saw. I knew what they saw.

I let them tell their stories, first when some tourist gatekeeper of the fort came quickly and then later, maybe a half an hour later, when a *Garda* came and talked to me and several other people who either saw what happened or said they saw what happened.

"Some of the witnesses said he stepped off the cliff, on purpose," the officer said to me, checking his notes, making new notes. "But you say he lost his balance?"

"I was watching him all the way," I said. "He lost his balance and fell."

"An accident then? He was all alone at the edge. All agree on that. But you say he fell?"

"An accident. He loved this place."

The *Garda* took my information on who Kenny was, taking special note that he was the son of Sargent Jones out of Ballyvaughan, and took my information, who I was and why we were here together. He had no idea that I was a writer when he heard my name. Or maybe it just didn't matter to him.

"An accident then," he said, again, as he finished taking notes and closed his notebook.

I wondered if he knew I was lying. Maybe it just didn't matter to him.

The nameless friend of Mully was beside me as soon as the officer was done.

"I called Mully. Told him what happened. I'll get ya back to Kilronan," he said. And he did, with nothing more to say until he dropped me off dockside.

"A sad day," he said as he offered his hand.

I nodded, shook his hand, said "Thank you" and offered up another 10 Euro. He waved it off, spoke briefly, unintelligibly to my ears, to Mully. And then walked away.

"I called his parents," Mully said. "You want me to get you back to Gleninagh?"

"Yes please."

And he did, with nothing more to say on the voyage back. Both he and Ian left me to sit alone at the back of the boat, watching at The Arans grow smaller and smaller as we headed East, the wake of the boat at first focusing my vision on the islands and then blurring into the vastness of the bay.

When the boat pulled into the dock, Mully helped me off, then shook my hand too, but still said nothing. He was a man no stranger to death, especially death delivered by the sea and the shores the seas have forever mercilessly crashed upon.

Ian walked with me for a little while, leaving me to start any conversation, which I did not. When we arrived at the parking lot at the pub, where my car was parked, he said: "You going to be OK? You need something?"

"No," I said. "A sad day. A sad accident."

He shook my hand, echoed "sad day" and then turned away. He headed to the pub, to tell a story I assumed. I decided to leave my car, to walk home. It was late afternoon. I felt tired and wanted to be alone, maybe sleep, maybe even get my head straight. As I walked, I wondered if Irish men always shake hands or if they did so because they thought American men always shook hands.

I wondered if Ian knew I was carrying a lie away from the Arans. Maybe he did. Maybe it just didn't matter to him.

* * *

The day came for the proper Irish Catholic burial of Kenny's body, augmented, maybe, by the even more ancient ritual release of his wayward Irish soul.

There was the clearly well-rehearsed religious ceremonies of priest and church and family; there was the seemingly scripted but clearly random ceremonies of friends true and feigned. I remember the day in glimpses of clarity and long stretches of blurred words and actions.

First there was the customary Irish wake at his parent's house, then the customary Catholic Church ceremony and burial, then the customary wake at the pub — which, while stereotypical in fictional Irish stories but often also true anywhere in the world, ended with disagreement over the character of the deceased.

Cathleen asked if I wanted to ride with her to the parent's house for the family wake, which I did. We didn't talk, as I remember, when I came down from my house to hers, and even Michaeleen seemed to sense sadness in the air and was timid. We didn't talk on the short drive over to the parents' house either. I have found such moments are the same anywhere in the world when a funeral is in process. In America, where I attended a few; in the Philippines, where I attended one very strange Catholic ceremony, and now in Ireland. I think people tend to expect quiet, want quiet, try their hardest to be quiet.

Of course, fracas-filled Irish wakes are the stuff of legend, in drama if not in the real world. And while I was itching to break the silence, and discuss that subject as it bounced around my brain, I watched and waited until we were within sight of the Jones home, one of several similar homes, side by side, with very little yard between them, lining each side of a dead-end paved road near Gregg. I guess this is what passes for a tract home in Ireland.

"Just what are we getting ourselves into?" I say, sensing the opportunity.

"Oh, thank God," she bursts out. "Silence was killing me."

"It'll not be what you might expect," she continues, scanning for a parking place well before the group of houses, where cars were parked haphazardly in a field just off the road. The exact location of the Jones house was obvious by the modern Mercedes hearse in the driveway.

"What do you think I might expect?"

"Lots of wailing, with the occasional loud cheer for the dearly departed. Maybe a fight or two."

"No drinking?"

"Well," she says, glancing at me as she pulled into a spot within sight of, but still a good hike from, the house, where I could now see a sporadic flow of people entering and leaving the front door. A crowd had gathered in street in front of the house, as nobody was driving away just yet.

"Not likely to be any drinking inside the house. Kenny's mum is a right proper Catholic woman and she simply would not have anybody but herself fortifying themselves for the day, at least not in her house. Step outside after paying your respects. There will be more than one flask of whiskey being passed around."

"Kenny will be inside?"

"His body will be," she says, turning the engine off and turning her full attention to me. "He'll be in a side room, maybe his bedroom. There will be a window open to let his spirit out, though I believe his spirit is flying now, somewhere out there at The Arans."

I shrug my shoulders. Not sure I believe in spirits, either the kind to escape through windows or the kind to fly over oceans. But I believe in other people's beliefs.

"They'll close the window a few minutes before they carry him out to the hearse and head to the church. They don't want the spirit to wander back in. Its got better places to be. And don't get between the body and the window. Bad manners if not bad omen."

We climb out of the car, to the obvious attention of the crowd waiting in the street, and we are near the door before I think of another question.

"Do I say something to the family, or just pretend like I'm taking a look at the body? I'm not much for looking at dead people. I like to have them alive, not dead, in my mind."

"That depends."

"On?"

"If his parents want to talk to you, they'll send a family member over to request it."

There seems to be a murmur of recognition as we pass the crowd in the street. I wished it were for Cathleen but I know it is for me, the last person to see Kenny among the living.

Just before we settle into the short line at the front door of those awaiting entrance and opportunity to pay respects, Cathleen stops, and faces me, her voice is a forceful whisper.

"Sargent Jones will want to talk to you, Matty. That's for sure. Maybe the mum. Depends on how she is holding up."

I take a deep breath and we enter. But it seems, now, that I am alone.

Cathleen, as I remember it, is a step or two behind me.

There are pods of people, some sitting in a front living room area, a few more standing a little farther in at one end of a long dining room table that has food spread wide on the other end. A few people are getting small plates of food, one rather large man has plates in both hands; I wonder how he will hold them and eat at the same time. Maybe he is collecting for two, probably not.

There are maybe half a dozen small groups throughout the room. One group, maybe 10 men in nice uniforms, stand quietly off to themselves. They are quiet, strong men, used to carrying the load for another man of their ilk. They are there with a purpose other than offering condolences.

A couple emerge from a side room, she crying and he holding her around her shoulder in a comforting way. I assume that is, was, Kenny's room.

As we walked, I glanced into the room where Kenny lay.

As I remember it, there were candles placed at the head and foot of the coffin and I noticed a mirror on the wall had a black cloth covering most of it. I could make out some of the writing on the mirror; it was some beer ad, related to football. It was clearly a boy's room, a little boy's room, little used and little changed over the years since the boy grew up.

Cathleen and I are fully separated as she sauntered over to talk to a group of women. I had my duties; she had her's.

I scan the crowded room, notice a wave of Ian's hand, first getting my attention and then beckoning me near. I get swept up with a bunch of men in nice suit jackets and ties but all looking about as uncomfortable in such attire as you can be. Jimmy is there. So is Mully, talking with a couple of men I did not recognize. Their conversation falls quiet when I approach. I don't like the feeling.

Ian puts his arm around my shoulders in a comforting way, or maybe a herding way.

"Sargent Jones has asked about you," Ian whispered. "Kenny's mum wants a moment of your time, he says."

"Crap."

He looked at me. His mouth said nothing but the little tilt of his head, a squint of his eyes, said: "You expected this didn't you?"

I had. I nodded.

Ian let me loose, and stepped away, just as the remaining group crowded around me for a moment. They curtly introduced themselves, possibly offering support as they offered their hands to be shaken as they expected an American would want, possibly simply wanting to see up close the man everybody had been talking about.

Mully was the final one to approach, the only one offering anything more than their mumbled names. He leaned close, and spoke in the softest voice I had ever heard out of the man.

"Parents hear the rumors. Kenny jumpin' and all. They asked me and Ian. I told 'em that's not what you told us. Not what you told the *Gardaí*."

He paused, glances around and took his volume down to an even softer level.

"You hear me here, Matty. You want to clear your conscience on some matter, this be the time. It won't leave that room. You know what I mean?"

I did, I nodded.

Mully escorted me the short distance to the kitchen where an older woman sat at a table, an older man standing beside her. There were two other women, of similar age, sitting with her but when they saw me they both quickly rose and stepped aside. As I entered, leaving Mully behind, the two women moved gracefully around me, inspecting me up and down as they passed.

It was just me, Kenny's parents, and God.

The woman was dressed in all black, with a strange combination of several strands of pearls and a fine chain with a small cross around her neck, hanging loose under a fatty chin and throat. She wore heavy makeup but it was clear that keeping it on, erasing the tear tracks, was a work in progress. Her eyes were bloodshot. Near her hands, which were clutching prayer beads, was a mannish black formal hat, a kind of short Abraham Lincoln hat, with a flourish of black ribbon attached. She would look very dignified in that hat at the funeral of her son.

Sargent Jones was out of uniform. I'm not sure why I expected him to be in uniform at his son's funeral. He wore a dark suit with perfectly starched white shirt and black tie. His full head of recently groomed hair was only slightly receding at the part but the slightly unnatural brown color may have been a willful crime of vanity as he had short, naturally grey sideburns. His face was a steely pale, not white but almost absent of color. His eyes showed no signs of tears and he looked at me with the focus of a detective well practiced in the art of drilling into the face of a suspect. He would look very aloof at the funeral of his son.

She glanced at me and then turned her attention back to the rosary beads. He nodded his head, in appreciation I guess, and then waved me to the chair nearest his wife's.

I sat and waited. The only sound was the "tick, tick, tick" of a beautiful old wall clock I could not help but glance at. The rest of the house had fallen silent, it seemed, and only a distant hum of voices from the outside provided any sonic relief.

"*Tae?*" he said, finally.

"Oh, yes," she said, glancing up, snapping her eyes from me to her husband and back to me. "Yes. We should offer you some tea? We should."

"Thank you, no."

She, again, fell silent and returned to her beads.

"Thank you for coming," he said.

"Of course. My condolences for your loss. I liked Kenny a lot."

"He liked you," she said, with her eyes still averted.

Both Sargent Jones and I know it is time to let her lead the discussion.

"Bragged about the American writer who listened to all his football stories," she continued. "Said you might write about him in your book."

"I was a new face for him to talk soccer to. The rest of the crowd at the pub had heard all his stories before."

I smiled a smile she did not see and he did not react to.

"He was excited about the trip out to *Dún Aonghasa*. Said you were interested in the place," she said.

"I was. It was a beautiful day."

I noticed the father gave me a funny look when I said that. Like he did not understand the statement.

"It was warm that day," she said, glancing up. "Sunny to the west, to the islands."

"It was."

"You two enjoyed the trip out?"

"We did. I did."

"What did you two talk about?"

"Not much on the trip out. It was very peaceful. Water was only a little choppy."

"Galway Bay is never calm. West winds," she said. "And at the ruins?"

I wondered if she were asking what we talked about at the ruins, but I was not sure. I paused. We fell into an uncomfortable silence.

"What did Kenny say, there at *Dún Aonghasa*," he said, pushing the conversation.

"Oh, yes," she said. "At the ruins."

"He told me the history of the place. He was very knowledgeable. Said he visited the place as a kid."

I glanced to the father as I spoke.

"He did love that place," she said.

"Was the wind up?" she continued. "At the ruins …"

He let out a kind of exasperated breath, and then cut to the chase.

"What mood was my son in when you talked?"

She turned her attention back to the beads, not wanting to witness what she was about to hear, what she feared.

"Kenny was happy," I said. "We had a great day. I had a great day. Right up to the moment of the accident."

Her gaze darted to me. His was always on me, unwavering.

"It was an accident. I saw him walk up to the edge. I saw him looking out over the ocean. I saw him loose his balance. I saw him fight to regain it. I saw him fall."

Kenny's mother resumed crying, continued her losing battle with her makeup. Not sure if it was pain or relief. Didn't matter really.

"Tragic accident," I said. "God is my witness."

As she cried, he spoke.

"Are you a religious man, Mr. Maybourn?"

"Not all that much. But I believe in God. Mostly I believe I'm an honest man."

As she cried, he continued: "I appreciate an honest man," he said. "And what did my son tell you 'bout me, 'bout his father, on his last day?"

The man wanted honesty, so I gave him honesty.

"He said he had been happy with you, at those ruins, on that island, sometimes, back when he was a boy. He said that was the last time you and he were happy together."

As the truth hit him, he flinched as if the words pounded like a fist into his guts. He nodded, reasserted the stern face of a man his stature.

"Thank you, sir," he said, then he reached his arms around the head of his wife and she buried her face into his perfectly pressed suit and shirt, smearing tears and make-up all over his shirt.

They said nothing else. I waited for a moment, and then stood up.

"I liked your son. I would have enjoyed more time with him. He had good stories."

Kenny's mum did not look away from her husband and he did not look away from his wife.

I walked out of the room. I glanced around to find Cathleen. I found her and sought refuge.

We catch eyes for a moment, then I walked directly out of the house in search of a flask of Irish whiskey. I walked up to the first knot of anonymous men I can find. They welcomed me with silence, and two flasks quickly offered.

I accepted one, took a hit, handed it back. The owner of the flask followed my drink without wiping the flask's mouth. For the moment, the day, I am one of them. Then, after a couple of deep breaths, I grab the second one, which is met with tight smiles and accepting nods, and took another hit.

"Don't blame ya, Yank," the second flask's owner said, also following up with a drink of his own.

Cathleen joined us shortly. I noticed her approach, as did the group.

"You holdin' up?" she asks.

"I've done what I could."

She reaches out, touches my shoulder, lightly and for only a moment, but then stands beside me, for all to see. "You're a good man, Matty."

The whiskey, and the moment, have taken my breath away. So I say nothing.

I glanced back to the group of anonymous men. Nothing need be said there either.

We say nothing, Cathleen and I, as we walk farther away from the house.

I don't think we shared more than a dozen words the rest of the day. You get swept up at such times; carried by the crowd, by the tradition.

We stood outside and waited for the casket to be carried out. Six men in uniform did the heavy lifting. We then fell in with the rest of the precession, driving to a modern and modest Catholic church in Gregg, where the funeral mass was unexpectedly brief and seemingly old-school, surprising with The Reverend Ronan leading.

There was little remembrance but no real celebration of the life of Kenneth Angus Jones. There was a prayer for salvation for the soul deceased, a prayer of comfort for the grieving family, a prayer of thanks to God for Christ's victory over death. All very canonical if not bluntly clinical. The Revered seemed at ease, but almost distant in his duty.

After the service he announced that the funeral would be for family only and, finally appearing at ease, he pointed out that "eulogies for the deceased would be left to friends and family and drinking establishments," which was met with a murmur of either humor or shock, or maybe a bit of both.

Cathleen, sitting beside me but at a respectable distance, leans in close and whispers a bit of explanation into my my ear.

"The church is returning to some traditions. Baptism, communion and funerals are much more solemn these days," she says.

I hadn't thought they were any other way, but then it was my first Irish Catholic funeral mass.

A family-only burial in the cemetery beside the church followed.

As Cathleen and I drive away, I wonder if the Catholic Church still frowned on burying suicide victims in hallowed ground. I wonder if the man upstairs had played me like a rook on a chess board, an often insignificant but occasionally pivotal castle providing shelter in the midst of a maelstrom.

Maybe it was just the two shots of the Irish.

As we arrive back into Gleninagh, she asks if I want to be dropped at the pub or taken home.

"The boys will likely be there," she says. "Tellin' stories and lies."

"The pub please."

And she takes the road toward the sea instead of the road to the highland.

"Can I buy you a drink," I ask as we near the pub. "For the excellent taxi service?"

"Thank you, no," she says, as she bypasses the usual parking lot. "Seimus will be there. He'll be warmed up, his not being at the funeral."

After she pulls up near the front of the inn, and I open the car door and get ready to slide out of the car. I look at her, and wait until she looks at me.

"Are you afraid of him?"

She shakes her head, smiles, a tight-lipped little smile but a smile none-the-less.

"No. But I can handle just so much sadness in one day. No need of more sadness, more drama."

"See you soon, Cathleen," I say as she turns away and I slip out the door.

"Take care, Matty."

* * *

Evidently, while I as at the formal wake and the funeral, the informal wake was steaming ahead at Cassidy's pub. I could hear muffled evidence of the dark festivities as I crossed the inn's entryway and neared the pub's entrance. Opening the door and stepping in, the wake was in full voice.

Many of Cassidy's regulars, and Cassidy himself, were already there, having been at the Jones house earlier, but then skipping the church. I knew them and they knew me and most gave me notice, a few gave me a nod of their head. There were also a few strangers though, who noticed me only because others paid attention. I attracted their attention as well. I scanned for Mully or Ian, down at their usual end of the bar, glanced to Séamus usual table, even looked to the end of the bar with the television, to where some soccer game would usually be playing and Kenny would be parked. The television was dark and none of my usual drinking buddies were to be seen.

I was not in much of a mood for meeting new people so I almost turned around immediately. But I caught Cassidy's eyes and his hand as it waved me over to an open spot at the bar. One drink, I decided.

The noise emanating from the pub had been deceiving, I decided as I traversed much of the space to get to my host. Most of the attendees were talking quietly and drinking quietly, except for a few of Kenny's one-time, if not current, friends who somehow thought they were supposed to be the leaders of the wake and drink too much and talk too loud while telling stories everybody either knew, or suspected, were lies.

I settled in against the bar and Cassidy approached with a beer and a double of Jamison's in hands.

"Some of the boys want to buy you a beer. You'll be drinking free for a while," he said. "The Irish is on me."

I picked up the beer, turned, and raised a toast to the unknown benefactor in the crowd. Then I returned to face the barkeep, pushed the beer away and pulled the whiskey close. Cassidy and I exchanged nods of the head. Not one to waste, the beer was quickly removed and deftly placed in front of the nearest empty glass, an action to which the temporary owner of the glass quickly nodded to Cassidy and then to me.

I took a big swallow of the whiskey, let it flow over me.

"Not your first today?" Cassidy said.

I shook my head. "But my last," I added.

He smiled at me, then turned to attend to others.

As I nursed the last measure of my Irish, I could hear the loudest of the young men reminiscing about the dearly departed, telling stories about his "younger" days, a strange descriptive for a man dead just before his 24th birthday.

Having rarely if ever seen them in the pub, much less heard them talk to Kenny, I took their sometimes baleful babble of remembrances of the deceased being a happy-go-lucky kind of guy as nothing more than beer-induced bullshit.

I found out shortly, when I finished my drink and decided it was time to take that long walk home, that Séamus had apparently not been buying the "happy Kenny" storyline either.

I pulled out a tip for the barkeep; glanced around the bar and smiled at anyone looking back at me, and then headed for the back door.

I found Séamus, smoking by himself, as I exited on the dirt parking lot side.

"Kenny in the ground, uh?" he said, glancing at me, his smoldering cigarette bobbing gently in his mouth as he talked, his voice low, almost as if he was taking to himself and did not expect me to pay him any attention.

He leaned on the side of the building, his bad right side against the wall. He looked like he hadn't slept much, or maybe that was his usual look and I was just never close enough to tell: bloodshot eyes, unshaven face, scraggly hair lying haphazardly this way and that.

For the first time I noticed a little twitch in his bad leg that caused his entire body to convulse irregularly and the stream of smoke from his cigarette to break spasmodically and float up in front of his face, like Indian smoke signals.

I could not help but stop and stare, deciding too late that staring at a tired, probably drunk man is never a good idea, especially when you are tired and little drunk yourself.

"Got some fodder for that feckin book of yours?" he asked leaning away from the wall, standing as straight as I guessed he could, and awkwardly grabbing his cigarette from his lips with his bad hand.

I must have given him a questioning look.

"Funeral and all. Bullshit Irish wake. All enough local color for one day?"

I shook my head at him like I would if dismissing a petulant child. Again, not the best of choices.

He looked away from me, inspected his cigarette, now little more than a butt. He put it back to his lips, held it there, then using only his bad hand, slowly, clumsily, pulled a fresh cigarette from his shirt pocket and put it, too, to his lips, before transferring the smoldering butt back to his bad hand. He then painstakingly lit the new one with the butt before tossing it to the ground.

"To Kenny," he said, taking a deep draw on his new smoke.

First I wondered if he learned the cigarette slight-of-hand so he could hold a drink with surety but still light up a smoke. Then I wondered if he actually liked Kenny, in his own equally crippled way. My wonderings lasted only a moment.

"I asked ya how that feckin book of yours is comin'?"

"I'm not writing much. More research, really."

"Ya, not being Irish and all, must need a lot of research."

"I guess."

"That what you doing?" he said, tilting his head to the door and the pub beyond. "Research? When you drinkin'?

"Some, I guess. Mostly just enjoying a beer and talking with people."

"Quite a focus group, I'd say."

It was a funny choice of words. Surprisingly astute. I wondered how much of his Irish ruffian act might be just that, an act to keep people at a distance.

"Everybody has a story," I said. "Some you hear first-hand. Some second-hand. Getting a feel for everybody's history, I guess."

"And me? People talk much about me?"

I smiled, shrugged my shoulders.

He smiled, maybe the first time I saw him smile, and nodded knowingly.

"I'd like to hear it first-hand sometime, maybe," I said. "I like to talk to people, not about people."

He nodded again.

"You've a story, I've heard," I continued. "Listening to you. Mully. My neighbor. Maybe I'll hear her story sometime too."

Séamus' smile disappeared as quickly as it came. His gaze hardened. His face went lifeless. He pulled the cigarette from his lips. I knew I had made a mistake, maybe a big mistake.

"Tell you one thing," he said, spitting out his words. "Her solitude is her own making. The *Sean-Bhean bhocht* refuses to come out of that cold stone house. So what her man left her. Not the first widow to America. Won't be the last."

"Ah," I said, nodding but understanding only half of what he was talking about.

"She wants to be a widow," he said, throwing his half-smoked cigarette to the ground like he was suddenly sick of it. "Feckin London husband left her and she's ashamed. She's better off."

His voice faded off into a growl. "Could be better off."

I could see his frustration, his anger rising, from somewhere I could not see, did not want to see.

"She wants to be alone. Deserves to be alone. Guess both of us deserve to be alone."

There was something really bitter, really sad in his words, in his view of her, of himself, of the world.

As I have probably said, one of my skills, I think, is that I read people well, often think I know the right thing to say. That is ofter counterbalanced by my habit of almost always saying the truth, as I see it. Both traits have often led me into trouble.

"You're too young to be such a sad shit," I said.

Séamus was, apparently, in the mood for neither truth nor empathy.

"An' you're a feckin pretender," he snapped back. "You come down from that house on the hill, down from your soft life in America. Drink with us and study us and take your feckin notes. One day you'll go off, fake your Irishness, write your book and make us all look simple and happy. Quiet Man 's a joke. A feckin joke. You're a feckin joke. Feckin American joke."

As his rant grew, and his volume grew, I took a couple small steps back, gained some distance from his anger.

He stopped, took a breath. I thought about just turning and walking away. But I was also never all that good at quietly walking away.

"Sorry you feel that way, Séamus. Really I am. You were dealt a bad hand, I know. But why do you have to act like a sad fucking old man all the time?"

He looked at me with a funny look, amusement tempering anger, maybe. Then a strange little grin came across his face. I braced for a possible fight or flight moment.

"That I am, Mr. Maybourn. A sad fuckin' ol' man. But you fuckin' Americans made me that way."

We stood in silence, for a moment. Then I turned and walked away. A few steps away from the pub I turned back to look, he was entering the pub, his limp very noticeable.

* * *

When I got back to the house at Gleninagh, I answered some emails, wrote a little but mostly sat at the keyboard and thought meaningless thoughts.

Finally, as the day settled into dusk, I made myself some coffee. Made it strong. I returned to the keyboard, with ideas running around my head like leaves blowing in an early November north wind: haphazardly but with a known source and, maybe, an unknowable purpose.

When I thought about Cathleen, remembered her tenderness on The Burren and at the funeral, I returned to the phrase that Séamus had used. It took a few tries at spelling in Gaelic before I found it: *Sean-Bhean bhocht.*

I found several references on the web, the most interesting of which was an essay on Irish feminism by Kathryn Conrad. With the caffeine in pitched battle with the earlier alcohol, I did not fully understand the depth of the essay, but I stashed it away for future reading if not comprehension.

In rough translation *Sean-Bhean bhocht* meant "poor old woman." Its origin, apparently, is an Irish folk song from the late 1700s, the period of one of the many failed Irish rebellions against British rule, this one when the French failed to aid Ireland at a pivotal, promised time. Also known as the United Irishmen Rebellion, and inspired by the American and French revolutions, that particular failed rebellion provided yet another generation of poor old women who lost their husbands, sons and hope.

While my cloudy-minded research revealed an overabundance of Irish history, it shed little light on Séamus's obviously complicated relationship with Cathleen. It shed no light what-so-ever on my increasingly complicated relationship with her.

Cloudy-minded research rarely leads to much of value.

Caibidil a hocht
(Chapter 8)

When it comes to famous writers, exaggerated egos and actual brilliance favors no nationality nor ethnicity. There have been great writers from all points of the earth, including at least one great Icelandic writer I know of: Nobel laureate Halldór Kiljan Laxness. Genre or perceived literary seriousness of subject matter does not matter either. If you were to put Hermann Hesse and Stephen King and their often inflated egos in the same room there would not be enough room for either of them to breath.

Not even in my wildest dreams have I ever dreamed of being spoken of in the same breath as James Joyce, but I do not discount my ability to write a story somebody is willing to pay hard-earned cash to read, or see later on the big screen, whether in the old-fashioned movie house or on a high-definition, wall-mount home television.

I know, however, that I am a better mimic than I am an originator. My characters are often shallow, often strongly influenced by someone I know or think I understand, and sometimes a pale shadow of a great character written by a great writer. I often read the works of the Nobel laureates, then try to mimic aspects of their style of writing in some way, usually resulting in awful poetry that I want nobody to read but sometimes slightly lyrical prose that makes its way into my novel *de jour*.

I guess that is why, with my research piling up and my Irish novel waiting impatiently for me to stop procrastinating and start producing pages to drop into an empty, untitled manuscript box, I was drawn again and again to the pile of 30-or-so books I purchased during the week of my arrival at Gleninagh North. They were stacked near my writing table into three, unbalanced cairns: Irish history, Irish geography and, the largest, Irish writers. I grabbed three books from the writers stack at random and then re-stacked those left behind, also at random.

I was familiar with the Irish classicists, of course: the works and personalities of James Joyce, Oscar Wilde and C.S. Lewis. They were probably the only Irish writers, other than Walsh, that I had read before my current sojourn. At least the only ones I knew were Irish by birth despite any later English claim. I settled on a poetry collection of Seamus Heaney, a novel by Patrick Kavanagh and a short story collection of Brendan Behan.

Behan was a rough-edged 20th century Renaissance man and writer of all genres. He was an IRA member, an alcoholic who drank with the world's most famous alcoholics and a literary candle in the wind who died at the age of 41. He was born a Dubliner and died a Dubliner, and wrote in both English and Gaelic, the latter a language he reportedly taught himself in his 20s. He is best known for his semi-autobiographical novel "Borstal Boy", written in the late '50s, that is both an advocacy of the Irish Republican movement and a condemnation of the morally bankrupt violence it had come to represent. I passed over the novel and went for a makeshift collection of his writings called *The Wit of Behan*, a sample of which was a line attributed to him which all modern writers know by heart: "I am a drinker with writing problems."

Kavanagh, best known as a poet but also the author of the novel "Tarry Flynn", died in Dublin only a few years after Behan but lived life at a much more measure pace and, hence, was into his 60s when he passed. I avoided his poetry and instead went for the 1940s era novel, which I learned was only published after his poetry started making fans and money, and then published reluctantly as it was originally banned in his ultra-religious home country by the Irish Censorship Board for being "indecent and obscene." I loved it, devoured it in one long evening, and its reflections of rural life in the 1940s seemed to fit perfectly in with timeframe into which my novel was congealing.

When it came to Heaney, there was no other thought than to get a book of his poetry. He lived into the Third Millennium, dying in 2013 at the age of 74 with the 1995 Nobel Prize for Literature in his pocket. Well, maybe not literally in his pocket. Although I think I would be buried with such a thing.

Instead of picking up one of Heaney's later, more famous works, I had carried home a late 1960s collection called "Door into the Dark".

It was Heaney's book that Cathleen noticed, late one day, when she was scanning my hurriedly organized but still cluttered house on Gleninagh North, the first time I invited her into my Irish inner sanctum.

It was the week after we'd buried Kenny. I had been avoiding the pub, for some reason. Maybe because I wanted to gain distance from the rumors and the truths surrounding the young man and his fate. Maybe to avoid Séamus.

I had been avoiding Cathleen as well, for an entirely different reason, one I tried not to contemplate. Let's say I was enjoying my solitude, but I also knew I owed Cathleen a dinner for her gracious tour excursion of The Burren and for her supportive taxi service on funeral day.

I invited her up the hill for dinner and discussion on a fine late summer Gleninagh day.

* * *

An almost cool breeze is blowing in off Galway Bay.

She arrives at the suggested time, 7 p.m., knocks at the front door and enters after my welcoming yell from the kitchen area. My front door faces north, and sunset is two hours away, so she enters in a late early evening shadow. The first thing I see, as I walk to greet her, is her smile and bright green eyes and a pink sweater she has thrown over her shoulders. I think I have never seen her in pink; it looks good with her black and grey hair.

"Welcome," I say, as I move close, drying my wet hands on the small towel I carry while on kitchen duty, and give her a perfunctory kiss on the cheek.

"Dinner's 20 minutes away. Drinks and crackers and cheese?"

"Splendid," she replies, after giving me a reciprocal, perfunctory kiss on the cheek.

She smells like flowers. I small like roasting pork loin.

As I move away, I wave my hand around the room, invite her exploration.

She glances around the room, undoubtedly knowing the layout, the design, but examining the trappings of a new, unfamiliar occupant.

As I move to my bar, she sees my pile of books, and the three books currently on my writing table, and picks up Heaney's.

"Have you read 'Requiem for the Croppies'?" she asks.

"Yes," I reply as I drop ice into a shaker with pre-measured contents, and begin shaking two vodka martinis. "The image of the barley growing in the killing fields, that was beautifully disturbing."

"The 1917 uprising was beautifully disturbing," she says, returning the collection to its place on my table.

"Heaney is loved here," she adds. "A thinking man. An honorable man. Not a stereotypical Irish man, all drunkard and angry at the world. Like Behan."

"I like Behan."

"I appreciate him, his talent, his voice. I don't think I would have liked him much, tho'. Think the same of Hemmingway."

I finished shaking and pour the martinis.

"Do you like them with olives or twist of lime?"

"However you take 'em."

"Twist it is." And I decorate the two glasses. They are in simple, small tumblers as I am without the correct, classic martini cocktail glasses.

She notices.

"Not my bar."

"I'll bring up a couple. I rarely use them at my house."

"I bet you have the perfect glasses for Irish on the rocks."

"Of course. And they're not a bit dusty."

I smirk. She smirks. Our jokes have become more subtle. Our discussions more subtle.

"I have some green salads in the fridge," I say. "Then roasted pork served warm. My mom's American potato salad, served cold. Thought I'd keep it simple and cool."

"Sounds lovely. Thanks for the invite."

"OK if we sit outside?" I say. She nods.

"Please grab the munchies," I say, pointing to a tray on the kitchen counter. "I'll bring the drinks."

I lead the way out the front door, to the two chairs and small table located just outside on a small cement deck, to one side of the walkway to the front door. It is not as nice has her backyard garden but it does afford sun in the morning and shade in the evening and a great view of the bay to the north.

Michaeleen has been waiting out front. Lying outside the shadow and soaking up the dying sun. He is a good friend and is not disturbing another male doing his business, but he jumps up and bounds over as we come out and find our chairs.

"He has been mooning for you," she says as she places the tray and sits. He approaches.

I move to protect the food but he ignores the plate of Bree cheese, crackers and berries, and seeks my attention.

"Away," she says. He ignores her.

After setting down the drinks to each side of the tray, I reach down and scratch his neck.

I then turn away, sit, and after looking back to Michaeleen, say "Enough."

He turns and lies down a few feet away, out of the shadow.

"Feckin all," she says. "Minds you better than me."

I pick up my glass, and then she hers. "*Sláinte*," I say and we drink.

We sit for moment, in silence. She makes herself a cracker with cheese. I take another drink. She breaks the silence.

"Just so you know," she says, "if ya going to be looking for another kiss tonight, its your turn to lead but I'd not be fightin' it."

She sounds a lot more old Irish than modern English when she drinks, or becomes comfortable. Clipping her word-ending "g" and such. Has she always spoken like that? Am I just now noticing?

I look at her and laugh. She, either teasing me or showing that my finding humor in her words is not funny, looks deadpan.

"Good to know," I say.

"Just tryin' to get us beyond that awkward stage of courtin'. That's what's happenin', I'm gussin'?"

"My being clumsy used to pass for courting. I'm not sure it still does."

"Does where I'm from."

I nod.

"I should apologize for being distant lately," I say.

"You had a difficult time, with Kenny and all."

"I mean after Black Head."

She sighs. Takes a big drink from her martini.

"I told you before, Matty. You think too much. It was a moment. A feeling I had and, I think, you had."

I nod.

"I did," I say. "So let's move on from that awkward stage."

"Ok," she says, looking at me with that deadpan look again. "But remember that I am *usually* a good Catholic girl."

Still not sure if she is joking.

"Three questions?" I say.

She shakes her head, a slight smile comes across her face, but accompanied by a suspicious squint.

"We ask each other three questions," I say. "Get some things out of the way."

"Not much for speed dating, but probably productive I would guess," she says. "You first."

"Are you still married?"

"Not for much longer," she says, quickly, unequivocally. "You want the longer version I assume?"

"My question, your answer," I say.

And she goes into a slightly longer version.

It is funny, sometimes, the differences you get in someone's life stories from the person who lived them and from the crowd who think they know that person and their stories.

As she talks, I finish my martini. She told me about her marriage, about her attempt to endure what seemed to me to be a relationship, a marriage, borne more of chance than of fate. She told me of its beginning in the hospital where she worked in a suburb of London. Where she met a man with a good Irish sounding name whose family had lived in England for three generations. He was an electronics engineer of some sort; she didn't elaborate and I did not really care. She told me of its ending, when the winds and winters of south Galway Bay blew their love and their marriage onto the unforgiving rocks of a future both realized they did not want. I understood, perfectly.

"Old story, just grew apart," she says. "An' I guess it wasn't worth fighting for."

In the end an annulment had been sought. After her husband did not fight it, local church leaders approved and she just had to wait a while longer for the formal approval from somewhere above in the Irish Catholic Church bureaucracy.

"Reverend Tom had to push the Bishop to allow it to go to the Marriage Tribunal, but he did. And it happened. New Pope, new rules," she explains.

"So you are looking at the new old Miss Auchmuty," she adds.

I look at her, smile but want to giggle.

"Yes, I know. And now you know why I don't mind still being called O'Brian."

Her turn. She did not ask about Maggie, either because she knew what she needed to know or knew that was a subject for a different day, should the need arise. Instead, she wanted to know about my children, and I was proud to tell her about them. I think she envied my pride.

When I am done being proud, I see she has finished her martini as well.

"Another?" I ask.

"Oh yes," she says.

I take her glass and, with mine, go into the house. When I
return with a second round, I notice she has prepared half a
dozen crackers with cheese and a berry atop. They are scattered
on the tray but she is eating one and Michaeleen is standing
beside her, eating something and focused on her. I can only
assume the reason for both.

She sees me notice.

"Still knows the hand tha' feeds him," she says, somewhat
proudly.

I hand her the drink, sit and begin to nosh. Michaeleen looks
from her to me and back to her, trying to figure out which is the
easy mark for another tasty morsel. Neither of us offer, and he
retreats back to the evening sun in frustration, but still licking his
lips.

"Your turn," she says.

I think about asking about her lack of children, but think
that would be rude if not none of my damn business. I want
badly to ask about her relationship with Séamus. But decide,
again, probably none of my damn business. Both were subjects
for a different day, should the need ever arise.

I ask and she talks about her work. About her ghost writing,
mostly medical journal articles for doctors, a modest industry
driven mostly from the contacts she'd made in London. I was
fascinated that she gained work from America, too, and even
from someone she called "Doctor Olga" from Russia.

"Olga is studying the effects on childbirth issues in the areas
surrounding Chernobyl, birth rates and deformities and such
terrible things," she says. "She'll have to leave Russia one day.
Her results are not appreciated at home."

Her turn.

I think she'll ask about my books being turned into movies,
about the *la la land* that is Hollywood. But she asks about my first

published work and I told her about the ghost story I wrote that appeared in an anthology that almost nobody other than the authors read. I was proud of that story, even though I made only about $150 in royalties off it before it went out of print.

"Hope you had a good night out with those riches," she says.

My final question is about her house, her history on Gleninagh North. She says the house was her grandparents on her mother's side. She and her brother, a grocery store manager in Cork, were born and raised in Ballyvaughan; she was educated in Galway, including nursing school. The house was given to Cathleen by her grandmother, after her parents died younger than they should have, and left the grandmother without family nearby. Cathleen's *seanmháthair*, her "old mother" she affectionately called the old woman, eventually died alone but happy sitting in the garden behind the house she had shared with her husband for 42 years.

"I came home to bury her and found out the house was mine," Cathleen says. "Kevin had lost his job. Times were rough in London, that crash in 2008, you know? I figured it was meant to be that I move back. So we did. The marriage was on rough times, too, but that move was the beginning of the end, you know?"

I nod.

Her final question to me, as we sit with empty glasses but enjoying every moment, is worded about as pointedly as a question could be asked to an author.

"This book you're plannin', it is going to be a great book or just a profitable book?" she says. "Is it for love or money?"

"I think I'll not make much money off it," I say. "After the screenwriters get done with it, Jasper and his entourage may make some money off it. Will it be a great book? I don't know. I doubt a really great book is in me."

She shakes her head.

"You think too much Matty."

I know, I think.

"Time for dinner," I say.

The evening rolls gently on from there. Dinner is just OK. Michaeleen only protests a little when he is shut out from the house and the dining table opportunities. The pork is a little dry, too long ignored in the oven, but Cathleen does not complain and just puts a little more of the salad dressing on her salad so she can moisten up the main course. She declines a third martini and I open a bottle of Pellegrino water.

Over dinner, we talk mostly about Irish literature, which she knows a lot about and I know really very little. After, I make coffee and I serve a desert of expensive cheese cake I bought just for the occasion. Cathleen wants only a small piece and does not eat it all. Not much for sweets, I file away for future use.

As she finishes her coffee, she goes over to my pile of books and brings one back to the table.

"The Kavanagh book is a good read for you," she says. "The time of it makes sense for your story, I assume."

"It does," I say.

"You read it yet?" she asks.

"Nope. It's been sitting there, shamed to say. Hasn't called to me yet."

"He's a farmer who wants to be writer, a shy loner that wants to be a wild lover. One could say it's a quest for the meaning of life. For a man, that is."

"Huh," I say. Not sure where she is going.

"Is that your quest Matty?"

"I'm not sure where I am going, to tell the truth," I say, not really sure where I am going with my answer either.

When the silence of my uncertainty fills the room, she fills it softly.

"Time for me to go," she says.

Darkness is just falling and we have spent nearly two hours together. Seems like the evening went too fast.

"Thanks for everything," I say as I escort her to the door.

"Thanks for dinner," she says, turning at the door to face me. "Next time I'll fix up some good Galway seabass. Michaeleen hates fish. He'll leave us alone."

She does not have to ask again if I am going to kiss her goodnight on this fine evening.

* * *

I had actually expected Sinéad's manuscript to be emailed to me as a Zip File, or DropBoxed, or some other form of modern transmission I would need help opening or downloading. But it arrived perfectly word-processed and printed on the purest of a slightly off-white paper, delivered neatly boxed in a Swiftpost package dropped off at the pub despite my name and proper address clearly printed on the label.

"*An Post*, that's our Irish postal service, refuses to deliver anything up your hill," Eileen said as she handed it to me, after first seeing me enter the pub, followed immediately by an almost theatrical departure and return with the package held as gingerly as a box of cupcakes, or a suspected bomb. "I think it is Cathleen's dog. That beast picks who he likes and doesn't, and apparently doesn't like the postman."

She handed it towards me, but sort of kept her gentle grip on it as she did so, like she was waiting for the well-deserved explanation of the contents as reward for her good care of it. I figured if I told her, she would spread the story around properly,

248

with haste and with only the slight embellishments allowed to the town gossip.

"This is from Ms. O'Reardon, the young woman helping me with my book tour. You remember her from the Galway talk?"

Eileen nodded, and absent-mindedly gave me a slight wave of her hand as if to say "And what more?"

"It's a book she's working on," I said. "Wants me give it a look."

There was no wave of the hand, in subtle request for more, but a silent tilt of her head conveyed the same intent.

"Bit of historical fiction, she tells me. About someone named Dolores Price."

"Dolours," she responded, pronouncing it as "de-lorrs" and stretching the "rr" out a little. "Not Delores," she continued, pronouncing it with slight disdain as "de-lor-is", as I had pronounced the name.

I was silent. She lost me somewhere and she knew it.

"Price was IRA," she said, before she glanced around and, seeing nobody within earshot continued in a softer voice. "A revolutionary right down to the marrow of her murderin' bones. Part of the London bombing by the Provos in the '70s. The Provisional IRA, really nasty part of the army, you know?"

I had some idea of the labyrinth history that was Irish Republican Army, its various offshoots, its morphing over the years from nationalists to revolutionists to terrorists and back to nationalists with their own legitimate political party, with the politically acceptable name of *Sinn Féin*.

"I've read her name several places," I said. "Died a few years back. Drug overdose or something. Married to an actor I met once, Stephen Rea."

That was about the extent of what I knew, so I shut up, but Eileen did not seem to have any desire to go farther into the subject at this time and place. I knew enough not to push it, at this time and place anyway.

"What's the title?" she said.

I placed the package on the bar, and started to unwrap it. She took the opportunity to grab my beer glass, slip quickly behind the bar, and return with a fresh Smithwick's and a glass of Porto for herself. By the time she returned, the wrapping was off, an unread card-sized envelope was tucked into my pocket, and the box was opened, revealing a 24-point title *Beidh ár bás Teacht*" and below that, in slightly smaller type, "*Our Death will Come*" and "By Sinéad O'Reardon".

Eileen bent her head to get the proper reading angle as she set down the pair of drinks.

"Sounds like something actually worth a read," she said, then her gaze snapped to me. "No slight meant."

"No slight assumed."

"Good, good," she said. "'Tis a play off *tiocfaidh ár lá*, our day will come. Know it?"

I shook my head.

"The phrase has come to be a desire for a united Ireland. All sorts of uses, from Joyce to pop music. Ever read 'Portrait of an Artist'?"

I had, but remembered little, so I shook my head and invited her to continue.

"It's a line in the book about the death of freedom fighters. Their day will come, maybe their righteous deaths will come. Maybe Ireland's day will come. A united Ireland. I assume she's writing about Bobby Sands and the other IRA jailed. Price spent many years in prison in England after the bombing. Almost died from a hunger strike. You know Sands, don't you?"

I remembered he basically killed himself through a hunger strike. What a fucking terrible way to die. I nodded.

"Anyway, it's sort of a rally cry for IRA members on trial for many years. There's a famous photo of it as graffiti on a bullet-marked wall in Belfast. Powerful statement. Her title, and origin. Sounds like something worth a read."

Eileen then paused and took a drink of her Porto.

"Now tell me a little about this young woman intendin' to mount the Irish tiger."

As I closed the box lid, and the pub's *de facto* cleaning lady grabbed and crinkled up the packaging after a slight delay to see if I objected, I began to give her the dime store version of what I knew.

"Sinéad O'Reardon. Can there be a more Irish sounding name in this country?" I asked. "Goes by Jenn, though. Jennifer. That the proper translation?"

"Acceptable," Eileen said. "I'm glad she writes under Sinéad. Good Irish name for a hellion I would say."

I nodded and went on with my short, mostly true story. I left out the part about Lamb's Alley.

* * *

I got back to my house after finishing my beer, putting the box into my car, taking a walk along the beach for no good reason other than it was a nice early summer evening. I poured myself a short one of my *good* whiskey and opened the box again. If I was going to read a little about an old Irish hellion written by a young Irish hellion, I figured I needed to be in an Irish hellion mood.

I camped out in a living room chair, backlit by evening light floating in a front window, my Connemara sitting on the chair's flat wooden arm. Instead of starting at the beginning, I began as a good editor or agent starts, with a couple random hits. I pealed up 40 or 50 pages and found myself in the middle of a disturbing description.

… the sixteenth day. I had stopped noticing what was happening inside my guts, inside the marrow of my bones, days ago, when I realized it was simply my body was telling me I was starting to die. I told my guts to shut its weakling mouth, do what it had to do and quit bothering me. Ignoring the gnawing in my stomach was easy, actually, and seeing my bones becoming more and more pronounced was more a curiosity than anything. But the aching in my joints, my hands and feet and, even more, my elbows and knees and hips gripped me, tight. Even my neck creaked and cracked and refused to move as it had always moved, which made reading and writing in my diary painful beyond the painful words I was writing and straight to the core of the painful thoughts my words flowed from, like the viscus oatmeal my mum would pour from the breakfast pot into her seven children's bowls on cold Dublin mornings when I was four or five. A large dollop for the boys, a smaller dollop for the girls; we had to learn to do with less from an early age. Only my eldest sister, 17 and pregnant by a boy who would never come home again after being caught alone by a pack of Protestant drunkards and beat to death in the street just down the block from where we lived, got a larger portion. She was, after all, eating for two. And the baby could be boy, a good lad who would grow up and join the cause and, maybe, take revenge for his father.

I was trying not to think about my mum that day, instead I was thinking about dear Michael, who had died a few months before, after the Brits had butchered him during a forced feeding. But his spirit still hunts these halls and my dreams, both awake and asleep. God damn to hell those that killed him. But it was not Michael who came to me, either in my dream or in my insanity, sat beside me on the cot in my cell, stoic and stone-faced. I thought he was Gandhi, but he seemed to know my mistake and corrected me in the most polite of ways.

"Amarajeevi Sriramulu," he said in an accent I could not place.

"Potti. Call me Potti," he continued, now talking with an Irish voice coming out of an Indian mouth. "It will get easier now. Believe me. In the end, you just fade away like a flower whose bloom has passed and its color withers into the glare of the sun. It is warm, and quiet, and the world will shrink. It will become so small you can hold it in your hand. It is dharma. It is most beautiful."

I would have believed him, this Mr. Potti, were it not that he looked very much like the desiccated, mummified remains of an Egyptian Pharaoh, pulled out from some tomb after an eternity of dry, slow decay.

"You will be immortal, you know," he said.

Did I really want to be immortal? Not if it ached like I am aching now. I closed my eyes and told myself to find another ghost.

For a moment I knew I was alone, and I noticed the pencil in my hand had torn the square of toilet paper I had been writing on. I tried to change my grip on the pencil and continue whatever I had been writing. What was it? A note to my sister? My own obituary? I couldn't focus long enough to know for sure. Fear spread over me. Fear of dying and nobody noticing. But then someone noticed.

There was a man sitting beside me, this time a monk of some sort, wrapped in a green cloak. He looked like a painting of St. Peter I remembered: tall and old and weathered, white hair, balding on the top of his head but flowing like streams down each side of his face, joining, briefly, then separating and flowing further down his neck and chest. He looked saint-like, I guess, but one about to die …

I read on. The words flowed. Like any good read, some things came and went, some things were remembered for a moment or two, and some things were etched for later, deeper thought.

There was this Irish word, this idea, she explained in some detail before you realized you were getting it explained: *troscadh*. A Gaelic word referring to fasting, or self starvation, as a means of protest in ancient Ireland. It was apparently often a personal statement; you fasted on the doorstep of an offender and, if you died, that brought great shame on the offender. Legend has it that St. Patrick was no stranger to the hunger strike.

In a few pages I understood that was what Dolours Price was doing, what Bobby Sands would later die doing. Having a prisoner, having a protester, die on the British government's doorstep would be politically embarrassing, even a prisoner who participated in a car bombing of London's Old Bailey Central Criminal Court that injured 200 innocents.

After being charged with great fanfare and resolutely convicted of the bombing along with her sister and eight others, in a media showcase trial in the Great Hall in Winchester Castle, Dolours served seven years of a 20-year sentence. Her hunger strike, ostensibly to get herself and her sister and the rest of the convicted transferred to confinement in Ireland, lasted 204 or so days because the British started a practice of very forcefully feeding the strikers. Hers included the daily torture of having tubes forced down their throats and liquid nutrients poured down. The practice ended when another striker, Michael Gaughan, died due to complications of the forceful feeding.

In Sinéad's book, Michael eventually came to Dolours, as her preferred ghost in her nutrition-starved hallucinations. But the conversation was not some affirmation of the IRA cause, of the IRA means, it was mostly Michael detailing the trial he was facing, in the highest of high courts, where he was awaiting judgement for his black heart and his black deeds. Dolours also found herself questioning her motives, her friends and her enemies, a gnawing guilt that she carried with her throughout her life, buried in a shallow grave, like the Belfast single mother of 10, Jean McConville, who Dolours reportedly helped kidnap and murder and bury for the rumored crime of befriending a member of the occupying British army.

I continued to bounce around the book and found some sections equally as fascinating as the Kafkaesque starvation scene, one about life in Belfast's Divis Flats housing project where the Northern Ireland Catholics were kept in a virtual prison complete with a guard tower which occasionally rained bullets down upon IRA snipers taking pot-shots at British soldiers. The snipers camouflaged themselves by firing from within the labyrinth of apartments filled with working class families and children that had to hide in their apartments' inside rooms to prevent a stray bullet from lowering the possible rebel recruit population by one.

Another section had Dolours moving, like a phantasm herself, through her first day of freedom after she received the Royal Prerogative of Mercy, a release due to her "anorexia nervosa." She bounces off people and ideas, old and new, intoxicants old and new. She careens between glancing blows delivered by hero worshipers filled with guilty praise and religious zealots filled with damnation. Ultimately she gains a taste of the addictive lifestyle that would eventually take her life some 30 years later.

Another was a beautiful, tender scene of her and her husband, the actor, remembering better days—the birth of their two sons, and quiet days in blissful self-exile in France—on the day of their decision to divorce.

There were some rough, in need of being rewritten, passages in Sinéad's pages as well. But the weaknesses in her structure were more than overshadowed by the stunning strengths of her prose.

After reading sixty or eighty pages, total, refilling my Connemara once, I put the box of pages back together and checked the time. 10 p.m. Galway time; 5 p.m. New York time. Too late to reach Young Saul but just the right time to reach his father.

I dialed the general number for the agency, the number I always used, and when a young, alluring voiced receptionist answered on the second ring.

"Meyers Talent Agency. This is Monica, how can I be of assistance?"

I simply announced myself. "This is Matthew Maybourn."

There was a pause, only the slightest of pause, as she checked her database for my name and status. "You are calling from Ireland, Mr. Maybourn?"

Everybody who worked for the Meyers was on the ball when it came to clients.

"Mr. Meyers is out of the office. May I take a message? Or is there something I can help you with?"

"I am looking to talk to Saul senior."

There was another slight pause.

"May I ask what your call is in reference to?"

"The next great Irish novel," I said.

"Yours?"

"Maybe."

"Give me a moment, please."

She was true to her word. There was only a moment of dead air until old man Saul came on line.

"Matthew," he said, as if he were talking to someone on the other side of his large, perfectly polished teak-wood desk adorned with all the accoutrements of a literary powerbroker but conspicuously missing a computer. "You timing is, as always, perfect. I've been thinking of you. Is that project for Jasper progressing? When are we going to make some money off that?"

"Its good, Saul," I said. "All good."

"Junior's gone for the evening. Opening of some Japanese chef's new Latin-Asian fusion hot spot in Harlem. God protect us all."

I laughed. He appreciated reaction to his humor.

"I'm actually looking for you, Saul. I've got something for you."

Saul paused. Saul seldom paused.

I was originally signed by Saul when he read my first draft of my first book. It wasn't his *aperitif* but he knew the color of money when he saw it on the table and he cut the deal, made money for both he and I, but handed the details off to his 20-something son eager to make a splash some 20 years ago. He took me to the best restaurant in Manhattan in 1998, treated me like I was the most important person in the world, compared me to Hemmingway, and then told me he was passing me off to his son. It was just business; he was more into the Nobel Literature Prize crowd and I was looking like the John Grisham, if not

Stephen King, crowd. When I was in town, I would see him, drink with him sometimes. But we never talked business after his son took over.

"Your new book?"

"Someone else."

"Yes …" he said.

"Irish writer," I said. "Young. Tattooed. Brash."

"Subject?"

"IRA revolutionary. Woman. Young. Tattooed. Brash."

"You had me at tattooed."

"I know I did. Anyway, she has this manuscript. It is great. You won't make a lot of money but the awards will pile up like dog shit in Central Park in July."

There was another pause. Twice in the same phone call. That might be a first.

"What's her name?"

"Sinéad O'Reardon,"

"Oh, my, the gift that keeps on giving. … and its a book about the IRA?"

"Sort of."

"Good enough. Send it to me."

Saul then paused for a moment, again. Three in the same conversation. Probably a once-in-a-lifetime event.

"So, Matthew. Your new book. Are you planning to send it to me or junior?"

I paused. I thought for a moment. I wondered.

"Probably you," I said. "Jasper might not like it."

"Screw him," Saul said. "What does Hollywood know of great writing?"

"They buy it."

"That they do, Matthew. Send it to me. I'll get you some awards. Any particular college you want an honorary MFA from?

I've been waiting for something from you I could handle. Send it to me, Matthew. Look forward to reading it."

I knew Saul was speaking the truth. You could just tell.

"Thanks for taking the call Saul. See you in the city sometime. Give my love to Bosma. Tell her I can still smell her perfume."

"You can smell her perfume on the moon, Matthew."

"I know, that's why I miss it."

I was quiet; he was quiet. The whiskey must have been scrambling my mind; not sure what his excuse was.

"You getting any love there, Matthew? You need to get some love. It's all about the love you give, and the love you get. You know that, don't you?"

"I'm learning, Saul."

"Learn fast. Life is short."

"I'll have Sinéad send you her pages."

"Do that. Then send me yours when you are ready."

"Have a good evening Saul."

"Get to bed, then have a good morning, Matthew."

We hung up. I turned back to the box of pages from Sinéad. I had to read more.

* * *

It wasn't plagiarism; not really. It was researching for a story that would pay *hommage*.

I was reading the script from "The Quiet Man", and the conflict between Victor McLaglen's "Red" Danaher and John Wayne's Thornton seemed to both irritate and attract me. Red was often a forced if not totally fake character, clearly secondary in the plot to the Irish love story, yet also clearly pivotal.

McLaglen, actually Victor Andrew de Bier Everleigh McLaglen and born a Londoner rather than a Irishman, made a career of being a character actor but he won a best actor Oscar in 1935 for director John Ford's early Irish ode, "The Informer", a film exploring the not-so-romantic aspects of the Irish War of Independence in the early 1920s. He was perfect for the role of Red in Walsh's "The Quiet Man", and Ford knew it.

The cinematic chemistry between he and Wayne was undeniable.

In one heated exchange between Red and Thornton, on their road to one of Hollywood's classic fight scenes, the bullying soon-to-be brother-in-law says: "I'll count three, and if you're not out of the house by then, I'll loose the dogs on you."

The brutish Irish ruffian was not talking about his canines but his fists, and the reluctant American boxer's response made it clear he was neither amused nor intimated.

"If you say 'three' mister, you'll never hear the man count 'ten'."

There was a reason for that exchange to be sticking with me: I had been thinking a lot about Cathleen, and about Cathleen and Séamus, and about Séamus all by his shitty little self.

My life is mile-marked with big decisions made, acted upon, and then ridden with The Fates, the three sisters of destiny, to wherever they dropped me. It happened when I left junior college to join the military, and when I left the military to go back to college. It happened when I decided I wanted to be a writer, and decided print journalism was the first mysterious door in the career labyrinth I was opening. It happened when I blissfully, blindly decided to marry; when I introspectively accepted divorce. It happened when I decided to put away my fears of repeated failure and married once again.

Such a point of decision, of accepting what was to come, was rapidly coming for my book. My scene was set, most of my characters had quietly settled into their personas, their backstories, and their current stories were starting to take on lives pretty much out of my control, if I let them. I could decide who lived and who died, who found love and who found misery, who had profound visions and who were dumbfounded. Or I could just let the river flow.

As often happens in fiction, and in life, pivotal decision points come before you know they are pivotal; twists of plot, twists of fate, happen before you know they are pending.

In my fiction I get to play the role of God.

In my life, especially in this period of Irish emersion, I suspected that I had somewhat less of an omnipotent role. I wondered if I were just a character actor in some larger plot line. Was I John Wayne, or Victor McLaglen?

Like characters in the expanding world of my book-in-work, I would just have to live a day at a time and see where God's plot line led me.

On this day, it was a little brisk in the morning; it was starting to feel like my Irish summer was beginning its post-solstice wane into fall. I felt like a hike, and hiked down the backside of Gleninagh North, with its barren rocks and hidden life and air full of imagination. The hard landscape put some hard thoughts into my head. When I returned, I felt like writing, and sat and wrote for several hours, well into the afternoon.

I wrote about manly things, mostly about the rock-hard world of men at war.

Twenty pages of cartwheeling free-writing that would turn into maybe a dozen pages of focused finished work travelled through my fingers. When I came up for air, I liked what I wrote and decided to reward my effort with a beer or two at the pub. I was still feeling strong, so began a walk down the front side of Gleninagh North. Cathleen was gone for the day but Michaeleen was roaming and he walked with me to the bottom of the hill where I rejected his advances and he, at first, pouted and then turn his back and pranced away.

It was a game we played often.

When I arrived at Cassidy's, flung open the outside door, stepped in like I owned the place and let the day's bright light shout out my entry as the door slowly closed behind me, I realized it was Saturday and the pub was quite crowded. There were the regulars, of course, but also the local weekenders and a decent number of tourists. Mully and Ian were the first people I saw, leaning at their usual spots at the bar near the door. I assumed they had been working as someone smelled of sweat and fish and vaguely of diesel. Cassidy was his usual blur of movement, serving them up as quickly as they were emptied. Eileen was at the far end behind the bar, sipping a Coke it appeared and talking intently to another woman; with her back turned, it might have been Cathleen or it might not. Looked like Cathleen. I could count the times I'd seen my neighbor in the pub on one hand, but this could be another.

Other lesser known to me regulars were in their usual spots in tables, at booths or sidled up to the bar, and a small busload of tourists were filling the rest of the place. The only noticeable difference in the locale of the regulars was Séamus: he was sitting at a table near the bar, a little ways from where Mully and Ian stood. He was as usual by himself, sitting and sipping his whiskey, in his own world.

I glanced at him, then to Eileen and her guest, who, after Eileen softly said something to her, turned her head, glanced at me, then Séamus, then back to me. It was Cathleen, and she didn't smile at either of us.

My writer's imagination was still bouncing around my head and, as a writer, I had this feeling that this was what's called a prelude to a plot twist.

"Matty," Cassidy called out as I passed from the doorway into the darker bar area. Mully and Ian and a couple of the weekenders let out their usual echo: "Matty!"

I had gotten past the uncomfortableness of such greetings and answered back with a booming: "*Tá mo liopaí tirim!*"

I was getting much better at my Gaelic vocabulary, if not my pronunciation. Best I could tell, my greeting response was telling everybody my lips were dry and wanted a beer, and, as no one ever corrected me, I assumed my translation was close enough.

Initially, I was going to go over and say 'Hi" to the ladies but the two seafarers parted and made space at the bar for the landlubber at the precise moment my pint of Smithwicks was delivered. It would be rude to decline the invitation, plus one mustn't seem too eager when it came to women, in Ireland or anywhere.

And for all I knew, they were discussing me anyway.

"Ah, vanity, my favorite sin," Shakespeare said, I think. Or it was from some non-John Wayne movie. Sounds more like Marlene Dietrich.

Anyway. I sidled up to the bar.

With the usual welcome, it seemed like any other day in the pub: Mully, Ian and me just passing time. It stayed that way for only a short while.

At first, we three talked small talk. Mully and Ian had been on a fishing charter early in the day and were drinking a little of their earnings and telling fishing stories. You know how fishermen are. Cassidy was too busy to do much but say it had been too long. It had only been two days since my last visit, but you know how bartenders are.

The fishing stories ceased, so I figured it was my turn.

"Good day of writing," I said to the pair, holding my glass up in a mock toast. "Rewarding myself. Took a hike over The Burren early, too. I find it good for clearing the head and then filling it with words."

"So that great Irish novel finally comin'?" Séamus said, loud enough that we three, and several other people at the bar near us, heard.

I hadn't even considered that he could hear the conversation.

"It's coming," I said, turning my head to glance his way.

"Good," he said. "Bet you can't wait to get the feckin hell outta here."

He had turned his head to look my way.

He sounded like the drink in front of him was not his first. Not drunk yet, which I had seen too many times, but well along that Jameson road.

I shrugged my shoulders. "Not really," I said before turning back to the bar.

Ian picked up the conversation, trying to steer it back to a more civil tone.

"You've been doin' some traveling this summer," he said. "Cork and Dublin. The Arans. Well, that wasn't all that much of a memory, I guess."

"Inishmore was beautiful," I said, then I held my glass up to the air, silently toasted Kenny as I often toasted my father when drinking alone.

"I'll remember that day as long as I live," I added when the toast, and a good gulp of my beer, was done.

"That was a fine thing you …" Ian said, before he was interrupted.

"Kenny was a tool," Séamus said, again loud enough that we three and several other people at the bar, heard.

I glanced his way again. He and I locked eyes, for a moment, but I said nothing, then turned my back squarely away from him, hoping the subliminal message would sink in.

It didn't.

"Clear he jumped off that cliff. Feckin tool. And you feckin lied. Hear you're a good liar. Seems like all you Americans are good liars."

There was a pause in his rant. I couldn't see but assume he was drinking up a little more courage as I heard his glass slam down to the table before he continued.

Both Mully and Ian turned their heads to face Séamus, probably giving him a good stare-down. I pretended to ignore him.

It didn't do any good.

"Feckin Americans think you own the whole damn world. Tellin' people what's right and wrong. Tellin' people they got to go fight in some feckin hell hole country nobody gives a good Irish crap about."

If I thought he would listen, I might have argued geopolitics with him, but decided his anger was not worth the attention. He was in a shitty mood and I would just leave him to his good whiskey and bad mood.

Ian saw what I saw; heard what I heard; again tried to steer the conversation to a different place.

He did not steer it to a better place.

"Burren is a fine place to wander," he said. "I've lived all my life here. Hiked around as a kid, all over these rocks. Not so much anymore. I hear you and your lovely neighbor been spending time out there."

Ian was trying to make small talk, I know, but as soon as Cathleen entered into the conversation he knew he made a mistake.

We all knew he'd made a mistake.

"Glad that book's getting' on," Séamus said. "We all be feckin glad for you to get the hell out of here."

"O'Dennehy!" Eileen called out. I was surprised she could hear, from where she and Cathleen stood. "Mind your tongue now."

I glanced from Eileen, to my beer, to Séamus, as she spoke.

And there was silence, for a moment, from Séamus and from the crowd. Then, with his head turned away, he spoke in a lower voice that was, intentionally or not, not low enough for me not to hear.

"Ya, ya," he said. "Feckin American writer, whole feckin country …" His good hand danced in the air as he spoke, like he was pulling strings of a puppet. "… all high and mighty, act like someone we should bow down to ya while takin' all ya wants from us."

I swiveled around, faced his anger, without really thinking about what I was doing. Maybe I should have thought a little more about it. I stared at him, which everybody could see even if he couldn't. He grabbed his whiskey glass again, finished its contents, and again slammed the glass back to the table. It sounded like it might break, the glass and the rant, but neither did.

"Feckin widow's all impressed, ya being a famous writer and all." He turned his head to look at Cathleen, but clearly he was talking to me. "She'll find out ya not worth a good Irish crap when ya take all ya want and fly away. Irish woman not good enough for ya. You'll go home and marry ya another blonde *fraochÚn*."

There was was a bit of a gasp from several in the crowd.

"That's it," Cassidy snapped. "Uncalled for."

Truth be told, I was not completely sure what he just said, but I assumed he was talking about Maggie, and he was not saying something nice. And that, I guess, was the point when I made a decision that I was going to kick Séamus' ass. Or at least try.

I turned back to the bar, set my beer down, then turned back to him and stepped toward his table. Somebody's hand tried to grab my shoulder, Ian maybe. I could hear Eileen yell again. Not really sure what she said. Maybe she was yelling at him, maybe at me.

"You got something to say," I growled, "you say it to my face."

He said nothing, so I punched him in the back of his head. Not hard, just enough to get his attention.

He turned his head slowly, looked at me. I recognized the look: the wicked little crooked smile, with one side of his mouth, his face, drooping just a touch. I had seen the smile before, especially that day he abused the young Burke boy in this very bar. But I had never been close enough to see the palsy in his face.

"You feckin hear me now?" he said, slowly standing up, rising out of his chair' maybe a bit more clumsily than usual, either from the drink or from anger. It didn't matter.

"Yes I do," I said. "I told you before, you're a sad fucking man, Séamus. Maybe all you want is pity. But you'll get none from me. I've got no time for a man who wants to wallow in his own shit."

"You want me to say what I think to your face, I will," he said. "Leave Cathleen alone. Go home and find your whores. You don't, I'll bloody ya every time I see ya."

We were face-to-face, one big step apart. I stepped a half a step closer.

"Whatever problem you have with Cathleen, you take it up with her," I said. "What she thinks, what she wants, you talk to her about it. Not me."

On cue, Cathleen appeared, standing near Séamus and me. Maybe she had been there for a while and I just did not notice.

"You two, you stop this," she said. "I'll not be a prize to be fightin' over."

"This is not about you," I said, shaking my head, glancing at her but keeping my attention on the man standing a sucker-punch distance away, keeping special attention on his right hand.

I had sucker punched him, I could expect nothing less from him.

"Matty, please," Cathleen said, pulling on my arm. I shook her loose.

I looked square back to Séamus. His crooked smile looked a little more pronounced.

"Finally found ya feckin button, uh?"

"You call my dead wife a whore?" I said. " Ya, you found it."

"What if I did?"

"What if I take you outside, and beat you, you sad little fuck."

I could have been mistaken, but I think Séamus' smile faded, just a little, for just a moment. Then his smile returned with a vengeance.

"Like to see ya try to do that," he said.

I took another half pace closer. It was the staged-for-television weigh-in before a boxing match, or two kids with puffed chests on the playground at recess. Maybe not; I could smell the whiskey on his breath as he breathed.

"If you're trying to intimidate me, you're doing a piss poor job," I said.

His smile seemed to fade again, just a little. I hoped he wondered if he had bitten off more than he could chew.

I wondered if my ego had just pushed me to make the same mistake.

I waved my hand toward the back door of the pub. He, too, waved his hand toward the door.

"Our American guest first,' he said.

I thought for second he might just hit me if I led the way out of the pub and, as I stepped toward the door, but kept my head on swivels: looking ahead, looking behind.

There was a noise in the crowd. A crowded murmur of surprise, of shock, of anticipation. I could hear someone say "Yank's goin' get hurt." Someone else said "Séamus pretty drunk." Still another said something like "twenty on that". The murmurs became a hum of noise, of movement, to escort us out the door.

As I cleared the door, my head still on the swivel, I realized I had left Séamus several steps behind. Either I was almost running or he was lagging, or dagging. I stepped off to one side, away from several parked cars and toward a little clearing of mowed grass. Good a place as any to bleed a little.

When I turned, Séamus was taking off a jacket I hadn't noticed he was wearing, rolling the sleeves of a shirt. I pulled off a sweatshirt I was wearing over my head and threw it to the side. Under it was a t-shirt; one of my U2 tees, from the "Beautiful Day" tour, with the boys all in black and looking like a middle-aged gang of posers.

Felt like a poser myself.

The crowd spilled out of the pub behind us, circled around us. Talk continued but I could not make any of it out. Séamus looked at me, that smile on his face. I tried to show him my best poker face, but I was never very good at poker faces. As stupid men and dumb boys have done forever, we stepped close to dance.

I remembered his fight with the Burke boy. I remembered his stance: leading with his bad side. For a second, I stood like I was preparing for a wrestling match, crouched and my hands held waist high and open fisted, flashing back so many years to those smelly, sweaty high school mats and the crowded, noisy gyms.

More murmurs. Someone laughed. "The hell he doin'?" someone said.

I stood a little straighter, clinched my fists and moved in, leading with my left foot but rocking back and forth on my both feet. As I got close, his heavy breaths, the smell of whiskey, greeted me.

"Want to run, don't ya," he said,.

"I'm not some drunk kid."

"You'll fall the same."

More murmurs.

I started to circle, not to his bad side but to his good side. More murmurs.

Taken a little by surprise, he backed a step, moved to circle away, but I was half a step ahead of him, stayed close, and my first left jab also caught him by surprise. While it was a weak offering on my part and glanced off his shoulder, it reiterated my previous message: I was not some drunk kid, and he will not be leading this dance.

Séamus stepped back again, looked a little confused. I continued to jab my left, forcing him to move awkwardly to present his bad left side while protecting his good right side, coiling his punishing right-hand punch for action.

Around us, some of the spectators stood idle and watched, others moved a little closer to get a ringside view of our little dance of destruction. I thought I saw Eileen and Cathleen among the men. I could not be sure. At that point, I was alone.

It was then that Séamus made his first move. Stepping close, he presented his weak left side, inviting attack. I obliged him, offered a half-hearted right punch that glanced off his drooped shoulder and glanced off his tucked head. All the while, I watched his right hand.

"Best you got?" he said.

"Nope."

He squared up, stood face to face with me, and stepped forward. His right fist was poised at chin level, to protect his face but also ready to strike; his left held low, again inviting attack to his weak side. This was the offer the Burk boy had blindly accepted. I did not.

I ignored his left hand, his tempting target, and circled to my left, forcing him to turn awkwardly, to keep his dangerous right hand free and poised. We circled. When I figured I was half a step ahead in the dance, I jabbed my left again. He was ready for it this time and knocked it away easily with his right. But then I took a quick right step forward and quickly followed my left jab with a roundhouse swing from my right, but not to his head, over his bad arm, where I knew it would glance harmlessly off his shoulder and tucked head, but to his unprotected left midsection. He saw it too late, tried to bring his atrophied left arm down to protect, but it was too weak, too little, way too late.

I could hear the dull thud as my punch hit home. Everybody could hear the thud. Séamus groaned. Everybody could hear him groan.

More murmurs. A shout of surprise—or was it joy?—from somewhere.

"Told ya," someone said. It might have been Mully; maybe someone else.

Séamus stepped back. I stepped forward, chased his retreat. He regained his stand and, stepped forward, again leading with his bad side and inviting attack. I declined and circled, forcing his same awkward response.

I could see the anger growing in his face, but I could also see his grimace as he stretched his left arm out.

"Nice punch," he said. "For an old man."

"Thanks," I said, jabbing my left as I spoke.

He blocked it again. I stepped in to my right but this time faked my right to his left midsection. He carried his left hand lower, better to at least try to protect his side but leaving his head more exposed than ever. My right might have found his chin if I'd wanted.

He was also slower that I thought he'd be, than I remembered. Maybe he was drunker than I thought. Maybe my anger, my adrenaline rush, made me feel faster. I cautioned myself of overconfidence, but I somehow knew, then and there, that if I did not allow him to hurt me, I could hurt him, again and again.

"You have enough of this?" I said.

"Not quite yet," he said.

His clarity of words scared me. Maybe I had more to fear than I thought.

I nodded, started to dance to my left.

He stepped back, frustrated.

"Stand and feckin fight," he said.

"Fuck you," I said, still dancing, still focused only on this right, ignoring his trying to offer his weak left.

Again I waited until he was half a step slow in circling and jabbed my left. Again he blocked it and, as before, with his good hand expended and his left almost useless, I triggered my right, this time with as much as I could put behind it. With his left now caught in the no-man's land of protecting both high and low, I swing low, found his midsection, forced only a little lower by his left arm pushing my punch down in reaction. But, again, my fist sunk deep into gut.

Another groan. More murmurs. He staggered backward. I stayed close, circled. When I was half a step ahead of him, I jabbed. Instead of being deflected by his right arm, my jab surprisingly caught him square on the side of his face. A heartbeat later, his right caught me by equal surprise, a glancing blow on the side of my head after I did not pull it away fast enough.

Murmurs. A yell, probably from someone who had money on Séamus.

It hurt. It jarred me. For the briefest of moments all I saw was his bad left hand and his seemingly open head on the left side. It was tempting. It was what the Burke boy had seen, and attacked, when he was hurt, when he had been jarred by that right.

I shook my head. "No. No," I reminded myself. And I returned to circle left. Again I jabbed, again it found his face unprotected, but this time I jerked away, pulled my punch a little as moved my head away.

His right swung hopelessly and his eyes told me he had no idea if I were coming back with my left to his head or my right to the target of my choice.

I moved in, pounded my right into his body. He groaned, maybe from the punch, maybe from the frustration of his realization that this dance was likely nearing its end, and not ending well for him.

But the dance did continue, unchanged except he lowered his bad left even more to protect his now abused midsection, and, after forcing him to deal with my left jab, my right merely went over his arm and caught him squarely on the chin. It rocked his head back and hurt my hand, a lot.

Still the dance continued, except he returned to protecting his head from my right. So I pounded his gut again.

He groaned. Part of the crowd groaned. He stepped back, several steps this time. It was clear my left jabs to his head hurt, but it was my rights to the body, to his head, that was taking the greatest toll. He was grimacing. There was blood at the corners of his mouth. He favored his left side, his bad side, even more than normal.

"I don't want to hurt you, Séamus," I said. "But I will."

The fight would be over soon. He knew it; I knew it; the crowd knew it. He had once been a good soldier, and a soldier knows when a battle cannot won.

But he shook his head, beckoned me forward with a wave of his right hand.

So we danced only a little more.

I dodged his desperate right a few more times, a couple glancing blows came close but did more damage to my blocking forearm than anything.

I stayed close, continued to circle to his good side, continued to tie him up and often continued to connect with my right, mostly to his body, maybe half a dozen more blows.

Everybody could see I was a good step ahead of him now. I could almost attack him at will, and whether he blocked my jab, or took it and then futilely tried to counter punch, my right, my almost free right pounding his guts or, at least one more time, rocking his head. It could not be defensed.

I was punishing him, as he had punished the Burke boy, as he had probably punished Cathleen's husband more than once.

When that realization came to me, I stepped back.

"End this Séamus," I said, praying he would end this. My face hurt; but my hands really, really hurt. Braden had been wrong: this bareknuckle stuff was absolutely no fun, especially if you were not 20-ish and full of alcohol and testosterone.

Séamus stood. Looked at me. Dropped his hands to his side; I did as well.

We just stood, breathing deep, looking at each other.

He knew what I wanted.

"Never should have cursed your wife," he said, dropping his face, his eyes, as he apologized.

I nodded. He raised his gaze to me, nodded as well.

There as a roar from the crowd, actually a cheer from some and a moan from others.

"Now," I said. "I'll buy us a whiskey, if you care to argue some on your opinion of us feckin' Americans."

He nodded. I nodded.

Men can be simple beasts.

He turned and led the precession back toward the pub. I followed. I knew he was hurt, but he tried as best he could to walk upright, to not show it. The crowd followed me, some handing money over and some collecting it. As I passed Mully, I noticed he was collecting it, a lot of it. He smiled, gave me a slight nod of the head, as I passed.

"Your drinks will be on me," he said as I passed.

I saw Eileen, standing off to the side, shaking her head as mothers often do at petulant children.

Cathleen was waiting at the door, however. She stopped Séamus. I stopped. The crowd stopped. She said something to him in a soft voice I could not understand. "I'm fine," he said back to her. She then touched his face, looked at his eyes like a ring doctor would look at a fighter. When she touched his side, he grimaced. She poked more.

"You might have a cracked rib, but I think you'll live," she said, now clear for all to hear. "You piss blood, you get the hell to a doctor. You hear me?"

He nodded and she let him pass. He stepped into the bar and then it was my turn.

We draw near.

"How's your face feel?" she asks.

"Hurts a little. But my hand really hurts," holding up my right and noticing there was blood on it. His or mine, I could not tell. What I did know was that it happened the one time I caught him on the face. "Think I broke it."

She touches my face where Séamus had landed his one good blow.

"You'll have a black eye, that's for sure," she says.

She then grabs my hands, one at a time, and probes each. She gives a quick visual inspection, then a cursory squeeze, to my little used left.

She takes her time on my battered right. She squeezes my hand, then each finger on that hand. I grimace but don't let out the scream I want to let out.

She stops in mid-inspection: "Good you took your ring off," she says.

I realized, for the first time, that I had taken off my wedding ring. I touched my front pants pocket, where I always stashed it when I needed to take it off. It was there. I realized, too, that it would not fit back on my swollen hand anytime soon.

"Maybe you broke somethin'," she says, continuing to probe my right hand. "Maybe not."

I smile. She does not.

"Feckin boys," she says, just before she turns and walks away, away from the bar and toward Gleninagh North.

I walked into the bar.

It was maybe the strangest sight I'd ever seen. The place was empty; those who had not come outside to see the fight, the tourists likely, must have fled through the inn entrance door. Séamus was already sitting alone at his table. He was rubbing his face, stretching out his left arm, his left side, wincing each time he did so.

Cassidy and Eileen were the first through the door behind me.

But Mully was first to speak: "A bottle of Connemara for the combatants, barkeep, and a beer for any that I took their money."

I walked up to Séamus.

"Somebody's bought us a drink?" I said.

He looked at me, waved his hand toward a chair at his table, grimacing as he did so.

"Little drunk already, ya know" he said.

"And I took full advantage of that," I said, shaking my right hand repeatedly.

He smiled. I smiled. Both of us hurt when we smiled.

As I sat, the crowd poured in and took their places at the bar or at their tables and booths. There was plenty of talk, mostly murmurs I could not understand. But nobody bothered us except for Cassidy, who arrived shortly with the bottle of whiskey and two glasses. He said nothing as he came and went.

"Feckin Americans always wanna talk it out," Séamus said when Cassidy was out of earshot and as he poured us two-fingers worth each.

"It's what we do," I said as I raised my glass in toast.

And talk it out we did, over that drink and one more — two whiskeys are my limit; after that, I want to talk but make little or no sense. The first one we downed quickly, as a painkiller; the second we sipped as a conversation lubricant.

We spent a few minutes talking about his dislike for America, specifically some unnamed American general and his Irish army's service in a peacekeeping mission that turned out as peacekeeping missions unfortunately often turn out: with the bloodshed of locals delayed but not avoided and the immediate if intermittent bloodshed of the peacekeepers. While I could argue the logic of the war in Afghanistan, led by America but involving many of its usual allies, I could not argue with his opinion that, in the end, it was a total failure of nation building and cost a lot of good soldiers their lives, and in Séamus' case, one man's future.

We talked a little about his world. Among other things, I learned his government pension was enough for him to live on. That and the fact that he was sitting on about 80 acres of prime farmland east of Gleninagh North, inherited from his parents but rented out to men who could actually farm it. We talked a little about my world. About the only thing he wanted to know about was some of my experiences in Hollywood, about my books being made into a movie.

I wondered if he had a book in him. I am of the belief that there is at least one book in every person: the personal memoir of their life.

The thing we did not talk about was Cathleen, and I was damn happy about that.

I moved to leave the table first, when my second whiskey was breathing its last breath.

"I'll go and nurse my wounds," I said, as I stood up.

"Ya," he said. "And I've been blabbin' like a drunk."

"Me too," I said.

There was still half a bottle of the Connemara; I pointed to it, then waved my hand toward him.

He shook his head, stood up, grimaced.

"Then we'll drink it another time," I said.

He nodded.

"And, Matty ..." he said, as we two stood, face-to-face, "Should not have said that about your wife. Not usually *that* much of an arse. Sorry that."

I held out my bad right hand to shake his good right hand.

"Let's not talk of it again," I said.

When we shook hands, he squeezed hard and I grimaced.

"Broke your hand on my face, I be thinking?"

"Maybe."

"Something to remember me by."

He laughed. I smiled. My face still hurt too much to laugh. We both grimaced.

Cassidy stepped up as we completed our little bromance.

"The bottle will behind the bar for ya, Matty," he said.

Séamus protested. "That darlin' be for either of us, I be thinking," he said.

"For the combatants, the man did say, but it's Matty's bottle," Cassidy snapped back at him.

They both looked at me.

"The spoils, I guess," I said.

The three of us laughed; two of us grimaced as we did so.

As I walked home, I felt like a man, like John Wayne. Or maybe it was a little boy again.

* * *

I felt like John Wayne, and not Victor McLaglen, a little later that day, too, after I came home, laid down on the couch because I was feeling a little woozy, and nurse Cathleen came to visit.

There was a knock, gentle at first, but when I was slow to get up and to it, it repeated with a little more energy behind it.

I opened the door and see her standing, her hair twisting around her head as a late afternoon wind pushes her my way, her hands holding down the hem of a simple paisley-print knee-length skirt as it battled against the wind, a bright-white blouse with its open collar turned up as if intended to frame her face and its sleeves rolled up as if to be ready for work.

I would have said she was stunningly beautiful but her face held firm in what she wanted to appear to be a bad mood.

I stand, looking, for a moment too long.

"You going to invite me in?"

I step aside.

"Just so you know …," she says, walking in, with Michaeleen following closely behind. "… don't be expecting me to be sleeping with you. *Mister Maybourn*. I'll sure as hell not be some reward for winnin' a feckin fight between feckin boys."

She looks at me, at my face and then at my hands, as I close the door behind the two of them.

"And why don't you have that hand in some ice?" she says.

I shrug.

She walks in as though she owns the place, heads to the refrigerator, looks and finds ice. Michaeleen circles around my legs a couple of times but, when I don't offer a scratch, he heads to his favorite spot on carpet. I walk back to the couch and lay back down. I am half sitting up, my head on a big pillow.

Cathleen returns, sets a wine bottle bucket of ice down on the floor beside me. She leans over me, inspects my bruised face again, touches it gently.

"Oh my, you going to have a beaut of a black eye," she says.

She inspects my left hand, but finds little pain on my part and little of interest on her part.

Finally, she inspects my right hand. It hurts when she grabs it with her two hands; it hurts like hell when pinches the two outside fingers.

I wince. "Ouch," I say, confirming the obvious.

She gives me a look of loving disapproval. I have seen the same look: in my mother's face, in the faces of aunts and friends and strangers, in Maggie's fondly remembered face.

"What a child," she says just before plunging my hand into the ice bucket.

"And you be makin' you livin' typing out words with those hands. Feckin silly thing to do, Mister Maybourn. Ya know that?"

"Yes, Missus Auchmuty," I say, stretching out the words like a whining child.

She again gives me that look of loving disapproval.

She sits down on the floor beside the couch, her legs tucked up under her. One arm rests on my right shoulder, the other tucked into her lap. Her head rests on her arm that is on my shoulder. She starts to talk. It is not a conversation, really, as she really does not seek any response. It is like she is singing without song. I listen to the lullaby.

She talks about things I only half understand, half remember. There are stories of her childhood, of her house. There are stories of Ireland, and the Book of Kells, and something about the Four Masters, I think that is what she called them.

I listen to her, let her words wash over me, say nothing as I fall asleep.

When I awake, it is dark outside with only a single light on in the house. I am covered with a patchwork quilt I had lying on the back of the couch. My hand is out of the ice and feels a little better. I listen for the sounds of another being breathing in the quiet house. Cathleen is gone, but Michaeleen is still lying on his chosen carpet, watching me, keeping watch over me.

I wondered if she was peeved when she left, peeved that I had fallen asleep, peeved that her dog wanted to stay with me rather than go home with her.

I got up, slowly, and open the front door. He got up, circled around my legs a couple times. I gave him a quick scratch this time, with my left hand. When I stop scratching, he walks out the door, his duty done and reward gained.

I looked down the hill and see a light on at Cathleen's house. I want to go down, to knock on her door. But I don't.

Whatever this is, that is not the way it will be.

Caibidil naoi
(Chapter 9)

My time on Gleninagh North was feeling as if it were running short. A trip to Belfast, the finale of my book tour, was two weeks away, my Irish summer was beginning to fade, and the first draft of my Irish book was blooming just as fast. The timeframe and setting of the new work was sketched, the cast named if not fleshed out, even the plot was now more an outline than a series of ideas.

But mostly I felt a strange urgency to spend more time with Cathleen. Her story, our story, was still a blank page.

I guess that is why I set up a *real* first date night, as in out in the public for all to see.

I had noticed that there was an evening of modern dance at the National University in Galway. A work-in-progress by an English-born dancer currently living in New York City, a female soloist who had danced with Merce Cunningham and carried the extravagant name of Valda Setterfield, and a Dublin choreographer with the understated name of John Scott, who probably wished he had a more extravagant name.

The dance was based on Shakespeare's *King Lear*.

"Lear? On the dance stage?" I remember her saying when I invited her, standing in her back yard as I passed her on my way off for a jog. "I never figured you for a dance fan."

I shrug. Smile.

"Is it a date, then?' she says.

"Do you want a date?"

"I thought you'd never ask."

"So is it a date?"

"It is," she says. "And I'll make us an early dinner before we drive in. That Galway seabass I've been promising. Good with you?"

"Perfect," I tell her, as I head off, jogging down the hill with a little more spring in my step.

The day of the date came. The dinner was as good as I expected. The afternoon was warm and the breeze soft, so we sat outside in her garden. There was good French white wine, which she left for me to open and pour as she ferried back and forth from her back door and kitchen, first with a cut apple and nuts, then with a *caprese* salad, and finally with angel hair pasta covered with the fish in a butter and olive oil sauce.

"Usually we Irish just fry it up, but I felt this 'd be a little more Euro," she explains.

As promised, Michaeleen does not seem to like the smell of fish cooking or being served and leaves us alone. Last I see him, he is up behind my house; he'd probably spend the evening on his favorite carpet in my front room had I left the door open for him, but he'd settle for the padded chair on my back porch.

Time and conversation passes easily but when dinner is done we are running a little late to get into Galway, so she offers to drive and I let her. She knows the back roads to get around the city and she has no fear on the roads, as I still do. We arrive in plenty of time.

The dance program is splendid. At some point, after intermission, she takes possession of my right hand and holds it chastely on her thigh. I glance at her when she does so, but she is watching the program and does not return the glance. The second knuckle on my ring finger, where I usually wear my wedding band, is still swollen. I probably broke the damned

thing. I wonder if she notices the ring is missing. She doesn't ask;
I do not ask.

After the dance, I drive, and either meander or take a couple
wrong turns, on our way home. We talk about the program,
dance in general, and Shakespeare's *King Lear*. She had seen a
classic performance in London at the Globe by actors who knew
how to read Shakespeare. I am envious.

When we get back to Gleninagh North, I park in my usual
spot and walk her down. She leads; I follow.

We walk past the gate to her back-yard garden, to the
downhill side of the house, where we enter her front yard,
through another gate in the stone fence. I have seen her front
door a hundred times as I drove up or walked up and scanned
the large, single front window for her movement. But I have
never really noticed its details: its small, perfectly manicured
grass lawn bracketing a graveled path from the road to a small
cement slab at the front door, the two planters, one to either side
of the cement, with flowers, a sign on the front door, a woodcut
of a yellow flower with the word *Fàilte* imprinted on it: welcome.

It seems too decorated, too cute, for Cathleen. Maybe it is all
an *homage* to her grandmother; maybe I just don't know her very
well.

I have visited her kitchen, through the back door that leads
to the garden, and it is all business: clean and organized to the
point of being sterile. That is my vision of Cathleen's world. But
as we near her front door I realize there is undoubtedly more to
her world.

She stops at the door.

"Care to finish that bottle of the French?" she asks.

"I would like that."

She ushers me into her house, through a heavy wooden door
framed with metal, weathered but sturdy.

The front room smells clean, but with clear evidence of not-so-fresh cut flowers, a faint smell of the sea, or maybe just the evening's fish, and the even fainter, but vaguely remembered, musk of a woman's world.

I like it before I even take a casual look around.

The front room is a great room, with two levels: the lower as you enter by the door is small but filled with a pale-colored cloth couch of proper proportion to the room, as well as a leather armchair of comfort and utility, with reading lamps perched on reading tables to each side, and steamer trunk serving as a center coffee table. There is a vase of cut flowers on the table; they are past their prime but still fragrant if not artful.

Farther into the room is a raised area, maybe a foot or foot-and-a-half higher and accessed by a short set of stairs to the right side, where the dining room is located. The room has a large wooden table with seating for six and a large, lidded soup tureen of antique earthen-color centered on an off-white tablecloth. There are two wooden cabinets, one low and the base for a piece of what I think is ceramic sculpture, and one taller, with glass doors and shelves filled with dining ware and glasses.

The interior walls of both rooms are sand-colored stone and off-white mortar, like the outside walls of her house, only scrubbed of its grime but not its history. There is little art in the room, aside from the sculpture. The walls are bare except for a modern abstract hanging to one side of a small fireplace located on the opposite wall from the front door. It is simple, tasteful, and feminine in a subtle but distinctive way.

"Very nice," I say, realizing I am taking more than a casual look around.

The room would be bright, I assume, when the lights come on or the daylight bathes it through the big window to one side of the front door. I think the window is situated so that defused northern daylight would stream in.

I can picture her sitting there. I like the picture.

Tonight, near 11 p.m., the house is lit by a single overhead lamp and a faint light creeping in from kitchen, which is on the far side of the dining room. As I scan the house, I notice a staircase, also to the right side of the dining room, leading up to the second floor and the bedrooms, I assume.

I glance around for Michaeleen; I have never invaded the space of the "man of the house" and wonder how he will take the incursion. But he is nowhere to be seen, inside or outside. I wonder briefly if he, too, is out on a date?

"You have a beautiful house," I say, as I close the front door and step deeper into Cathleen's world.

She does not seem to hear me, or care to respond. She walks in, taking off the lite blue sweater she had been wearing all evening and exposing a sleeveless, starched white cotton shirt. The sweater is thrown onto the couch as she walks through the room, presumably headed to the dining room and the kitchen beyond in search of the wine.

I stand quietly, close my eyes, and the male imagination takes over …

I almost see her stop at the top of the two stair steps leading to the dining area. She turns.

"We'll wait on the wine," she says, looking back to me. She is silhouetted by the light from the kitchen.

At first I hesitate, unsure of what she means. Then I understand, walk to the stairs, and take a step up. As we stand, her face is slightly higher than mine, but she bends down slightly and pulls my face close as I wrap my hands around her waist and pull her body near. We kiss. And kiss again. Our hands roam. My lips roam and find the side of her neck and the opening at the top of her blouse.

"The last of the wine," she says. And I open my eyes and
return to the moment.

I guess I look startled, or maybe I am blushing.

"I don't think I'll ask where your mind was wandering," she
says.

"Best you don't," I say.

She comes down the steps with the bottle and two glasses.

Michaeleen is prancing behind her. As she nears, she waves
to the couch and chair arrangement; I sit on one end of the
couch and after two glasses of wine are poured, she sits beside
me. We are close, but separate. Michaeleen lies nearby, watching
us; watching me. He is still the man of the house of this house.

There is soft music floating around us.

"Nice music," I say.

"CD player," she says. "Little old fashioned, I know. But I'm
a little old fashioned. In a lot of things, I would say."

I nod. Say nothing.

"Brian Boydell," she continues. "He's passed, but a fairly
modern composer. This is from the '60s, I think."

We are quiet for a moment, but I recall her soft voice from another time, remember her telling me stories as I fell asleep while she tended to my bruises. I want to hear that voice again, telling me stories.

"You started to tell me something, the Four Masters," I say. "The night I hurt myself."

"The night of that foolish fight? Then you fell asleep on me?"

"Ya," I say. "Such is life."

"Such is life," she echoes.

"The Annals of the Four Masters," she continues. "The Four Friars. Could better be called, *Annála na gCeithre Máistrí*. A history of the original people of this island, from Noah's time to the time the friars compiled it, wrote it. Good source for medieval history, really. Vanity project for a local land baron."

She sips her wine and snuggles in a little closer. I put my arm around her as she draws near. She could have been describing how to overhaul an engine and her voice would still have been beautiful.

"Mostly just names and places and dates, really, and not all of it above question. But there are some lovely little hints of stories. There's story about one *Rí O'Fionnachta*, a sort of king or land baron, from what's now County Down. It says that during his reign snow fell that tasted like wine; sounds like a fairy tale, but then if you break down the name, the word *Finnachta* is the union of two other words. *Fionn* is white and *sneachta* is snow, so the king was Snow White."

And the stories go on. I like them all.

When the wine is finished, her stories are finished. It could have been 10 minutes; it could have been an hour. We are quiet again.

"I should go," I say.

"Yes," she says, "I do have a meeting in Galway early."

We untangle. She walks me to the door.

"I enjoyed the date," she says. "I like dating."

"I do too."

I kiss her. It is a lingering kiss, a longing kiss.

I wonder if she, too, envisioned an evening that ended differently.

* * *

They like to say Glaway Bay was the only area of Ireland relatively untouched by the Easter Uprising against British rule of 1916, and the Irish War of Independence and Civil War that followed, but even an American outsider could clearly see that really was not true.

Galway was the western headquarters of the British Army while the IRA was relatively weak in the area as the hotbeds of the turmoil on all sides were in Dublin, Belfast and Cork, among other places. Maybe the most egregious act was the 1920 killing of a Galway city Catholic priest, reportedly at the hands of British forces. That led to a local business boycott of Belfast-area goods in protest of treatment of Catholics by the British in general and especially in the Protestant loyalist's Northern Ireland stronghold.

Even during the Civil War, there was a relative peace in Galway despite clear divisions of the population into Pro-Treaty and Anti-Treaty camps.

But the threat of violence in Galway was always on the minds of locals: the threat of British vs. IRA clashes, and then the threat of a bloody breakdown of the uneasy co-existence of Irish nationalists with passionately different views of the Irish nation's future in the wake of the treaty that created an independent Ireland without Belfast and with British forces still on its blood-stained Irish soil.

That threat of violence was also on the mind of the director and writer of *The Quiet Man* film.

There is an almost throwaway line, when Danaher and Thornton are about to fight, when Danaher asks the betting crowd "So the I.R.A.'s in this too, huh?" To which another character responds: "If it were, Red Will Danaher, not a scorched stone 'o your fine house'd be standin'."

If there was only the threat of violence in Galway area, there was more than enough actual violence for all of the island of *Eire* in Northern Ireland, in Belfast. Throughout the Irish fratricide that is universally and euphemistically known as "The Troubles", violence was a part of every family if not every life. *Na Trioblóidí*, as it is called in Gaelic, officially began in the late 1960s and officially ended with the Good Friday Agreement of 1998, but there were troubles long before, and the troubles linger.

Everyone I talked with in Galway and everywhere I went in Ireland, had their personal stories of being touched by The Troubles, sometimes lightly, from a distance; sometimes brutally, from close range.

Maybe Sinéad had the most knowledge on the subject, as her book proved, but she was too young to have lived much of it. She had distant connections, mostly through her mother, who apparently had her fair share of painful direct connections. But Sinéad, like me, was more of a historian on the subject, and her generation, for the most part, was more interested in moving beyond the past and into the future.

Cathleen, too, was mostly a student of the dark days; a reader of books but with little direct connection as far as I knew.

With Pádraig, back in Cork, I had had the longest discussion on the issue. He had his story to tell but he admitted it was a story of intentional avoidance rather than active involvement.

The Harringtons at the pub, especially Eileen, had their stories to tell, but mostly second hand stories heard and retold over the bar that may or may not have been mostly true stories.

Ian, early on, had pointed out Mully as a man with a story to tell. And every story in Ireland in the last 100 years was shaded in some way by The Troubles. But it is not the sort of thing one casually asks about, and despite a couple opportunities where the subject arose when he and I were alone, Mully never offered.

That changed on my unexpected sea excursion to Northern Ireland.

With my reading in Belfast coming up in a couple weeks, everybody offered up tourist suggestions, things to see and things to do, even Séamus, who told me of a good pub, of course. Sinéad had a suggested itinerary, but she made known it was only a suggestion. Despite huge and heartfelt public relations and tourism promotional campaigns, Belfast was not your normal tourist destination.

Mully, however, offered me much more than simply a tourist itinerary. He offered me an adventure.

"I could take you up there, me and my deck hand here," he said one day, as we stood at the bar, he and I and Ian, keeping our lips wet. "An' ya can't really say you've seen Ireland 'til you see it from the sea, with the land off your shoulder."

I was confused, and I guess my confusion must have been evident.

"Take a sail up to Belfast," he said. "My lass needs to run 'fore the wind. Been too long tied to land."

I thought I understood. He was offering to ferry me up on, instead of my taking the train or flying. But I looked to Ian just the same.

"He's talking about his Laurent Giles," Ian explained. "Fifty-one footer. 50 years old and still the most beautiful vessel I ever had the pleasure of steppin' foot on. *Aislinge*, he calls her."

He pronounced it something like "ash-ling", I think.

"Woman in peril. Needin' a steady hand," Ian continued.

I looked at Mully, just to make sure I understood what he was offering.

"Be my pleasure, if you can change the plans I'm sure that young lady has made for you," he said. "Tides are favorable. Weather looks good for the week 'fore your reading. We'll give you a week before you're due there but should only be five days at sea. Nights at safe harbor. Ain't as young as I used to be. Any problems we just rent you a car. You and Ian drive on in while I stay with my lass. Will need to run out and leave ya there, run before a storm that may be coming, get out of Belfast quickly. 'Course, nothing like a little storm on the sea to get your heart beatin' strong."

I would bet my pocket cash that he had run before a storm once or twice in his life, probably more; I'd bet my bank account that this discussion was the most consecutive sentences Mully had uttered since I met him.

I learned long ago to take gifts freely offered by people you respected, especially gifts you really, really wanted to accept. An adventure at sea, up the Irish coast, while writing a book about Ireland, was a gift that would keep on giving years later.

"I can pay the fuel," I said.

"You Americans … think you can buy the wind," he said, with a bit of sarcasm that passed for humor. "God willin' won't need much diesel."

I figured there was no use arguing with a man such as Mully, so I didn't.

"Be my pleasure," I said. And plans were made for passage up, with the two of them making their way back alone at their leisure, while I did my business in Belfast: the reading and a city to explore.

Sinéad did not like that I was leaving my travel plans to the winds of fate, quite literally. She made that clear when I called her that night. But I told her we would leave a week early and assured that only a shipwreck could change her plans. She did not really like that either.

"Oh, that makes me feel more confident," she said.

But she agreed, changed my train reservations to just the return trip and said she would reserve the hotel for three days early, just in case. I agreed to call her from the road, or sea or ports of call or wherever. Keep her informed on our arrival date.

The day arrived and Ian picked me up in his car.

I had told Cathleen of my plans and of the itinerary, but she wasn't around to see me off; she didn't go for that "seeing your man off at the dock" cliché, I guess. Cathleen did not get into many of those "Irish woman" clichés. But she did offer to pick me up from the train station on the day of my return.

Michaeleen barked me a farewell, however. It was a funny kind of bark, almost a howl; I wondered if he noticed my travel bag. It was strange to be off for an adventure and only a neighbor's dog to wish me a safe journey.

Ian and I drove a little north to pick up the ship.

Mully's Laurent Giles was, as Ian had said, the most beautiful vessel I had ever set foot on as well. The *Aislinge* was a classic, wood-hulled beauty built in England by true craftsmen in the late 1960s and early '70s. It was a sailing yacht but with more than enough diesel muscle to take on the open sea, even the often rough northwest coasts of Ireland. When I first saw it in moorage, after being driven up the coast by Ian, I wondered if two men were enough to take it to sea. Then I realized if one of the men was Mully, two might just be one too many.

With me, there would be only three on my unexpected adventure at sea.

That first morning, I stood on the sparkling teak deck, in front of the main mast, feeling a little like Odysseus tied to the mast, as we powered out of Galway Bay against the wind. Mully was at the helm, of course, and Ian scurried around preparing to set sail. It was a great feeling as the wind and the waves lightly pounded the boat. I had always liked the sea: the smell of the wind, the taste of the spray. There was something almost primeval about it.

As we neared the mouth of the bay, I noticed Ian was working the rigging for a big sail up front and the main sail where I was standing. I figured it was time to climb in beside the captain for the open ocean. There was a partially enclosed area where Mully stood at the wheel, and plenty of seating behind that, under a back sail that would swing back and forth for steering. I learned more about the ship and its sails, and their names and uses as the voyage went on. But initially I stood just behind Mully, holding fast to railing on the inside of the cockpit. He noticed my move, but initially acknowledged my movement with only a glance to ascertain my place in his world.

"Good spot, Matty," he said finally. "Stay there for the time."

It was not a request.

A few minutes later, as we cleared the mouth, and the wind and waves changed in force if not direction, I stood mostly still — holding on to a railing meant for such things and rocking back and forth on legs unaccustomed to the rolling of the sea. I watched two men at work with an almost complete lack of knowledge of the work being done.

Mully barked out commands, either in Gaelic or in some universal nautical language that only seafaring men know. Ian responded with action and the occasional grunt of recognition.

In an indescribably fast order of occurrence, a small sail was set behind me with little fanfare; then a larger one up front popped into place and almost immediate effect, exerting a pull on the ship that caused me to loose my balance and almost fall, much to the amusement of Mully, who glanced my way but after seeing me clutching the rail to gain my balance turned to other matters. Finally, a middle sail, one that appeared could be swung side-to-side, was set and popped into place, to one side of the vessel.

A few minutes later, after some more indecipherable discussion, the diesel went quiet and the indescribable sounds of a sailing ship under full, favorable sail set in. Maybe I should say "lack of sounds," as while there were some vaguely mechanical sounds emanating from somewhere within the ship, the sound of the wind and creaking of wood and stretching of sails became dominate.

"My lass loves to run," Mully said, now in an almost normal volume, as we settled into our trip up the coast. I wasn't sure he was talking to me or himself.

"Make yourself comfortable," he added, this time clearly to me, waving his hand to the seating area to the back of the ship. I left my rail and settled in with a view of the Irish coast to my right, the wide Atlantic to the left, and a wake soon extending to the horizon in the back.

Ian came from his scurrying about the deck, his work done for a while I assumed. He grabbed a bottle of water from somewhere, offered one to me, which I declined. I should have not had such a large breakfast I decided. Ian, too, settled down for the ride.

That first day, Ian was mostly quiet, but every hour so he would comment on some point on the coast. "That be Connemara," he said at one point, pointing to the mainland. "That be Inisbofin," at another, pointing to an island as we made passage between it and the mainland as we continued north. Sometimes there was a little history in the discussion; other times just a point on a map that navigators of the Irish coast knew by heart.

When the sun was high, at some unnecessary-to-define midday hour, Mully mumbled something to Ian, who then asked if I was hungry. Breakfast was still hunting me, so I declined. He then disappeared below deck and returned shortly with simple sandwiches for the two of them and a travel mug of undefined liquid for the ship's master.

"This'll be your job starting on the morrow," Mully informed me as he munched.

Ian's sparse travelogue then continued.

"Headed into Belmullet," he said as evening drew near and I could see we were entering a harbor of some sort. "We'll dock here tonight."

After that first day, I studied maps of our transit and tried to identify the points along the coast myself.

"That be Glencolumbkille," I said to Ian after we cleared Belmullet and had sailed open water north for most of the second day but were finally nearing land again.

He laughed and corrected my pronunciation. "But your navigation is true," he said.

We played the game each day, as we were on the water for eight or 10 hours each day, often running at six or eight knots.

Sometimes I had the names and the pronunciations right. More often I had one or both completely off and he would correct me.

That second day we made Sligo Bay, heading mostly northeast. The third we made Dungloe, heading mostly north. On the fourth we made Rathmullan.

"A day out of Carrickfergus," Ian said as we neared Rathmullan. "Belfast just up the way."

I had enjoyed the voyage about as much as anything I could remember enjoying since before Maggie was diagnosed. I took notes, but remembered it much better than I could describe in mere words.

Starting on the second day, and each of the remaining days in transit there-after, we had fallen into a pattern. We would wake early, after a night of restful sleep in the slightly cramped but still luxurious cabin, to strong tea with honey and simple breakfasts of breads with jams or cereal with yogurt or milk. I watched Ian put out the food and clean up the galley the first morning and from then on I took it as being my job. After breakfast, we would put out under power. Once in open water, there would be short time of calculated but almost frenzied sail work, mostly by Ian; occasionally he would allow me to help with the ropes.

Mully said little or nothing, but from where we sat he would have had to yell for me to hear him anyway. I wondered if all sailors, or just Irish sailors, were habitually short of words. Maybe it was just sailors on sailing ships. There was something, almost magical, in the lack of sounds. Like a spell that nobody wanted to break.

For the most part, I just prepared and cleaned up after breakfast and the light lunch of simple sandwiches of cheese and meat, nothing fancy. Mully's midday drink of choice, I learned, was strong tea with honey. Other than that daily duty, I watched and listened and learned.

Most of each day, I would find a spot on the ship were I was out of the way but watchful of all that occurred on deck. Ian would sit near me most of the time, as we continued our game of location and navigational sights and that night's expected port-of-call.

The days passed slowly, luxuriously: often warm and sunny, occasionally overcast and less warm. There was a rain squall one day, and it was accompanied by changing, unpredictable winds, which caused Mully to bark Ian into action. Just before the rain came, Ian handed me a slicker, told me to stand near Mully, and the three of us rode out the squall standing tall on deck at the ready, as men at sea have always ridden out such squalls.

By the third day, I was sunburned in the usual places, wind-burned over my face and neck, and I smelled the sea with every breath, tasted salt every time I licked my lips.

I have rarely felt as alive.

Each day, Mully remained mostly silent. He studied his maps, studied his weather radar, read the winds and the tide. He explained things when I asked, but I am hesitant to interrupt men at work and clearly this was Mully's work, his life's work. And he seemed to be at rest as he worked. I knew the feeling, to some degree. When my words were flowing, as I was writing a passage for one of my books it was not work. It felt like breathing.

Each evening, we found safe harbor. Each night we found a place ashore to eat; usually a simple pub within view of the harbor. Both of them knew the ports like they knew the sea that brought them there. At the pubs, Ian and I would have a beer. Mully drank only tea, strong tea with honey. We would eat, and the two sailors would talk of the day to come: the transit, the next port-of-call, the expected weather and sea condition. I listened and imagined that I, too, was a sailor, like them.

I had not felt as much a man for years, maybe as far back as when I was in the military, or a randy bachelor just after.

In the afternoon of the fourth day, with one more night's stop before putting in at Carrickfergus, near Belfast, there was an unexpected crew shift. Mully called Ian up, gave him some instructions I could not hear, and turned the helm over to him.

This was not unusual, Mully would occasionally turn over the helm to Ian, but only for a few minutes and then almost always to go below deck to answer nature's call. A couple times, Mully would move about his deck, changing something Ian had done, tightening or loosening rope tension here or there, or folding something in a different way. Ian would bitch about what he considered the unnecessary adjustments and Mully would ignore him, as all captains do on the ship they command.

But on that day, Mully came and sat beside me. He reminded me of a photo of Ernest Hemmingway, when the writer was older but still vibrant. All wild hair and beard and face scrubbed clean by the sea and the wind and the years of rugged, joyful life.

"Thanks for allowing me to give you this," he said. "I think you're a good man. I admire the way you handled Kenny's death. His parents. I admire the way you handled Séamus. He was asking for the beatin', and you give him a right good one. But he bled for Ireland, he deserves respect for that. You gave him that respect."

I did not know what to say. I just nodded and accepted the words, the gift.

"You're looking for stories of Belfast," he said, finally.

I nodded again; knew another gift was coming.

Mully pulled out a photo, wrapped in protective plastic, and handed it to me as if he were handing over the most precious

jewel he possessed. I looked at the photo: a young man, maybe
20 years of age, maybe younger, dressed in a dark jacket and
dark hat and holding a rifle in his arms as one would hold a baby.
I took the photo, studied it, nodded, handed it back with just as
much care. He returned it to his pocket.

"My son," he said. "Just before he was killed."

I could see the young man in the photo resembled the old
man who sat beside me and, I assumed, also what Mully had
looked like when he was in his 20s.

Mully paused, his jaw set, eyes focused on my eyes, the wind
blowing his unruly hair to and fro, and a backdrop of grey sea
rising and falling. For him, words were not as easy to master as
the sea.

"Details of this story stays here," Mully said. "Promise me
that."

I swallowed hard, nodded.

"He was IRA," Mully said.

I swallowed hard, again.

"Barely a man in '85. But he was man enough to join the
provos. You know, Provisional IRA?"

I did know. Nodded.

"He grew up in a bad place in a bad time. Belfast was a
feckin war zone in the 1970s and '80s. Not a great place before,
but really hard place then. Particularly if you were a Catholic,
and his mum was a repentant Catholic. A blessed, big old heart,
she had. Alice was her name. Ailise O'Dowd. Good Irish name
that. What a lovely young woman when I met her in '65. Looked
like Twiggy, you know? Long legs, short hair, big eyes you got lost
in. I was an officer on board an Atlantic cargo carrier."

He took a deep breath, a tiny smile flashed across his lips, a
momentary glint of happiness in his eyes. Then it faded.

"Story as old as the sea, her and I. Found out she was pregnant when I was an ocean away from Belfast. Gave birth when I was gone, too. Her letters were not angry. Just telling me the truth, giving me her love from afar. My letters sent money, not much love, though, not really."

He was silent for a moment. He looked beyond me, out to the open sea. I recognized, or imagined, a twinge of pain cross has face, an ache buried deep by the years but easily exposed.

"Thomas. Tommy boy, I called him. Ailise hated that. First time I saw him he was a toddler. Shy boy around men. Mum held him too close, maybe. Hard choice for her, my not being there. Just couldn't change, I guess. Didn't want a wife. Never wanted a wife. But had a child and had to stand up to that. Offered to move the two of them out of the city, out of all that trouble. Move them to Galway. Still had my mum there. Me mum would've helped. But Ailise would have nothing of it. No marriage, she said, then she'd stay with her family, stay in Belfast, despite all the anger, all the danger.

"Early years my boy was raised in Divis Flats. Terrible place. Gave her enough money to at least get the hell out of that hell hole. Much of her family stayed there, though. And Tommy still got into trouble young, early teens. Fights with the Prods in his neighborhood. I wanted to get him out of there. Take him with me. I was a captain by then. Still doing Atlantic transport. Could have brought him to sea with me, but he'd not leave his mum, his people.

"Can't blame him, I guess. Ailise wrote me that she wanted him to go, urged him to go. Told me he was hanging with the Provos. Looking for trouble. Found it one night. Shot dead by the Collar Dogs, the UDR. You know?"

I nodded. Ulster Defense Regiment, pro-British loyalists, unofficial soldiers.

"The Prod's IRA," I said.

He nodded.

"You've done your research, Matty. Good. You understand there was a lot of hate. Blood in the streets. Terrible days."

Again, silence between us. Only the rush of the wind, the sounds of the sea surrounded us. Again, I could see the man's pain etched on his face.

"Got the news of Tommy in a letter. Last one I ever got from my lovely Ailise. She told me the sad news, sent me that photo. Last one she had of him, she said. Never sure if she was proud of it, or ashamed of it and wanted that image out of her life. She told me to stop sending money. Said she didn't need it anymore. That's my last memory of her, a feckin letter from afar, bringing me sad news.

"Last time I saw her, in the flesh, when I offered to take Tommy away, she was already an old woman. Her beautiful hair had gone long, limp. Her eyes empty. That's the way I see her in my dreams. The price I pay, I guess. Those twenty years raising a Catholic boy in Belfast had to be hard. But that was her choice. Tommy did not really have much for choice, I figured. Should have had a better life than dying a teenager in a senseless gun battle in a tragic war that everybody knew had to come to an end."

He paused again. Looked at me, studied me, like a sea captain looks at the sky and the swells and the wind just before he makes decisions that he will have to live with, maybe die with.

"I was angry about that. Angry that people do such stupid things. I guess that's why I agreed to help smuggle IRA arms into the north."

The wind continued to blow his hair around. The grey sea continued to roll. My guts tightened. The Troubles truly touched everybody, in some way. In surprising ways, sometimes.

"You want to hear it all?" he said.

"It stays here," I said.

"Good," he said. "I want to tell it to someone ta' who it might matter. Not going to live forever."

"Neither am I."

"Words in a book, Matty, they can live forever."

I shrugged. Maybe true.

"They approached me in Galway. I always took my breaks from the sea there. Me mum had passed and the old house in Rathmorgan was mine. Young man approached me at a pub in Ballyvaughan. Likeable enough kid. Reminded me of Tommy Boy. Told me he knew my son, was a friend of Tommy. Told me how he died, how they gunned him down in the street with his back turned. Told me his people were friends to Ailise. Told me they were taking care of her. Protecting her. He said I could honor Tommy, help her, by helping the cause. Made the mistake of listening to that young man instead of giving him a beating right then and there.

"That meeting turned into another meeting, in Galway with another man, older man. Little less likable. Nobody tells you their names, just hint at who they're aligned with. IRA, Provos, INLA. Hard to keep track of the heroes and the thugs. Some of them were revolutionaries, some just thieves and murderers wearing that black national mask. Hard to know who was talkin' true, who was lying. Couldn't trust anybody, really. Man said he was Fenian, American supporters of a United Ireland. He knew I would be captaining the *Traverse Bay* in a couple months' time.

"*Traverse* was container ship, sailing to and from America. He knew it would be handling cargo out of Boston, mostly to Bremerhaven, in Germany. Knew we'd be making a stop in Dublin. He knew more than I did about the whole feckin thing.

All I had to do was look the other way in Boston, he says. Make a stop in the night off County Donegal, he says.

"I guess I didn't say 'No.' So next man I met was in Boston. Looked like an American gangster, all leather jacket with a gun tucked away but not really hidden all that well. No names, of course, but he knew me and knew what I'd agreed to. Told me the cargo would be on-board when I took the *Traverse* out of port. Nothing to do but lay-up at the place and time he gave me, look the other way and make sure my night watch would look the other way too.

"A fishing trawler found us off Downings," he said.

"Passed there today," I said, vaguely remembering a place on the map.

"That's where it all went to hell," he said, grimacing, his voice fading off into he wind and the sea.

"I was told it was all medications and communications and such. No guns. But like I said, couldn't trust a one of them, especially the man we took on from the trawler. Things were taken off and a man came on."

He took a break from his story.

There was a look on his face, one I'd never seen on Mully and rarely seen on any other man. It was anger, yes, but guilt as well. He looked past me, out to sea, then back to my face. I wondered which truths he had decided to trust me with, and which he would keep to himself and carry to his grave.

"*An diabhal*. The devil. Let's just say that. That man I took on. I found out later he was some captain in the Provos. Connected right to the top, to God almighty Gerry Adams himself, they said. Had I known that, I might not have killed the bastard. Hell, maybe I would have anyway. He was a shit of a man."

I swallowed, hard.

"Anyway, the man came aboard my ship and started giving orders, to me and my crew. Told me he would disembark outside Dublin. A small craft was to meet us at dawn. Bastard took over my cabin, so he could hide away he said. But a couple hours later the man came stormin' onto my bridge and wanted to know who knew what onboard my ship? Who was on watch, at the helm? It was 'bout the time we heard over the radio that the trawler had been intercepted off the Culdaff, headed for Derry maybe, and had a cargo of guns and ammunition and explosives for the IRA. Not sure how he knew before I did, but the bastard said he suspected someone onboard reported the drop. He was crazy mad.

"He focused in on one of my boys who'd been on watch that night. Young lad from Glasgow, a British national. I has sailed with the boy couple of times. He seemed a good lad. Quiet, did his job well. But he'd been in the radio room at the time and might have seen what was going on. Might be he had reason, like I had reason. The devil was hell-bent on finding someone other than his people, his plan, to blame. Ordered me to send the boy up to meet him on the fantail. I knew what he intended. The boy either did the deed or didn't, but he'd not make it off that deck that night. I knew it. Couldn't let that happen. Not on my ship. I went to meet him on the fantail."

Mully went silent. I sure as hell had nothing to say. He looked out the sea behind me, then returned to me, and to his story.

"Just passed Red Bay," he said, waving his hand over his shoulder as if casually pointing. "Not much of a bay, really. Castle there, south of Cushendall. Fitting name, though. Ship was near there when I clubbed the man and threw his dead ass into the water."

Mully looked up, to the heavens. I wondered if he were looking for words, or looking for a bit of clear sky lightning to be sent down.

He looked a little like an animal watching for death from the sky.

He looked back at me.

"Not proud of what I did, Matty. But it had to be done. He was a murderin' son of a bitch, I found out later. Always sendin' others to do his dirty work. Sending young men off to kill and die and he'd just stand back and take whatever glory there is in such things. All the while, he's keepin' his hands clean."

Mully had always looked to me like a young man in an old man's body. But as I looked at him, his hair blowing in the wind with the sea rising and falling behind him, I saw an old man in an old man's body. There was this photo of Hemmingway, not too long before he shot himself, filled with depression and realization that his life had been fully lived but was near its end. Mully had that look.

"My hands are not clean, Matty," he said. "But I did the deed myself. I'll die with that deed, an' let God above judge me."

We just sat there, the ship driven by the North Channel winds, and the wind and the steady creaking of the ship and the sails the only thing to break the silence. Until I broke the silence.

"One question," I said.

He nodded.

"Why aren't you dead?"

His face brightened.

He laughed, loud, the laugh of someone who knew life was good and was enjoying every minute of it he had left.

"*An diabhal* was not a good man. I think other people knew that as well," he said. "Maybe there were people in the IRA, in *Sinn Féin*, who really didn't care that he just disappeared. I suspect he knew his drop boat was going to be intercepted. Suspect he was working for the money, anybody's money, and not the cause.

"Anyway, another man without a name came to me, in Dublin, asked me what happened. I told him the man had been drinking my Irish whiskey, full bottle of it, after the transfer went to shit. I said he'd went on deck and there had been some sort of an accident. Not sure if I was believed or not, but I was told to talk no more of it, and no other nameless man came to visit.

"The times were changin', at least some people were tryin' to change 'em. Maybe that man I killed was an obstacle to that change. Maybe they thought he'd finally paid God's price for his evil. Maybe. I guess I'll find out. I waited for a few months for a stranger to come up to me, on some dark street. But that night never came. That man never came.

"Anyway, nobody ever talked to me again about that night. Not the men with me on that ship. Not a man since. You're the only soul I ever told about my meeting with the devil. Not even a priest. Guess this be my confession box."

"Seems fitting," I said. "At sea."

"Does indeed," Mully said.

I knew we would never speak of it again.

I did a little research later, however.

I found news reports of a trawler being intercepted off County Donegal, but no mention of the *Traverse City*. Apparently an Irish Republic citizen and an American citizen were caught onboard, turned over to Irish Republic authorities and, eventually, sentenced to 10 years in prison in Portlaoise Prison, which is nowhere near Northern Ireland.

I also found a story about someone who could have been "that man" but might not have been. An IRA captain had disappeared. Lots of people disappeared in Northern Ireland.

I decided the story was not of a bad man dying, anyway. At least the story I wanted to tell. It was a story of a man who made a choice, first to help the revolution for a young Irish lad and then to rebuke the revolution for a young British lad. The story of a man who lived with the terrible consequences of his choice the rest of his life. That was the story I wanted, the one I took away from that day, in that North Channel confession box.

We pulled into Carrickfergus late that day. The harbor has an old castle that looks like it could have been a prison at some point in its life. Mully shook my hand as I disembarked onto an old stone quay, but merely wished me a safe return. Ian helped me ashore and made sure I had a taxi to take me into Belfast. Ian explained that they would spend the night but be out first light in the morning.

"Mully doesn't care for Ulster," Ian said as we waited for the taxi. "I think he has a bit of bad history here. Think there be some men who'd he just as soon avoid, if you know what I mean. Ship captain makes enemies if he's any good. Bad crew members and the like. Anyway, we'll be off early."

The taxi came. As I rode away, I wondered how much Ian knew and didn't know. I bet he knew nothing.

Old Mulligan was good with secrets.

How do you write what you know about a thing when you know almost nothing about that thing?

It is one of the great hurdles an honest writer must face. You can pretend to know about a particular place, a time, what is the mind of a particular person in that place and time. You can pontificate, pass what limited knowledge of the subject you possess on to people with less knowledge, and ignore the questions and comments of those who know more. I have never been able lie to myself about such things: I know my limits, personal and professional. I guess that is why I chose fiction as my genre of choice; when you make up stuff it is hard to get your facts wrong.

The problem I was facing with my Irish novel was making it sound historical while it had very little actual history in it. I was creating a place, a time, getting inside the mind of particular persons in that place and time, but very little of it had I actually lived. The truth is that you really do not know a thing unless you have lived it. Hemingway knew this, as did others, but in my mind he is the most honest advocate of simply writing what you have lived, of blending fictional storylines into real stories. The Ol' Man's fictional characters, I think, live in a world he had seen, and touched, and been touched by.

But, with much of Hemingway and with others, the ability to bring realism into a story is best when balanced with the ability to write something the reader will actually care to read. One can write something full of verifiable facts, full of dates and description and dissertation, and still not capture the nature of the place and time, and certainly not capture an audience. Many travelogues, and restaurant reviews, are that way: they describe a thing accurately yet do not allow the reader to really see it, or taste it.

Conversely, one can also write in a way that places the reader in a real place, in a real time, that actually never existed, a place and time as seen through the eyes of a person who, also, never existed. I have read great science fiction where I knew nothing was real and, yet, I believed that it could be or could have been, that it should be or should have been.

I guess that was the question that was rattling around my mind when I arrived in Belfast that first evening, as a writer trying to write an updated version of a 100-year-old Irish fairy tale.

When it came to Belfast, to Northern Ireland, to The Troubles, I wanted to write what I knew to be true, but knew that I did not live it and could not live it, and so could never really write something that had a snowball's chance in hell of approaching Hemingway's truth.

My book, whatever it ended up finally being, had to have my characters live through or die some period of the great Irish nightmare. But I wondered if I could ever really detail it, define it, defend or condemn it. I would leave that to Sinéad and to all the writers whose stories confronted The Troubles because they had, in some degree of proximity, lived it. I would let them wrestle with the beast that is "the truth".

My story, like the script of the film version of *The Quiet Man*, really had little need of the truth. At least that was the lie I was telling myself, a lie writers tell themselves to get them through the night and through the first draft of their books. And, anyway, I decided that I understood sufficiently the facts surrounding The Troubles, from my research, from Sinéad and Mully, and a dozen other people with lessor stories I had been told.

Or was that just another lie I told myself, I wondered, as I sat alone, finishing my first tumbler of whiskey, on ice of course, trying to fill idle time and drown a swirling maelstrom of thoughts.

As Cathleen liked to say, I'd been thinking too damn much.

Throughout my glorious voyage north, maybe the only problem was that I had too much time to think, too much to think about, to brood about. I pondered my book's past and future, reasons to live and to die, reasons to kill and be killed, and reasons to simply accept the fates and patiently await the end of my fictional world.

But my place, my future, in the real world was always there as well.

At the end of my first day in Belfast, I wanted to bury my wandering mind and make sure I slept solid on *terra firma* after several nights of being rocked to sleep by the ocean. I thought a little whiskey would do the trick.

The Northern Ireland bred Bushmills Single Malt 16, straight up, did the trick, I noted in my notebook the morning after. It was smooth but still kicked like a mule in heat as I sat on my barstool at a massive wooden bar in the spacious restaurant of the Ten Square Hotel, a modern reincarnation of a Victorian linen warehouse dating from the 1860s and located the heart of Belfast City Centre.

That particular barstool quickly became *my seat*. I hated sitting alone at a restaurant dining table and did not mind eating meals at a bar. After the first night, I took it as a good omen that the same seat was open when I wanted it and took it a bad omen if I did not take it. So over the span of my stay, my butt was in that chair four more times, once with lunch but this time with a pint, and three times for breakfast with a strong, overly bitter cup of a muddy liquid I was advised was "norn iron coffee". "Norn iron" was the nearest I could translate the slurred pronunciation of Northern Ireland the locals gave their general locality. The coffee, if it was really that, demanded sugar and milk, which I rarely needed but did in this case.

I lost track of my days, pleasingly so, at sea and without any schedule. So the events of my first two days in Belfast are jumbled both in my memories and in my notebook, pleasingly so. Time spent in Belfast is, however, beautiful and ugly and fascinating; a time out of mind.

I created my own walking tour of the City Centre the first afternoon, starting right after a small white taxi of unknown make picked me up at the Carrickfergus and then dropped me off at the Ten Square Hotel, where I immediately showered several days of sea salt and unforgettable adventure off before setting off to find a meal and my land-legs, and ending with my first Bushmills 16.

I was never really out of sight of the hotel. After admiring the Linen Hall Library, a library better described as a beautiful bookstore, almost next door to the hotel, I simply walked around and admired the magnificent City Hall building, which is the focal point of Donegall Square, the roundabout that circled the cathedral-like structure that I was to learn is the heart of the City Centre.

The City Hall building dates from the 1880s, when the good Queen Victoria finally decided to get around to calling Belfast a "city". It is surrounded by park-like landscaping but is built of a stone in a style that would make a medieval castle maker proud. Actually, I read somewhere its architecture is that of a Baroque Revival style that resembles London's Old Bailey, or so some staunch Unionists claim. It has an enclosed courtyard, which I could not see the first night and made a point of seeing the next day. But its most distinctive sight is its four towers—that castle thing again—and its lantern-crowned copper dome that has a patina of weathered green; not quite Irish green, but close.

The building, though, is also another example of the continuing internal struggle of the city and its division-wall-building neighborhoods. City Hall used to fly the Union Jack each day but in 2012, I read, the city council voted to limit the flag flying to certain days, like two weeks' of special days to the Unionist communities, a vote that was followed by a night of protest and sporadic violence.

Anyway, two leisurely trips around the building, around the square, was enough the first night for me to be seeking a pub and dinner, both of which I quickly found by walking up May Street, on the back side of City Hall and headed towards the River Lagen. The Duke of Hillsboro pub had cold Bass ale and a meat pie, and after the whiskey nightcap back at the hotel, I crashed hard.

Despite a good night's sleep in a real bed, the next day was still a day lost in transit.

It was a "slack day", as Sinéad had called it, a day she built into the itinerary of my Belfast reading just in case of sea-borne delays. Her phone message, which I missed while touring City Hall the day before, informed me she'd arranged for me to take a Black Taxi tour of Belfast that day, the driver of which would serve as a "stand-in guide" until she arrived. I could decline the tour, of course, but I trusted her, had no better idea, and carried low expectations for the tourist tour.

I should have known better that to question Sinéad's knowledge of my likes and dislikes, and reset my expectations when I was met by a driver of very high knowledge but few words driving in a solid-black unmarked Mercedes-Benz towncar.

"The good Mr. Maybourn, of Gleninagh North," the driver had said as he stepped quickly to open my door after pulling up at the hotel at the appointed time.

"Daniel's my name," he added, holding out his hand to shake after opening the door. "Sinéad told me you were a quiet man."

I guess I must have given him a queer look.

"I understand you're a man likes quiet more 'an noise. Likes to see more 'an being told. She said you'd want a tour without the history babble the usual American tourist wants. Said you know a bit more than the usual. "

"That was nice of her to say," I answered. "And how do you know her?"

"My nephew went to school with her, in Dublin. Her business came to me through him. Likes to make plans, wants them carried out, she does. Very precise. I like that in a woman. But you know that, I be guessin'. Said you already knew a good bit about my city and just wanted to see little more of what's in the history books. Get your bearings."

"Sounds right."

"Then I'll show you the neighborhoods, the murals. We have what the management calls the mural tour, but I'll be leaving off some of the list and showing you some others that I prefer. They tell the stories much better than I ever could anyway. If you have any questions, I'll give it my best."

Listening to Daniel, as little as I did that day, made me think he was an English import to the city. There was something different about the way he and others "Belfastians" talk. Daniel was born and bred Irish, I found out. But there was a definite, shall we say, English influence.

It was good to add an English lilt into my impressions of the Northern Ireland voice.

The more I saw that day, the more I put living faces to places, and physical places to locations in print, I decided Belfast was as much an English city as it was an Irish city. And the more I learned that day and since, I have decided the history of Belfast is the history of an English city for the current majority of its people.

"Norn Iron", as Daniel also pronounced his homeland, could also be a definition of the intestinal fortitude of the people. Like the rest of the island, the Belfast area was pretty much a land of unruly and unfriendly prehistoric Bronze Age and Iron Age warriors until the Anglo Normans arrived from England in the 12th Century and started building castles, importing a more docile population, and beginning the animosity between the conquering English and the native Irish.

But, I decided, if you want to see why Belfast's modern history and majority population leans toward the English, one must look not at what was built in Belfast from the 1600s through the 1800s but what was destroyed in the 1900s.

While I expected, and was not disappointed, with the mural evidence of violence and destruction wrought by The Troubles, it was the devastation and resilience of the city, both physical and mental, during and following World War II that surprised me.

The Republic of Ireland was officially neutral in World War II. It maintained diplomatic relations with Nazi Germany throughout the war but was a willing participant in supplying the allies with military intelligence and an unofficial safe haven for allied ships and aircraft. But Northern Ireland in general and Belfast in specific was fiercely loyal to the British cause and, thus, was considered fair game to the Germans.

The Belfast Blitz, as it has come to be called, was a series of four bombing raids by the *Luftwaffe* in April and May of 1941, the largest, the Easter Raid on April 15, reportedly saw 200 German bombers hammering the city's manufacturing centers. Almost a thousand people were killed and twice that number injured. The destruction of Belfast's historic buildings are a scar that can still be seen today. Outside of the bombing of London itself, Belfast suffered more destruction at the hand of German air forces than any other English city.

Great Britain never forgot Belfast's bloody allegiance, a famous quote from Winston Churchill after the war made his country's feelings very clear:

"But for the loyalty of Northern Ireland and its devotion to what has now become the cause of thirty governments or nations, we should have been confronted with slavery and death, and the light which now shines so strongly throughout the world would have been quenched."

Churchill, and leaders who followed him, also probably never forgave the Irish Republic's neutrality at a time of Britain's ultimate peril.

For that reason, not to mention a Protestant church pew full of other reasons, the majority of Belfast's population just has the feel of an English population.

I first felt a little like I was in London, that late afternoon when the taxi Ian had called dropped me off in the City Centre for the first time, as I caught my first sight of Belfast City Hall, the first landmark. It felt even more like an English city with Daniel and my Black Taxi tour, when I was more in the mood to notice details. I noticed the street-facing main entrance of the three-story hotel, with its carved faces two famous Brits, a famous American who once fought for the British, and an Italian who probably never expended an ounce of his almost endless intellect to far-away *Éire*: William Shakespeare, Isaac Newton, George Washington and Michelangelo.

While City Centre reminded me of London, the suburbs of the city through which Daniel drove me were like nothing I had ever seen.

My tour guide drove me slowly through a variety of neighborhoods, some populated with middle-class homes, nice homes of various vintage, some with not-so-nice houses and massive apartment complexes that would be called "the projects" in late 20th Century America. Each neighborhood had its distinctive feel and each had its wall.

Every wall was covered with a range of artwork from simple graffiti to beautiful murals. Some were windowless sides of businesses, or upper stories or warehouses, or standalone walls separating neighborhoods and people. Several were subtly gruesome, some stunningly beautiful. Many are indelible: a large building with an entire wall covered with an elaborate mural showing a rose garden and a bombed-church and the words "Peace cannot be kept by force" and "It can only be achieved by understanding" and a small building with one wall covered with a crude mural depicting a black-hooded, rifle-toting Loyalist fighter and the words "You are now entering Loyalist Sandy Row" and "Heartland of the South Belfast Ulster freedom fighters".

When asked, Daniel told me there are records of as many as 2,000 murals produced in the city and its suburbs since the artistic battle officially began, with some preserved and some painted, defaced, and painted over again.

"Our ever-changing exhibit started in 1908, they say, with one of William of Orange on a horse celebrating his victory at Boyne over James the Second. Protestant over Catholic. Lots of Orange murals after the partition in the '20s. Mostly patriotic

319

and religious in nature, but in the '70s and '80s it became an
artistic battlefield. The Troubles documented, some say."

Some of the oldest ones, I noticed, especially long Shankill
Road, show the faces and stories of those who died during the
height of the bloody years, including a much-photographed
image of Bobby Sands. The newest ones, however, are more
hopeful for the future instead of looking toward the past —
discounting one which pays macabre tribute to the tragic demise
of the Titanic, built in Belfast between 1909-12, and which has
become a curious tourist attraction.

"Covering up bad memories of those who lived through The
Troubles with the bad memories of people long since dead,"
Daniel poetically said, when I asked.

The Black Taxi tour with Daniel was mostly quiet, however.
It lasted almost four hours, with the mood broken by a stop in a
rural suburban pub for lunch.

"Can I offer you a bit of lunch at a neighborhood place,"
David had asked a couple hours into the tour.

"I would like that," I said.

And we stopped within a minute or two, at a clean, brick,
corner building in a neighborhood of clean, brick, row houses, a
place where the driver was known and I was welcomed after
being introduced to the regulars by another regular. It was called
Molly's and I could not find it again if my life depended on it. I
had tea—too early and too much reverence for the content of
the tour to start drinking—and took the recommendation of
smoked mackerel on thick toast with a salad. He had the same.
We talked a little about football, a little about my touring and his
annual vacation to Portugal, and a little about my book; nothing
about what he was showing me and I was witnessing. The only
time we talked local politics, or the politics of the local religions,
was when I asked about a flag on the wall of the establishment:

an orange field with a star in one corner and a red cross on white in another corner.

"Orange Order," he said, looking at my face to see if I knew.

I had some idea: Protestant fraternal organization, sort of the Masonic Order of the Loyalist side, to put it all too simply. Best known for their yearly marches, and the pride and derision derived, as supporters, if not the fountainhead of, Unionist extremist violence in The Troubles. I recalled something called the Royal Black as being a more exclusive, more secretive offshoot.

I nodded, did not being up the topic of the Royal Blacks.

"Not a member myself," he said. "What you might call a Protestant peacenik."

Sometimes, the more you find out about someone, the less you really know.

Anyway, even with that detour into his personal life, lunch was dominated by bland, pleasant discussion. I tried to pay for the meal for both of us, but he said Sinéad had taken care of it, and I did not doubt it.

She is, as David had pointed out, all about the plans.

When he dropped me back off at the hotel, he ran around to get my door again, but this time I beat him to the punch. I tried to tip him for his time, and his perfect, delicate, balance of infomercial, small talk and silence. He declined again; again evoking Sinéad's prior planning.

"Just write the truth of my Norn Iron," he said, as we shook hands again. "Write it as you seen it."

I think that is all anybody who has ever taken the Loyalist cause in Northern Ireland wants: the truth and the tragedy of both sides told.

I guessed that Sinéad had told him I was an American writer, but not what kind. Maybe he thought I was a journalist with the

New York Times, or a university professor, writing another version of the first draft of history but probably not a fiction novelist writing a love story based on a feckin fairy tale with history being only a backdrop.

As I turned and walked into the hotel, I wished I were a better writer.

Later that evening, after a nap and a shower, and a couple of whiskey on the rocks before and during a steak dinner at a City Centre restaurant with white napkins and mood lighting, but nowhere near the ambiance of Molly's, I thought, at least in some limited way, I knew Norn Iron better. Maybe I could, in a limited way, write about it a little more Hemingway-esque. Sleep came deep and dreamless that night; maybe it was finally being back on land and maybe the two drinks.

* * *

I was still brooding about my ability to write the truth as I sat on my barstool at the Ten Square Hotel, awaiting my regular tour guide.

She arrived promptly at 9 a.m., in business casual with a black skirt, blue blouse and dark green sweater.

"You look like you've been at sea for a month," she said as she approached, noticing, I guessed, the colorful sunburn and windburn outlines around my eyes from sunglasses and under my chin from keeping my head low while on deck.

"Does it make me look manly?"

"A little older, actually," she said, as I stood and we hugged in a kind of "old friend, if not father-daughter" way.

"Rugged, though," she continued as we parted. "That'll make the press photos better. More dignified. Not so much the pasty American."

"No offense intended, I assume," I said.

We both laughed as we sat down.

"So," I said. "I have a linguistic bone to pick with you."

"And that being?"

"Putting aside your Dublin friends and enemies, an uncle of a friend gets to call you Sinéad, but you're still Jenn to me?"

"Daniel?"

"Yes. And a prefect guide, I might add. Not as good as you, but perfect."

"Jenn is kind of a business thing, I guess. Representin' an American company, I guess. Most Americans, lots of Euros, can't handle the pronunciation."

"*She nade*," I said again. Two syllables, soft on the first and long on the "*a*" in the second.

"Good enough," she said. "But only if I can call you Mahon."

She pronounced it as one syllable; like "mound" without the "d".

"Modern Gaelic for Matthew," she continued.

I liked it. It sounded Irish to me: short, simple, to the point.

"I like it," I said. "Deal."

I knew I was not really a *Mahon*, but at least I had found a name for a character in the book. But there was no doubt in my mind this young woman was a *Sinéad*. She was Irish.

Cathleen was traditional Irish; Sinéad was modern Irish.

And I liked them both. A lot.

Sinéad looked at my coffee and bowl of oatmeal, both mostly consumed.

"You stayed away from the Ulster Fry, I see," she said.

I looked confused; she continued.

"Ulster Fry. Breakfast of eggs, meats, breads, tomatoes. All sorts of shite. All fried."

"Glad I don't know what the hell you're talking about."

A waitress approached. Sinéad glanced at me. I waved my hand over the remains of my breakfast. "I'm done," I said, declining an offered pour of more coffee. Sinéad asked to make sure I was putting the meal on the hotel tab, which I was. And she retrieved a few coins from a small purse to be left for tip.

"Good driving tour with Daniel?" she asked.

"Quietly brutal. I felt overwhelmed."

"City'll do that to you."

I nodded. She, I knew, knew how quietly brutal Belfast could be.

"Yep," I said.

She nodded.

As we stepped outside, I took another glance back at the façade, and the famous faces.

I was glad she chose the hotel she chose, for several reasons. Not the least of which is that it apparently is the hotel of choice for entertainment celebs visiting the city. I did not check the price per room, but I figured it was not cheap. Also figured it was either a reward for passing her manuscript on to Saul the elder, maybe her idea, maybe Saul's. Or it was the perfect setting for "Hollywood type" to be staying while in Belfast—looked good for the local press and all.

Probably Sinéad's doing, but Saul's subtle touch could not be totally discounted.

Whatever. I learned long ago to not look a gift horse in the mouth as they say, and staying at the Ten Square allowed me to glimpse Elton John and his entourage parading out late the previous afternoon after my Black taxi mural tour.

At least I think it was Elton John; that's my story and I am sticking to it.

I was going to tell her the story but I figured she'd know if Sir Elton was in town and I did not want her to spoil my story.

"So, everything still as planned?" I said instead.

"As planned," she said. "Free day today, just more time than there might have been. I'll tourist you until you say you're done. Reading tomorrow morning, then a slow Saturday train back south later in the day."

I counted the days.

"So today is Friday?"

"You really were at sea too long," she said. "You need any help getting home from Galway?"

"Nope. Cathleen will be there."

"Cathleen?"

I smiled. "You don't know everything about me, young lady."

"Damn glad o' that." She smiled.

That reminded me, I needed to buy a bottle of Jameson Black for the woman picking me up from the train station.

All and all, Sinéad had reacted well to my "get there when I get there" ocean transit north. I had phoned her on our last night in port before arrival, and she'd set everything into motion. The Black Taxi driving tour, she said, was set up as insurance for the uncertainty of my transit. We would have taken the same tour no matter the day, the only difference was that she'd not be accompanying me one day and would on the next. No matter, the reading would take place on Saturday at a bookstore simply called The Bookshelf in the Victoria Square shopping center.

"Anything specific attract your interest in the city as you drove around?" she asked, as we stood on the sidewalk and bustling Belfast's morning rush flowed around us.

"I have had enough of the murals, The Troubles and the Titanic, for one visit anyway."

She took me at my word. We made plans for a tour of art, both public and in gallery, a fine English garden, and an even finer dinner after a day of beauty, just to balance my opinion of the city.

"I have already checked out the City Hall square," I said. "But I do have my walking shoes on."

"I thought so," she said, pointing out her shoes, which for the first time I noticed were bright red tennis shoes that clashed with her business casual. "We're beyond my needing to impress you with my business attire."

She was way past needing to do anything more to impress me. I wished again, for just a fleeting moment, that I were 30 years younger. Then it came to me that in 30 years Sinéad would probably look exactly like Cathleen looks now, only with tats.

"Beacon of Hope?" she asked, as we walked down the street. "You see the *Nuala* yet?"

I had not seen it, but had read about it.

Maybe the most hopeful of Belfast's public art, if not the most interesting, "Beacon of Hope" is a metal sculpture by Andy Scott, erected in 2007 on the Queens Bridge, one of several which span the River Lagen in City Centre. It was nicknamed the "Thanksgiving Statue" by someone without much imagination, due to it being in an area called the Thanksgiving Square for reasons I somehow missed. But it was also nicknamed the "Nuala with the Hula" by someone with an overabundance of imagination.

We walked to the Queens Bridge, passing Victoria Square shopping center, where the bookshop was located, but not much else was of note as I could see. It looked like any other modern city center in Ireland, or England for that matter.

As we headed toward *Nuala*, we walked leisurely along the river for a while, passed something called Waterfront Hall:

nothing special as a concert hall I was told, but modern in design and another sign of hard-fought change coming to the city of walls and murals. Maybe the statue was another sign of change, at least hope for change.

"Strange name, *Nuala*," Sinéad explained as we stood on the bridge in the statue's ringed shadow. "Gaelic feminine, from Irish mythology, fair haired or queen of the fairies. At least Wikipedia says so. Not sure I've read that definition anywhere else."

I remember little of the nondescript scenery, and little of the insignificant talk, as we continued to walk along the river. There was something called the Big Fish, literally a big blue fish. Mostly I remember the pleasure of the casual walk and casual talk. We talked about my book, and her book. We talked as writers and friends would talk. We talked about state of the world and we talked about nothing. When the conversation lagged, Sinéad flagged a taxi.

"We'll drive by St. Anne's Cathedral," she said. "That's a must-see. Survived the war, survived The Troubles. She's not really all that grand but she's a tough ol' bird."

We passed the Albert Memorial Clock, maybe Belfast's most famous tourist landmark, on the ride to St. Anne's.

"The clock is leaning, like Pisa, you know," she pointed out.

I did not know.

"It was once the place where the sailors met the ladies of the night," she added. "Not so much anymore, but it does have a certain reputation. Young love and all. Damaged by a bomb the Provs took credit for, in '92 as I remember the story. You know?"

Another fact I did not know. Landmarks, like just about everything else in the city, means different things to different people.

Before the day trip ended I was shown a great overview of the lay of the land, literally, from Cavehill, north of City Centre.

Also had a good walk at Belfast Botanical Gardens, south of City Centre. In between, and much to my surprise, I gained a haunting reminder that in Belfast there is no escaping the faces of The Troubles.

Cavehill offers a great view of Belfast city, the Lough and the Mourne Mountains beyond. Some say the area was the inspiration for the location of Jonathan Swift's *Gulliver's Travels* as Cavehill might, to some, resemble the form of a sleeping giant. Nice story, but I did not see it.

The highlight of the walk around the Botanic Gardens was the Victorian glasshouse, with its humidity loving exotic plants and its ornate dome. It was a lovely place to take a peaceful step back in time, into the city's past.

But at the Ulster Museum, a stop we made to view some modern art, I was not only able to see the city's often bright artistic present and future, but also its inescapable past. The problem with intentionally trying to avoid The Troubles, I have come to realize, is that everything you see must be seen through the filter of those years. Like a bad wound, the memory and its aftermath can't be avoided.

The art show was called "Silent Testimony". The artist was Colin Davidson, and his art was a series of rough but deeply expressive portraits of people who had stories to tell: stories of loss resulting from The Troubles, stories of dead fathers, mothers, husbands, sons and daughters, and other family. One of the subjects was blinded by the violence, another paralyzed.

I didn't even have to read their stories. In fact I did not want to. I wanted to *read* the paintings, the faces; I wanted to see their loss, not what caused the loss. These were ordinary people, not the faces on the murals, but faces of the people who walked by the murals every day, who try as they might to walk past the images, The Troubles, but could never, will never. In Belfast, there is no escaping it. And I knew that however insufficient my ability to bring it into my story of Ireland, it must be there.

The day ended, at about 6 p.m., as promised, with a fine dinner at The Mourne Seafood Bar. The specialty is, apparently, a plate of oysters. I've never did like such things, though, so I had some good salmon and pint of ale. There was more good conversation but none of it about the Ulster Museum's show.

The next morning, as I sat at my usual seat in the restaurant's bar area, I relaxed over the bad coffee and selectively picked at an Ulster fry, which I had to try mostly because I was warned against it. As I nibbled, tested and rejected most of my breakfast, I read a newspaper and, like the Davidson paintings, understood that the loss and suffering was not yet a thing of the past.

There was an article in the paper about a man who was shot dead overnight in East Belfast, in an area called Short Strand. The man was a father of nine and apparently a "former member of the IRA." The man, the story reported, was one of the suspects in a shooting six months earlier of another man, a "former member of the Provisional IRA."

"Sinn Féin has denied speculation that Provisional IRA may have been involved in his murder," the article stated.

Somehow, I saw the face of one of the young women in Davidson's paintings when I thought about the nine children the murdered man left behind.

As I read, and sipped, and pushed aside the unpleasant aspects of the Ulster Fry, I jotted some notes.

First, I noted that despite desperate, heartfelt and probably productive efforts to move forward as a society, there is no escape in this city or in this country from nearly a century of violence that left both deep scars and fresh bruises. I guessed that I would get little argument from Sinéad, or anyone, on that point.

One tourist slogan I noticed states: "There's more to Belfast than walls." But there are all those damned walls. While the open warfare has waned, replaced by everyday sectarian benevolence and the settling of old political grudges, there is still a clear need to separate Protestant and Catholic neighborhoods, often with real walls when social walls do not completely serve the purpose of separating those who believe in a united, if not Catholic, Ireland and those who believe that there never was and never will be a united Ireland. There is no denying, no matter your Irish political persuasion, that both sides have been innocent victims and both sides have been justly vilified, before, during and in the aftermath of The Troubles. But there is also little argument that it will take the passing of a generation or two to allow the breathing space for the next generation to hide if not forget the scars and stop inflicting new wounds.

I also expounded on my observations from the first day, an observation I quite possibly would have to defend with argument should I say it discreetly to Sinéad and possibly with fists should I say it aloud in any pub in the Republic: that Belfast is not an Irish city but an English city that just happens to be located on *Éire*.

There was something about the City Centre, about Victoria's square and the Queen's bridge and Albert's tower, yes. But there was also something about David and his Black Taxi and his Orange order. There was something very English, very stiff upper lip, about how the citizens of the city, and *Norn Iron*, on both sides of the walls, hold themselves in the face of the aftermath of the Good Friday Agreement, in the face of a process that will take decades to fully come to fruition. I read that the possible, probable, eventual outcome will be a united Ireland but only after the Northern Ireland Protestant majority and the Catholic minority are reversed, which population trends suggest will happen, but not for a generation or two. At that time, there is expected to be votes, both in the north and in the Republic, on unification.

I would not want to bet on the outcome of such a vote, on either side of the border and the issue. I wonder if Belfast can ever be anything other than what it has been for centuries: an English city.

I decided as I finished my coffee and prepared to head off for the bookstore that I could never put that idea down in print. One needs to know when, and where, to keep your mouth shut and your opinions to yourself.

The reading passed without much to note. The routine at the bookstore was, well, routine. Sinéad was all business. The very British-sounding owner of the bookstore was all business. The well-dressed but fairly small crowd listened politely, asked mostly about Hollywood and Jasper Kelly, and bought a few books. The most interesting thing was when I realized I had a shadow, a photographer.

"BBC," Sinéad told me. "His name is Chukwuemeka. Wants to catch you in context of these readings. He'll be with the reporter at the interview. The BBC, they do things right."

She introduced the photographer to me at one point, said his name again. Wasn't sure if it were first, last or even mattered; could not repeat it if I tried, so his name slipped away in the blur that was the reading. Not only did he take some shots at the reading and the book signing, he asked and I acquiesced to a quick series of posed shots outside on the street with crowds of people moving around me. The photographer was very dark skinned, African of origin I guessed, but his accent was perfectly British.

Three hours later, after I called Cathleen and left a message telling her which train I would be on and my expected arrival time, I was surprisingly at ease.

I was lying to myself again.

I could write a great novel of Ireland and not fully understand or even adequately explain The Troubles. I decided on this new lie as I sipped a Coke and stood in a crowd in the Belfast Central railway station, awaiting the start of my trip back to Galway, and looked at faces of people I did not know but who I knew had, at least some of them, lived Hemingway's truth.

Any real understanding of The Troubles was beyond my reach, let alone my grasp. But I did not need to understand it all to detail the pain — the truths — that were in the faces, in the eyes, of people I did know, that I had seen, on the ocean and in the art gallery. I realized my life, however grand or barren, is, in the end, the only world I will ever know with any degree of truthfulness.

I called up my U2 playlist on my iPhone when I settled in for the trip. For some reason, I decided to start with *Achtung Baby*. I liked the album but rarely played it. The first song up on random was *Until the End of the World*. It seemed fitting somehow. The song really had nothing to do with Northern Ireland or The Troubles. It was about Judas and Jesus. But it made me think of Mully. I couldn't grasp why.

* * *

Cathleen waited for me at the train station.

There were several women waiting, as women have always waited for their men to return. In the opening scene in *The Quiet Man*, a solitary old woman stands and scans the train windows of a recently arrived train. The film viewer never finds out who she is waiting for, not John Wayne's Sean Thornton, that is for sure. It is, I think, a classic Irish image: the woman waiting, either in vain or with relief, for the train, for the return.

A dozen solitary men detrained with me. Maybe my train was one which middle-class businessmen used to return home from a day or week on the road. Maybe it was something else.

In addition to the men, there were also a solitary old woman moving gingerly—that is what reminded me of the film—as well as a couple of young couples bouncing with energy, and one family wherein a harried couple was trying to shepherd three well-dressed but wayward children and two large suitcases.

I first paused to see if the old woman needed a hand climbing down from the railcar; she did not: she moved slowly but with a firm purpose and firm grip on her cane.

The disembarking men looked around, searching, eventually finding a remembered face, a slight smile, a joyful wave, and the recognition that home is often not a place but a face.

Each time I return to Galway now, I too feel as though I am returning home.

I pick Cathleen out of the crowd of waiting women. There are others waiting: a few, with her dark hair and beautiful eyes, but they are younger, or older; they are taller or shorter, heavier or thinner. She stands out.

She looks around and has not yet seen me.

I stand and watch until her eyes fall on me, in the crowd, in the moment. A big smile comes across her face. Her eyes shine bright.

We allow the crowd to move away, first away from me, then past her, and then we step closer. I carry my small suitcase in one hand and a jacket in the other. We say nothing as we draw close and she leans in, gives me a gentle kiss on the cheek, a welcoming kiss.

"It's been a while since I was welcomed home like that," I say.

"Been a while since I cared to welcome someone home that way," she says, as she leans back and glances at me head to toe and back to head.

"You look like the sea agrees with you."

"You mean the sunburn?"

"That too, but there is, ah, a certain brightness to ya."

"Thanks."

We turn and start to walk, side-by-side, toward the exit of the station together.

"Thanks for picking me up."

"I'm glad I could do it," she says. "I had some business Galway. Told you that, didn't I?"

"Ya."

We walk in silence, like our minds are both somewhere else.

We find her car in the parking lot. Before I get in I look to the west, it is still a couple hours to dusk, but the sun is low. There is also, I think, an autumn chill in the air.

The Athenry station is easy to get out of, and we are heading west toward Oranmore quickly. I still do not know the roads very well, but I have good idea of the cities and towns, what road leads to what town. We talk a little, about nothing really. The weather, the fact that it is mid-August and fall is starting early in Galway.

"Not as colorful as America," she points out. "But trees are turning early this year. A good omen in Ireland, fall starting early. We are all about the fall. *Samhain*. Look it up. Quite a tradition."

The silence returns, for several miles, and it seems a little awkward.

"You're a bit quiet," she says, finally.

"Belfast. *Norn Iron*. You know," I say, attempting to imitate.

She smiles at my attempt.

"It's overwhelming, true enough. A lot to take in, to try to understand. Lot of sadness. Lot of hate. My visits there are as short as they can be. Can't wait to get back to Galway."

"I guess," I say, then the writer in me takes over and I search for the perfect words but can't find them. "There is something else."

"There is, isn't there."

The silence returns, and we drive on for a few minutes. Then she breaks the silence again.

"Care for a little walk before we finish the drive to Gleninagh?"

"I'd like that."

"I know a nice place for a view this time of day."

She proceeds to get me totally lost right outside of Oranmore, when she gets off the highway. We pass through farmland, much of Irish rural farmland looks similar: rock walls, green, sometimes amber pastures, varied animals and crops. We pass a place called Renville, then a place called Cregcarragh. It is land's end. It is flat and there are only farmlands stretching out like a finger into the bay, the west horizon is, maybe, the Atlantic.

She parks.

Without waiting for me, without speaking a word, she climbs out of the car and walks away, to a little high point. I scramble out and walk a step or two behind her. She stops, looks west, to the distance. She does not look back as I approach, but I hear her voice.

"America is out there," she says, looking past the land's end.

"Gleninagh is there," she adds, this time pointing out a high point on the south shore.

"It is beautiful," I say, as I stop an arm's length behind her.

"It is," she says. "Thought you might like it. But it is the saddest place I know Matty."

I look where she looks, to the distance, and try to see what she sees.

"I came here when my husband left," she says, finally.

I move closer, try to wrap my arms around her, but she moves away, just a step.

She turns to me. Her face tightens, her lips pursed together in thought. Her eyes focus on mine.

"I want you to know something," she says. "Know, truth be told, that I'm little more than a good little Catholic girl grown old. I came close to not being that good Catholic girl with you. Wanted it something fierce. But that'll not happen again. If that's what you want, I'll have none of it. I'll be a friend if that's all ya need now. But I'll not simply be your lover. That's not who I am. Know that."

I nod, like I understand. I wonder if I really do understand.

Again a moment of harsh silence, of desired distance.

"So, where do we go from here?" I say, finally.

"We move on. Or we don't."

I look at her. I think she is shaking. It is cool here on the water's edge, but it is not *that* cold.

I wish I had a drink in me, maybe it might make me braver. I'm glad I don't have drink in me; it surely would make me say something stupid, if not cruel.

"Is it really that simple for you?" I say.

I guess I don't need a drink to say something cruel.

"It's not simple at all, Matty," she says. "I have no idea of my future. If you're even a part of it."

She pauses.

"I've made some mistakes in my life," she says. "I think there's not enough life left to make many more."

She pauses again, then it flows, in rhythm, like the lapping of the waves on the bay.

"I'm not sure how I sit in your mind, as you look forward, seek your future. But I want to make clear to you what I want, what I'm willing to accept.

"I look at myself, at my heart, and find it empty sometimes. I look at my future, too, and find it empty sometimes. I don't like the view. Sometimes I don't like the view from my own house. I look up that hill and see that white cottage in a different way these last months. I think of what the view would be from the swell of Gleninagh North. How it is different than just down where I am. How the sun would shine a little brighter in the spring and the breezes would blow a little more pleasant in the summer.

"Women, at least in the Irish Catholic house where I was raised, begin by allowing the possibility of a better future, of love, whatever the hell that is. Then we wait, if fate is kind, for that chance to be offered. Romance? It can be a grand thing or a pitiful, painful thing. And marriage? A husband? If fate is not unkind, you like him and accept him and maybe grow to love him. If fate is unkind, you endure.

"Happiness, maybe love, or only a sterile comfort as you grow old. Those are a woman's choices. That and whether to give herself completely or deny herself reluctantly, each in the good Catholic way.

"And I think of you, clean and mostly honest, and, despite what you say, so sure of your future. But you talk none of it."

I nod; think I understand.

"I've been thinking about that, my future," I say. "I know I'm going to write a good book, just not sure if I'll finish it here or back home. Not sure where my home is, I guess. I do know I am lonely and don't want to be. I knew that from the moment I met you. Lately I've been less lonely, been thinking a little different of the future. I just don't know …"

She nods.

"I see you, hear you," she says. "I can't always understand what you be thinking, but never really understood men. I do know one thing for sure, though, a man's future is his to decide."

She turns again, looks west.

I step up behind her, wrap my arms around her. This time she does not protest.

She pauses. Her hands come up, pull my arms a little tighter around her.

"I know what it is like to lose someone. I'll not say it's the same, but the only men I've ever loved are gone to me. Alive, but lost to me just the same. Know this, I'll not ask for all of you, if you even have that to give anymore. I'll not ask for your past, for you to forget, but if we move on, I'll want your future. Me and only me."

There is a big lump in my throat. I want to speak. I want to say something elegant, something from the heart, something poetic. But I say nothing.

I nod. I understand. I wonder if she can tell.

I am shaking, but it is still not *that* cold. I wonder if she notices.

We stand that way for another moment, or maybe it is an hour. The sun is setting over the heights of Gleninagh North.

Finally, she breaks my embrace. She turns and again looks at my face.

"That's all I'll say about that," she says, then she smiles a smile without joy.

I smile too, also a smile without joy.

She wants me to say something, I think, to give her some idea of what is on my mind. I search for something, words from the heart, something poetic. But I say nothing.

I am such shithead sometimes.

She waits. Then she leans forward, gives me a kiss on the cheek, and begins to walk back to the car.

The drive home is in silence.

When we arrive at her house and park, I pull out the bottle of Jameson Black from a pocket in my suitcase.

"A little thank you gift for bringing me home," I say. "A dull gift now, I guess."

She takes it. Looks at it. Looks at me.

"It will be of use this winter," she says. "Lovely old houses, ours. But chilly as hell in winter."

She turns and walks toward her house. Michaeleen has taken note of the car and us, sprints near and then stops abruptly. He looks at Cathleen, then looks at me, then turns and walks back toward the house with her.

"Cathleen," I say.

She turns. Michaeleen turns with her.

I really want to say something, anything, from the heart, poetic or not. But nothing comes.

"Thank you, Cathleen," I say, finally.

She nods, smiles a smile without joy.

"Have a good evening," she says, before she turns and continues to walk away.

Michaeleen looks at me, and he does not look all that happy either. He, too, turns and walks away.

I wonder if he too knows I am a shithead sometimes.

* * *

The day after my arrival back from Belfast, after a late afternoon trip to the grocery to restock my larder and refrigerator, I found myself alone, literally and emotionally.

There was a note under my door. Written on the outside is "Matthew". I am not sure I have ever seen Cathleen's handwriting, but I knew it was her's. I carry it inside the house, put it on a counter while I put away my purchases, and then pour myself a drink, a stiff vodka martini on the rocks, and carry the letter, my drink and my expectations out past the kitchen, out the back door, to the stone wall, where I sit.

I look out to the rock highlands, to The Burren. There is a perfume in the air: the fragrance of herbs, of sage and mint maybe, mixed with wild rose, now past its prime but still announcing its presence.

I expect the note's contents are filled with beauty, with clarity, with the equal portions of the mystery of romance and rejection: words of love, words of disappointment if not anger, words of farewell. I take a drink and open the envelope. It was not what I expected.

She is simply notifying a neighbor that she will be out of town for a few days, to London for a meeting with a client, and she had left Michaleen with a friend in Galway. I bet he hated that. I was almost hurt that she had not left my buddy in my care, but then again I might not be his buddy for much longer.

Expectations. In literature and life, rarely are they met.

I took another drink, a big one; set the glass down again, fold the note and put it back into the envelope, put it into my shirt pocket, over my heart, I realize.

I then looked out toward The Burren. There is a cold wind blowing from the west, from the Atlantic today. The landscape looks like it has been swept barren by the winds.

Caibidil a hAon Déag
(Chapter 11)

I am what some might call a formulaic writer, which is both
good and bad. It is why I have never won a major writing prize,
other than the ones book publishers give to writers who made
them a lot of money. I have made fair amount of money for my
publisher, my agent, and myself. Reward enough, I say.

Most literary works, throughout time, were written to a
certain "formula" with the formula that was expected or
appreciated in the writer's time in history and place in the world.
Two of the oldest known literary works, the ancient Greek *Iliad*,
and the even more ancient *Mahabharata*, were likely written as
epic poetry because that is what writers did in that age.

Almost all modern literary works are, in truth, formulaic: all
good and not-so-good mystery, the perfunctory steamy romance,
the by-the-book legal thriller or the *He*-man shoot 'em up novels.

But the writers of even great modern novels work to a
formula, that being completely different stylistically than
anything else ever written or read.

Sometimes it actually works: Norman Mailer's late 1960s
personal-journalism-as-literature masterpiece *The Armies of the
Night* or Jeffrey Eugenides' early 2000s blur of sexual identity,
Middlesex. Both Pulitzer Prize winners.

When I say I write to a formula, I mean that my genre of
crime novels have a certain rhythm, a certain sequence.

When I decide one of my story ideas, which I have a ton of,
is ready to become a novel, I have three things sketched out,

sometimes actually written in first draft: first is an introduction that will grab the readers somewhere deep, somewhere at a certain level of base instinct; second is a male character that has a heroic backstory, the logical motivation for unexpected future action, and at least one dramatic personal flaw, usually more, that allows for sometimes unheroic moments; third is an ending that wraps up the storyline and wraps up the reader into a warm fuzzy resolution blanket and a that feeling that, ultimately, life is good.

As the book progresses, and especially as it nears its end, the introduction changes very little. That is the inception of the story, you see, and if it were not pretty good thematic soil to begin nothing else would have grown from it. The *resumé* of the main male character often changes, but usually in subtle ways or due to dramatic icebergs that surface in the course of the writing which require justification or at least background explanation.

The ending, too, rarely changes. The details will morph, as my books carry me as much as I create them along a storyline. But the ultimate resolution of my hero's story I know. I must know it because even if the story does not end at that point, everything is anticlimactic after that point.

So, as I sat at my computer, half a French press carafe of strong black coffee already consumed and its delivered caffeine already roiling my brain, I fully expected I was ready to get cranking and start filling in the many blank pages in between the 20 or so passages I had already written on my great or maybe not-so-great novel of an American in Ireland.

My brain was excited but my fingers were paralyzed.

The problem, I decided, was that I had no formula for this strange, new life; this strange new story.

In the week since my return from Belfast, I wished, actually prayed in my own humble way to "the man upstairs," as I like to say. I needed someone or something to tell me what I should do. I was at one of divergent roads in my life. I knew it, I could feel it in my guts, in my heart.

I had, early on, written an ending to my Quiet Man sequel. Basically, an Irish-American boy meets Irish girl and lives happily ever after in Ireland. Jasper wanted a sequel to the movie and I damned well had to give it to him. That is the way the readers would expect it to end, the way Hollywood would expect it to end. But with everything I had learned, everything I had experienced, I wondered if it really should end that way.

My personal ambiguity was leading to a critical ambiguity in my novel's storyline.

Freud would have a field-day with that parallel quandary.

If a character in one of my books were to face such a decision, such ambiguity of action, I would simply create a plot device to subtly tell him what he should do, to justify to the reader what he was about to do.

I might simply write a scene where the man's dying wife provides foreshadowing, where he remembers one of the last times they talked.

"There are more good women in the world than there are good men, and you're a good man," she might say, in a final strong moment of her strong life, when her husband had the tears in his eyes. "Please keep me in your heart forever, but if you're lucky enough to find more love, you deserve it."

That bit of cliché might actually work in a romance novel, maybe, but Maggie and I had no such talk.

Our last few talks were not the stuff of bad tearjerker movies. In real life, real people do not talk of such things. The one that will carry on with life never even hints at things such as new love and remarriage in intimate, final or near final conversations, even if, down deep, the thought has crossed their mind. And the one that is dying? They might say what they think other people want them to say, out of love mostly, but I doubt that dying makes one care all that much about the future, theirs or anybody else's.

Dying is all about the present, and the past, both all too short.

I might also write a different scene that might tell my character what he should do. I might write one where a family member, maybe a daughter, or a friendly confidant, would give justification for taking this road, instead of another, at a moment of life's road's divergence. Life might even come full circle: good advice given would come back as good advice accepted, maybe.

"I remember what you told me, daddy," the man's daughter might say, either at a small table at an intimate coffee shop or over a Skype connection with a thousand miles between them. "Everyone deserves to be happy. To be happy you have to take chances in life, take chances with love. That's life. Sometimes you get hurt and sometimes you find happiness."

That, too, might work in a book, but Ally and I would have no such talk.

I am not even sure a man would want to talk to his daughter about the possibility of his life, of her life, changing in such as way. It would be unfair to put her in that position: to choose between the memory of her mother and the happiness of her father. It would hurt her, I think, even if she did not admit it to his face.

It had to be the man's decision. His family could accept his decision to move on when he was ready, forgive his decision if they disagreed; they would never forgive his forcing them to move on before they were ready. He had to live with that decision, and with the consequences, on himself as well as those he loved.

If I were a really good writer, one writing a really good book about Ireland, I might write another scene, one that actually sounded real. It would read like the brief conversation I could imagine having with Séamus, maybe one I wish I could have with Séamus.

I would hear a car drive up near my house, a car that sounded different than mine or Cathleen's.

I would go to the front window to see an old, muddy Land Rover. I would stand and watch as he gets out of the car, thinking first that he was coming to visit Cathleen. But then, with his usual degree of struggle, he would make his way up the hill toward my door.

I step out to meet him.

"Mister O'Dennehy," I would say.

"Mister Maybourn," he would answers.

"Not here to fight, and I've not had a drop all day."

"Since there be no fight, and since you're up her for some good reason, may I offer tea then?"

"Not today. Something to say and want to get it over with, get to my bottle."

"OK."

Séamus would straighten himself up, stand as tall as he could, I think. There is a certain set to his face, to his jaw. He is here for business.

"Cathleen and I had a good talk while you were gone."

"OK."

"Well," he would say, kind of still deciding what he wanted to say. "We talked. She and I. She made clear her view of the future, her's and mine. Guess there is none. Guess I knew that before. Probably talked 'bout that before, but I'm a little hardheaded, you might say."

I would say nothing.

"Kind of known for having a hard head."

He smiles, so I smile back.

"How's that right hand of yours?"

"Cracked a couple knuckles, I think," I would say, shaking my right hand.

"Good. Hard head of some use."

I would nod. We would smile again.

"Not such a good thing when it comes to women, though."

"That's my experience too," I say.

"Anyway, not here to talk such things," he would say, still unsure of his words. "Cathleen made it clear. She wants me to move on. Took that to mean that she wants to move on. Wants me to quit droppin' my shite all over her life. Didn't come right out and say it. But you know her, too damn nice of a woman to say hurtful things. Assume I'm not telling you anything ya don't already know."

"I didn't know she talked to you."

"Well she did."

"And did she talk about me?"

He looks at me, smiles.

"That," he would say, "that, as you once told me, is between you and her."

I nod. Stand accused of the things I done.

He is looking at me, saying nothing. So we both stood there, said nothing.

"You came up here to tell me that?" I, finally, would say.

"No," he says, once again forcing himself to stand as tall as his body would allow. "Came up here make something clear to ya."

"OK."

"Not my place to tell you what to do. None of my feckin business, I've been told that more than once. But loved her once, and she loved me I think. No more, but once. I know you know. Even a blind man can she now eyes you with a certain bit of happiness in her mind. She's not been happy for a while. Part of that my fault, part just the stones that come with the fields. None of us getting any younger and she has some happy years due to her. I can't do that for her, not now, not anymore. I think she has some hopes for those happy years due her."

He then looks at me, with the same look I have seen before, when he is ready to fight to prove his point.

"What I came here to tell you is this, man-to-man" he would say. "You got to do what's best, for you. I know you got family. Know you this famous writer. Hollywood type. I guess you just might belong to a world bigger than me, bigger than Cathleen, bigger than this little spot of God's green earth. I ask you, though, as the decent man I think you are, if you're leavin', then leave us without too much damage. And know this, Mr. Maybourn, if you lie to her, if you steal her hopes for those better years and then hurt her, I'll take that real personally. I get a chance, I'll be takin' another shot at kickin' your ass. And this time I will not be drunk, so know this too, the outcome might be a little different."

We stand there for a moment longer, in silence. He is done talking.

"You sound like her father," if I were writing it, my character would say.

"Good," he would say in response. "Not my intention, but if that's the way you see it, good."

We stand there for another moment, in silence.

"Thanks for the visit, Mr. O'Dennehy," I would say, finally, then add "I look forward to having a drink with you from that bottle of Connemara."

He nods.

"See you at the pub, Mr. Maybourn," he would say, finally, as he turns and starts to walk back to his car.

I watch him until he drives away, down the hill and past Cathleen's house. I wonder if she saw us.

That might work, I think to myself, as I sit at my computer with my brain bouncing and my fingers idle. But then I realize such a conversation seems fake, like something I might have thought about writing but then thought better of it. Nobody, least of all Séamus, was going to make my decision for me. He, too, might accept whatever happens between she and I, but he would never approve, and might never forgive.

No, old boy, I told myself. This is all yours to get right or to fuck up.

I got up from the table, went to my liquor table and brought back my bottle of Jameson. I put a touch, just a touch, maybe an ounce, in my coffee. I was not sure it would help my writing but it might help my mood.

The next drink of coffee was like a slap in the face, and maybe it was just what I needed.

"You fancy yourself an Irishman then, well, feckin act like an Irish man then," I wrote, not sure of which of the characters in my book might say such a thing, but liking it none the less.

I liked it, that bit of dialogue, but then it was probably too early for me to start drinking.

*　*　*

I did not have a drink the day of the BBC interview, nor the day before. I merely put on the show that I was the classic heavy drinking writer.

I actually cleaned up the house, and stashed away my liquor, except for a bottle of the good French vodka, the vermouth, and the remaining Connemara brother. I thought it might look good in a photo. I also shaved, and though I probably needed a haircut, I decided a little wild-writer look might look good in a photo as well. I wore a button-down Oxford, light blue. Color looked good on me, Cathleen had informed me when I told her the interview day was coming.

Two weeks after my return from Belfast, with Fall approaching with more surety, she and I had settled into a kind of planetary relationship: we revolved around each other but stayed at a balanced, cold distance. For the most part, now as before, we worked, passed each other as we began or ended our day, smiled and waved or exchanged a few words on the weather or the wind or the waves.

I took her out to dinner once, to an Italian place in Ballyvaughan. I had asked nervously, almost expecting to be rebuffed. She accepted gracefully. Another time I ran across her at the pub sitting with Eileen. We ended up walking home together. Both times we talked about our days, our work, the coming of fall, and then, maybe, my first Galway Bay winter. I did not attempt to kiss her and she did not seem to care. She brought me a dinner one night. She said it was leftovers but it looked fresh to me. It was a stew and after a good day of writing during a bad day of weather, the stew washed the cold rain away.

I wondered as I ate her offering in lonely silence, if she had seen me that morning or others, my back to the front window, pounding away at the keyboard, my music box quiet. I wondered if she noticed my lonely silence, and if it was why she brought dinner.

The day of the interview, I noticed that she was outside, working in her back yard, and as I looked on I saw a strange car pull up and stop. The same photographer who shadowed me in Belfast emerged from the car, with an older man, a reporter whose last name was Jenkins, Sinéad had informed me.

I have done many interviews, big time and small, in-person and "phoners". And, like readings, they usually took on a familiar pace and structure. If the reporter was good, he'd have all the background info researched and in his notes. He or she might check a fact or two, just to prove possessed knowledge. Then they would beat around the bush with a standard question or two. Not a "What's your sign?" kind of question, but often close. Questions asked mostly to get a feel for how I talked and how talkative I was. I am usually talkative. After all, they are usually doing me the favor, or at least my publisher the favor. Finally, there would be half a dozen questions that cut to the chase. Questions I actually had to think about, think how they would sound in print, and questions that often allowed me to figure out what angle the writer's story was going to focus on. I almost always tried to say what they wanted me to say, what fit a pre-written storyline. Rarely would I blow off a question—give it a short, curt answer—usually if they asked about Hollywood and Jasper, or about my personal live, which had happened a couple times after Maggie's illness became public.

Basically you tell an interviewer what you want them to say about you, the story you want to tell.

If they want to build a different story, a big flaming made-up story — as one sensation-seeking entertainment reporter did when "Kiss of Death" was about ready to hit the Red Carpet, when her big question was about my smoking pot on-set with Jasper — you simply say nothing. Avoid any answer to what could be a "Do you still beat your wife" question, and make them make their crap up if all they want is crap. It galls them to have to do so, but they often will do it anyway.

I could tell from almost the first words out of his mouth that it was unlikely this very British and very proper Mr. Jenkins made crap up. People who wear tweed jackets with elbow patches rarely come anywhere near that stuff.

"Lovely house, lovely view," he said as we shook hands. "Very Quiet Man I must say."

He introduced the photographer. We smiled at each other and shook hands, again, but I again missed his quickly pronounced name filled with that unusual consonant structure. I think he liked being anonymous, though. Photographers are often that way.

Jenkins wanted to see the house, inside and out, which not only allowed him to see how I lived but also gave the photographer opportunity to snap a few shots of me in my environment. They had worked together before, had a dance down. As we moved around the house, and then entered through the front door, the photographer moved around with his camera in action and the reporter danced in-step, staying out of his way and out of his shots.

The rainstorm had passed and it was a fairly warm fall day, so I offered and we settled on two chairs outside in front for our talk.

With our small talk, I learned a little about him: he was based in Dublin, but often covered America and Americans; he did news as well as features. I liked that, as such reporters often were more, shall we say, substantive.

Before we got down to business, he pulled out a phone, asked if he could record the discussion, and I agreed. He then proceeded to ask a couple of background questions. Just checking on facts he already knew. Then he asked me how my summer in Ireland had been. Where I had traveled to, what sights I had seen. I told him a little of my travels, of my readings, of my visits to the Burren and my voyage up the coast. He knew of the adventure with Mully and Ian. I guessed Sinéad had dropped that little nugget. It made me sound more Irish and manly. True and brave, and all the crap.

Then we got to the real questions; and as such interviews usually are remembered, I recall them in a Q&A format, as such interviews are often printed:

"I understand this is a rather different literary effort for you, as you were asked to develop your current project as a favor to Mister Kelly. He owns the film rights to any sequel to The Quiet Man, I understand, and intends to produce one. Does such a change of ultimate audience alter at all your approach to your writing?"

"It is different, but I am embracing the difference. I have had three of my novels make it to big screen, but they were written without the big screen

in mind, written for the reader. I am trying to do that here, but knowing what Jasper wants to do with the story is always there. I would like to tell you that my story, the way I am writing this novel, is uninfluenced by the big screen. But that would be a lie, and you would know that, and the reader would know that. What I am trying to do, however, is to write a book that will keep my audience turning the page, that will tell a good story about Ireland, that will be worthy of having a good movie made from it. I am sure the screenwriters, should this particular story ever make it to their hands, will see their own vision of how to tell the story for their audience. The two are seldom the same, they cannot be."

"Mr. Walsh's story and Mr. Ford's film, in many ways, are different stories. Which are you relying on the most for your work?"

"I am not sure I am relying on either. I am influenced by both, how could I not be. But each tells a story. I think they tell the same story, really, just in a different language. Hollywood, Ford and his screenwriter, Frank Nugent, told a story of how America viewed Ireland, in an idyllic sense, a fairytale sense. But we now know it was a time and place they really knew very little about. And then there was John Wayne. Everything he touched, especially at that time in his career, was tailored for him. He was larger than life, so the film makes his Sean Thornton larger than life. Walsh, on the other hand, tells a story of Ireland, of a certain time, a story he too imagined, yes, but with details he knew, he actually lived. But his American returning home, his Sean Thornton, is a fiction as well. How an Irishman would visualize an American returning to Ireland. It is a bit of a fairytale, too. At least that is how I see it, how I read it. Now that I think about it, I guess my story's Sean Thornton will be more of Walsh's fairytale than Ford's. But my story is about more than Sean Thornton."

The reporter jotted down a note triggered by my last sentence. I knew we would return to that at some point, after his initial questions were asked and it was time for follow-up.

"I read somewhere that after the story was published in the United States, Mr. Ford purchased the rights for $10, and that his studio wanted him, and the principal actors, to do another American western before they would finance his Irish film. Hollywood works in peculiar ways. I am told you are writing this novel primarily as a personal favor for Mr. Kelly. That you were hesitant at first. Is that true?"

"First, I read that story of the $10 rights fee too. Not sure if I believe it either. Sounds too Hollywood for me. Second, if you are asking me if I am being paid by Jasper, the answer is yes, of course. He is paying dearly. Before I accepted, I made him buy me dinner and drinks in New York City. I made sure it was a very expensive meal. But really, I am doing this because I am a writer and, once he and I talked it through, I wanted to write this story. Maybe, also, I think I can grow as a writer by doing this. Will the book make money? I don't really care. It will make some, and if they make a movie of it, that too will come with pay. I do not give my work away. Jasper and I are friends, true. And I know there is some rumor out there that I am doing this for free. But business is business. Now what I will do with whatever I make from this project? There is a couple charities my wife and I were involved in. I am looking at endowing those. There is also a group in Dublin I have an eye to support. When that time comes to spend more of Jasper's money, if you are interested in those charities, we can talk more about that."

"I would like that. I was told she was an extraordinary woman. I read a newspaper article detailing some of her charity work, of her activities during her illness. Quite extraordinary. So, excuse me, but since you mentioned her, is there a story about her, about your trips to Ireland, which you would care to share?"

(I paused before continuing. I noticed he wrote something about my pausing before I continued.)

"Thank you. She was a special woman. But she was a private woman mostly. We enjoyed our visits to Ireland, she and I. And I did pick this

location to live this summer because of her having a business connection to Galway. I am staying in a house owned by her boss, a very lovely German lady who loves Ireland. You know that story?"

He nodded. Maybe he did, maybe he didn't; I noticed him jotting down some notes.

"Maggy loved Galway. I liked it. But no real story to tell about that, about her. We had some history here. Shallow history, but history. I have much more now."

"Yes. I understand you have had quite an adventurous summer here. We spent the night at the inn down the hill last night. I had a pint. Smithwick's, your beer, I understand. We heard some stories about your summer, much more colorful than the very informative, very dull, summary your Irish assistant sent us. She is a very good agent, I would say. Adventurous summer, this? A funeral, a fight, and other experiences, I am told. The sea voyage and all."

"You know Irish pubs, I assume. So you can only believe half of what you hear, maybe less. But I guess I have done the Hemingway thing, a little, I suppose. I have not killed anybody or been shot or got arrested or anything that would be newsworthy. Too old for those sorts of things. But this has been a very different experience for me. It may sound a little cliché, but I have tried to immerse myself in this landscape, to the extent I am able and allowed. The people here, once they got over my knowing Jasper, have been very welcoming, very honest, very direct with me. Sometimes uncomfortably direct. Not that I have enjoyed everything, been particularly proud of everything, nor do I care to talk about all my experiences. I'll let other people tell you those stories. But it has informed me. It has shaped my view of Ireland in a way no story or no movie ever could. My experiences as an American immersed in the Irish past and present, will undoubtedly weave their way into the story. Some of it may actually sound as though I have some idea of what the hell I am writing about."

"That does bring up a point, sir. Knowing what you are writing about. There is, out on the blogosphere, those who say it is wrong for a non-Irishman to write a sequel to a story written by an Irish writer as well respected as Walsh. How would you defend your hire?"

"There is no defense I care to offer. The criticism is fair, to a certain extent. But I do have a track record of writing good books that people read. Not exactly great literature, I'll give you. But good books that people read. In a way, and I mean no disrespect in this, this story might be better written by someone from the outside looking in. Not that this book, and any film that may come from it, is meant for an American audience only. Jasper's international distribution people would kill me if I said that. But it is, as the original film and in some ways Walsh's story was, not really meant for an Irish audience only. I take my jobs, just as Walsh took his jobs wherever and whenever he could. He wanted to break into the American reading market, I am sure. And his story being published in the Saturday Evening Post was probably big for him. To answer your question, though. A writer who knows Ireland innately would write a different story, a different sequel, I am sure. Would it be better than mine? That would depend on the writer. I suspect that someone wasting their words blogging about me could not write it as well."

He smirked. But did not take any other notes. Question asked and answered.

"I'd like to talk a little about the new book. I understand you might not want to give details at this time, but in general tone, shall we say. Walsh's story gives you characters to work with, but you have said your book is not simply a chronological sequel. Can you give us some hints?"

"The storyline, at least the beginning, requires no hints. Everybody knows, or probably will know before they even pick up the book, the story of Sean Thornton and Mary Kate Danaher's courtship. So I need to pay some sort of homage to them, to what happened to them. But I've always desired

more of Red Danaher, the great character created by the great Victor McLaglen, and even the classic Catholic priest, Father Lonergan. There is depth about those characters that was left untapped, I think. I could go there. There is also history, the events in Ireland and the world. Sean and Mary Kate, for all the idyllic world they lived, they also could have been influenced by history, by what was happening. Given that, the world is wide open to what will happen in my story."

"It sounds as though you are making clear this will not simply be a continuation of a storyline we all know, that there will be new characters. The faces, the personalities of the characters we know, are really set in the public mind. But the new characters, where have you found the faces of the new characters?"

"Funny you use the word faces. I have always found characters in the faces of strangers. People I see. People I pass on the street. People I simply find on Google. I really do not use people I know well, those people have their own personality firmly in my mind. But strangers, people who I can take sketches of their face and place it in a different place and time, those are usually the basis of my characters. And I find them everywhere. In the pubs, here in Gleninagh, or other places I have travelled. I know some people, especially here, but there are always others, strangers. There are some great faces there. And on the trains, on the streets, as I travelled the country. In strange places sometimes. I took notes, made character sketches, of several faces from an art show I saw recently, the Davidson paintings at the Ulster Museum."

"You saw the show?"

"I thought it was stunning. On several levels. There are stories behind the faces, The Troubles and all. But, take away the specific reason for the sorrow and the anger, you have faces of Irish people whose wrinkles, whose scars, whose grim smiles, have been drawn by sorrow and joy for decades. People showed loss and bliss in their faces in Walsh's story, in his time, and in the Ford film. The scene of John Wayne grimly reliving his boxing past

*are, in my opinion, very powerful. There will be loss and anger and joy and
bliss in my story, in my story's time. Maybe one of Davidson's faces will
morph into the face of one of my characters."*

"Those paintings, those people whose lives were so
influenced by The Troubles, lead us to a question I assume you
know I must ask. You talk about the history of Ireland playing a
role in your book, so, the revolution, The Troubles, that history
that is so central to Ireland after the time period of Quiet Man.
Can an American write about those times, about those
experiences, when you did not live it?"

*"I guess I have to answer that question two ways, no and yes. Can I
write about the revolution and The Troubles in any great detail, with any
great authenticity? Of course not. I would not even try. But the troubled,
tragic history of Ireland in the 20th Century is as much as character in The
Quiet Man, in any story dealing with the country or its people, as the hard-
drinking, hard-working farmer, or the good Catholic woman, the wise country
priest. The tragedy, the way it colors all of modern Irish history, has to play
its part. Walsh understood that but did not include it in his story. Ford
understood that, and had it written into the story, briefly. Walsh's best works
had the revolution as a key element in the storyline, but he chose to not cloud
his fairytale with it. It was not important to his intended audience, an
American audience. But Ford, and his screenwriter, in the 1950s, could not
ignore it even though their story, too, was a fairytale meant for an American
audience. I will need to at least acknowledge its presence, the specter of the
revolution in Sean and Mary Kate's time, and the foreshadowing of The
Troubles. Maybe more."*

"Maybe more?"

*"There is more to Ireland than the revolution, The Troubles. There is
history of tragedy, invasions and famines, bloody religious and political feuds.
But I think the Irish, have always looked forward, to better times, and they
work for those better times. Ireland is constantly changing and yet, I think, is
incredibly slow to change, especially in the eyes of those looking from the*

outside, even to Irish immigrants, my grandfather. There is an Irish idyllic that is hard to change, to the rest of the world, especially to Americans. The world that Walsh created still exists, in the some idyllic if not in modern reality. Just as the world that Seamus Heaney moved in, took his readers to, still exist, also in another idyllic. Even from Brendan Behan, there is a— idyllic is not the word—there is a familiar darkness that still exists in the Irish psyche. I think my story will acknowledge that darkness, and the darkness that was the revolution and still is The Troubles. Every story about the Irish, the country and individual people, should show them moving forward but always acknowledging both the darkness and the idyllic, what I call the Irish fairytale. My story will. … But in the end, my story will be story of people … The greatest Irish stories, I think, are the stories of people, told among friends, in a pub over a pint or a whiskey neat. That is the story I want to tell."

"Quite well said," Jenkins said.

"Thank you," I said. "I practiced that."

He laughed, one of those subtle, reserved laughs I have found the English like. I laughed a little more heartedly. I heard the camera snap off a series of photos as I laughed, the first time since the start of the interview I was aware of him.

For Jenkins, I think, the interview ended there. I think he had what he wanted, what he needed, to write a story of a "maybe not so ugly" American writing an update of an Irish classic that history treats with equal portions of affection and distain. At least I hoped that was the story he was writing, and writers usually read other writers pretty well.

He had a few brief, housekeeping questions as he wrapped up the interview. Most I answered and quickly forgot. One, however, required some thought before I answered, and some reflection after.

"Is there a calendar for the project?" he said. "A deadline in your mind? Your publisher gave me no estimate as to when your book will be delivered to them, let alone a date of publication. I assume, though, that Mr. Kelly's people want their story yesterday. May I ask the status of your book, on its writing? Will you finish it here or back in America?"

"I am deep into the first draft, and I try to not screw with my books too much after the initial writing," I said. "I will find a good Irish editor to work with, I have always valued a good editor, to help me. Then the publisher takes the child away and puts that child into foster care, or maybe it is finishing school. To answer your question, when will I be finished? Maybe by the end of the year, early next year at the latest. And where will I write, where will I finish it? I cannot picture not being Ireland when I do so. I have come to love this place. I think I might stay, even after, if Ireland will have me."

Jenkins looked at me as I finished my answer. I could tell he wanted so bad to ask a follow-up, but he did not.

Maybe he thought that was another story for another day and another interview.

Maybe it would be.

* * *

A couple weeks after my BBC interview, when it appeared on line, I prepared myself for critiques, in no particular order, from Cathleen, Ellen, Jasper or at least Jasper's people, and undoubtedly from Sinéad. And there would be the boys at the pub; I knew that my fair share of abuse would wait.

I don't read my interviews, nor my book reviews; other people's reactions tell me all I need to know.

I did not go to the pub the day of the story's posting. And while I saw Cathleen, she said nothing about it as we exchanged

359

pleasantries. I guess she thought I wanted some distance and, by damn, she was giving me that distance.

Sinéad sent me an email almost immediately, just to make sure I had seen it online. I had. That is what Google notifications are for, for those vain enough to want to know what other are saying about them or snoopy enough to be what to know what others are saying about someone else. She made no comment, no critique. Maybe she was waiting for my response, or waiting for her bosses back in New York to respond. Maybe she was waiting for my opinion of the interview, which would never come.

No, my first critique came late in the day from Jasper's personal assistant. Carrie, as I remember. A text popped up with the sender identified as merely a 310 area code number not in my contacts.

"Nice interview, Mr. Maybourn. Sounded very Euro," she wrote. Then she asked if I could take a Skype from Jasper. "5 p for you. 9 a for us." She had correctly judged the time. I could, and did. At 5 p.m. my time, his smiling face was on the screen when I answered his electronic request.

"Matty," he said. "My wandering Irish lad, how you doing? You talk funny yet?"

"Feck off," I said. "Other than that, not much."

"Been a while," he said. "Good to see you, even if I am looking up your nose a little."

I adjusted my computer screen and its camera a little.

"You too Mr. Hollywood."

We laughed. He looked good but kind of unkempt. Hair a little wild and stubble beard.

"When was the last time you shaved, dude?" I said.

"What do you mean, this is the look this year. GQ, Matty, you see the cover of GQ in September? I look good. Anyway, I'm working on a sci-fi project, lost in space kind of thing. All the rage these days. A little out of the world adventure with a handsome face, a woman in a tight suit and whole lot of CGI. Audiences love that stuff. No monsters, though. Staying away from aliens and all that space gore stuff. This is good science, at least that is what I am told. We stole some NASA ideas and taking a trip to one of Saturn's moons. Mimas. Film's called 'Eye of Mimas'. Ever seen a photo of Mimas? Looks like an eyeball. Got a great ending. Real 'Woo woo' stuff. I'll be on set most of the day, that's why I'm calling now. Hope it's not a problem for you."

"It's 5 here Jasper. You're just giving me a reason to drink."

"That's what Carrie said. I thought it would be later than that. Anyway, I'm working away here. How you doing?"

"Good," I said. "Really good. I think I have a story for you."

"I never doubted it," Jasper said, his face drawing near his camera and becoming more distorted on my computer screen. "You write good stories."

"Not really why I am calling," he added. "But as long as you want to tell me …"

I noticed as he leaned back in his chair, somebody moved near, then a feminine hand set a coffee mug in front of him. Red hearts and the words "Poppa Bear" in black.

"So, cocktail hour your time, uh, Matty. Have a little bit of the Irish in my honor."

He leaned forward, grabbed the mug, leaned back and offered me a toast.

"Give me the trailer, Matty. Give me the trailer."

I thought it interesting that he was sipping his morning coffee and I was planning for an evening Irish whiskey. California and Ireland were not quite half a world away, but it was close.

I also thought it interesting that he was already moving on to his next movie. He was always planning his next step. I liked that about him.

"So the story picks up like 20 years after the movie," I said. "Sean Thornton and Mary Kate have had some good years. Tough years for Ireland, the revolution an all, but they have worked the farm and raised a son and seen him off to America for a good education. Dual citizenship and all. They also want to get him away from Ireland, from the aftermath of the civil war, from the coming war in Europe, you know?"

"Wait. Wait. I can't play a 20-year-old kid."

"That's the beauty. You get to play Sean as an older man in the 1930s, made up to look older. Then he dies. You get to die well on screen. I promise. Then the son, Seanusy, goes off to war as an American. You know Ireland was mostly neutral in World War 2, right?"

"No shit?"

"History, buddy. History. They write books about such things," I said. "Anyway, he fights in Europe. What do you want to be, a sky-pilot or a ground-pounder, your choice. You also get to pick some young teen heartthrob to play the youngster going off to war. That will be good for box office and all, I would guess. And when the war is over, his life in America is not what he expects, not what he wants out of life. So Seanusy comes home to Ireland. He is older now, and here is where you can play him again. And there we all have good and bad times, you know: war memories, an old mother, a young woman he falls in love with. An Irish lass, all dark hair and beautiful green eyes."

"Love it," Jasper says, then he takes a sip from his cup and tips it to me again. "Love … It! Finish it before the end of the year and we can get this thing moving next year. I mean, don't rush it, you know. But I'm not getting any younger, you know."

Then he sets his coffee cup down. Leans forward.

"Neither are you Matty. Neither are you."

Oh, oh. Hollywood is getting serious.

"The book not really why I called, Matty. Wanted to talk about you, catch up with my friend. How you are doing? I read the BBC interview. Great stuff. You look good. Sound smart. you made me and the project look good. Great stuff. But you know, you come across a little sad. I know you are working on the book. But I got to ask you: you finding some happy there? I know you've had some adventures. Traveling the country old school. On a train? Really? Now going down to the sea with men, that's something I'd like to do. Hell, I heard you even had a little heart-to-heart with the police out on some island. Some tragedy. Sorry about all that. But that's life, isn't it. That's all adventure.

"I also heard you got into a fight over a woman. That's real adventure. Love that."

I wondered where he got his news. The BBC? Sinéad? The feckin blogosphere? All of the above?

"Don't believe all you read, Jasper," I said. "And nothing of what you hear."

"Not the point, *Matthew*. Not the point," he said. "Point is, are you finding some happy? You moving forward? Look, my friend, you can tell me to fuck off later, but I'm going to tell you straight. You like it straight. You gave it to me straight. The high road. You've been walking the high road, Matty. Nobody can ever say you didn't take the high road. Not your kids. Not your friends. Nobody. You've taken the high road."

I looked at him. He looked at me. We were no longer half a world away.

"You going to tell me to fuck off?" he said, finally.

I nodded. "Thinking about it."

"Well, while you're thinking about it, I'll get some breakfast in me. You get a little touch of the Irish in you and think about what I said. Then you get back to writing."

"You think all we do is drink in Ireland, Mister O'Kelly?"

He laughed a little. "When in Rome, Matty. When in Rome." Then he smiled. "Good to talk to you. See ya soon. Hollywood, out."

After he hit a button on his computer, he was gone.

* * *

I tried to write the rest of the evening after talking with Jasper. I could not write, even with a little touch of the Irish to loosen me up.

I tried to sleep after I tried to write. I could not sleep, despite another little touch of the Irish. My mind wandered but landed nowhere. I bounced from work to life and back to work, again and again—from reality to fiction and to the netherworld between. Finally I slept, stirring at dawn's twilight. I remembered a snippet of a dream with Maggie, pleasant but without clear definition.

Getting up to take a piss, I looked at myself in the mirror. I saw myself, but again, without clear definition.

I decided a morning hike was in my future.

Next thing I knew, I was walking up behind the house, up on the edge of The Burren, where I found myself walking often these days. Just as I reached the top of Gleninagh North, I noticed a bird in the air, a hawk. I watched the bird as it slowly circled out over the rock landscape and then dove. It disappeared from my sight somewhere down the slope from the rocky crest. I wondered of its fate.

And, as I have always known, fate cannot be scripted.

A moment later, I saw it rise above crest, its wings working hard against the wind and dragging something in the air beneath it.

I walked again. Back to the house, back to my bed. I was very tired.

When my eyes opened again, the sun was high—late morning, early afternoon?

I thought about the bird. The choice it made.

I laughed, a little, as I thought of the bird circling. *Could a bird think too much?* My laugh turned louder, uncontrollable, as I thought about how stupid that sounded.

I got up, looked at myself in the mirror.

I walked downstairs and went to the front window, looked toward Gleninagh.

I thought about Maggie, and I thought about Cathleen. I thought about Ally and Sean, and Jasper, and a dozen other people's faces and voices, some living and some dead. Then I thought again about Maggie, and about Cathleen. I thought what had been, what was and what could be.

I started to cry, softly at first, then deeper, from somewhere deep inside me.

Something inside fell away. Something rushed by, like the wind, like the wind that first carried the bird gently then released its grip and allowed it to fall, allowed fate to play its inevitable hand.

I stepped outside. Barefoot. The dirt felt good. The tears felt good.

It was that moment—that instant, that heartbeat—that I heard something behind me, something moving softly across a field and toward me. Startled, I turned my head sharply.

Michaeleen stopped his advance. He looked at me. I looked at him.

My crying stopped just as suddenly as it had come.

If I were the kind of writer that went in for such silly things, I would say he was smiling at me.

"I look really stupid, don't I?"

He just smiled.

"Don't you laugh at me, dude."

He just smiled.

I laughed at the thought our conversation, of his smile, and assured in some way he moved closer. He sat down beside me and looked out to where I looked. To Gleninagh. Then he looked back to me. Stood, as if waiting for me to lead.

We stood there for a while. Maybe a minute, maybe more.

Then I turned back to the house and invited him in while I shaved and showered and dressed in the best slacks and shirt and jacket I possessed.

He and I then stepped outside.

When I started to walk down the hill, back toward his house, he followed a step or two behind. I think that dog knew exactly where I was going.

* * *

Irish courtship, at least in *The Quiet Man* myth that comprises both the story and the film, is a lesson in a marriage ritual that no longer existed in the early 20th Century when the story was filmed, let alone in the 21st Century. In the story, briefly, and in a longer form in the film, the courtship of Sean and Mary Kate has no real wellspring, the moment when the man gets on his knee with ring or a poem or heartfelt words in hand, and asks for the woman's hand in marriage.

Instead, there is a familiar dance of a mythological Irish time and place: a formal request to court by the man, approved by the bride's family with or without the prospective bride's consent, chaperoned time spent together under the watchful eyes of someone trusted and hired for such tasks, or a member of the local clergy, hopefully followed by an acceptable compatibility agreed upon by the intended pair, and finally an acceptable financial arrangement agreed upon between the man, or the head of his family, and the woman's head of family.

Ah, the age of the dowry.

As I walked quickly and resolutely down Gleninagh North, I thought about the courtship in the film, and how it would change, needing to be updated, but not forgotten, in my story. It was a point still unwritten in my book: would my story be one that looks back or looks forward? Would it be a story set in the age of myth or in the age of the split atom?

One's mind wanders as one circles, seeks, and approaches the unknown.

I glanced toward Cathleen's house and noticed her car was absent, considered but rejected any more delay, any more waiting for the right time and place, and continued my hike down the hill, to the pub on the chance that she was there.

Michaeleen followed me as I strode past his home, bouncing along now only a step behind.

I was glad I did not have to do the Irish courting dance of old, of Walsh and Ford and the Irish myth. I just needed to find her, beg her to forgive my indecision and accept me, if she will still have me. At least that is how I pictured it.

I should have known that, if there was one thing I had learned, in all my research, in all my adventures, in all my imaginings as an American interpreting Ireland and the Irish, nothing in Ireland is as simple as the American mind understands it.

Down the hill, the gravities of the earth and my heart and the moment pushed me on, past the road and onto the now familiar path that cut short the distance to the pub and to the bay beyond. But there was a certain rising wind, from the southwest, carrying me as well.

"Cathleen," I would say. "I am such a shithead, I am so sorry for putting you through what I have put you through but …"

No. No. Sounds wimpy. Just get to the point.

"Cathleen. If you'll still have me, I want to marry …"

Formal? Too formal? Blunt? Too blunt? Too forward? She actually hasn't said she'd marry me, has she? You know what assuming something, especially something as fragile as love, makes of you and me.

"Cathleen. I love you but …"

But? No buts. I either loved her or I didn't. If it was a different love, a more mature love, even a love with more distance than the poems of romantics or the romantics of youth, she might understand, might accept. But love could not come with 'buts'.

I walked, and thought about what I would say, could say, over and over, as I walked.

Maybe that courtship thing was not such a bad thing after all.

I glanced at Michaeleen.

"You want ta' be me chaperon?" I said aloud, knowing he, alone among my Irish friends, would not mock my accent.

He ignored me, either unwilling to accept the job or unwilling to accept my mocking Irish accent, and we continued our jaunt across the field.

I saw Cathleen's car parked in the back lot of the pub. My heart be a bit faster. The parking lot was not full, but it was close. What day was it? Friday? Yes, Friday. What time? She liked this day of the week, this time of the day, to stop off and spend some time with Eileen; her work week was done and plans for the weekend to be made, if they were not already.

My heart was pounding, and I guessed it was not just my double-time military march. What was I going to say? What was I going to do? I thought of the circling hawk.

I should have a poem in hand, at least a letter filled with wonderful words. That's how I should do this. I should have a ring, even a simple one, from here, in Ireland. An Irish cross or something. Or was she the diamond kind of girl? Na.

I should have something. But I had nothing but an urgency.

I was ready to dive to earth and there was no stopping and reconsidering.

Life's little details could be dealt with later.

The regulars might be in, and maybe some tourists, but it was too early for the working folk, for the Friday night working-man revelers. You spend enough time at a place, you get a feel for its moods.

I rushed the back door, jerked it open and stepped inside. Michaeleen barked as the door swung closed and he was denied entry. The bright light of the day was suddenly the dim light of the pub; I wasn't blind, but it was close.

"Matty!" came the call and response, Ian's squeaky tenor the first, loudest and most recognizable. Mully's more distant, more subtle, bass was there, too, a heartbeat lagging. The good barkeep Cassidy's baritone a full beat behind, but loud and clear, like a call to prayer, or to drink. With Cassidy, other voices, some vaguely recognized and some unknown, rang in; after months of the ritual greeting, the vaguely known regulars and even boisterous tourists often joined in, just to feel part of the pub crowd.

Lately, amid the heartfelt and feigned greetings, I had begun to think of Kenny's missing, toneless, empty echo.

I liked it that I missed his voice. When one drinks at an Irish pub, one should toast those missing as much as those present.

There was another sound too. Unusual. Music. A guitar played off to one side. The pub often had jam sessions on Friday and Saturday nights, but usually later in the evening.

As full vision reappeared, I found my sailing odd couple in their usual leaning positions.

"Evening boys," I called out. "What a great fall day in Gleninagh."

"That it is, Matty, that it is," Ian said.

"You've been a distant friend," Ian continued, as I cautiously entered and scanned the room for Cathleen, or at least Eileen. The good Gleninagh gossip would undoubtedly have a cookie trail for me to follow. "You been well?"

"Perfect," I said, continuing to scan the room.

"Up to your ass in that book, then, you big shot writer?" Ian said. "You missed that BBC man. Stopped off, bought the house a round. Bought our kind words about ya."

"Bet that was a load of shit," I said, turning to Ian for moment, smiling at my friend.

"Nothin' like the load of literary *shite* you delivered ta the BBC," Mully chirped in.

"Wasn't it, though," I said, turning my attention, my smile to another friend.

"Pardon me gentlemen," I said as I turned back to my scan of the room.

Small talk with the odd couple would wait.

I was in full glide mode, circling, circling.

The bar was half filled. There were several tables filled with what looked like tourists, and Cassidy was purposefully returning from one with empties in hand and orders to be filled. Séamus was absent from his usual booth, and his solitary, slumped form did not jump out to me as being in an unusual place, at a table. I could see the guitarist, though, set up in the far corner. I had seen him before: a college kid from Galway that was occasionally allowed to busk tips from tourists. I remembered him mostly because he once played a nice version of Radiohead's "High and Dry." I always doubted that the good barkeep knew what the lyrics spoke of.

But no Cathleen.

And no Eileen, it first appeared, until: "You missed her."

I looked over to the bar again, behind the far end stood the woman of the house. With her was The Reverend Ronan. Both had tea cups in hand.

I turned to Ian and Mully. "Business beckons, good sirs," I said.

"A beer awaits if business is bad," Ian said.

"Whiskey awaits if business is good," Mully said.

They knew me too well. Nothing in the world like old sailing buddies.

I stepped to the end of the bar, and Eileen leaned over close.

"Haven't seen that life in your step for quite a time," Eileen said, in a soft voice for my ears only. "Lookin' for Cathleen?"

I nodded to her. She smiled.

"You two ready to finish this *seachain* dance you been doing?"

"I guess that is to be decided."

She looked at me. It was that look that women give men when they know the man is full of crap.

"I know," I said. "I know. So?"

"So, she was here, short while ago. Just left. Wanted a walk, she said."

"Ah," I said, nodding. "Castle or quay?"

"What do you think?"

"The quay, the beach."

Eileen smiled, nodding.

"She's 15 minutes gone, and no place but an empty home to go after. She's not gone far."

She'll still be on the beach, then.

I gave the good Gleninagh gossip a tip of an imaginary hat, then turned to the good reverend.

"Business question for you sir?"

The reverend smiled; the gossip looked perplexed.

"Church business?"

"Yes sir."

"Always open for business, then."

Eileen still looked a bit perplexed.

"Can a dog be a proper chaperone for a good Catholic girl at the beginning of a courtship?"

The reverend's laugh was followed, by a second or two, by the laugh of the gossip.

"Well now," he said, after a moment.

I waited; Eileen waited.

"If the dog in question truly has the girl's interests paramount. But if we are talking about the dog I think we are talking about, I hear he might have divided loyalties."

"True enough," I said.

"Then there needs to be another."

He smiled. I nodded. Eileen laughed again.

"Well then," I said. "May I ask for another bit of business from the church? Will you accompany me on a task in need of a proper chaperone?"

The reverend took one more sip of his tea, gave the lady of the house a tip of an imaginary hat, and waved his hand for me to lead the way.

I turned and stepped toward the door, the reverend in tow.

The guitarist's music played, but there was a noticeable lack of usual any noise besides that. The regulars watched. The tourists watched the regulars to see what they were looking at. By the time I reversed course again, turned back from the door, toward the musician, I would have guessed every eye was on me. I approached the music man. He saw me, maybe thought I was going tip him. Instead I pulled out my wallet, pulled out a couple 20 Euro notes and, with fanfare, showed them to him. He stopped playing. Now there was almost total silence.

"You got an Irish love song in ya," I said.

"Does the Pope wear a feckin big hat?" he said.

I nodded. Dropped one of the notes in his guitar case, but continued to show him the second.

"That's for the song," I said. "This one's for a short walk down to the beach with me."

I then dropped the second note into his case.

As I turned, he moved like a college kid offered free beers. Before I could make it to the door, he had placed his guitar in its case with his earnings, closed it, and quick-stepped to be only a couple of steps behind me and the reverend.

When I exited the door, Michaeleen awaited.

When I cleared the building and started down the path to the beach, I glanced over my shoulder and noticed the dog and the reverend and the minstrel were forming a bad conga line, a few steps behind me. Twenty steps down the trail, I glanced again and noticed the conga line had grown: Eileen was next, then Ian, then Mully, then a multitude of faces half known and half unknown.

There were murmurs, and laughs, and shouts. There were questions asked and answers given. I even thought I heard wagers being called for and wagers being taken. What would they be betting on?

I stopped, and turned.

The bad conga line stopped.

Michaeleen and the reverend and the minstrel and the town gossip stopped in a somewhat orderly fashion; they looked at me, awaiting my next move. Ian and Mully, side by side at the head of a pack, stopped and kind of looked around, up and down the shore, like they were trying to appear as though they were not following me. They were not convincing. The crowd piled up behind them, like cars at a wreck on the highway, some bumping into each other, others slipping off to the side to see what the pile-up was all about.

I noticed someone was jumping up and down in the back of the pack: Cassidy. I wondered if anybody remained in the pub.

"You didn't expect us to just sit and wait, did ya," Eileen said.

Michaeleen barked.

I turned and returned to my walk. The bad conga line followed. The murmurs, and the laughs, and the shouts resumed. What could they betting on?

Five minutes later, I was at the beach. Half a dozen steps onto the sand, I stopped. The conga line stopped, piled up again, and fell into quiet.

I looked to the west, toward the Atlantic, toward America. Nothing.

I looked to the east, and there at a little distance but clearly visible, was Cathleen.

I stopped circling and dove.

Cathleen was walking, strolling really, down the beach. She moved slowly, and my fast pace, matched by the conga line, allowed us to close in quickly. The sun continued its slow slide away behind us, and I noticed my shadow stretched out toward her. The wind blew lightly, but still noisily, from off the water. Maybe it obscured the sounds of the conga line. Maybe she was lost in thoughts, as such strolls are wont to cause one to be. She strolled on, without looking back, for twenty or thirty paces as we continued to close in.

Then she turned. I was maybe ten yards behind her.

First she looked startled, then confused, then she recognized me. Her beautiful face, the sun shining off her pale skin and her jet-black hair, lit up like a second sun in the sky.

I stopped. The conga line must have stopped and piled up again, as Michaeleen barked and the murmurs rose into questioning shouts.

"Are we there?" someone said.

"Where?" another said.

"What's happening?"

"Just watch, ya fool."

"Ya, ya. Are we there?"

I stood and looked at her.

She stood and looked at me, then looked past me for a moment, to the crowd, and then she started to laugh: a loud, echoing laugh as she looked back to me.

Her laugh was the laugh of the gentle sirens, of joyful little girls, of women who find humor in the world. Without even being aware of my steps, her laughter, and the wind, carried me nearer.

There may have been more noise, more murmurs and shouts, behind me, but I paid no notice.

A couple yards away her laughing stopped and I stopped.

"You Americans," she says. "Do ya have to make a show of everything?"

"What?" I say.

She glances behind me. I turn and look.

The bad conga line has piled up into a small audience: Michaeleen, the reverend, the minstrel and Eileen in the front and center, the sailing odd couple and Cassidy off to one side but close, a crowd of twenty or so people craning their necks and bodies in an effort to see past others and see what was happening.

Mully has stepped off to one side to get a good view.

"Well, that's strange," I say.

"Feckin strange," she says.

I step closer. Her beautiful green eyes glow unlike anything I have ever seen. A dozen different things flying through my head: half a dozen things I could, should say.

"Now?" the minstrel calls out.

I turn my head and see him, guitar in hand and Eileen carrying his guitar case.

"Should I play now?"

I shake my head. No.

I turn back to Cathleen.

I smile, shrug my shoulders, and then hold out my hand.

"Can we walk together for a while?" I say.

Her smile fades; a "quit feckin around" look comes to her face.

"There is another question here …" she says. "Isn't there?"

"Yes. But let's walk a little while I think about what to say."

She takes my hand, turns and I step beside her.

"You think too feckin much," she says.

We walk side by side, in silence.

Then I stop. She stops. We face each other and I take her other hand.

Guitar music fills the air. A song starts.

"Sure a little bit of Heaven fell from out the sky one day,
and it nestled in the ocean, in a place so far away."

There are no more murmurs, only shouts and cheers and someone calls out "That's the one." And the song continues.

"And when the angels found it, sure it looked so sweet and fair,
they said 'suppose we leave it, for it looks so peaceful there'."

Michaeleen barked.
Several voices became a bad, echoing chorus.
I knelt to one knee, and sank into the sands of Galway Bay.

An deireadh agus an tús
(The end and the beginning)

There is an Irish blessing which *mo grá*, my love, ran across in his research and just *had* to recite it to me:

May you have honest work to occupy you,
a hearty appetite to sustain you,
a good woman to love you
and a wink from the God above

Matthew seems pleased by the discovery; he says it is a fit thing to end his book. I try not to dash my man's excitement, but I have to tell him that there must be a hundred Irish blessings of a similar vein, most of them not written by Irishmen.

"It doesn't matter, *mo mhuirnín*, the words work," he says, with his still atrocious Gaelic pronunciation. He thinks he is calling me his "darling." I'm not sure where he read that, but being his "little maiden," however archaic, is sweet enough.

As he talks, he raises his metallic grey eyes from his computer screen, his smiling face is aglow with the light of the screen and the dimming evening light coming through the windows and into his writing space.

"So," I say, as I pick up the half-eaten lunch plate I'd brought him a few hours before. I am surprised that the dog did not finish it for him, it being ham and all. "What's flowing today from that keyboard of yours?"

"A short story, the New Yorker wants to take a look at one. I told them it would be about modern rural Ireland. It is finished really, just can't quite end it."

"Not really very good at endings, are ya Matthew?"

He leans back in his chair, folds his hands in his lap, pouts his lips like the child he sometimes wants to be.

"Just saying," I say, as I set the plate back down on the dining room table where he spends his days writing. I then lean over him and run my hand through his course grey hair, now a little unruly and in need of a cut. He needs a shave too, but I like the look of his being a little unruly.

"Just saying," I repeat.

He reaches up, grabs my hand, brings it to his lips, gently.

"That's what I want the blessing for, to end this. So you can read it."

"Then end it," I say. "It's cocktail hour, if you'll be of the mood."

He kisses my hand again, and then lets it go.

In the six months we'd been married, we had settled into habits. New habits for both of us, no doubt, but comfortable, married-couple habits nonetheless.

Matthew and I were wed the week before Christmas, in the church where we said goodbye to Kenny. He said it felt funny, like Kenny was there. It kind of creeped me out, but that is how he sees things sometime. He lives his life as if it were words on a page of one of his novels.

The Reverend Thomas Ronan officiated our marriage. Ally and Sean, and Ally's young man, were there; Matthew flew them in from America. The children were a little quiet and reserved when it came to me, especially Ally, in whose face I could see another woman. Both of the children were raised well, though, and they loved their father as much as they loved their mother.

They said the right things to me; they took the high road, as Matthew likes to say.

It was a small ceremony, only a few Catholic doctrine details to be dealt with, and there was just a small party at Cassidy's after. We decided we'd take a holiday in the spring, and over much of the winter Matthew was often knackered from long hours of writing on his book while I was busy editing another self-help book for another London doctor. My only interaction with his book was correcting his often-flawed Gaelic, his occasionally questionable Irish history, and rare bad grammar, all of which I did without much comment on his storyline.

The big party came in the spring, in June, when his work was done and just before we headed off to the Azores for our holiday. Mr. Kelly rented out the Lough Cutra Castle: *the whole feckin place.* We had a long weekend there, with family and friends from Ireland and England and America; even one from Germany, Matthew's old friend Mrs. Hench. A lovely old woman, she was. It was stunning, surreal experience. Thought it was too "American", too ostentatious, but who was I to stop it? It was almost a paparazzi moment, with television cameras and such. Mercifully, Jasper's press people only allowed the circus to go so far. I did not like the big show, feckin Hollywood in Ireland, but who was I to stop it? I suppose it was good press for the book and the movie, but it was a little too Red Carpet for me.

It was magical, though. And who was I to stop it?

That was Jasper's gift to Matthew and me, I guess. He had only asked for some slight changes in the book, which was delivered to Saul in March, then to Jasper in April, and to the publishers in July. It is planned for a holiday season release this year, I understand, and he'll have to do a book tour, of course. I'll go to America with him, when that time comes, for two weeks. I look forward to having him show me around

Philadelphia, him being the tour guide. I'll let him go it alone on the Irish and British stops, except London. I'll show him London. I've put a lot of my work aside for a while, but I've accepted a big editing project starting in the fall.

And I've spent enough time finding out how I fit into his life. It's time he finds out how to fit into mine.

But that is tomorrow, and the day after. We live day-to-day, really. And today is a fine day on Galway Bay.

"Come down soon or I'll start without ya," I tell him as I carry the lunch plate to the door, glance around the room to make sure nothing else needs to be taken and cleaned. He is not the tidiest of men. Sometimes it feels good just to tend to a man. Archaic, I know, but it is sweet enough for me.

"Be right there," he says, as he returns to his computer. "I just have to end this damn thing."

We have settled into a good life, he and I. While we sleep together each night in my house, in a new bed we've bought, he has his own house.

Else's wedding gift to him was her Gleninagh house. A gift to us actually, she told me at Lough Cutra, when she said how much she loved my grandmother and told me to call her 'Else". We plan to connect the two houses with stone walls, an expanded garden, a walkway. The upper house will became our guest quarters, and his writing room, which it is already, as well as Michaeleen's own feckin dog house. We put a doggie door into the back, leading into the kitchen so as to not spoil the view from the front. The dog usually sleeps in his old house with us, but I often find him lazing around in the high house when Matthew is writing.

And when Matthew writes, he spends much of the day there, often alone, after breakfast and before cocktail hour and dinner. Sometimes I ring a bell and he hears it and comes down.

Sometimes, like today, he's playing his atrocious music and I need to come up to get him.

After I pick up his dishes, and give him a kiss on the top of his grey-haired head, I leave him to finish.

"*Slán go fóill*," I said, knowing I would, in fact, see him soon.

I stand outside the door for a moment and looked to the bay; it is pleasant, the view from Gleninagh North.